The Hippopotamus

STEPHEN FRY

The Hippopotamus

HUTCHINSON
London

This edition first published in 1994 by
Hutchinson

Random House UK Ltd
20 Vauxhall Bridge Road, London SW1V 2SA

Random House Australia (Pty) Ltd
20 Alfred Street, Milsons Point, Sydney, NSW 2061, Australia

Random House New Zealand Ltd
18 Poland Road, Glenfield, Auckland 10, New Zealand

Random House South Africa (Pty) Ltd
PO Box 337, Bergvlei, 2012, South Africa

The lines quoted on pages 28 and 30–1 are from 'A Father's Advice'
by Mark Beaufoy

The lines of verse from 'The Hippopotamus' by T. S. Eliot are taken
from *The Complete Poems and Plays* by T. S. Eliot, reproduced here by
kind permission of Faber and Faber Limited and the Estate of T. S. Eliot

A CIP catalogue record for this book is available from the British Library

ISBN 0 09 178412 3

Set in Plantin by Intype, London
Printed and bound in Great Britain by
Clays Ltd, St Ives PLC

For Kim, *alter ipse amicus*

The author would like to thank Matthew Rice for his invaluable help with the shooting scenes. Any inaccuracies in that quarter are entirely his fault.

The broad-backed hippopotamus
Rests on his belly in the mud;
Although he seems so firm to us
He is merely flesh and blood.

'The Hippopotamus', T. S. Eliot

Foreword

You can't expect an arse like me to tell a story competently. It's all I can bloody do to work this foul machine. I've counted up the words processed, a thing I do every hour, and, if technology can be trusted, it looks as if you're in for 94,536 of them. Good luck to you. You asked for it, you paid me for it, you've got to sit through it. As the man said, I've suffered for my art, now it's your turn.

I don't claim that it has been a wholly grotesque experience. The Project, as you insist on calling it, has kept me from drinking at lunch-time, from drooling after unattainable women and from quarrelling with the unspeakables next door. At your suggestion, I have been leading a more or less regular life these seven months and I am told the benefits can be read clearly in complexion, waistline and eye-whites.

The routine has been fixed and perversely pleasurable. Every morning I have risen at round about the hour most decent people are thinking of one more shot before bed, I have showered, descended the stairs with a light tread, champed through a bowl of Bran Buds and guided my unwilling slippers studywards. I switch on the computer – a procedure my son Roman calls 'jacking into the matrix' – goggle with disgusted eyes at whatever guff I've set down the night before, listen to some more of those bloody interview tapes with Logan, light up a Rothman and just bloody well get down to it. If the day has gone well I'll disappear upstairs for a round of light celebratory masturbation – what Roman would no doubt call 'jacking into the mattress' – and I won't so much as think of a bottle till seven-ish. All in all a proud and pure life.

The problem with renting a house in the country is that suddenly everyone wants to know you. I am endlessly having to fend off Oliver, Patricia and Rebecca and others who seem to think my time is limitless and my cellar bottomless. Every once in a while the Bitch will unload a son or daughter for the weekend, but they are both big enough and ugly enough to look after themselves and don't need me to help them roll their joints or fit their coils. Next week Leonora will be moving into the house I've given her and be permanently off my hands. She's far too old to be clinging to me.

No, on balance I would say the thing's been a huge success. As a process, that is, as a process. Whether the *product* has anything to recommend it is, naturally, for you to say.

I am fully aware that there's a deal of tarting up to be done. I assume you'll make some decision about whether or not to create a unified point of view ... a consistent third-person narrative, an omniscient author, an innocent eye or an innocent I, all that Eng. Lit. balls. Since half of it's in letter form you could always titivate here, dandify there and call it an Epistolary Novel, couldn't you?

My favourite candidate for a title is *Other People's Poetry*, I have a feeling however that your filthy marketing people will regard this as a notch too poncey. It seems to me to be the best title, the only title. So whatever cheap alternative you dream up instead, to me this book will always be *Other People's Poetry* and nothing else. Your suggestion, *What Next?* or *Now What?* or whatever it was, strikes me as a touch too Joseph Heller and a whole smashing uppercut too market-led, as I believe the phrase is. Otherwise I'm rather fond of *The Thaumaturge*; that would go down as my nap for place. No doubt you'll come up with your own clever-arse idea. Roman thinks *Whisky and Soda* would be rather neat.

The details here below are more or less accurate. If you develop a publisher's yellow streak, you can always change the names and dates – buggered if I care. Meanwhile, on delivery of this, the second quarter of my advance is due: I'm off back to the smoke to find myself a tart and a bar, so sling the cheque over to the Harpo, in which place too a message can be left, delivering itself of your professional opinion, for what little it's worth.

E.L.W.

One

The fact is I had just been sacked from my paper, some frantic piffle about shouting insults from the stalls at a first night.

'Theatre criticism should be judgement recollected in tranquillity,' my wet turd of an editor had shrilled, still trembling from the waves of squeal and whinge that actors, directors, producers and (wouldn't you just believe it) pompous, cowardly prigs of fellow-reviewers had unleashed upon him by fax and phone throughout the morning. 'You know I support my staff, Ted. You know I venerate your work.'

'I know no such bloody thing. I know that you have been told by people cleverer than you that I am a feather in your greasy cap.'

I also knew that he was the kind of anile little runt who, in foyers and theatre bars the West End over, can be heard bleating into their gin and tonics, 'I go to the theatre to be entertained.' I told him so and a full gill more.

A month's salary, deep regret, the telephone number of some foul rehab clinic and my lance was free.

If you're a half-way decent human being you've probably been sacked from something in your time . . . school, seat on the board, sports team, honorary committee membership, club, satanic abuse group, political party . . . something. You'll know that feeling of elation that surges up inside you as you flounce

1

from the headmaster's study, clear your locker or sweep the pen-tidies from your desk. No use denying the fact, we all feel undervalued: to be told officially that we are off the case confirms our sense of not being fully appreciated by an insensitive world. This, in a curious fashion, increases what psychotherapists and assorted tripe-hounds of the media call our self-esteem, because it proves that we were right all along. It's a rare experience in this world to be proved right on anything and it does wonders for the *amour propre*, even when, paradoxically, what we are proved right about is our suspicion that everyone considers us a waste of skin in the first place.

I boarded the boat that plies its fatuous course between newspaperland and real London and watched the *Sunday Shite* building grow upwards in space as slow knots were put between self and dismal docklands and, far from feeling mopey or put upon, I was aware of a great swelling relief and a pumping end-of-term larkiness.

At such times, and such times only, a daughter can be a blessing. Leonora would by now have high-heeled her way, it being half past twelve, to the Harpo Club. You probably know the place I mean – can't use the real name, lawyers being lawyers – revolving doors, big bar, comfy chairs, restaurants, more or less acceptable art on the walls. By day, smart publishers and what used to be called the Mediahedin; by night, the last gasp of yesterday's Soho bohemians and washed-up drunks taking comfort from the privilege of being sucked up to by the first gasp of tomorrow's ration.

In the back brasserie Leonora (hardly my idea, a name that tells you all you need to know about the child's footling mother) hugged, snogged and squealed.

'Daddee! What brings you here in the daytime?'

'If you take that slithery tongue out of my ear, I'll tell you.'

She probably imagined that a slightly famous daughter and her even more slightly famous father displaying easy affection for one another in such a manner would provoke envy and admiration in those of her tight-arsedly bourgeois generation who only ever saw their parents for tea in hotels and wouldn't think of swearing, smoking and drinking with them in public. Typical bloody Leonora; there are pubs all over the country where three generations of ordinary families drink and swear and smoke at each other every bloody night, without it ever crossing their minds that they are simply sensationally lucky to have such a just brilliantly fabulous relationship with their wonderful daddies.

I dropped the Rothmans and lighter on the table and let the banquette blow off like a Roman emperor as it took my weight. The usual dirt averted their eyes while I took in the room. Couple of actors, nameless knot of advertisers, that queen who presents architecture programmes on Channel Four, two raddled old messes I took to be rock stars, and four women at a table, one of whom was a publisher and all of whom I wanted to take upstairs and spear more or less fiercely with my cock.

Leonora, whom I had never wanted to spear, the gods be thanked in these unforgiving times, was looking thinner and more lustrous-eyed than ever. If I didn't know it was unfashionable I would have supposed her to be on drugs of some kind.

'What's all this?' I asked, picking up a portable tape-recorder on the table in front of her.

'I'm profiling Michael Lake at one,' she said. 'For *Town & Around.*'

'That fraud? His dribble of three-act loose-stooled effluent is the reason I'm here.'

'What can you mean?'

I explained.

'Oh Daddy,' she moaned, 'you are the limit! I saw a preview on Monday. I think it's a perfectly brilliant play.'

'Of course you do. And that's why you are a worthless key-basher who fills in time sicking out drivel for snob glossies until a rich, semi-aristocratic queer comes to claim you for a brood-mare, while I, for all my faults, remain a writer.'

'Well, you're not a writer now, are you?'

'A jessed eagle is still an eagle,' I declared, with massive dignity.

'So what are you going to do? Wait for offers?'

'I don't know, my old love, but I do know this. I need your mother off my back until I'm sorted out. I'm two months behind as it is.'

Leonora promised to do what she could and I skedaddled from the brasserie in case the Lake fake was early. Playwrights more than most are not above throwing good wine or bad fists when the valueless offal they have vomited up before a credulous public has been exposed for what it is.

I sat at the bar and kept an eye on the mirror dead ahead, which gave a full view of the influx from the entrance door behind me.

The lunch crowd twittered around the bar area awaiting their meal-tickets or their spongers; the daytime scent of the women and the sunlight pouring through the window created an interior atmosphere so distinct from the dark, flitting nimbus that hangs over the place at night that we might have been lapping in a different room in a different decade. In America, where boozers are often under the street, like the cutesy bar in that ghastly television series they repeat every day on Channel Four, a daytime atmosphere is positively banished. The punter, I suppose, is not to be reminded that there is a working world going on outside, lest he start to feel guilty about pissing it away. Like an increasing number of niminy-piminy Europeans, Americans bracket drinking with gambling and whoring, as deeds to be done in the dark. For myself, I have no shame and don't have to steal off to Tuscany or the Caribbean to be able to drink guiltlessly in the sunlight. This casts me as a freak in a lunch-time world where the fires of anything vinous are extinguished by spritzing sprays of mineral water and the blaze of anything hearty is drizzled in balsamic vinegar or damped down with blanketing weeds of radiccio, *lollo rosso* and rocket. Christ, we live in arse-paralysingly drear times.

Once, since we're on the subject of designer lettuce, at a luncheon for literary hacks, the novelist Weston Payne prepared a salad of dock, sycamore and other assorted foliage collected from the residents' garden in Gordon Square. He dressed these leaves in a vinaigrette and to universal applause served them up as *cimabue, putana vera* and *lampedusa*. One grotty little pill from the *Sunday Times* went so far as to claim that *putana vera* could be bought in his local Chelsea Waitrose. A bottle of London tap-water chilled and passed through a soda-stream was slurped with every evidence of delight under the name of *Aqua Robinetto*. Very fitting really. After all, for twenty years Weston's novels had been palmed off as literature to these same worthless husks without their ever noticing a thing. I sometimes think that London is the world's largest catwalk for emperors. Perhaps it always was, but in the old days we weren't afraid to shout out, 'You're naked, you silly arse. You're stark bollock-naked.' Today you only have to fart in the presence of a dark-haired girl from the *Sunday Times*, whose father is either a sacked politician or a minor poet like myself, and you'll be puffed and profiled as the new Thackeray.

You can't imagine, if you're younger than me, which statistically speaking you are bound to be, what it is like to have been born into the booze-and-smokes generation. It's one thing for a man to find, as he ages, that the generations below him are trashier, more promiscuous, less disciplined and a whole continent more pig-ignorant and shit-stupid than his own – every generation makes that discovery – but to sense all around you a creeping puritanism, to see noses wrinkle as you stumble by, to absorb the sympathetic disgust of the pink-lunged, clean-livered, clear-eyed young, to be made to feel as if you have missed a bus no one ever told you about that's going to a place you've never heard of, that can come a bit hard. All those pi, priggish Malvolios going about the place with 'do you mind, some of us have got exams tomorrow, actually' expressions on their pale prefectorial little faces. Vomworthy.

It seems the popsy up on a stool next to mine read some of the off-pissedness in my face, for she gave me a long sideways stare, unaware that I was inspecting her inspection by way of the mirror. She slipped her bony but appetising buns off the stool and made for a chair in the corner, leaving me the sole occupant of the bar pasture, to graze the gherkins and crop the cashews alone. Knew her from somewhere. Five got you two that she was a diarist for the *Standard*. Leonora would know.

The great dramatist was ten minutes late, naturally, and strode through to the dining area without seeing me. The smirk on his face indicated that he had either fooled the generality of my erstwhile colleagues, no difficult thing, and been praised for his abominations, or he had heard the delightful news of my dismissal. Probably both. He wouldn't remember of course, because they never do, but it was I who discovered the little prick in the first place. That was back in the days when I used to shuttle around the fringe nightly and sit through performances by companies with names like Open Stock and Shared Space; a time when my nod could guarantee transfer from an upstairs pub in Battersea to a plush drama-brothel in the West End. Michael Lake had written what in a better world would have been a perfectly ordinary play, but which was rendered extraordinary by the banality, illiteracy and po-faced sulkiness of just about every other new work that had been written that year and for the last five years before it. In a dung heap, even a plastic bead can gleam like a sapphire. Nineteen seventy-three that must have been or, at a pinch, four. Now, of course, it wasn't possible for the man to write a note to his milkman without it being lavishly mounted to universal praise at the National Theatre ... the *Royal* National Theatre, I beg its creepy, arse-licking pardon. The few fires of good anger and proper passion that had flickered in his early work had been pissed out by an insufferably pompous state-of-the-nation gravity and a complete indifference to the audience or awareness of the theatre. He, of course, as one of the generation that disdains the definite article, would have said 'a complete indifference to audience or awareness of theatre', as if Audience was a formless notion, instead of a live tangle of coughing, shuffling humanity, and Theatre an intellectual concept entirely divorced from actors, scenery, lighting-rigs and wooden boards. Never mind that Theatre transformed his humourless texts as best it could into just about bearable evenings and Audience funded his Suffolk watermill and lurid collection of Bratbys . . . they shouldn't expect his thanks for it. On the contrary, the general scheme was that we should be grateful to him. Cocky little arse-wipe.

'More of the same,' I said to the barman.

'Let me get this . . .' a voice, female, at my elbow.

'One of the finest phrases in our language,' said I, without turning round. I could see in the mirror that it was the bony-bunned creature, levering herself back up on to her stool. Absolutely *love* small women, they make my dick look so much bigger.

'And a Maker's Mark for me,' she added, pointing to a bottle high on the bar shelf.

A proper drinker, I noted with approval. Your experienced lapper knows that barmen always initially mishear the name of whatever brand you specify. 'Not Glenlivet, Glen*fiddich*! No, you oaf, not a lager shandy, a *large brandy* . . .' Always find the bottle with your eye first and point at it when ordering. Saves time.

A hint of something Floris-ish, or at a pinch Penhaligony, wafted up as she settled herself. Adequate breastage and a slim white throat. Something neurotic in her bearing, you get to spot that quickly in female bar-flies, most of whom are usually on the brink of the kind of hysteria that smashes glassware or slaps innocently by-standing faces.

Roddy poured a large measure into a highball glass and she watched him closely. Another good sign. I was a close chum for a time of Gordon Fell the painter, before he got knighted and began to think himself too high for low company; we went out on the nasty together fairly regularly throughout the Sixties. Gordon always drank Old Fashioneds, had done for thirty years. Never took his eyes off the barman for a second while they were being prepared, like a blackjack player eyeing the deal. One afternoon Mim Gunter, the old witch who wielded the optics at the Dominion Club in Frith Street, a favourite pissery, was off sick and her son Col had to take her stand at the bar. Well, Col was only sixteen, poor lad didn't have the first clue what an Old Fashioned was, and bugger me if Gordon hadn't the foggiest either. I tried later to calculate how many hours of his life Gordon had spent watching while they had been assembled before his unblinking eyes, but ran out of napkins to do the sums on. I knew that Angostura bitters came into the formula somewhere, but that was all I knew. In the end we had to ring Mim in hospital where she was all gowned up and ready to be wheeled into the theatre to have the cancer cut from her throat. Our SOS tickled her pink, of course. Ten feet from the phone, the other side of the bar we were, but we could still hear her screeching the foulest insults at the hapless Col down the line and telling the doctors to bugger off, 'this was business'. She died under the knife two hours later, Gordon Fell's Proxy Old Fashioned taking its place in history as the last drink she ever mixed.

The point is, we watch the barman, but we don't take it in. It's the reassuring movement of the hands, the pleasing fitness of bar stock and cocktail apparatus, the colours, the noises, the rich, speaking scents. I've known non-drivers unable, in the same way, to recall routes they have taken daily in taxis for years.

The placing of the glass on its paper coaster, the discreet pushing-forward of the ashtray and Roddy's quiet withdrawal having been accomplished, we were free to talk.

'Good health, madam.'

'And yours.'

'Have I a feeling,' I wondered, 'that we've met?'

'That's what I was asking myself when I was here before. I decided you were too forbidding to ask, so I disappeared to the corner seat.'

'Forbidding?' I've heard this tosh before. Something to do with jowls, eyebrows and a pugnacious, Bernard Ingham-like set to the lower lip. 'As it happens,' I said, 'I'm a lamb.'

'And then, sitting there, I realised you were Ted Wallace.'

'The same.'

'You may not remember, but . . .'

'Oh hell, we haven't done the deed, have we?'

7

She smiled. 'Certainly not. I'm Jane Swann.'

Said as if the name was a reason for my never having sauced her.

'Jane Swann. And I know you, do I?'

'Cast your mind back to a small font in Suffolk twenty-six years ago. A baby and a rising poet. The baby cried a great deal and the rising poet made a promise to turn his back on the world, the flesh and the devil. A promise that even the baby didn't believe.'

'Well, fuck my best boots! Jane . . . Jane Burrell!'

'That's me. Though in fact it's Swann now.'

'I must owe you any number of silver napkin rings. And a library's worth of moral guidance.'

She shrugged as if to say that she didn't believe me to be the kind of person whose taste in silver napkin rings or moral guidance coincided with her own. Now that I looked there was that in her cast of features which recalled her ghastly parents.

'Never got much of a chance to get to know you,' I said. 'Your mother threw me out of the house not half an hour following the baptism. Barely laid eyes on her or Patrick since.'

'I was always very proud of you, though. From a distance.'

'Proud of me?'

'Two of your poems were set texts at school. No one believed you were my godfather.'

'Bloody hell, you should have written to me. I'd've come and gabbled to the Sixth Form.'

Too true. Nothing like the parted admiring lips of a seminar of schoolgirls to make a man feel wanted. Why else would anyone try to become a poet?

She shrugged and took a sip of her bourbon. I noticed she was trembling. Not trembling perhaps, but shivering. She had about her an air that reminded me of long ago. Leaning forward as if she wanted to pee, leg jogging up and down on the bar-stool stretcher. There was something . . . images of wooden draining boards, Dividend tea stamps and pointy bras . . . something forlorn.

I looked at her again, the little signals came together and I remembered. Jane looked now exactly as girls in the early Sixties did when they returned from visiting an abortionist. An unmistakable confluence of gestures and mannerisms, but one which I hadn't seen in a girl for years. That blend of shame and defiance, of disgust and triumph; the urgent appeal in the eyes that encouraged you either to mourn the desolation of a life utterly ruined or to celebrate the victory of a life made magnificently free, a dangerous look. I remembered only too well that if you guessed the girl's mood wrong in those days and congratulated her when she wanted to be comforted, you got a fountain of tears and a fortnight of screaming recrimination; if you consoled and sympathised when what she fancied she needed was applause and praise for a proud and heroic stand, you got a zircon-edged swipe across the chops and scornful laughter. Why the expression on my new-found god-daughter's face should have put me in mind of the atmosphere of those sordid and unmissed times, I had no idea. Women haven't needed to look as vulnerable and guilty as that for thirty years; that is a man's office now.

I coughed. 'Which poems?'

'Mm?'

'Set texts. Which ones?'

'Oh, let me see. "The Historian" and "Lines on the Face of W. H. Auden".'

'Of course. Of bloody course. The only two that ever make the anthologies. Tricksy rubbish.'

'Do you think so?'

'Certainly not, but you'd expect me to say so.'

She favoured me with a sad-eyed smile.

'Same again, Roddy.' I rapped the bar.

'I often read your theatre reviews,' she ventured, sensing that the smile had been a touch too obviously sympathetic.

'Not any more you won't.'

I told her of my sacking.

'Oh,' she said, and then, 'oh!'

'Not that I give a stuff,' I assured her, in a manner that admitted no condolences. I unloosed my thoughts on the current state of British theatre, but she wasn't listening.

'You've time on your hands then?' she said once I had run down.

'Well . . . I don't know so much about that. There's a more or less open invitation to fill the restaurant column in *Metro* . . .'

'I'm not a writer, you see, and I don't know enough . . .'

'. . . and there's always room for just one more definitive book on the Angry Young Men . . .'

'. . . you are virtually family, after all . . .'

I stopped. There were tears forming in her lower eyelids.

'What is it, my dear?'

'Look, do you mind coming home with me?'

9

In the cab she stayed off whatever it was that was distressing her. She sketched a short autobiography, enough to show me that she wasn't as bright or pretty or stylish or interesting as she had seemed sitting at the bar. But then, no one ever is, which is why it's always worth having shares in whisky and cosmetics.

Five years earlier, barely twenty-one, she had married a man, Swann, who traded in paintings. No children. Swann was currently in Zurich sharing his duvet with a Swiss girl, degraded enough and powerfully enough built (if Jane's bitchy glossing was to be believed) to appreciate his bruising bedroom habits. Jane's father Patrick had been gathered to God some six summers, which come to think, I knew, and Rebecca, the mother, still gadded about between Kensington and the Brompton Road pretending to be smart. Rebecca's other child, Jane's brother Conrad, whom I remembered as something of a turd, died in a car-crash. Pissed off his head, apparently. Good thing too. There's no excuse for crashing a car sober.

Rebecca was one of the few women I ever met who . . . well, it is a fact that women do not enjoy sex. It has become almost a matter of religion for them to deny this, but it remains a fact. Women put up with sex as the price they pay for having a man, for being part of what they like to call a 'relationship', but they can do without. They do not feel the hunger, the constant stabbing, stomach-dropping hunger that tortures us. The bugger of it is that whenever I say this I am accused of being a misogynist. For a man who has spent his entire life thinking and dreaming of women, skipping after them like a puppy trying to please his master, ordering his entire existence so that he might be brought into more contact with them and judging his life and worth solely according to his ability to attract them and make them desire him, it comes a little hard to be accused of a dislike of the sex. All I feel is profound worship, love and inferiority mixed in with a good deal of old-style self-loathing.

I know the arguments . . . Lord, who doesn't? Desire, they tell me, is a form of possession. To lust after a woman is to reduce her to the level of creature or quarry. Even worship, according to a reasoning too damned tricksy for me to follow, is interpreted as a kind of scorn. All this is, I need hardly tell you, the supremest bollocks.

Some of my best friends, as you would expect of a quondam poet, are chutney-ferrets. So too, as you would also expect of a quondam theatre critic, are some of my bitterest enemies.

You couldn't ask for a better controlled experiment to help us settle this business of the genders than the world of the nance, now could you? Gaysexuals, bottomites, benderists, settle on a name you like, taking such problems as the queer-bashers, the newspapers, the virus, the police and society as read, lead a pretty fabulous life. Lavatories, parks, heathland, beaches, supermarkets, cemeteries, pubs, clubs and bars vibrate to their music of simple erotic exchange. A man, bent, sees another man, bent. Their eyes lock and . . . bang, sex is done. They don't have to know their partner's name, they don't have to talk to him, they don't even, in the back rooms of dark metropolitan nightclubs, have to see his bloody face. It's a male world, ordered in a precisely male way, according to the devices and desires of a strictly male sexuality. Do those big hairy faggots who pose in magazines with leather collars round their dicks and rubber tubing up their cack-alleys think of themselves as oppressed? Do gay men tarting themselves up for a night in a club whine about the vile sexism which insists they must be made attractive in order to be inspected like cattle? Do they hell.

Sometimes, in my dreams, I imagine a world in which women enjoy sex: a world of heterosexual cruising areas in parks and promenades, heterosexual bars, heterosexual back rooms, heterosexual cinemas, heterosexual quarters of the town where women roam, searching for chance erotic encounters with men. Such an image is only conceivable in one's fantasising bedroom, jerked into life by an angry fist and a few spastic grunts. If women needed sex as much as men did then – duck, Ted, duck, run for cover – then there wouldn't be so many rapists around the place.

We live in the world as given, and no doubt anthropologists and zoologists can tell us that it is biologically necessary for one of the sexes always to be hungry and the other to be mostly bored. Men have compensations, after all, for the agony of their endlessly unfulfilled desires. By and large, we run the world, control the economies and swank about with laughable displays of self-importance. This isn't a whinge. I merely want the simple truth understood and out in the open: men like sex and women don't. It has to be recognised and faced.

Women's constant rejection of such a self-evident fact doesn't help at all. Whenever I point it out to my women friends they instantly deny it; they will claim to be regular masturbators; they will claim that the idea of a good

11

anonymous fuck is a real turn-on; they will claim that only the other day they saw a man whose bottom reminded them a little of Mel Gibson and that they got really quite juicy thinking about it. *Only the other day?* What about only the other *minute?* What about every damned sodding bloody minute of every bloody damned sodding day? Don't they see that women should pop open the champagne and celebrate the fact that they are not slavering dogs like men, they should revel in the biological luck which allows them to be rational creatures who can think about the benefits a partnership with a man can provide, who can think about motherhood and work and friends . . . who can just plain *think* unlike us poor bastards who spend days that should be spent in work and higher thoughts having to realign the sore and swollen cock under the waistband of our underpants every time a set of tits walks by? Of course women get the itch now and again, we wouldn't be here as a race otherwise; of course they have genital equipment sensitive enough to ensure that sex can, when embarked upon, cause shiverings of pleasure, barks of delight and all the dirty rest of it. But they are not, lucky, lucky, lucky things, for ever *hungry,* for ever *desperate,* for ever *longing* for the base physical fact of getting their bloody rocks off. I mean, the fact is, it's five in the afternoon as I write this, and I've already tossed myself off twice today. Once first thing, in the shower, and again just after lunch, before sitting down to this. Any honest tart will tell you, sympathetically, like a nurse, that men, poor dears, just have to spit their seed. Why women should wish to claim parity in the matter of this gross imperative beats me.

As it happens, because of my trade, I've met a great many famous men, men of good report. Do you know, without exception, those I've known well enough to be able to sit with round a whisky bottle in the small hours have all confided to me that the real motivation behind their drive to become famous actors, or politicians or writers or whatever, has been the hope, somewhere deep inside them, that money, celebrity and power would enable them to get laid more easily? Whisky can rot through the layers that mask this simple truth: ambition to do well, a desire to improve the world, a need to express oneself, a vocation to serve . . . all those worthy and nearly believable motives overlay the bare-arsed fact that when you get right down to it all you want to do is get right down to it.

I owe whisky that. Not a drink many women of my acquaintance are much given to, but it has saved me. Without it I should be even more of a lost and bewildered old cunt than I am. If it weren't for those late scotch-soaked nights I should have gone through life convinced that I was uniquely dirty and uniquely dangerous. The ruination of a promising career, the occasional run-in with the police and the destruction of a couple of marriages is the price whisky exacted for allowing me to see that I was not alone: solid bloody bargain.

But . . . that's enough of that. I can get carried away. If you want catchpenny theories about the Sexes and all that, you can find shelves in bookshops devoted to nothing else. *Men Biting Back, Women Biting Back From Men's Biting Back*, responses to responses to counter-responses: it's like the days of the Cold War, every publication by the other side is read, every posture analysed, every twitch on the web detected and every cultural shift pored over. God knows there are columnists, cultural commentators and semi- academics enough to keep the Gender Wars industry arming and rearming for ever. Anyway, who gives a fuck what a parcel of undereducated journalists have to say about anything?

No, I fart this noxious guff in your faces not because it's important or new, nor because I want to engage in a sterile debate about it, but because you have to understand something of my mood and disposition that day Jane found me and dragged me off to Kensington. Her mother Rebecca, I was about to note before I leapt astride my hobby-horse and galloped off for a few paragraphs, was probably the only woman I've met who really seemed to enjoy sex for sex's sake with a relish and a need that could compare to a man's desire. She was also the only woman I've ever met whose favourite drink was whisky. A connection possibly.

Jane's house found itself somewhere near Onslow Gardens. There was money in her purse, no question, courtesy of her Uncle Michael no doubt, and, like every rich, ignorant girl these days, she passed herself off as an interior decorator.

'People saw what I'd done with the flat,' she said, as the taxi drew up outside a standard South Kensington white-pillared portico, 'and asked if I could help them out too.'

The interior lived up to my ripest expectations. Hideous flouncing swags for curtains, raw silk instead of wallpaper, you can picture the whole sham shambles for yourself, I'm sure. Barbarically hideous and as loudly wailing a testament to a wholly futile and empty life as can be imagined. Just how fucking idle, just how rottingly *bored*, do you have to be, I wondered, to sit down and dream up this kind of opulent garbage? She was standing in the middle of the room, eyebrows raised, ready for my gargles of admiration. I took a deep breath.

'This is one of the most revolting rooms I've ever stood in in all my life. It is exactly as hideous as I expected, and exactly as hideous as ten thousand rooms within pissing distance of here. It's an insult to the eye and fully as degrading a cocktail of overpriced cliché as can be found outside Beverly Hills. I would no more park my arse on that sofa with its artfully clashing and vibrantly assorted cushions than I would eat a dog-turd. Congratulations on wasting an expensive education, a bankload of money and your whole sad life. Goodbye.'

That's what I would have said with just two more fingers of whisky inside me. Instead, I managed a broken, 'My God, Jane . . .'

'You like?'

'Like isn't the word . . . it's, it's . . .'

'They tell me I have an eye,' she conceded. '*Homes and Interiors* were here last week, photographing.'

'I'm sure they were,' I said.

'You should have seen the place when I moved in!'

'Such a sense of light and space,' I sighed. Always utterly safe.

'Men don't usually appreciate such things,' she said with approval, moving to the drinks table.

'Fuck off, you mad, sad bitch,' I said inside, while 'Even a man couldn't fail to be knocked out by this skilful, tasteful blend of the ethnic and the domestic,' said my cowardly outspread arms.

'It was Macallan, I noticed,' she was saying. 'There is Laphroaig if you'd rather.'

'N-no, the Macallan does.'

She brought them over, folded a leg under herself and sank down on an ottoman, which was moronically tricked out in a design which would turn out, I supposed, to be taken from some Mayan funeral shroud or mystic Balinese menstrual cloth. The grand idea behind such a squalid episode of cultural rape and the other equally feeble, equally impertinent conceits that littered this appalling room, I supposed, was that Jane would dispose herself there, surrounded by friends, the diversity of whose drinking habits would justify the ludicrous range of unopened liqueur, aperitif and spirit bottles on display, while gentle yet probing conversational topics were flicked like

14

shuttlecocks about the room. Instead she sat, still trembling like an adolescent, with nothing more for company than a raddled has-been who once knew her parents. And he, despite the gallons of free whisky on offer, was wishing himself violently elsewhere.

She swirled the drink in its tumbler.

'The first thing you have to know,' she said at last, 'is that I am dying.'

Oh, marvellous. Ideal. Simply perfect.

'Jane . . .'

'I'm sorry.' She lit a cigarette with jerky movements. 'That was crass, actually.'

Damned right. Nobody seems to understand that in such matters the tact and sympathy should come from the one who is about to die, not the poor bugger who has to take the news. She'd come to the right shop, though. I've known enough death not to be nice about the forms of it.

'Are you quite sure?'

'The doctors are unanimous. Leukaemia. I've run out of remissions.'

'That's a smeller, Jane. I'm very sorry.'

'Thank you.'

'Scared?'

'Not any more.'

'I suppose it's hard to tell when the axe might fall?'

'Soon, they tell me . . . within three months.'

'Well, my darling. If you've made peace with your enemies and said goodbye to your friends, you shouldn't be too sorry to leave the party early. It's a grotty world and a grotty age and we'll all be joining you soon enough.'

She smiled a thin smile. 'That's one way of looking at it.'

'The only way.'

Now that I knew, of course, I could see it in her. It was there in the brightness of the eye and the tightness and pallor of the skin. The boniness of body that I had read as neurotic rich girl's pseudo-anorexia, that too might in justice be attributed to sickness.

She leaned back, and breathed out. Just showing off now, I thought. The exhalation seemed to me to be designed to demonstrate how mature and wise her death sentence had made her, how it had 'put things in perspective' and set her curiously free.

'I told you that I wasn't scared,' she said, 'and I'm not. But at first I was. Simply hysterical. Tell me . . .'

'I'm listening.'

'I don't really know where to begin. What do you think . . . what do you think of priests?'

I sat down. Here we go, I thought. Here we ruddy go. The laying-on of hands. If not priests, essential oils; if not essential oils, needles; if not needles, herbs; if not herbs, lumps of translucent rock and etheric sheaths.

'Priests . . .' I said. 'Are we speaking of the Romish or the Anglican kind?'

'I don't know. I take it you're an atheist?'

'I sometimes slip, but broadly speaking, yes. I try not to think about it. The cassocked buzzards have been wheeling in the air above you, have they? Fighting for scavenging rights to your soul?'

'No, no . . . it's not that. Oh dear . . .'

She got up and paced about, while I sat, gripped my whisky and waited. I thought about life as a restaurant critic, wondered if there were the seeds of any late-flowering poetry in me and reflected, with the intolerance of the healthy, that leukaemia was an affliction that I would be perfectly capable of snapping out of. Brace up and walk it off, woman, I said to myself. If you can't tell a few white corpuscles to piss off out of it, what are you?

At last she turned, a decision arrived at.

'The point is,' she said, 'that a strange thing has happened. In my family. I don't understand it, but I think it might interest you. As a writer.'

'Oh ah?' Whenever people say, 'as a writer, you'll find this very fascinating,' I prepare myself for thunderous boredom and numbing banality. Besides, what kind of writer was I anyway? She was trying to flatter me into attention.

'I thought, as you aren't . . . ah . . . *occupied* at the moment, that you might be able to help me. Something needs investigating.'

'Well, my dear, I don't know exactly what you had in mind. I'm not what you might call an investigative journalist. I'm not actually any kind of journalist at all. I can't really imagine what a failed poet, failed novelist, failed theatre critic and only marginally successful failure could possibly offer.'

'Well, you know the people concerned, you see, and . . .'

'Woah!' I held up a hand. 'Jane. My darling. Angel. Poppet.

16

In sappier happier days, your mother and I used to stick it away. That's all. I haven't seen her in a coon's age. She said goodbye to me twenty-odd years ago in a blizzard of flung christening cake and savage abuse.'

'I'm not talking about Mummy, I'm talking about her brother.'

'*Logan?* You're talking about Logan? Jesus suffering fuck, woman . . .' I tried to say more, but the Cough had come upon me, as it does these days. It starts as the smallest tickle in the throat and can build, though I say so myself as shouldn't, into a not unimpressive display. Something between a vomiting donkey and an explosion at a custard factory. Jane watched without sympathy as I choked and wheezed myself to relative calm.

'You knew him,' she repeated, 'you knew him better than most. And you are, don't forget, David's godfather.'

'Well,' I panted, wiping away the tears from my cheeks, 'as it happens I haven't forgotten. Sent him a confirmation present only the other week. Got a cutely pi response.'

'Cutie pie?'

'Pi, as in . . . oh, never mind.'

Nobody can speak English any more.

'So you knew about *David's* confirmation, but not about mine.'

Lord, what a whining old sow.

'I told you,' I explained patiently, 'your mother won't have anything to do with me. I saw her three or four years ago at Swafford and I could see then that she still hadn't forgiven me. Your Uncle Michael, on the other hand, has a large nature.'

'And an even larger bank balance.'

This was not worthy of a reply. It was true that I valued Michael's friendship highly and his sister Rebecca's not a whit, but I liked to think that there was more to it than money. But then, I liked to think that the world venerated poets and that one day wars would end and television personalities be wiped out by a fatal virus. Between what I liked to think and the cold veridical state of things fell one hell of a shadow.

'I would want you to think of this as a commission. I'm not an especially rich woman . . .'

No, of course you aren't, are you? You've pissed it all away on Lalique flacons, Peruvian birthing-blankets and Namibian labia-jewellery, you senseless cow.

17

'. . . but I could offer you a hundred thousand now and the rest . . . either later or left to you in my will.'

'A hundred thousand?' I caught sight of myself in the artfully, fartfully tarnished mirror above the mantelpiece. I saw a red mullet, gaping, pop-eyed, purple and very, very greedy.

'A quarter of a million all told.'

'A quarter of a million?'

'Yes.'

'This isn't *lire*, is it? I mean, you are talking about pounds sterling?'

She nodded gravely.

'I don't . . . Jane . . . a quarter of a million is a lot of money and is, I won't attempt to deny it, quite monstrously appealing to me. But I don't know if I have it in me to do anything for anyone which, in any kind of honesty, is worth a tenth of that sum.'

'You will have to work hard,' Jane said.

I could see from the set of her mouth that nothing I could say was going to make much difference to her. Her mind, like her face, was fully made up.

'And you will have to work fast. Whatever you uncover I need to know before I die. That is if I do.'

'Er . . . if you do what?'

'If I do die.'

'If you do die?'

'If I do die.'

We were beginning to sound like a couple of pissed Nigerians.

'But you said . . .'

'No, the *doctors* said, the doctors said that I was going to die. I don't believe I am. That is the point.'

Well, there it was. If she did get around to giving me a cheque, it would in all likelihood be signed 'Jessica Rabbit' or 'L. Ron Hubbard'.

'I believe that I have been saved, you see.'

'Ah. Right. Saved. Yes. Lovely.'

She rose and went over to a lacquered bureau, smiling the seraphic smile of the irretrievably crazed.

'I know what you're thinking, but it isn't like that. You'll see.' She took a cheque-book from the bureau and began to write. 'There!' She tore off a cheque and waved it in the air, a pennant of good faith drying in the breeze.

'Look . . .' I managed. 'Jane. In all honour, or such tatters of it as I have remaining, I shouldn't take your money. I don't understand what it is that you want me to do, I doubt that I have the capacity to do it and it is, to put it nicely, a racing certainty that you are not in your right mind. You should see a . . . a chap.'

What I meant by 'a chap' I wasn't sure. Doctor, psychiatrist or priest, I suppose. Frothing hypocrisy on the part of a man who doesn't believe in such ordure, but what the hell else is one supposed to say?

'I want you to go to Swafford. I want you to tell the family that you are writing Uncle Michael's biography,' she said, handing me the cheque. 'You are probably the only person alive he would allow to do such a thing.'

A properly signed and dated cheque for one hundred thousand pounds lay on my lap in front of me. My bank had a branch near South Ken tube station. I could be out of the house and filling in a deposit slip in ten minutes.

'There are,' I said, 'professional writers who will compile family histories for you at a fraction of that price. Vanity publishing, they call it.'

'You don't understand,' she said. 'You won't be writing a family history, you will be reporting a phenomena.'

'Phenomenon,' I muttered irritably.

'You will be witnessing a *miracle*.'

'A miracle. I see. And what kind of miracle precisely?'

She paused. 'I want you to go to Swafford and make your reports,' she said. 'Write to me constantly. I want to see if you notice anything. You think my mind has gone, but I know that if you go there, you will see for yourself what there is to be seen.'

I left the house and rolled up the Brompton Road, reflecting as busily as a wet mirror on a sunny day. Jane was mad, certainly, but her cheque was crossed and endearingly sane. It was a question now of how to wangle an invitation to Swafford. It was a question of how much work I had to do for the money. It was a question of what kind of work I had to do for that money. I damned the woman for not telling me what to look out for. If she had given me the slightest indication I could then have at least contrived to bolster her delusions by seeming to confirm them. But what were those delusions? My last visit to Swafford had been amusing enough but hardly revealing of miracles.

19

Two

Lord Logan knelt down between his sons and pointed to the tower. David looked up. Through the night mist he saw the clock face, newly painted gold on blue.

'Very smart, Dad,' Simon was saying. 'Is that real gold?'

Lord Logan laughed.

'Gilt.'

'It is gold in the drawing room though. You said.'

'In the drawing room, yes.'

'And in the Chinese Room, Dad, and the chapel.'

'Gold leaf.'

'Gold leaf,' Simon repeated with satisfaction. 'The decorators showed me the book. Every single page was pure gold.'

David was screwing up his eyes. The electric light spun the mist all around the clock into a yellow ball that suspended itself above the stable yard.

'Now then,' said Lord Logan. 'What's the time?'

'Uh oh,' said Simon, putting his hands over his ears.

David looked too and saw that it was about half a minute to ten o'clock. He counted down the seconds in his head.

Lord Logan hugged the boys to him and made a tick-tock noise with his tongue. He felt the warmth of David's hand in his and the chill of Simon's.

David listened for the grinding whir that came before the

chime. One of the big hunters was stamping in his stall and, farther away in the kennel block, David heard the whining of the beagle pups.

No sound came from the clock. They were not standing directly in front of it so David supposed their angle made the hour hand look more advanced than it really was. He began a fresh count-down from ten. Simon had told him once that you could accurately count seconds if you put the word 'alligator' between each number.

'Ten alligator, nine alligator, eight alligator, seven alligator, six alligator . . .' David said to himself.

Simon removed his hands from his ears.

'Dad!' he said reproachfully. Only these holidays had he switched from Daddy to Dad and he liked to use the new word as much as possible.

'You see?' Lord Logan jigged with pleasure.

There was no doubt that, whatever their angle to the clock, it was now a clear minute past ten.

'But I *liked* the bong,' said Simon.

'Ah, but you don't understand. There's a control fitted. It still chimes during the day, but when it's dark, it doesn't.'

'Brilliant! That's brilliant, Dad!'

'Something had to be done. The twins were being woken up every hour, on the hour.'

'I know, Dad,' said Simon. 'My room's just down the corridor, don't forget.'

'Ah well,' said Lord Logan, standing up and dusting his knees with the back of his hand. 'That's another thing. Come on, David, you're not too big . . . hup!' David jumped on to his father's shoulders and they made their way back to the house. 'Now that you're thirteen, Simon, we ought to take you out of the nursery and give you a proper bedroom, don't you think?'

'Oh boy,' said Simon.

'I mean, if you're going to be joining the guns on Boxing Day.'

'Daddy!' Simon kicked the gravel in excitement. 'Oh boy, oh boy, oh boy!'

Lord Logan hitched David up further on to his shoulders.

'Woof! I'm getting too old for this, Davey.'

David knew, however, that although he would soon be twelve, he was small and light for his age and that his father could have carried him five miles without a murmur.

*

21

A fortnight later David lay on his bed and stared at the ceiling, just as he had the night before. The night before had been Christmas Eve when all children lie awake to surprise their fathers. Not that it would have been Lord Logan himself, Simon claimed.

'He gets Podmore to dress up and dump them in our rooms.'

'No, I bet it is Daddy. He'd enjoy it.'

David had not managed to stay awake long enough to find out. Tonight he would certainly stay awake. He absolutely had to.

The brand-new alarm clock, a Christmas present from Aunt Rebecca, ticked on his bedside table.

Half past one.

The most important thing was not to wake up the twins. They were more than a year old and, since the muffling of the stable clock, they had started, in Nanny's words, to sleep through. But you never knew with the twins. They were always capable of creating an uproar. So that they would be especially tired, David had spent an hour entertaining them in their cots earlier in the evening. He had drawn pictures for them with crayons and pulled faces, hummed tunes and danced stupidly around the room until it was time for the goodnight visit.

'They seem rather hot, Sheila.'

'Yes, Lady Anne. David has been exciting them.'

'Davey?'

'I was just reading to them, Mummy.'

'Oh. Funny boy. Never mind, at least they'll sleep. Won't you, my darlings? Night night, Edward. Night night, James.'

A quarter to two.

David stood up and pulled a pair of dark brown corduroy trousers over his pyjamas. He put on his games pullover from school, which was navy blue with a roll-over collar, and chose a woolly hat and black plimsolls, also from school.

Looking at himself in the mirror, he wondered if perhaps he shouldn't smear boot polish on his face. He decided not to. It would be simply disastrous if he couldn't wash it off and everybody saw traces next morning.

Two o'clock.

He looked out of the window. Still dry. A clear night in fact, with just a hint of mist. That would mean a good hard frost and that would mean no footprints. God was on his side. God and Nature.

David returned to his bed, shook a pillow out of its slip,

folded the slip neatly and pushed it up inside his jumper, securing it behind the waistband of his pyjamas and trousers.

He went to the door and tip-toed out into the corridor.

The door of the twins' room opposite was open; a twenty-watt night-light threw a weak yellow glow into the passageway. David could hear the twins breathing in time with each other.

As he passed the door of Simon's old room David edged himself closer to the wall, to avoid a loose board in the middle of the floor. Nanny was the only grown-up who slept near by, but she could wake up at the slightest sound, so he had to be most terribly careful.

David inched along the wall towards the pass door that led into the main part of the house. During the day you could bounce balls, slam cupboards and scream and shout in the nursery wing without ever being heard, but at night the smallest sound was magnified. His breathing alone seemed to make a dreadful amount of noise. The walls, the carpet, the roof, the radiator pipes, everything shifted, clicked and hummed like parts of a machine.

He opened the door. There came to him a faint scent of cigar smoke and the important ticking of a long-case clock. The north passage lay ahead and beyond it the stairs. David let the door swing silently behind him and stole forwards with the great Seven League Boots stride of the stealthy. He couldn't remember exactly how many guests were staying; he thought at least twelve, with another ten or eleven coming the next day for the shooting. To be sure of things, he would have to go by the bedrooms as though each one were occupied by a very light sleeper.

He took the centre of the corridor now because he knew that there were cabinets and tables set along the walls with china and silver and glass on them which would make a lot of noise if he brushed against them.

He was about half-way down, with the marble gleam of the staircase now in view ahead of him, when a sudden sound brought him to a stop. A yellow line of light had appeared under the door of the room he was passing, the Hobhouse Room. Frozen mid-stride, David strained to listen, mouth open, blood hammering in his ears. He heard the silken rustle of a dressing-gown being drawn on.

With a bolt of fright he remembered that there was no bathroom in the Hobhouse Room. He leapt along the corridor in a panic, stopping by the long-case clock at the end where he flattened himself against the wall. He leaned back and panted as quietly as he could, trying to synchronise his breathing with the great gulping beats of the pendulum that swung inside the clock beside him.

He heard the door of the Hobhouse Room open and foot-steps approach.

David couldn't understand what was happening. He wanted to scream out 'But the bathroom's the *other* way!'

The footsteps came closer and closer. David held his breath and closed his eyes tight. The vibrations of the clock went through his body, each tick like an electric shock.

The footsteps stopped. 'He's looking at me,' thought David. 'I can hear him breathe.'

Then came the sound of fingernails gently tapping on wood. There was a bedroom door the other side of the clock from David. The Leighton Room, where Aunt Rebecca always stayed. David heard her whispered voice.

'Max? Is that you?'

A man's voice close by David answered, hoarse and cross.

'Let me in, it's bloody freezing out here.'

The door opened and closed.

David waited. Laughter and other sounds came from inside the Leighton Room. He knew that Aunt Rebecca loved games of all kinds. He decided to gamble on the likelihood of her and the man, Max, staying in the room for some time. David took a deep breath, stepped forwards and headed for the staircase.

His route was meticulously planned and rather complicated. He had to go first to the library, then to the kitchen, then outside through the scullery into the stable yard, and finally back through the kitchen to the library again.

It was dark at the top of the stairs. David took off his plim-solls so that their rubber soles wouldn't squeak on the marble. He went down slowly, feeling the corners of the picture-frames on the wall as he descended. His hand found the corner of the last painting, a huge Tiepolo every inch of which he knew, so now he could be sure he was on the last step. At the bottom, he turned left and went quickly across the open hall, the short-est route to the library.

Half-way across the hall he ran into something huge, some-thing sharp and bristly that hugged him and stung his face. The shock was so great, the sense of being so completely in the grip of what he could only suppose to be a ghost or wild animal, that without meaning to he shouted out; a short howl of pain and fright.

At the very moment he cried out, David realised that what he had run into was only the Christmas tree. Disgusted with himself at such cowardice, he spat a needle from his mouth, stepped back from the tree and listened. There were no sounds of any movement upstairs: no shouts, no sleepy grumbles, no wails from the twins, only a gentle tinkle from the decorations as the tree recovered from the collision. David's panicky yell had probably not been so very loud after all. In his head he replayed the sound and realised that really it had been no more than a husky gasp.

Circling the tree warily, David made for the library.

In the library the smell of cigar smoke was so strong it made the hairs at the back of his legs prickle. It was warm too; a faint orange glow in the fireplace showed that the fire had not yet died. David closed the door behind him and felt for the light switch.

Blinking at the sudden brightness, he looked about the room. He was glad to see that the shutters were closed. There would be no oblongs of light thrown on to the South Lawn, which would have been visible to anyone looking out of a window from one of the upstairs bedrooms.

On the fifth shelf, behind Lord Logan's enormous desk, there was a neat line of twelve old books entitled *Crabshawe's History of the Countie of Norfolk*. They were bound in sand-coloured leather and stamped with gold lettering.

David moved his finger along the line, like a browser in a bookshop, until he came to Volume VI, which he pulled out and laid on the desk. He inserted his hand in the gap on the shelf and felt for the lever. He pulled hard and was shocked by the great twang of the spring as it released the catch. By day the mechanism seemed as quiet as a whisper.

The whole section of shelving swung open and David went through the secret doorway and into the room beyond.

He couldn't find a light switch in this room, so he had to work by the light spilling in from the library. He could see enough, however, and sense even more: the heads of fox and stag bearing down on him, the light aroma of gun-oil and the thudding of yet another big clock.

He made for a small bureau against the wall, between two gun cabinets. On the bureau was a large padded leather book from Smythson's of Bond Street. 'Game Book' it said. Simon had given it to Daddy two Christmases ago. David remembered excitedly asking to see it, expecting it to be a book perhaps like Hoyle's, some sort of encyclopedia or dictionary of games and pastimes. He had not been pleased to find out that it was just blank pages, with ruled ledgers headed 'Date', 'Breed', 'Guns', 'Number killed' and so on.

Behind the game book there was a small drawer. David pulled it open and stirred the contents with a finger until he found – amongst the rubber bands, fishing flies and squares of lint – a key, around which his fist closed with a relieved and determined clutch. Now it was time to go down to the kitchen.

He took the greatest care to avoid the Christmas tree as he crossed the hall. Once he knew it was there he could see it quite clearly, of course, standing guard over the staircase like a huge and shaggy bear.

David shivered at the sudden breath of warm air that met him when he opened the red baize door and went down the steps into the kitchen.

Moonlight came in through the high semi-circular windows; it gleamed on wickerwork hampers that had been laid out ready for the great breakfast. David edged round the central table, sat down on a chair at the end nearest the stove and put his plimsolls back on. His elbow touched a piece of grease-proof paper on the table. He lifted a corner of the paper up and could smell smoked ham. Immediately his throat began to contract and spasm. He turned away and breathed deeply, but had to bury his face in his forearm to muffle the sound of his dry retching. After a while he stood and wiped the tears from his eyes.

At the far end of the kitchen was a door which led to the sculleries and pantries. David went through and turned on the light.

The machinery in the cold-room hummed and down the end of the passage a large black cat came up to him, stretching its legs as it walked.

'Sh!' said David.

The cat twined itself around his legs and began to purr.

'Come on, then,' David said and the cat accompanied him to the larder door.

The second shelf of the larder, neatly ordered, contained sugar, flour, tins of baking powder, packets of yeast, sachets of gelatine, spices, cake decorations and cartons of candied peel, all in huge catering-size packs. There were children's party napkins there too, boxes of meringue nests, bags of confetti, waxed paper jelly-bowls and tins of Playbox biscuits.

David took out the pillow-case from under his pullover and began to fill it. He dropped a piece of angelica on the floor for the cat, who sniffed, shook a paw and stalked out, disgusted.

When the pillow-case had been filled with the right things, David left the larder, switched off the light in the passageway and returned to the kitchen.

With his pillow-case over his shoulder like Father Christmas, he let himself out of the back door.

He walked through the night, clouds of vapour coming from his mouth and nostrils. He felt happy and charged with energy and vigour.

The outhouse he was heading for used once to be part of the laundry buildings and lay between the stable block and the gamekeeper's cottage. Simon called it the 'B and L' room now, for beaters and loaders.

The moon, high in the starlit sky, shone on the door and lit the iron padlock with a lick of silver. David took the key from his pocket and unfastened the lock.

Far away, in the spinneys and copses, the pheasants shifted in their roosts. Rabbits fled from barking vixens, owls swooped on scampering voles and, back in the yard, the black cat that unseen by David had slipped with him out of the kitchen, batted a dying mouse from paw to paw.

Sitting on a large box marked 'Eley', David straddled the machine. He pulled back the brass lever and hummed a little tune to himself as he engaged the treadle.

II

Simon jumped out of the Range Rover with Soda, his spaniel bitch, and looked amongst the crowd of beaters for a sign of his brother. Eventually he saw David standing apart from the others, stroking the head of one of the labradors. At a whistle from Henry the gamekeeper's lad, the dog turned and sprinted towards the group of pickers-up who were making ready to leave. David, deprived of company, looked up in Simon's direction. Simon immediately pretended to be scanning the sky and smelling the wind.

Ahead of him lay the drive, a long avenue of beech, oak and elm. Simon closed up his gun, brought it to his shoulder and sighted into the air above the trees.

'Blam!' he whispered. 'Blam!'

A giant hand landed on his shoulder. 'If a sportsman true you'd be, Listen carefully to me, Never, never let your gun . . .'

Simon joined in, '. . . Pointed be at anyone. When a hedge or fence you cross, Though of time it cause a loss, From your gun the cartridge take, For the greatest safety sake.'

Lord Logan nodded.

'Sorry, Dad,' said Simon, breaking the gun. 'I was just . . . you know.'

His father shrugged with a smile. He looked over his shoulders like a conspirator and drew a silver hip-flask from his coat pocket. 'Chivas Regal,' he said. 'One nip only. Don't tell your mother.'

The whisky stung Simon's throat and tears started in his eyes.

'Whooh!' he said. 'Thanks, Dad.'

Lord Logan screwed the lid back on and looked down at Simon's dog. 'Whisky and Soda,' he said and winked.

Simon laughed. Today he was the only gun with his own dog. Everybody else would have to rely on pickers-up to retrieve their dead game. Soda was Simon's dog and she would bring his kills back to him personally.

'We're numbering eight, we're moving two!' called Henry.

Lord Logan looked in the direction of the drive, where the drawing of numbers was under way. 'Have you drawn?' he asked.

Simon shook his head.

'Good,' said his father. 'Best not. Let the older guns fight it out, eh? We'll double-bank you behind Conrad.'

Simon's face fell. 'But I want to be at the front!'

'Conrad's a dreadful shot. You'll do well.' Lord Logan's mouth wrinkled in the special distaste it reserved for whines and whinges.

Simon blushed. 'Thanks, Dad.'

'Well, then. Let battle commence.'

Simon kept a few paces behind to watch the effect his father had on the others as he joined the main group of guns. Men and women stepped back, eyes sliding covertly in his direction. Everybody smiled. Simon knew that some were smiling because of the preposterously perfect condition of his father's clothes, the shining Purdey guns, the gleaming new leather, the perfectly made hat from Lock's, the hand-warmers, the cartridge belt, the tailored tweed coat and the tight narrow leggings that tapered down from his broad bulk – dark stockings over moleskins. Dad knew too and he didn't care. He liked the best of everything and said so often enough. Mummy's friends and family were in the tattiest old tweeds and muddiest boots and thought highly of themselves because of it. Dad let them smile. He knew they smiled for other reasons too.

David and the other beaters had gone off round to the wood behind the avenue. The guns and loaders, all men, were beginning to arrange themselves, two to a peg. Simon went up to one of the loaders.

'Just chuck us some boxes,' he said.

The grown-ups had a loader each and a pair of guns, so that they could keep shooting with one gun while the other was being loaded. Simon did have two twelve-bore guns, but one was an over-and-under, a present from Aunt Rebecca who, being a woman, had no idea that over-and-unders were not on; they were fit only for foreigners, armed robbers and weekend nobodies. The barrels on a proper shotgun, everybody knew, had to be side by side. To make matters worse, Aunt Rebecca's gun had a box lock instead of a side lock, which put it completely beyond the pale. Therefore, beautiful as it may have been and ideal for a private and solitary rough shoot, Simon had left it behind. He prayed that Aunt Rebecca, who was milling about around the back with Uncle Ted and a group of women and spectators from the village, wouldn't notice. Simon did have another shotgun, a four-ten which he had grown up on, potting at crows and rabbits, but after a long debate with himself he had decided that he should take just his one dependable old twelve-bore and do his own loading.

He filled the pockets of his Barbour with cartridge boxes. Soda danced around him displaying all the excitement and pleasure that Simon was trying hard to conceal.

He saw his seventeen-year-old cousin Conrad, drawn at number three, and took up a position behind him.

'Oh bloody hell,' said Conrad. 'Don't stand behind me. I don't want to die.'

Simon blushed.

'I'm a good shot,' he muttered.

'Got a bloody dog with you, too, have you? Well, I'm not having any running-in.'

'She won't run in,' said Simon indignantly.

'Well, she'd better not.'

'Sh!' Lord Draycott, an elderly man further along the line, scowled at Conrad from under a rather wide cloth cap.

Conrad snorted contemptuously. 'It's pheasant, for God's sake! They're virtually deaf.'

'These are wild birds, Conrad,' whispered the man next to Conrad, whom Simon recognised as Max Clifford, a friend of his father's. 'Sporting birds. They startle easily. They're not hand-reared as they are in Hampshire.'

Somehow, in Max's soft tones, the word 'Hampshire' came out as a terrible insult. Conrad reddened and turned away. Simon settled himself. Soda sat neatly beside him, tongue out, panting gently. Quiet descended.

Simon continued to recite 'A Father's Advice' to himself, under his breath.

'Keep your place and silent be, Game can hear and game can see. Don't be greedy, better spared, Is a pheasant than one shared.'

A cock pheasant strolled out of the wood and into the main drive towards them, clucking loudly. Someone laughed.

Simon felt inside his pocket and drew out two cartridges.

'If 'twixt you and neighbouring gun, Bird may fly and beast may run, Let this maxim e'er be thine, Follow not across the line.'

The pheasant continued its strut down the avenue, neck thrusting arrogantly backwards and forwards.

Simon pushed the cartridges into the barrels and closed the gun.

'Stops and beaters oft unseen, Lurk behind some leafy screen. Calm and steady always be, Never shoot where you can't see.'

The pheasant's cheerful walk slowed. He peered doubtfully ahead and seemed slowly to become aware of a line of pink faces, of brown, green and russet tweed and of shining gun-metal ranged against him. He checked his swagger and set his neck forward in goggling disbelief, which reminded Simon of the cross-eyed barman in Laurel and Hardy films.

Simon breathed hard through his nose and swallowed.

'You may kill or you may miss,' he whispered to himself, 'But at all times think of this, All the pheasants ever bred, Won't repay for one man dead.'

The pheasant threw a glance back into the spinney he had just left. Simon thought the bird had made some connection. With a rising note of outrage in his throat, as if trying to send some desperate warning signal to his family and friends back there in the wood, the pheasant rose.

At the same time, Lord Logan brought to his lips a silver horn and blew. Deep within the woods a mighty roar went up and the beaters began to stamp and strike the ground.

Simon licked his lips and banged his feet into a solid two o'clock position, weight forward on his left leg. His right thumb flicked the safety catch. The other guns rose from their shooting-sticks. Soda squared herself.

All at once the air was filled with squadrons of rocketing pheasants. Gunshots sounded everywhere like harsh coughs, and little puffs of smoke blossomed in the air.

Simon had practised this in his head so many times. The birds had to come high to clear the trees, which is why the guns were positioned where they were. But they came so fast: three or four hundred flushed in one go. By the time Simon could sight they were already over his head. He followed one bird up from the cover and fired off the first barrel just before his gun reached the vertical. He brought the gun down fifty degrees, followed another bird and managed to loose off again, aiming for the beak.

He had broken his gun and was scrambling to reload when a shout came from the woods.

'Steady boys: whoa, whoa! Hold hard!'

The last few pheasants fluttered past and Simon heard echoes of the closing volleys of gunshot rattle off the windows and brick-work of the house half a mile behind them. The first

31

flush had taken perhaps forty seconds and he had only just managed to get off both barrels. Conrad had fired off fourteen rounds. There rose a barking and yelping through the trees.

'Go on, Soda!' shouted Simon. 'Go on, girl!'

Soda sprang forward and dashed into the woods: Simon thought he might have downed a bird with his second barrel. Soda would have seen.

A shout went up.

'Look! Look!'

Simon saw, now that the gun smoke had cleared, that the air ahead of them was full of what appeared to be falling petals. The pickers-up were standing in bewilderment, their dogs circling them and whimpering as a coloured blizzard swirled about.

Simon heard Aunt Rebecca's voice behind him. 'It's . . . for God's sake . . . it's *confetti*!'

'Bravo! Charming!' said Uncle Ted.

'Bloody hell!' said Conrad.

Soda trotted out of the spinney with a pheasant in her mouth which she dropped at her master's feet.

Simon looked down in disgust. 'It's a runner,' he said. The bird was still alive, its beak opening and closing, its crooked, wrinkled legs working frantically. Simon picked it up and twisted its neck until he heard a crack.

The others gathered round.

'What the hell's going on?'

'This is the only bloody kill!'

Simon looked up in embarrassment as everyone crowded round him.

'What do you mean?' he said.

'We mean,' said Conrad, 'that no one else has bagged a single sodding bird. That's what we mean.'

Simon didn't understand. The first flush in a well-stocked cover like that should mean a kill of at least a hundred birds.

Lord Logan took the pheasant out of Simon's hands. Henry, the gamekeeper's assistant, was hurrying forward towards them, an expression both of wild fury and of complete puzzlement on his face.

Lord Logan examined the pheasant. There were little silver balls caught up in its gorge.

'Silver shot?' someone exclaimed. 'That's going it, even for you, Michael.'

Simon saw his father's eyes flash for a second under his heavy brows.

'This is not shot,' he said, rolling a single ball between his thumb and forefinger. 'Nor is it silver.'

He put the ball in his mouth and crunched it between his teeth.

'Sugar!' he said mournfully. 'Just sugar.'

Simon took a fresh cartridge out of his pocket and began to unpick the end. Into his father's outstretched palm he poured out a heap of coloured hundreds and thousands, silvered sugar balls, rice and a wad of confetti.

'Christ!' said Conrad. 'Sabs. It's the bloody sabs.'

'Sabs?' said Simon. 'They wouldn't . . .'

'Sabs! Sabs! We've been bloody sabbed!'

The cry went up and gathered into a roar that mingled with the chuckling of the pheasants as they settled back in their roosts and mingled too with the weeping, squealing laughter of one of the beaters who had lagged behind the others and now lay on the ground, deep in the wood, wriggling with happiness and, true to his trade, beating and beating and beating the ground with small fists.

Three

Dear Uncle Ted,

    This is just a note to thank you so much for your present. I'm very sorry you couldn't make the service itself, but I do understand that your life is immensely busy.

    Mr Bridges, my English master, tells me that what you sent is a first edition, which is extremely valuable. I am very touched by your generosity. I have never read the *Four Quartets* before, although we did *The Waste Land* for GCSE which I enjoyed enormously, so I am looking forward very much to reading and understanding these new poems. Are they connected at all to Beethoven's quartets, I wonder? My favourite poet is Wordsworth at the moment.

    The confirmation was magnificent. The Bishop of St Alban's spoke to us all beforehand and reminded us of the solemnity of the occasion. When the moment came for him to lay his hand upon my head I found myself crying. I hope you don't think that was wrong of me. I think I was moved more by the idea of the apostolic succession than by anything else. Christ laid a hand on Peter's head, Peter became Bishop of Rome and he laid a hand on the head of everyone else who became a bishop. Even though we broke with Rome in the sixteenth century, the bishops of the Church of England can trace themselves by a hand laid on the head, all the way back to Christ.

When I bit the wafer I was surprised by how tasty it was. I had been told by everyone that it would be disgusting – like cardboard. Actually it reminded me of the rice-paper that you find on the underside of a macaroon. The wine was very sweet, but that's how I prefer it anyway.

You said that you hoped confirmation would live up to its name and that, as well as confirming my faith publicly, the service would confirm something in me privately. Well, I suppose it has, really. Everyone is agreed that the world is getting to be a worse place year by year. There is more crime, more poverty, more corruption, more distress. I think that Grace, which we talked about a lot in confirmation classes, is probably the only thing that can save the world. That's very idealistic I know, but I think it makes more logical sense than anything else. Grace is about looking *inwards* not outwards. If everyone looked inwards to their own souls, or psyches or whatever word you want to use, then all the sins in the world would disappear. If only we could all put up our hands and say 'the problems are all my fault' there would be no problems.

Simon has been made house captain this term and is in the first XV, so we are all very proud of him. He wants to go into the army after school, but Daddy wants him to try for Oxford. I'm not sure what I want to do, not the army anyway. I would truly love, more than anything else, to be a poet like you.

After all, what else is *worth* doing?

> *The world is too much with us; late and soon,*
> *Getting and spending, we lay waste our powers:*
> *Little we see in Nature that is ours;*
> *We have given our hearts away . . .*

It's now after prep and I've just found a very marvellous line in the *Four Quartets* that talks about how the stones of a building don't reflect light, but actually *absorb* it. I think that is saying something about the love of God.

I hope you will absorb my love and thanks for a wonderful present.

Lots of love

David
XXX

I tried my damnedest to recall whether myself at that age, I had been quite such a pi, punchable little shit as this. I remembered listening to illicit jazz and climbing ladders to catch the house-master's daughter undressing; I remembered all the fights, farts and fidgets of a bog-standard, bog-quality British education; I remembered howling with injustice, roaring with passion and grunting with loneliness; I remembered talking about poetry, certainly, and pledging that the poets of the future would grab mankind by the balls and give such a vicious twist that the whole human race would scream for mercy. But wanking on about Grace and sin? Spraying out pissy dribbles of Words-worth sonnetry? I don't think so. 'The Bishop of St Alban's spoke to us all beforehand and reminded us of the solemnity of the occasion' indeed. Did the sanctimonious squirt think he was writing a letter to a godfather or an article for the school magazine? 'I would truly love, more than anything else, to be a poet like you.' Did he mean he would love to be, like me, a poet? Or was he crawly (and idiotic) enough to mean that he wanted to be the kind of poet I was? Cold Christ and tangled Trinities, what an anus.

4 Butler's Yard
St James's
LONDON SW1

Dear David,

What a remarkable letter. I am delighted that my little present has hit the mark so surely.

I too was disappointed not to be amongst those present at your confirmation. I recall my own with exceptional clarity. Chichester, not the loveliest of our great cathedrals – squat and ugly as a toad if the truth be out – but holy in my memory. The service took place on one of those afternoons that occur only in the past. Sunlight kissed the altar-table, the chalices, patens and candlesticks, the bishop's mitre and our young neophyte heads with a golden rim-light calculated to cause the sternest atheist among us to whinny with unconditional faith.

Utter balls, naturally. The only thing gleaming with light that afternoon was the dew-drop depending from the bish's nose.

There is no doubt, whatever one's perspective on these matters, that the numen created by a gathering-together of people united in one common spiritual cause is as palpable as the ground they kneel upon. Whether this is truer in an Anglican cathedral than in a Buddhist temple or a front-parlour séance of crackpot spiritualists is not within my province to say. I *am* pleased, however, that you are getting something out of old Tom Eliot, whom I did indeed know. He published me at Faber and Faber when I was starting out. Said some rather nice things about me – then again, towards the end, he said nice things about a whole fleet of talentless ninnies, none of whom you would have heard of, nor ever will hear of again. There was a man called Botterill he was absolutely sold on. Who reads Botterill today? Why, even fewer people than read me, and that is saying something.

However, that is neither here nor there. I wanted to say, principally, how impressed I was by the sentiments expressed with such courage and conviction in your letter. My only other godchild is your cousin Jane, and as you know, I am not on speakers with that side of your family, so I count myself very lucky in having an intelligent and interesting godchild with whom it is a pleasure to correspond. It'll be your holidays soon, I suppose. It would be a great treat if we could get together and see if between us we can't get to the bottom of this business of art and life. I wonder if it would be possible for me to come over some time in the summer and stay at the Hall? We would be able to read, think, talk, sip cordials and pick daisies together, or as Burns prefers, we can 'pluck the gowans fine'. My own son (you remember Roman?) will be with his respective and disrespectful mother over most of the summer holiday so I shall be alone and in sore need of some intellectual and spiritual stimulus.

Outrageous. Ted, you fucker, is this what you've come to? Cadging country-house visits off your godchildren? Admit it, you sad old bugger, the only 'intellectual and spiritual stimulus' you were ever in need of was a quick shag in the shrubbery with a domestic. I did need a way in to Swafford, however, if I was to earn my lovely lovely money. It was also possible that the company of a mooning romantic might disgust me enough to egg on some new and crunchy verse of my own.

So why not mention the idea to your parents, old lad, and see what they think? It's been an age since I've seen you and, dissipated and disgraceful as I may be, my promises at the font do mean something to me. Perhaps your youth will inspire me to write poetry again. I find that time and age have corrupted my powers and that, as your favourite poet observes, 'the vision splendid' does indeed 'fade into the common light of day'.

> *Whither is fled the visionary gleam?*
> *Where is it now, the glory and the dream?*

P-U! I had to leap up and pace the room whistling and humming and kicking the wainscoting to take the taste of that one away.

So, here's looking forward to a summer of discovery and amusement,

Your affectionate godfather

Ted.

Oh, you howling old hypocrite, what a beast you are, what a dread cruel beast. What a great, slavering, wicked and contemptible monster. How can you hold up your head? How can you look yourself in the face? How can you sleep? You horrible, horrible man.

Dear Uncle Ted,
    Your letter made me dance. Mummy or Daddy will be in touch soon. I hope you can stay at least a whole month!

> *. . . neither evil tongues,*
> *Rash judgments, nor the sneers of selfish men,*
> *Nor greetings where no kindness is, nor all*
> *The dreary intercourse of daily life,*
> *Shall e'er prevail against us, or disturb*
> *Our cheerful faith that all which we behold*
> *Is full of blessings.*

Counting the days,

Love

David
XXX

II

Swafford Hall
Swafford
Norfolk

Sunday, 19th July 1992

Dear Jane,

Your first report, as promised, from within the walls of Troy. My letter to your cousin and god-brother, if there is such a thing, worked like a charm. Little Davey all but sent me his pocket-money to cover my train fare, so keen was he for me to come. Unless I poo things up horribly, I'm here for as long as I behave myself.

Liverpool Street Station has been turned into a sinister and unacceptable mixture of an Edwardian amusement pier and a daytime television studio since last I looked. Absolutely disgusting. Since your cheque seems inexplicably to have been honoured, I travelled First Class. There's only one smoking car on the whole train as far as I can see. In Britrail's futile attempts to ape airlines (in itself a deranged project – about as sensible as going into a barber-shop and asking for a Lindsay Anderson cut) they litter the compartment with a laughable in-carriage glossy called 'Executive' or 'Top Traveller' or some such pukey garbage. Thank Jesus I'll soon be dead. Sorry, that sounds a little callous in the light of your illness. You know what I mean.

Anyway, after an hour and a half's worth of scenery had streaked past my window, the train banged to a testicle-strangling halt at Diss Station and collapsed the little pyramid of Johnny Walker miniatures I had been constructing on the table in front of me. I saw a youth on the platform, tossing and catching a bunch of car-keys like a gangster with a silver dollar. A glossy black spaniel sat by his side exposing its tongue to the air as is the custom of such creatures. The bungling manner with which I attempted to pull my suitcase widthways through a narrow compartment doorway must have told him who I was. It is unlikely he would have remembered me from four years ago, the last time I infested Swafford.

'Hello, sir,' he said, taking the case and deftly twisting it free. 'I'm Simon Logan. Welcome to Norfolk.'

'Good man. Ted Wallace.'

'This is Soda. My spaniel.'

'It's an enormous pleasure, Soda,' I said, dropping a fore-finger on to the animal's muzzle by way of greeting.

Simon led me to the exit.

'David wanted to come too, but I thought you'd enjoy the two-seater.'

A two-tone Austin-Healey stood in the car-park, ice-blue over ivory. A Rank Starlet car, I thought to myself, sort of thing Diana Dors would be photographed in, tossing back her scarfed head with a gleam of teeth and a glitter of winged sun-glasses. You're probably too young to remember Diana Dors, but I put this in at no extra charge. I had been hoping for Michael's well-stocked Rolls-Royce, of course, but the boy was clearly pleased with this machine, so I clucked appropriately.

'I left the roof and window pieces at home to leave room in the boot for your luggage. So long as it doesn't rain, eh?'

I looked up at a huge East Anglian sky, innocent of clouds and blue as . . . my poetic powers have been sucked clean of simile. I can't think what it was as blue as. As blue as blue. As blue as the Virgin's panties. As blue as it was.

Once the town of Diss was behind us, the Austin's engine note and the unmarked lanes created the pleasing illusion of a mild and dusty Dornford Yates England. One half-expected to see horses rearing in shock at the unaccustomed sight of an automobile and slack-jawed villagers nudging one another in wonder. In fact we saw no one. A sheet of stillness lay over everything and we ripped through it like a speedboat across a lake. You probably haven't heard of Dornford Yates either, but there you go.

In the rush of air my forelock flapped in my face as I looked right and left, stinging my eyes. Simon, whose hair is unfashionably short, looked straight ahead, every concen-trated second at the wheel sustaining him in something close to orgasm. I judged him seventeen and only newly licensed. He is the kind of boy who would take his driving test the morning of his birthday and find excuses to drive twenty miles to buy a box of matches. Soda was wedged happily behind us, the tip of her tongue whipped back by the wind till it met the base of her ears.

A silver gleam caught my attention in the distance, across a haze of fields whose crops were just on the turn from green to gold.

'What's that?' I bellowed.

Simon cocked his head.

I stabbed a finger and yelled. 'There! Shiny thing, like a church.'

'Oh, that. Silo.'

'What?'

'For grain. Cheaper to build that than reroof an old barn. Better storage.'

'Ugly bugger.'

I noticed too that the country seemed, Noël Coward jokes about Norfolk aside, *flatter* than I remembered it. This wasn't possible, but there was no doubting the increase in width and depth of view. It was the hedgerows of course, or rather the absence of them. It must have been twenty years ago that they had started to pull them down, but my old man's memory still expected them. In the same way, if Westminster council decided overnight to allow traffic in Piccadilly to flow in both directions I would probably never notice, because I always think of Piccadilly as a two-way street, for all that it must be decades since they buggered it up. Now, here in East Anglia, what with the denuded fields and those great giant's bolsters encased in bin-liner that serve the office of straw-bales and these new and nasty aluminium silos, the landscape resembles something frankly American – you know those great wheat fields in Iowa where, line abreast, massed combine-harvesters roll over the horizon like Panzer divisions? I am a city pigeon of course, needing hard paving-stones beneath my feet and air I can bite, but rural England, for all that, has its place in my heart and I don't like the idea of hooligans arsing around with it.

Simon was amused.

'Got to think of the yield,' he shouted and then – the aggressive cry of despoiling landowners everywhere – 'you want to eat, don't you?'

But hedges are still thickly planted, I noticed, around the approaches to Swafford Hall. There's nothing quite so enlivening to an unregenerate snob such as myself as the sight from a car of flashing parkland trees half-obscuring and half-revealing the chimneys, windows and columns of a great house, like a stripper teasing with a veil. We ate up the lime avenue and the full vulgar glory of the place swung, as L. P. Hartley would say, into view, and then I saw with a stab of regret and self-reproach that there was a boy sitting half-way up the baroque steps that poured from the front portico like a thick stream of molten lava. He stood and shaded his eyes in our direction.

I had deferred any thoughts of how I was going to shake off this wretched child. He had served his purpose by getting me invited here; the last thing I wanted was to trail about the place coping with pretentious adolescent drippery or, worse, being forced to listen to myself dole out my own dime-store apothegms. The answer, perhaps, would be to set him a task of some kind, to devise a devilish assignment that would keep him out of my hair. 'Write me something extensive in *terza rima*,' I pictured myself saying. 'If you're going to be a poet, you must learn to master the forms.'

Simon blew up a cloud of grit and gravel in a sharp and senseless sweeping handbrake turn in front of the house. David came down the steps blinking dust from his eyes.

'Hello, Uncle Edward,' he said, smiling and blushing.

He is a comely boy indeed. Never having had any relish for my own gender, such coltish charms increased my blood pressure by not a bar – indeed I consider his looks a little ridiculous in a male – but I can think of any number of writers and artists of my acquaintance who at the very sight of him would swoon and moan and clutch at a passing vodka for support. Simon is handsome in a colourless way, like an old photographic portrait. He is respectably growing out of his spots and into a conventional English – or in his case of course, half-English – manhood. David's complexion, however, is quite astonishingly clear; in all my life I have not seen skin so wholly without blemish. There is something a little freakish there, I think. I assume you know him better than I do? At all events, his downcast eyes and crimson cheeks speak of a virginal modesty rare in the young today. He bids fair to be fully the kind of prig his letters have threatened.

'Davey, you young hound, well met,' said I, heaving my corse from the car.

What is nowadays almost universally called, with mock

inverted snobbery, a 'real live butler' was standing at the threshold.

'Ah, Podmore, is it not?' I flapped a hand in his direction after a moment's concentrated hesitation, a hesitation designed to show me sifting my memory, recalling and discarding the names of at least twenty other butlers with whom I was on familiar terms. Comes easily to you, my dear, but we Bohemians have got to strive for the effect of insouciance.

'Good afternoon, Mr Wallace. Nice to see you again, sir.' Not that he was fooled for a minute, I dare say.

David had taken my suitcase from the boot of the Austin with a proprietorial air that told the world that I was, certainly as far as he was concerned, *his* guest. Simon waved over his shoulder and launched the car, with a crunching spin of the back wheels, away on some other errand.

Well, well. Here I was. How long I would stay depended, I supposed, on the kind of reception Michael gave me. Your idea of telling him that I would like to write a biography is all very well, but.

The fact is, and I didn't tell you this earlier, Jane, but I know for certain that at least two fairly prestigious hacks have tried before now to biograph Michael Logan with little success. Swafford Hall is known in journalistic circles as the Writs Hotel.

I'm not saying it won't work – after all Michael trusts me, trusts me rather as Guy Burgess was trusted, in the belief that anyone of such naked indiscretion and unreliability must be loyal and true – but I feel you should know that some other approach may prove necessary in the end. *Nous verrons ce que nous verrons.*

David had reached the top of the steps, the weight of the case listing his slight frame.

'It's all right, Mr Podmore,' he said. 'I'll show Uncle Edward his room.' *Mister* Podmore? Disquietingly bourgeois.

'Had I better punch in with the parentals before we go any further?' I wondered, sensing the prospect of the long terrace tea that melts seamlessly into veranda cocktails, on which I had set my heart, recede into the distance.

'Mummy's shopping in Norwich this afternoon,' came the happy reply. 'And Daddy's in London. This way.'

I forbore to ask when Michael was expected back. The trick of being a good guest is never to ask any questions about the composition of the household. Hosts, even the

43

grandest, are nervous creatures and interpret curiosity as evidence of dissatisfaction.

'Perfect,' I said, lumbering up the steps.

David had at least, in bagging the Landseer Room for me, swung me first-class accommodation. Have you ever stayed there? The room is huge, comfortably bedded, well supplied with Chippendale and Hepplewhite and generous of view. Of particular interest to me, for I am a man who loves his tub, there is a connecting bathroom stuffed to a level of Babylonian profligacy with costly oils and unguents and whose shower and bath are equipped with taps which can be operated from a console beside the bed. Only Michael Logan could be potty enough to employ servants who have nothing better to do than fill baths and then go to the expense of fitting machinery which can do their job for them. The curtains at least are operated manually, which is a great blessing, there being few pleasures in life higher than that of waking to the sound of a housemaid swishing in the daylight.

There is a price to pay for everything however, and in the case of the Landseer Room the reckoning comes in the form of the preposterous painting that hangs over the fireplace. This disgraceful quarter-acre waste of canvas depicts a spaniel of some kind straining alert and proud on a high castle rampart which gives over a vast Speyside strath or glen or whatever they call valleys in Scotland these days. The work is entitled, if you have a bucket handy, *Lord of All He Surveys*. There are other bedrooms, I know, which offer more acceptable art, including a passable *Deathwish of the Cumaean Sybil* and a more or less juicy *Zeus Ravishing Europa with Dryad and Nymph Standing By in Antic Pose*, but none has the style and comfort of this room, so I am prepared to let the spaniel pass for the sake of the fragrant bathing and amiable views. One of the things I shall have to ask Michael is whether he buys his art by the hundredweight or whether he uses his eye. I am at least denied the unspeakable horrors of the Hobhouse Room, whose dread *For Found Is the Lamb that Once Was Lost* can provoke nightmares and bucking hysteria in all but the most iron-willed. You ever met Oliver Mills? An old crony of your father and me. Screechingest of screeching queens, a depriested director of films and television – you must know Oliver. Anyway, he was once found skittering up and down the corridor outside the Hobhouse Room wrapped in an eiderdown and wailing, 'Lead me to a garret, a servant's hovel, a kennel, a Forte hotel, *anything*!' Naturally, Muggins had to swap rooms with him.

But the lordly spaniel surveying his domain (or should that be demesne?) I can take, especially since the other lordly spaniel, David, had sweetly taken a lot of trouble to cater for my every whim.

'Ah!' I said, sighting the drinks table. 'Everything is as it should be.'

David followed my eye to the tall, green, glittering forest set in its twinkling crystal sea. 'It is whisky you like, isn't it, Uncle Edward?'

'Before we go any further, old darling,' I said, 'shall we dispense with the Uncle? Ted will do, just plain Ted.'

'Right,' said David. 'Ted. As in Heath.'

'A boy of your age has heard of Ted Heath?'

David was startled. 'He was the Prime Minister, wasn't he?'

'Oh, *that* Ted Heath. Thought you meant the band leader.'

'Band leader?'

Christ, I abominate children. And Christ, I abominate my receding memory.

'Well, Davey,' I said, 'think I'll . . . ah . . . take a bath and conceivably a short nap.'

'Oh . . . right.' He hid his disappointment well. 'Absolutely. You know where everything is?'

'Rather.'

He backed to the door. 'I'll . . . when you come down . . . there's the South Lawn which is . . .' he pointed to the wall behind the bed, '. . . that way. I'll probably be hanging about round there if you want to . . . you know. Chat.'

I felt a bit of a swine.

'Davey,' I said, looking at him straight. 'It's simply wonderful to be here. We're going to have a splendid time. Thank you for asking me.'

His face lit up. 'Thank you for coming. There is so much . . .' He paused, shook his head and left the room, closing the door behind him.

Sleek and soft from patchouli oil and glowing with good malt, I sat an hour later, a sheet of Swafford Hall writing-paper in front of me and the view across the lawns and parkland beyond. I would concentrate on the drudgery of writing this letter to you later, but for the moment there was no reason not to tickle the Muse's tits and see if she mightn't start to express. It was unlikely a poem would come in such peaceful circumstances, but you certainly won't get if you don't ask. I listed, as is my custom, such few words as my mood and the scene suggested.

Held
Surface
Gaumy
Suspension
Ataractic
Gross
Weight
Mollity
Burst
This
Spread
Suzerainty
Piss-gold
Widened
Hotter

I examined this list for some quarter of an hour. The rare words often annoy the punter, but they never think, they never stop to *think* about a poet's life. A painter has oils, acrylics and pastels, turpentine, linseed, canvas, sable and hog's hair. When did you last employ such things routinely? To oil a cricket bat or mascara an eyelid, perhaps. Come to think of it, you've probably never oiled a cricket bat in your life, but you know what I mean. And musicians: a musician has entire machines of wood, brass, gut and carbon fibre; he has augmented sevenths, accidentals, Dorian modes and twelve-note rows. When did you ever use an augmented seventh as a way of getting back at your boyfriend or a bassoon obbligato to order pizza? Never. Never, never, never. The poet, though. Oh, yes, the poor poet: pity the poor bloody poet. The poet has no reserved materials, no unique modes. He has nothing but words, the same tools that the whole cursed world uses to ask the way to the nearest lava-tory, or with which they patter out excuses for the clumsy betrayals and shiftless evasions of their ordinary lives; the poet has nothing but the same, self-same, words that daily in a million shapes and phrases curse, pray, abuse, flatter and mislead. The poor bloody poet can no longer say 'ope' for 'open', or 'swain' for 'youth', he is expected to construct new poems out of the plastic and Styrofoam garbage that litters the twentieth-century linguistic floor, to make fresh art from the used verbal condoms of social intercourse. Is it any wonder that, from time to time, we take refuge in 'gellies' and 'ataractic' and 'watchet'? Innocent words, virgin words, words uncontaminated and unviolated, the very mastery of which announces us to possess a relationship with language akin to that of the sculptor with his marble or the composer with his staves. Not that anyone is ever *impressed*, of course. They only moan about the 'impenetrability' or congratulate themselves for being hep to the ellipsis, opacity and allusion that they believe deepens and enriches the work. It's a bastard profession, believe me.

Well, well . . . I can make any number of excuses, but I suppose the real truth is that the energy has gone out of me, has been weeping from me for ten years. Too many appearances on 'The Late Show' and Melvyn Bragg, too many easy offers to anthologise and edit, too much regard and petting, and lately, far too much of the old electric soup. I crossed out the list of words, scrawled 'FUSTIAN!' in angry letters across the page and stored the sheet of paper in the desk. I would have screwed it up and tossed it away were it not that a deranged university in Texas has paid me for the rights to all my papers.

'Papers?' I had asked when approached by their Professor of Modern Poetry. 'What do you mean papers?'

'Hell, you know . . . notebooks, drafts, correspondence . . . papers.'

What kind of self-conscious and insufferably twee belle-lettriste ponce keeps *notebooks*? I asked myself. Utterly absurd, but the money was good, so I sat down one weekend and forged dozens of likely-looking rough drafts of my better-known poems. It was the greatest lark alive, scrawling inde-cipherable Greek in the margin, writing 'but Skelton????', '*mild und leise wie er lächelt*', 'see Reitlinger's *Economics of Taste* Vol. II, page 136' and 'No, no, no, no, no, no! Close the field, close the field!!!' in different-coloured inks across the pages. At one point I wrote 'posterity can suck my cock' in pencil and then erased it. It took less than four years for an American graduate to uncover this and write to me asking what I had meant by it. She came over to England three months later on a research fellowship and found out.

Forgive me for rambling, my dear, but you've no idea what a relief it is to get all this off my chest. Besides, since you haven't told me what to look for, I've nothing else to write about yet.

Anyway, despairing of poetry, I was pouring myself another glass of scotch when the telephone next to my bed rang.

'Ted, it's Anne.'

'My love!'

'Quite. Settled comfortably in?'

'Snugger than a bugger in a rugger scrum.'

'Then come downstairs, I want to talk to you.'

She was in one of the south-facing drawing rooms, looking out of the window. She turned at the sound of creaking floorboard and favoured me with a welcoming smile.

'Ted, it's actually tremendous to see you.'

I joined her at the window, kissing each cheek and then stepping back to examine her. A taking little creature she has always been; fair hair, good cheekbones, eyes as blue as et cetera. I don't know how much you know about her, she's only your aunt by marriage, so I'll fill in a little for you.

She had met Logan while he and I were still clumping around in uniform. He hadn't a button in those days and she was the daughter of a bust and useless earl. While engaged on some footling divisional exercise in the Thetford Chase area, Michael and I, as the only subalterns in our distinctly shabby regiment who didn't say 'pardon' or hold our knives like pencils, had been taken by the CO for dinner at Swafford Hall, then a mouldering heap so cold that your breath stood out in the drawing room and the women's nipples peaked like bakelite studs. Anne was eleven years old at that time and had been pressed into the traditional child's service of handing out olives and smiling sweetly at the guests before being packed off to bed. I hadn't noticed her much, except to see that she had dog hairs on the back of a rather plain velvet dress.

In the car on the way back, with the CO nuzzled against his shoulder in a rumbling stupor, Michael had turned to me.

'Tedward,' he whispered, 'some day I'm going to marry that girl and buy that house.'

'Not before I've been made Poet Laureate,' I had said.

'It's a deal.'

The driver turned round and winked. 'And I'll be leader of the Labour Party,' he said.

'Shut up, Corporal,' we snapped in chorus, 'and watch the road.'

The CO had woken up and puked fiercely all over Michael's mess-jacket.

What happened to that driver I have no idea. For all I know he did become leader of the Labour Party. I never took much of an interest in these things. It is a certain truth that they didn't make me Poet Laureate and that they wouldn't if I were the only British poet left alive, which, as a matter of fact, I happen to believe I am. Michael left the army, with me, the moment our two years were up. Ten years later he had married Lady Anne and within another two the noble father-in-law's embolism burst and Michael bought Swafford off Alec, the new Lord Bressingham, a sneaky young tyke who looked a cross between Bryan Forbes and Laurence Harvey and was only too pleased to fold the cash in his lizard-skin wallet and skip to a flat in Berkeley Square. It was a kinky little caprice of fate, all of a piece with Logan's guiding star, that Alec Bressingham then spent the next five years giving that money right back in the form of gambling chips at the string of casinos that Michael then ran in May-fair. Alec even contrived to shoot himself in a Logan-owned hotel. Anne hadn't worried too much, the lad was only the remotest kind of cousin and she had always suspected him of anti-Semitism, a taint she could smell anywhere, like so many who marry into the tribe. She acquitted me of the vice, however, probably because I was so brazen in hailing Michael as 'you old Jew'. She is usually pleased to see me, so long as I behave myself.

I finished my inspection of her.

'And it's just as tremendous to see you, Annie,' I replied. 'You're looking younger. Lost some of that fat.'

'Michael's in town. Hopes to make it down for next week. Sends you a punch in the belly.'

I noticed she had half an eye still on the window. I followed the direction of her gaze. The South Lawn, as I assume you know, slopes down to a lake, in front of which, on rising ground, stands a miniature version of the Villa Rotunda, built as a kind of summerhouse. Anne saw me watching her, shrugged and smiled.

'David's in there,' she said. 'Ted, I think it's simply the best thing that you've come.'

'Ah,' I said, non-committally.

'I'm so worried about him. I ought to tell you . . . it's a little strange . . .'

She broke off. Simon was standing in the doorway.

'Mother, I'm going off to Wymondham to see Robbie. That okay?'

'Yes, darling.'

'I might stay the night.'

'Fine, fine. Make sure you tell Podmore you won't be in to dinner . . .'

He nodded and left. Anne sat down.

'Army, I understand?' I said, joining her on the sofa.

She seemed confused. 'Army? What army?'

I pointed to the door. 'Simon.'

'Oh. Yes. Yes, that's right.'

'Seems mad,' I said, waffling on to give her a chance to unburden herself of whatever it was she wished to unburden herself. 'I only went in because they would have hurled me in the slammer if I'd refused. The idea of someone actually wanting to sign up when it isn't compulsory . . . done his Wosbie, has he?'

'No . . . it's not Wosbie any more. It's the . . . the RCB, or some such.'

'Yes,' I growled affably, quite content to play the part of the trumpeting old war-horse. 'Quite. "The Professionals", they call themselves these days. An ability to keep the port decanter from touching the table as it goes around is not enough. You have to be able to speak Cantonese, strip a tank-engine, lead a discussion group on Post-Traumatic Stress Disorder and know your men's Christian names.'

'Ted,' she said at last, a pleading note in her voice, 'you're a poet. An artist. I know you like to . . . to make fun of yourself, but that's what you are.'

'That's what I am.'

'I've never understood much of your work, but then of course one isn't supposed to, is one?'

'Well . . .'

'But I do know that you must think a great deal about . . . about, oh I don't know . . . *ideas*.'

'A young poet once said to Mallarmé, "I had the most marvellous idea for a poem this afternoon." "Oh dear," said

Mallarmé, "what a pity." "What do you mean?" said the young poet, stung. "Well," said Mallarmé, "poems aren't made of ideas, are they? They're made of words." '

'Oh, do be serious, Ted, just for once. Please.'

I had thought I was being serious, but I duly switched on a pensive expression and leaned forward.

'We're all rather concerned that David is turning out oddly.'

'Oh yes?'

'It's nothing,' Anne put her hands to her cheeks like a flushed maiden, 'it's nothing you can put your finger on. He's an absolute dear. Terribly kind, terribly thoughtful. Everyone thinks him perfectly sweet. He's never in trouble at school. He just doesn't seem to be quite . . . of this world.'

'Daydreamer.'

'Well, that's not quite it. I think he's not . . . *connected* to us. Does that make sense?'

'It's an age when privacy counts, you know.'

'At a dinner party last weekend he said in a very clear voice to the wife of our local MP, "Which animal do you think has the longest penis?" She gave a hysterical laugh and snapped the stem of her wine glass. But he persisted. "No, which do you think? Which animal?" At last, out of desperation, she suggested the blue whale. "No," he said. "The male rabbit-flea. The erect penis of the male rabbit-flea is two-thirds the length of its body. Don't you think that's the most marvellous thing?" Then he saw we were all staring at him and he flushed scarlet and said: "You'll have to forgive me. I'm not very good at conversation." I mean. Ted. Wouldn't you call that extraordinary?'

'Certainly,' I said. 'I mean, poor *female* rabbit-flea. I trust she has been blessed with accommodation elastic enough for such a frantic attachment. But in truth,' I added hastily, for I saw this was not the answer she required, 'David is fifteen. Fifteen-year-olds are always odd. They like to rattle the cage, to tug on the leash, to find their . . . their *space*, I believe the expression is.'

'You'll know what I mean when you've spent any time with him. So distant, so detached. As if he's a visitor here.'

'Well I'm a visitor here,' I said, rising, 'and it's a lovely feeling. But certainly I'll observe him if that's what you want. I expect it'll turn out that he's in love with the gamekeeper's daughter or some such.'

'Hardly. She has a hare-lip.'

'That needn't be a bar to love. There was a whore in Rupert Street had a hare-lip. Gave the most delicious . . .'

I decided to leave the story for another time, bowed a crisp farewell and set my compass for the South Lawn.

David had emerged from the Villa Rotunda and was now on the lawn in front of it, lying on his stomach and chewing a plantain stalk.

'Good bath, good nap?' he asked.

'Didn't manage the latter,' I said, lowering myself on to the bottom step of the stone stairs that ran up to the summerhouse.

He looked at me through squinting eyes. 'The summer-house suits you,' he said. 'Same noble proportions.'

Cheeky sod.

'You speak truer than you know,' I replied, looking over my shoulder at the structure behind. 'John Betjeman's nick-name for me was the Villain Rotunda.'

He smiled dutifully and removed the stalk from his mouth. 'Have you been crying?' he asked.

'Touch of hay-fever. The air is thick with pollen and other unnatural pollutants. My soft-tissues are geared for London you see, with its wholesome sulphur and nutritious nitrogen.'

He nodded. 'I saw you through the window with Mummy.'

'Oh ah.'

'Were you talking about me?'

'What on earth makes you think that?'

'Oh,' he stared down at a money-spider chasing around his finger tips, 'she worries about me.'

'If you were advertising for a mother in the Situations Vacant column of a newspaper and wanted to frame the job description you couldn't come up with a phrase better than "Must be prepared to worry twenty-four hours a day." It's what mothers *do*, Davey. And if for ten minutes they stop worrying, that worries them, so they redouble their worry.'

'Well I know that . . . but she worries more about me than about Simon or the twins. I see it in the way she looks at me.'

'Yes, but the twins have got a nanny, haven't they? And Simon, with the best will in the world, Simon is . . .'

'Simon is what?'

52

I hesitated to use the words 'ordinary' or 'dull' or even 'unintelligent' which were probably unfair.

'Simon is more conventional, isn't he? You know, head boy, rugger, army, all that. He's . . . safe.'

'Meaning I'm *unsafe*?'

'I bloody well hope so. I'm not having any godchild of mine going about the place being anything other than wild and dangerous.'

David smiled. 'I suppose Mummy told you about the dinner party the other night?'

'Something about a rabbit-flea?'

'Why are people embarrassed about sexual things?'

'I'm not.'

'No?'

'Certainly not,' I said, taking out a cigarette.

'You have sex a great deal, don't you? So everyone says.'

'A great deal? Depends what you mean. I take it when I can get it, that's for sure.'

'Simon says he saw you with Mrs Brooke-Cameron once.'

'Did he? Did he indeed? I trust we put on an entertaining show.'

He stood up and brushed the grass from him. 'Shall we go for a walk?'

'Why not? You can cut me a stout ash-plant and tell me the names of the wild flowers.'

We headed towards the lake and copses beyond.

'In my opinion,' he said, 'people are more embarrassed about love than about sex.'

'Ah. What makes you think that?'

'Well, nobody talks about it, do they?'

'I thought they talked about little else. Every film, every pop song, every television programme. Love, love, love. Make love, not tea. All you need is love. Love is a many-splendoured thing. Love makes the world go to pieces.'

'Well, that's like saying they talk about religion because they say "Christ!" and "Oh my God" a lot. They *mention* love, but they don't actually talk about it.'

'And I wonder,' I said, 'if you have ever been in love?'

'Oh yes,' said David. 'Since I can remember.'

'Mm.'

We walked on in silence for a while, skirting the lake. The skin of the water was twitching with waterboatmen, dragon-flies and a tangle of skating insects I could not identify. A heavy, meaty smell of water, mud and rot rose from the margins. David was looking all around as he walked, eyes darting in every direction. It wasn't quite as if he was looking for anything, I thought. I was reminded instead of a game called Hector's Room I'd played up in Scotland once at the Crawfords' place. You ever played it? You are shown a room for a minute and then you bugger off while everyone else goes in and makes one small adjustment each, they move a lamp, take away a wastepaper-bin, swap a couple of pictures around, introduce a new object, that order of thing. Then you have to go back in and identify as many of the alterations as you can. The Crawfords had first played it in their son Hector's room, hence the name, and the real design, I have always thought, was to show the men and women exactly where each other's bedrooms lay, to facilitate late-night handkerchief-pandkerchief. That's certainly the only benefit I ever got out of it. Anyway, there's a very particular expression on the face of a player when he returns to an altered room, a slow smile, and a sweeping, darting gaze, with sudden suspicious but amused whippings-around of the head, as if the furniture and fitments might still be caught in the act of moving. David's manner reminded me quite precisely of that moment in the game.

'I suppose what I meant,' I said, 'was more "Have you ever been *in* love?" foul phrase though it may be.'

David had stopped and was scrutinising fungus at the base of an alder.

'Of course,' he said. 'Ever since I can remember.'

'Hum. Let me be coarser still, Davey. Have you ever been in lust?'

He looked up at me and said slowly, 'Ever since I can remember.'

'Is that right? And have you ever done anything about it?'

He coloured a little, but said fiercely, 'No. Absolutely not.'

'Is there a particular favoured one?'

'Do you remember,' he said, 'that Boxing Day Shoot four years ago, when those cartridges were tampered with and all that confetti flew out?'

'Vividly.'

'Everyone thought it must have been the New Age types that lived in the East Lodge. The ones that made lutes and kept a goat.'

'It was mentioned, I remember.'

'Anyway, it wasn't them.'

'No?'

As we wound our way back to the house he told me what he had done. He hasn't sworn me to silence or any such nonsense, but never having been wildly entertained by the pompous ritual of shooting, I have absolutely no intention of telling anyone else anyway. Besides yourself of course. I will, over the weekend, work it up into an amusing anecdote for you and send it separately.

It was only later that evening, while I was changing for dinner, that it occurred to me that he had never answered my last question to him.

III

It's Monday now, getting on for seven in the morning and I've spent a great deal of the night writing this letter.

I was in a foul mood after dinner. Nobody stayed up to drink with me and nobody wanted to play cards or do anything fun. I went upstairs and moped in my room.

It's hard to explain such a fit of the sullens. You can try and rationalise it. It may be that I am blue-devilled because I feel guilty about abusing the Logans' hospitality: I am, let us be frank, acting as your paid spy. This seems an unlikely explanation for my current state of mind, which I think owes more to Anno Domini.

I lay in the room, under the great baldachin of a tester, chasing the summer-night itches around my body. One little prickle awoke another and another, until I was bucking on my bed like that little girl in the exorcism film. The same thing went on in my mind, mental itches popping like bubbles. Not enough whisky before bed, this was the problem.

At sixty-six I am entering, I thought, the last phase of my active physical life. My body, on the move, resembles in sight and sound nothing so much as a bin-liner full of yoghurt; my ability to concentrate, the only skill aside from egotism that a poet needs, has faded. Marriages have gone phut and professionally I am regarded as a joke. The Right-Wing Poet they call me. Typical arsing impertinence. Just because I don't subscribe to all the mealy-mouthed orthodoxies of the academic cosa nostra, just because I am a sucker for a title and a well-bred air, just because I know the difference between politics and poetics, just because I have some sense of national belonging, just because I think Kipling is a better poet than Pound (a view, incidentally, that even boat-shoe-wearing academics have been coming round to of late), just because, in short, I have my own brain on my own shoulders, they choose to ignore and belittle me. Fuck 'em. Fuck 'em all. No need to: they're already fucked. But none the less I have this feeling, this feeling I cannot quite be rid of, a feeling that I have, at this period in my life, been turfed off the newspaper for a good reason – no, that's not it, clearly I have been sacked for a good reason – what I mean is that I got myself sacked quite deliberately.

And the daftness of things – that was keeping me awake too. You must have experienced one of those moments when life seems limitlessly absurd? Especially with your current sentence of death hanging over you. I find they come most often with me when I am looking from the window of a moving car or train. You catch sight of something perfectly ordinary, such as it might be bluebells nodding on an embankment, or a family picnicking in a lay-by, and suddenly your mind can no longer support the notion of a whole world full of life and objects and fellow-humans. The very idea of a universe appears monstrous and you become unable to participate. What on earth does that tree think it is up to? Why is that heap of gravel sitting there so patiently? What am I doing, staring out of a window? Why are all these molecules of glass hanging together so as to allow me to look through them? The moment passes, of course, and we return to the proper realm of our dull thoughts and our duller newspapers: in less than a second we are part of the world again, ready to be irritated into apoplexy by the stupidity of a government minister or lured into caring about some asinine new movement in conceptual art; once again we become a part of the great compost heap. Our absence is so fleeting and our control over it so negligible that an act of will cannot reproduce the experience.

Peter Cambric, whom I knew pretty well in the Seventies, a bit before your time probably, was harried until his death by the story of a hunt he went on in 1964 in South Africa. He bagged a couple of elephants, alone enough to damn him in today's eyes, but managed to pick off a couple of bushmen too, which even back then was considered pushing it somewhat. A hundred years ago one would have been able to round off such an anecdote with the words, 'The whole thing was hushed up, of course.' In 1964, though, things got out and Peter's life was made miserable everywhere he went: his name, rather like that of poor Profumo or one of the Watergate band, was for ever linked with this one scandal. The thing of it was that Peter was always a magnificent shot and rumour would have it that he had taken good aim at these natives. This was a little hard to credit, for Cambric came from a progressive family, spoke from his seat in the Lords in the Liberal interest and consistently voted against hanging. The construction put on the affair was that he had mistaken the Kalahari clicking of the bushmen for the call of an ostrich of some sort. This was enough to allow Cambric entrée into the drawing rooms of the mighty but not quite enough to free him of his whiff of impropriety. Anyway – I draw breath – all this has a point, because one Cheltenham Gold Cup day in the mid-Seventies I shared a car back to London with Peter and we sat in the back getting thoroughly nasty on a clutch of freebie bottles of Hine or Martell or whichever cognac house it was that sponsored the race in those days. Cambric confessed to me that he *had* taken careful and deliberate aim but that he had an excuse. It seems that one of these strange moments I have described stole over him of a sudden. The whole scene, the *veld*, the trees, the game, the bearers, the very sky above, all became quite unreal to him. Existence stopped meaning anything. Life itself was no longer of even passing significance; neither his own nor anybody else's. The moment he had loosed off the second bullet, however, he had come to his senses and dropped the rifle, breathing 'Oh my God, oh my God,' as the truth sank in.

'What I experienced, Ted,' he told me, 'was nothing short of ecstasy.'

'Ecstasy?'

'I've read a lot of Mother Julian and *The Cloud of Unknowing* since that day. The mystics. Ecstasy means "standing outside of yourself". From the Greek.'

'Mm,' I said. 'Yes. You are aware, my old darling, that all this would sound pretty wobbly in court?'

'There is a higher law,' said Peter, with the sententious gush of the well brandied, and we left it at that.

As I lay there itching, I cursed my own disposition which, when confronted with the hopeless nonsense of things, has always succumbed more to accidie than ecstasy. When push-off comes to shove-off, a man must have a reason to get out of bed in the mornings, something more than the threat of bedsores at any rate.

I threw off the covers and waddled with bare cracking feet to the drinks tray. I stared at the bottles.

'God's cock,' I said to myself. 'It's nearly four in the morning. Surely I haven't come to this?'

I stood there staring at those whisky bottles for upwards of an hour. Behind the tall green necks a sliver of light between the curtains whitened and the sound of birds filled the air. Couldn't stop the tears from falling. Petulant tears, frustrated tears, grieving tears, angry tears, maudlin tears, guilty tears . . . I didn't know what kind of tears they were. Just tears, idle tears.

Walkies, I thought to myself, grabbing a full bottle and pushing my feet into a pair of shoes. Best go walkies.

Choosing not to risk the complexities of the great front door, I let myself out through a french window in the drawing room and lingered on the terrace for a while, sniffing the dawn air and trying to convince myself that it was of a superior quality to our own London vapour.

In spite of the evidence of life all around me, the birds as mentioned and the spewing vegetable life of borders, shrubs and trees, I was conscious of an absolute deadness all around. London though, London at half past four in the morning, absolutely zings with life. The blasts of the newspaper vans thundering through empty streets, the hissing micturations of the derelicts, the quick staccato of cheap stiletto clicking down alleys, the rattle of lonely cabs and, in squares and streets, a louder singing of blackbirds and sparrows than the countryside can ever know, all these sounds are animated and given meaning by the quality that all great cities share: an acoustic. Everything rings in town. The rural world is absolutely without resonance, reverberation or echo, absolutely without the ring of civilisation. Which makes it fine for an occasional repairing lease or weekend excursion, but debars it wholly from suitability as a habitat for man. Country people, of course, think otherwise: if they had their way they would carpet Piccadilly and the Strand with moss and set wisteria creeping up the walls of Buckingham Palace, just to stop any sound from being allowed to ricochet. As with sounds, so with ideas. Shout out a thought in the capital one morning and it's printed in the Londoner's Diary in the *Standard* in time for the West End final edition, screeched over in the Harpo Club that same evening and derided as old hat in the pages of *Time Out* the following week. Value-less, beyond question, revolting, certainly, but surely indicative of a livelier atmosphere than obtains in arcadia, where ideas bounce like a punctured tennis ball on a peat-bog.

There is one thing, I concede, that the countryside does

very well and that is dew. And the dew it was, as I leant on the terrace balustrade clutching, but not drinking from my whisky bottle, that caught my eye. The wide tract of grass that glides down to a ha-ha, and the rougher grass beyond where the horses sometimes grazed, was, as one might expect and demand, soaked in quantities of pretty and appealing dew. It was a track of darker grass running down the centre of the lawn that drew my attention however, a trail that marked where someone had recently walked. A gardener, gardener's assistant, gamekeeper or indoor servant, even in these unmannerly times, would surely keep to pathways, I reasoned, so who – a quick check of the watch – who from the household would be abroad at three minutes shy of five o'clock?

I followed, drenching a perfectly excellent pair of buckskin brogues as I went. A fig for that, thought I, like a Salvation Army maiden discovering Life in a Sixties screenplay, this is Adventure. I pursued the scuffing spoor of whoever had gone before until I reached the end corner of the lawn where it sloped down to the deep ha-ha. The browner, barer ground here, banked against the sun and starved of irrigation, did not take dew, or if it did, soaked it up instantly, and I could see no more tracks to follow.

Unless my mysterious quarry had springs in his heels powerful enough to enable him or her to carry the ha-ha, they must have struck right, towards a dark, dense area of laurels and rhododendrons. I made my way towards it, feeling, by now, rather an arse.

The place, one of those margins that gardeners cannot do anything with, was so thickly planted with sinister shrubbery that I could see no way to enter. I stood at the edge, brandishing the bottle like a mace, and listened. Not a sound came back. The grass at my feet was lusher again here, but bore no traces of human presence. I turned and made my way back to the corner of the lawn, greatly puzzled. Much against my will, I started to think of your word 'miracle'. Don't think me mad, but tell me, my dear, have you witnessed someone . . . my mind rebels violently against any such thought . . . someone *flying*? Ludicrous, obviously, yet . . . let me know if this squares with what you want me to discover.

I was conscious of a sensation not unlike that which overtakes you when investigating a mysterious night-time noise that denies you sleep. You stand on the stairs, heart pounding and mouth open. You proceed to eliminate the obvious: creeper tendrils tapping against the window pane; your dog, wife or child raiding the larder; floorboards creaking as the night-storage heater activates itself. None of those fits the noise, so, fighting a rising panic, you begin to consider less likely causes: a mouse in its death-throes; a bat loose in the kitchen; a child's toy left running; the cat accidentally (or deliberately) treading on the remote-control unit and rewinding a video cassette, but none of those quite explains the particular sound either and so . . . if you are anything like me, you trot hastily upstairs, dive back into bed and cover your face with a pillow, preferring not to know.

I walked back to the edge of the ha-ha and looked over it to the parkland beyond. I could see no sign of footprints there, but perhaps I was at the wrong angle. Feeling like twelve types of dick, I slid down the bank and hauled myself up the steep side of the ha-ha, the full bottle of the ten-year-old my only weapon. Once on the level of the park I walked forward through the thick grass examining it for signs of human passage. Nothing. Not a trace. I looked backwards and saw the clear marks of my own progress. No one could possibly have come this way. I moved forward again and suddenly, with no warning, my toe stubbed into something hard and metallic. Leaping like a Scottish dancer, I let out a muffled yell. A hideous pain flew to my cold wet toe and a hideous stream of abuse from my cold wet mouth. It was a bucket, half submerged in a large tuft of longer grass, a heavy galvanised bucket.

I hopped there, wincing; my big-toe nail, which has a tendency to grow in, had jammed viciously into the end of the shoe. I uncorked the bottle and raised it to my lips. As the bouquet of the whisky arrived at my nose, I paused.

There was something inexplicably foolish and bathetic about this incident, yet also something intensely disturbing. A line of footprints leading nowhere: a man following them with a bottle of whisky in his hand: the trail ending with the kicking of a bucket. I am not, as you know, a fanciful man, Jane. I set no store by providential symbols, only symbols devised by man, yet I would be an arse-hole pig-headed bigot of a rationalist indeed if I failed to ponder this dream-like sequence.

I cursed and pushed the cork back in without tasting a drop, raised my arm high and let the bottle fall into the bucket with a clang and a crack. Just for the moment, I decided, I would allow myself a little superstition. Why not, while staying here, ease off the sauce a little?

Having renegotiated the ha-ha, I hobbled back to the house, slapping my thigh with irritation. With every step away from the ha-ha I grew in self-recrimination. What kind of man throws away a full bottle of ten-year-old malt? Perhaps it was not that I had drunk too much, more that I hadn't drunk enough; certainly I hadn't slept enough: above all I had failed to finish this first letter to you. The further drinking I decided to leave until later in the day, the sleep could be postponed too. But now I've said just about everything there is to be said, most of it inconsequential to a degree, I'm mongrel-bitch tired and my fist cannot form letters any more, so fuck off, my darling, and leave me alone.

Your devoted godfather

Ted

IV

David stared at the ceiling with something like reproach. The dreadful thing was upon him once more. No matter down what reeking gutters or up what transcendent steeples he forced his thoughts, still the blood thickened into that aching fibre and still his cheeks burned with that pounding heat.

'Down!' he panted. 'Down, down, down.'

He knew what was about. He knew full well how his balls were packed and straining with seed, how his tubes and coils forced and swelled with a pressure to unload. For a year at least he had experienced the soggy defeat of waking to the knowledge that the dam had burst unbidden during the night. What his body did in his dreams he could not control or be blamed for, but he would not, could not allow his conscious self to fall victim to this vile poking, pressing ugliness.

Four by the stable clock, fooled into action by the summer light of dawn.

David stood. He shivered as the shameful head of the monster rubbed with frictive drag against his pyjamas, for a wincing second prising open the slit at its head as it stabbed blindly at the fabric before finding the freedom of the flap and quivering upwards with a stupid prong of victory.

'Stop it, stop it!' David breathed. 'Oh, please . . . please . . .'

But nothing would stop it; not cold water, not prayer, not threats, not promises.

David stood by the bed and clutched the beast in fury, choking it.

'You . . . will . . . behave . . . !' he snarled, shaking it back and forth in anger.

The bastard thing. It won. Great ropes of semen flew from its tip and dropped to the carpet with a flat triumphant patter.

David threw himself on to his bed, sore, savaged and despairing. He sobbed into the pillow and swore that this thing must never happen again.

After a while, feeling better, he got up and began to dress.

He timed the last five words of his prayer to coincide with the five chimes of the stable clock.

'*Good, sweet, true, strong*, and *PURE!*' he breathed.

He hoped that by adding the word 'strong' he would be able to avoid calamities like that of an hour ago. Purity required strength. Where the strength would come from he could not tell. Not from purity, surely? That would be what his father called a catch–22. Strength came from within.

Well, he must be going. He loved it here, but it would never do to be . . .

He tightened up in alarm. Footsteps! He could hear them distinctly. Someone shuffling towards him. He heard a cough and a retching noise. Uncle Ted! There couldn't be the least doubt that it was Uncle Ted. What was he doing up so early? He was the kind of man, surely, who never rose before ten at the very least. David kept very still and, although it was pitch black where he was, closed his eyes tightly. Uncle Ted coughed once more and walked away towards, David judged, the laurel bushes.

Then Uncle Ted came back once more and stood right over him, wheezing and tutting and banging his foot so that dirt fell on to David's face. David didn't dare brush the crumbs of soil away. He simply lay in the warm earth and waited. He heard a scrambling and a thudding noise. Was Uncle Ted trying to find his way in? David held his breath. The sound stopped. There was silence. A wood louse crawled over David's cheek.

Suddenly there was a loud clang, followed by a great roaring and swearing. Uncle Ted was in the park! What on earth was he doing?

'Cunting, godding hell-bitch fuck-arse shite . . .' David heard, and then a small pop and silence. The small pop sounded like a cork being drawn from a bottle. David wondered if he was going mad. The next sound was another clang and then came the sound of scrambling close to him again. David held his breath once more.

At last, grumbling and puffing with annoyance, Uncle Ted turned and stamped away in the direction of the house.

Ten minutes later, the door of hinged turf neatly shut behind him, David crouched in the ha-ha and scanned the house for signs of life. Lowering his gaze, he saw the marks on the lawn and cursed himself.

'Of course!' he whispered. 'The dew! I really must be more careful.'

Four

12a Onslow Terrace
LONDON SW7
Tuesday, 21st July 1992

Dear Uncle Ted,

Your letter arrived this morning. I have read it over many times. Firstly because your handwriting is so difficult and I have had trouble with some ambiguous phrases. Secondly because there is much in it that puzzles me for other reasons. On the handwriting front, I spent much time wondering, for instance, what you meant by David's 'codfish chums'. I know that Davey is very much an animal lover, but I found this idea intensely peculiar until I realised that you meant 'coltish charms'. Then again, there is a reference to yourself as a Rotarian which struck me as unlikely. I have now decided that the word is 'Bohemian'. When I came upon the phrase 'let us be frank, I am aching as your pansy', I could only imagine that the whisky had got the better of you. I have since, by tracing out the letters and coming to an understanding of your pen-strokes, come to the decision that you actually meant to write 'I am acting as your paid spy'.

This leads me on to my main point. Ted, I do not want you to consider yourself a viper in the Logan bosom or a snake in Swafford grass. You made a reference at the very beginning of your letter to the Trojan horse and that is a bad anallegory too. You are an old friend and now a guest of Michael and Anne Logan. You stand godfather to one of their children. There is nothing so strange in your staying with them for a while, surely? Although it is true that it was I who asked you to stay at the Hall and also true that I am paying you to communicate your impressions to me, I have done so in the certain knowledge, *certain knowledge* that once you have been there for a while you will find that your own instincts as a writer and as a friend of the Logans will keep you there willingly. In fact I am sure that wild horses wouldn't drag you away from the place. You can no more call yourself a paid spy than a serious photo-journalist could call himself a snoop.

You may think that by going along in this business you are simply humouring the whim of a dying neurotic who is mad enough to pay you handsomely for it. That may be true. For a month now I have gone over and over it in my mind and asked myself whether or not I am imagining things. I went to see a priest some time ago and he told me that it was common for 'visions to attend the dying'. I saw a psycho-therapist who said the same thing in a different way: 'The hurt mind plays itself realistic images to mediate between its desires and dreaded reality. On a larger scale, society does the same thing with its cinema and television industries.' Some such stuff. But I know that what I know is what I know and that nothing can ever be the same again. I won't embarrass you by telling you that I now know that God exists, and that God is perfect and as real as this pen I am holding. Have you ever been in a hot country, a scorchingly uncomfortably hot place, and then walked into a cool cathedral or temple? Or come in from a bitter, cheek-aching winter day to the warmth of a fire? Imagine such a feeling of relief and welcome and pleasure to the power of ten, the power of twenty, any power you like, and still you haven't come near the sensation of coming into the presence of God.

I said I wouldn't embarrass you, but I probably have. You will say I've only embarrassed myself I expect, but that isn't true. I'll say no more about this for the moment.

I am so grateful that your first letter was so full. I didn't find it 'inconsequential to a degree' at all: absolutely every-thing you tell me is of interest. I don't even object to your making fun of me in the way that you have been. I suppose you are being rude because you hate me for making you feel like a prostitute or spy. I don't mind in the least, but I am sorry you have been feeling unhappy and 'blue-devilled'. What a charming expression.

Your story about Peter Cambric interested me greatly. I can't really beleive that, if he felt so 'at one' and in a state of 'ecstasy' he would have been able to do something so self-conscious as aim a rifle and then pull a trigger. One of my stranger therapists tried to induce a similar state of mind in me, as part of a process that was supposed to heal or cleanse my blood. Her technique had something to do with alpha and theta waves in the brain. These are necessary for Biofeedback which is the popular name for her technique. A group of us would be in a room together, lying on couches, all leukaemics and AIDS patients, and we had to relax totally until our theta and alpha waves were buzzing or radiating or emitting or whatever it is that they do, and then she made us communicate with our bodies.

'See your blood as a crystal stream, absolutely pure and absolutely clear,' she would say. 'See it gently flow and ripple and glide. But look, look deeper into the blood, there is a tangle of weed just below the surface. You think it's out of reach, but it isn't. You can reach, you can reach into the stream. Lean forward and reach into the stream and take the knot of weed, take it in your hands. It is like jelly. The consistency of jelly. Rub it between your fingers. You can press it and rub it between your fingers and feel it dissolve. As it dissolves you can dip your hands into the water and allow the dissolved residue to be carried down the stream. All the weed is untangled and dissolved and all its tiny particles now float freely and easily down the stream to be lost in the sea. Now the river is pure and free and clear again.'

All this would go on for hours and cost thousands as you can imagine. It works in your head up to a point. But, no matter how relaxed I was, whenever she told me to rub the jelly between my fingers I would look down at my hands (in my mind, this is) and something in my brain would force the weeds to become hard and fibrous and knotted and insoluble. I would force them to return to jelly, to something like the consistency of overcooked spaghetti, and then I would rub and rub, thinking I had won, but at the heart of the soft spaghetti this demon in my head would force me again to see another tangle of coarse, black fibre. And so it would go on, one part of me willing myself to dissolve the weed, another part of me forcing myself to recognise that the heart of the weed was malignant and unbreakable-down. When the session was over, as all the others did, I would smile sweetly at the healer, so as not to hurt her feelings (ridiculous when you think how much money she was making out of us) and say that I felt most amazingly at peace, but I knew that the little knot was still there.

I am the only one of that group alive now.

I must rush to catch the post. I want you to get this before Uncle Michael arrives.

Ted, I know I have done the right thing in sending you to Swafford. The length of your letter and your current state of mind show me that God, in his extraordinary way, has found a means to save both of us together in one action, as it were. You are my 'godfather', the word is not accidental.

Forgive me if all this is, as they say in America, 'too on the nose', but I'm not interested in shirking embarrassment any more. If my younger self could read this letter she could never in a million years beleive that I had written it.

Write as soon as you can and as much as you can. If there is any possibility of your borrowing a type-writer or word-processor it would save me eye-strain and head-ache . . .

Sending love and awaiting news

Jane

II

Jane,

Well, as you can see i have reluctantly consented to your request and tracked down a machine. This belongs to simon and appears to be quite unused. it does to words what the KRAFT company does to cheese.

apparently i bang the keys too hard, being used to mechanical type-writers. NOR DO I UNDERStand how the bloody shift key works. it either locks the capitals or denies me any at all. STill at least youll be able to read this if I can get simon or davey to show me how the printer is operated.

i enclose with this letter the story of david and the sabotage of the boxing day shoot for your edification. even if its irrelevant to your needs i thought you might enjoy it.

Your letter, contrary to your expectation, did not embarrass me at all. I dont know who or what you think i am, some sort of Henry wilcox or C. Aubrey Smith figure who goes all pink and stiff at the mention of emotion or faith. I'm a poet for fucks sake, not a treasury official. THE ONLY EMOTION that annoys a poet is cheap emotion, unearned emotion, borrowed emotion, the emotion of wish-fulfilment, emotion that comes from fantasy or guess work and not from the gut. at least that's what it says in the poet's manual.

BUT, pausing only to remark that there is no such word as 'anallegory' much though there should be, i'm not presuming here to judge your emotions. the weird thing (talking of weird you seem to have forgotten the golden rule 'i before e excepting after c'. You wrote 'beleive' in your letter. Perhaps you knew the right spelling but your subconscious mind couldn't commit itself to producing such a terrifying word as 'believe' in its entirety) the weird thing . . . what is the weird thing I was going to say? OH YES, THe weird thing about this word-processing affair is that you cannot go back and cross a word out. with a type-writer you can backspace and cover your errors in x's. It actually seems to be impossible here. one can absolve oneself of all one's sins and nobody will be any the wiser. Except oneself.

Talking of going all pink and stiff at the mention of things there has been a much fuller house this weekend than I expected. I mentioned in my last letter that I thought it rude to ask hosts or hostesses about the composition of a house-party, so i was surprised to discover that a girl claiming to be your best friend has been down here since Friday night. Goes under the name of Patricia Hardy, smells of cucumber juice and is the cause of much pinkness and stiffness in the undersigned. presumably you knew she was coming. I hope she's not here to spy on the spy.

I'll come to her and the others later. Where did I leave off last time? Monday morning. Yes. I finished my first letter to you, rolled wearily downstairs to post it in the box in the hall and dozed lightly with my head against a barometer on the wall for five minutes before managing to pull myself up the banisters, one rail at a time, finally falling on to my bed five minutes short of eight o'clock.

I AWOKE in time for lunch and managed to brazen out Annie's looks of blended astonishment and reproach in the small sitting room beforehand.

'Couldn't sleep. Bed too comfortable, everything too quiet,' I explained, but I could see that she thought I had been sitting up in my room all night quietly boozing myself into a stupor. Since I believe there are few things more transparently undignified in this world than a drinker making an effort to appear sunny and energetic in order to prove to the world that he is innocent of a hangover, I swallowed the insult of her look and declined her offer of a sherry without further protestations of innocence.

I shan't take you through every hour of every day: it's now Saturday and very little occurred on Monday and Tuesday that I judge worthy of notice. Simon was still away and Anne seemed anxious for me to bear David as much company as I could.

'He's very bright, they tell me,' she said. 'I'm afraid that there's not much stimulus for him in the holidays. Simon is that much older and has . . . different interests. As you know I was never exactly bookish either. Michael is wonderful with him, of course, but he's been so busy lately . . . do you remember his niece Jane? Jane Swann?'

Ha! Your name had come up for the first time. You haven't

made it plain whether or not your condition is known to the world so I made no mention of it, anxious to see whether news has reached Swafford.

'I should say so,' I replied. 'She's my other godchild.'

'Oh, of course, so she is. Jane was here in June, part of which covered Simon and Davey's exeat after exams, and she and Davey got on like a house on fire. All the more remarkable really because . . .' She broke off in some confusion.

'Because?'

'I'm not sure if you *know*,' she said, with the kind of upper-class emphasis which would have told me even if I hadn't.

'The leukaemia? Yes, Jane told me.'

'Really? I didn't know you were in touch. The most appalling thing. Jane invited herself here and . . .'

She thought better of saying whatever it was she had in mind to say. She knew about your mother and me, naturally, so perhaps she felt she was being tactful in not going on about your branch of the Logan family.

So you stayed at Swafford in June, did you? Is that when God smote you, or did you go as a result of being smitten? No doubt you'll let me know in your own good time.

(Extraordinary thing about this machine: when you type an apostrophe or inverted comma it can tell whether it should curl to the left or the right. Thus, when typing the dialogue above I would press the same key for quotes and it would automatically 'type it like this'. Damned smart. I'm beginning to see what all the fuss is about.)

The upshot of this conversation is that Davey has had me more or less to himself. He is a quick lad, no question about that, and I think genuinely interested in poetry and art and thought and the life of the mind. As is natural at his age, he believes that poetry's sole function seems to lie in the description of nature. Keats, Clare, Wordsworth, selected Browning and Tennyson, that sort of jazz. I delicately put him right.

'No, no, no, you chump. You must have heard the expression "the egotistical sublime"? These people aren't writing about dandelions and daisies, they're writing about themselves. Romantic poets are more obsessed with self than the most therapy-addicted Californian you can imagine. "*I* wandered lonely as a cloud", "*My* heart aches", "*My* heart leaps up".'

'But they love nature, surely?' We were walking through the park on the way to the village, where I wanted to stock up on Rothies. Michael only provides cigars for his guests. This would be Monday afternoon, three-ish. There was a beagle pup in need of exercise with us. Its function was to double the length of the walk, wee on my buckskins and attempt the stylish feat of snapping its jaws shut on darting butterflies.

'Listen, old darling. Nature is the shit we were born in. It's pretty, but it isn't art.'

' "Beauty is truth, truth beauty, – that is all ye know on earth, and all ye need to know." '

'Ye-e-s, but if you imagine that beauty is only available *out there*, you're going to have a grotty young life, you know. Don't imagine that celandine and meadowsweet, ranunculus and clover offer us our only path to truth, beauty and Vedic happiness. John Clare could wander the leas and dells in a loony trance because there were leas and dells to wander in. We have cities and edge-of-town big-shed architecture now. We have television and algae-wrap lymphatic treatments.'

'So we're supposed to write about those, are we?'

Get the 'we', Jane. I was thirty-eight before I dared put 'poet' in my passport and confess membership of the *genus irritabile vatum*.

'We're not *supposed* to write about anything.'

'Shelley said that poets are the unacknowledged legislators of the world.'

'Yes, and he would have looked ten kinds of idiot if everyone had agreed with him.'

'What do you mean?'

'Well, poets would then have to have been described as the *acknowledged* legislators of the world, wouldn't they? And get off their velvet-clad arses and start enacting. That wouldn't have suited him at all.'

'I don't see that that's a very helpful observation.'

'Well, *ex*cuse me.'

We walked on in silence for a while, the beagle pup leaping like a dolphin in the sea of long grass.

'Look,' I said, 'I love the fact that you want to be a poet. I adore it. But I cannot, in all conscience, imagine an occupation more . . . In fact, let's make a wager. I bet you, David Logan, I bet you that during my stay here you will not be able to name a single profession that has less use, less chance, less future, less point, less status and fewer prospects than the calling of Poet.'

'Sewage engineer,' he replied at once.

'Two scenarios,' I said. 'Scenario A: all the poets in England, Scotland, Wales and Northern Ireland go on strike. Result? It would be fourteen years before anyone outside Gordon Square or the offices of the *TLS* so much as noticed. Hardship, discomfort and nuisance quotient? Nil. Impact? Nil. Newsworthiness? Nil. Scenario B: all the sewage engineers in London alone go on strike. Result? Turds and tampons flopping out your kitchen tap, your feet squelching in scum and ooze where'er you walk. Typhus, cholera, thirst and catastrophe. Hardship, discomfort, nuisance, impact and newsworthiness quotients? High.'

'All right, all right, that was a bad one. Um . . . composer then. Classical music composer.'

'Well, closer. Modern composers do have a small audience, I grant you. But most of them, those who don't make the big money – and there is big money to be made even in what they insist on calling "serious" music – fill in time and earn their rent by writing film-scores, advertising jingles and public domain sound-tracks, conducting, teaching harmony and counter-point at conservatoires, that kind of thing. If they want to they can play bar piano in the evenings in a nightclub. A poet, though, what cabaret skills has he got? He has an even smaller audience, his work is almost exclusively confined, after all, to those who speak the same language: if he wants another job his only choices involve *other people's poetry*. He reviews. My God, how he reviews. In every newspaper, periodical, quarterly and magazine you can think of, he earns his daily Hovis reviewing other people's poetry. Or he teaches. Unlike the composer he doesn't teach the skills of his craft, he doesn't teach prosody and metre and form, he teaches other people's poetry. If he's a big cheese, he can edit the poetry list of one of the few remaining publishing houses that runs such a thing. He'll be publishing other people's poetry and anthologising other people's poetry. No doubt he can make appearances on "The Late Show", "Kaleidoscope" and "Critics' Forum" too, talking about other people's poetry. Jesus God, if I had the choice between coming back in this century as a poet or a composer I'd take composer and give half my annual income to charity in gratitude.'

Davey looked rather rattled by this outburst and I instantly felt the worst kind of pig. He thought for a moment, biting his lower lip. 'I know you don't mean all that,' he said. 'I know you're just testing my vocation. I know that there is nothing better to be than a poet and that you know it too.'

By this time we had reached the alleyway that leads into the main street of the village and I realised that a strange and wonderful thing had happened, or rather, a foul and horrid thing had failed to happen. I had spoken for half an hour with a youth who claimed to be a poet and he hadn't so much as hinted that he wanted me to read a single one of his poems. Perhaps this is the miracle, Jane, to which you have alluded . . .

That was Monday afternoon. Tuesday was a quiet day. We took a boat out on the lake and I drank Chablis and, at David's request, read aloud from my *Collected Verse*. Still no move from him to inflict any of his on me.

He thought 'Lines on the Face of W. H. Auden' was contrived, which I told him was like complaining that *The Hundred and One Dalmations* had a lot of dogs in it. He liked 'Martha, As Seen in a Slit of Light' and 'Ballad of the Workshy Man', but his particular favourite, naturally, was 'Where the River Ends', which I hadn't the heart to tell him was in fact inspired by the news that Gregory Corso and Lawrence Ferlinghetti's poetry was being set for school exams. He thought it was an ecological poem, a 'green' poem *avant la lettre*, about sewage outflow into the sea. Youth's a stuff I'll not endure.

Insanely, as if by the power of hypnosis, I found myself asking whether, since I'd shown him mine, he'd show me his.

He blushed like an overripe peach. 'You don't want to see it really,' he said.

'Well, can you recite any? Truly, I'd love to hear some.'

This from Ted Wallace, mind you, who'd been known to hurl himself into moving traffic at the prospect of verse recitation.

The poem was short, which was good. The poem was sweet, which was good. The poem had form, which was good. The poem was bad, which was bad. The poem was called 'The Green Man', which was unpardonable.

The Green Man

I sucked the earth and sucked it dry
Dry earth is dust, powder for the hair
I stretched myself and plucked the sky
Plucked sky is blue, a blue coat to wear

I licked the grass: licked it clean
Clean grass is hay; gold hay for the flesh
I hugged the leaves; squeezed their green
Squeezed sap is blood, and blood must be fresh

I sowed the seed, seed of my own
Sown seed is white, white as the breeze
Soon will be born, blood of my bone
Son of the earth and child of the trees

This man of straw, this god of mud
Blue is his coat, proudly unfurled
The precious green, the green of his blood
Shall bathe us all clean and ransom the world

I did warn you. It's like smelling someone else's farts, isn't it? He seems to be recording, in his own graceful way, a wank in the woods. In case you're wondering whether I lovingly committed this thing to memory, let me assure you I have copied it out from a painstakingly calligraphed manuscript which Davey presented me as a result of my having been (how could I be otherwise?) complimentary.

So much for Tuesday. Wednesday, however, was of the highest significance for Swafford, since it saw Michael's return from town. We understand he now hopes to stay for some time. He has a kind of telecommunications centre installed in his study where he can toil away stripping assets, defrauding pension funds and acquiring whatever it is that big cheeses like your uncle do acquire ... acquisitions I suppose.

On Wednesday afternoon David and I stood on the leads above the front portico and watched the helicopter land on the South Lawn. Michael clambered out, charged forward towards the house clutching his head (clutching his wig if grubby rumour is to be given house-room. I'll find out about that one day, don't you worry) and as soon as he had safely cleared the beating rotor-blades, looked up to where we stood. David waved, Logan waved back. I waved, Logan peered then waved and pranced. A welcome. A big bouncing welcome from a big bouncing man.

Down the wooden rungs we streamed, me gasping in David's wake; we clattered along the old nursery passage, tumbling down the back stairs and hurrahing into the hallway to greet him, like Jo and Amy March in the gooiest Sunday afternoon serialisation you can imagine. Your Aunt Anne, coming from the front drawing room, had won by a length and was first to be kissed. Michael, in his wife's arms, looked up as we braked our heels into the marble and skidded to an embarrassed halt.

'Davey! And Tedward! Ha-ha-ha!'

My God, you can only envy this man. Not his power and his wealth and his position, though frankly one can envy that too, but his authority and his – well yes, his power in that sense – his power within his family and his power over his family and the great radio beams of pure sodding charisma that he gives out so unsparingly and so unceasingly, much as weightlifters and literary editors give off BO.

Compare and contrast:

Last Christmas, Ted is invited to Helen's house, Helen being my second wife and the mother of Leonora and Roman.

Ted, not being a driver, makes landfall on schedule, as advised in writing and by fax to the household, at Didcot Station. Anyone there to meet him? In a pig's arse.

So Ted gets a cab to drive him the twelve miles. He arrives, and presses the doorbell with the tip of his plum-pudding nose, for his arms are all laden with presents.

Nobody comes, so Ted pushes and finds that the door swings open. He heads for the drawing room, staggering under the weight of his parcels. He reaches the threshold, cheeks ruddy with festive cheer, eyes twinkling like fairy-lights. Old Ted is the Spirit of Christmas Present, Henry the Eighth in one of his good moods, Friar Tuck and Clarence the Angel all rolled into one beaming bundle. He is Mirth, Jollity, Paternal Love and Yuletide Joy. He is chestnuts roasting on an open fire, he is a curranty wassail of mulling wine and plump mistletoe. His florid beam of bonhomie promises games, cheek-pinching, larks, piggy-back rides, jokes and mincemeat merriment.

His ex-wife, his only son, his only daughter, his only daughter's boyfriend and his only ex-wife's new husband look up from the television, where Cilla Black is presenting the Christmas edition of 'Blind Date', and say:

'Sh!'

'Oh, it's you.'

'Have you been drinking, Daddy?'

'Hi.'

'God you look awful.'

'Sh!'

Home-is-the-sailor-home-from-sea-and-the-hunter-home-from-the-hill, I don't fucking think.

This was no more than the kind of loutish, graceless, lumpen reception ninety-nine fathers out of a hundred are accorded every day of their lives. Nothing new or surprising in that. The only response to such brute behaviour, naturally, is to get so drunk and unpleasant that you do the bastards the favour of justifying their icy welcome and guarantee another just like it next time.

Moment of whining self-pity over, let me proceed. We had left your Uncle Michael (a man who had never in his life entered a room without everyone in it leaping to their feet and either clustering around him like tame gazelles or jumping out of the window in fright) standing in the hall.

'So, Davey . . . what do you hear, what do you say?'

'The strawberry patch is absolutely bursting. I had a look with Uncle Ted last night.'

'We shall have strawberries for pudding. Yes. A mountain of strawberries. Tedward!' Michael's bruisingest bear-hug. 'I heard.' Outstretched arms, shoulders raised, like Christ crucified.

Suddenly you could see that Christ's stance on the cross was in fact no more than a great middle-European Jewish shrug: 'I'm being crucified, my mother's at the foot of the cross and she's moaning that I'm not wearing a fresh loin-cloth. Oi!', that kind of shrug. The kind gentiles can't do. I took it to refer to my dismissal from the rag.

'Ah, well,' I said (my shrug, I could see in the hall mirror, gave me a sour and petulant dowager's hump), 'it's only a bloody newspaper.'

'Right! Only a newspaper. That's what I said when I sold it in '82. It's only a newspaper. Mind you . . .' He broke off and looked around him.

'So where's Simon?'

Annie had taken his arm. 'Simon has been staying with

Robbie. Tractor racing, as you very well know from the fax I sent you. He'll be back tomorrow morning.'

So Annie sends faxes to Michael telling him of the comings and goings of his brood, does she? I must say, Jane, that surprised me mightily, for I had been there in the drawing room on Monday, if you remember, when Simon languidly announced that he was staying away for the night, and Anne had hardly seemed to take it in at all. They say the only skill needed to be a financial genius is grasp of detail. Perhaps it applies to parenthood too, in which case I'm a dead loss, as it's all I can do to remember the genders, ages and names of my two.

Everyone satisfactorily greeted and hugged, Michael hurried upstairs to bath and change out of his financial suit and into the familial polo-shirt and shorts. The knowledge that he was upstairs made Swafford a different house. Hard to explain how altered the atmosphere was. It was as if we had been doing nothing over the last few days but filling in. I'm a few years older than him but he is still capable of making me feel like a four-year-old. All the more stupid of me, therefore, to break the news to him so suddenly on his first evening back.

'You want to do *what*?' His brows came together to form an expression which could have been either a scowl of thunderous rage or a frown of amused perplexity. In my rather watery fear, I interpreted it as the former.

'Michael, Michael . . . it's not . . .'

'So now you're some kind of hack? Some kind of . . . what is her name? Some kind of dirt-mongering Kitty Kelley? *The Private Life of Michael Logan*. No, no, worse than that, too tame. *The Private* Lives *of Michael Logan. The* Very *Private Lives of Michael Logan.* Tedward, Tedward. This is terrible.'

Oh shit. Oh shitey-shitey-shit-shit. I spread my hands.

'Michael, old walrus, I knew this would happen. I've gone and explained myself all wrong. It's not *you*, I'm not interested in *you*. Not you *per se*. It's the whole . . . the whole *thing*.'

'For a poet you have a less than wonderful way with words.'

I leaned back, flustered. The man had been so pleased to see me, so hugely and powerfully delighted. Now I had rushed in and hustled him. We were sitting alone around the dinner table, the covers having been cleared away, Annie having gone into the drawing room and Davey having bedded himself down for the night. There were strawberries and cream in us – Michael's words are never lightly spoken – the proper old-fashioned kind of strawberries at that, late fruiting, the kind you can twist the pith out of as easily as pulling a baby carrot from compost, not the modern travesty whose leaves snap off and which taste of stale cider; there was good wine in us too and a mellow cloud of Michael's Havana and my Rothies hanging in the air. I had thought the moment propitious.

'Bloody hell, Michael, you know me,' I said with a winning smile.

'That's what I'm afraid of,' he replied.

'Unworthy of you. I'm not interested in gossip or scandal . . . not that there is any, I'm sure, and if there is I don't care. I *say* biography, but I'm thinking as much of a kind of history, a kind of *outline*. You see, Michael,' I leaned forward again, 'I think the two great threads of twentieth-century history are the Anglo Saxon and the Jewish. It may be that next century it will be the Hispanic and the Arab, or the black and the Asian, or the Venusian and the Martian for all I bloody know, but for the last hundred years' (I was improvising madly here, of course) 'the Jew and the Anglo have more or less defined the entire shape of the globe, of intellectual thought, of art, of popular culture, of history, of . . . oh, I don't know . . . of mankind's destiny, if you will. Now, it's not uncommon for Jews to marry out of their race, nor uncommon for an Anglo-Saxon to do so. But you and Anne, you see, you make a particularly intriguing, a particularly *vivid* case-study, the outlines stand out. You're not just *any* Jew, you're maybe the most powerful in Europe. Anne isn't just *any* Anglo, she's from one of the oldest families in Britain, whose ancestors have ruled, rouéd and ruinated for over a thousand years. Her mother's connections mean there's a spot of Russell, as in the Prime Minister and as in Bertrand, in the mix, and there's a helping of Marlborough and Churchill too, with a side-salad of Cecils and Pagets. So your family is a union, an interweaving of the two great threads. Perhaps the tradition of Anglo-Saxon and Jewish dominance in the world is over, from Christ to Marx, Einstein, Kafka and Freud, by way of Shakespeare, Lincoln, Franklin, Jefferson and Colonel Sanders. Your offspring, your marriage, your family, it all becomes almost a symbol, doesn't it? I'm not interested in whether you've been faithful to your wife, Michael, or what dirty deals you may have done in your time. I really think there is a most marvellous book here.'

Fer-rankly . . .

Michael stared at me for what seemed a week. 'I'll think about it, Tedward.'

I smiled. 'That's all I ask.'

'You're staying a good long while. There'll be time to discuss later. Let's go join Anne.'

So we left it at that.

Have I done right, Jane? I think he's swallowed my story – why shouldn't he? It's bloody convincing – and I don't think I've queered the pitch for any other developments. But I wish, I wish, Jane, my dearest of dear, dear things, that you would tell me exactly what it is I'm supposed to be looking out for.

Give me time to stretch and pour myself another whisky and then we'll look at Thursday.

III

Thursday saw what we might call the opening of the house for the summer. When I heard that others were coming, it occurred to me that for Davey I was something in the nature of an advance guard and that the reason he was so especially pleased to have me early was that he could form a prepared alliance against any nasty grown-ups that were coming later and not be relegated to the status of Left-Out Child or Hanger-On. This was a hasty and ill-formed diagnosis, as we shall see.

We had a conversation about people in which we found ourselves pretty much in agreement. I said that I was nervous of meeting anyone new and Davey said he was in much the same case. He remarked that it was hardly surprising we thought the same about things: we were after all, he explained, to all intents and purposes the same age.

'You've gone all funny on me now, young walnut. What do you mean?'

'Well, I'm fifteen years from the cradle and you must be about fifteen from the tomb.'

Not *precisely* the kind of words you expect to hear from neatly brushed and polished youth, but he has a point of course, *bis pueri senes* and all that.

The first house-guest to turn up was your chum, Patricia. My lord, Jane, there's a pair of breasts if you like.

She had come on her own, recuperating from a 'devastating' affair with Michael's underling, Martin Rebak. You probably know this. Rebak, CEO of Logan's (it stands for Chief Executive Officer and is a sort of cross between a managing director and a chairman I believe), was her man for a year: there was talk of marriage and eternal love, but then he cruelly upped and tupped a PR girl leaving Patricia simply squelching in misery. Michael rather sportingly told this CEO that he was a cunt and a beast and he and Annie have, as it were, officially taken Patricia's side. The CEO's still 'in place' in Simon's words (Simon came back from his tractor racing this morning) and slightly miffed to be the recipient of Logan's old-fashioned Mafia boss disapproval. Whether Michael's sympathy for the beazel springs from a

81

desire in him to sauce her himself, only the Lord and yourself (probably) knows. There are *rumours* to the effect that Michael is a consistent and conscientious putter-about, but there are rumours about everybody. That the rumours are nearly always correct is neither here nor there for the moment.

Still, what a piece. She doesn't appear to be wearing the willow for her lost love, in fact she's brighter than a bag of buttons and merrier than a gallery of grigs.

'I remember *you*,' she says to me after bestowing a kiss on Podmore, I mean . . . *Podmore* . . . 'you're Ted Wallace! There was an article about you in the *Evening Standard* yesterday. You've just been sacked from something haven't you? A. N. Wilson wrote defending you and Milton Shulman said you were a disgrace to the good name of critics.'

'As Myra Hindley is a disgrace to the good name of child-murderers.'

'And we met twice,' she went on. 'Once at a launch for something, was it a Ned Sherrin theatrical-anecdote book at The Ivy?'

'You won't believe this,' I said, 'but I have missed every one of Ned Sherrin's theatrical-anecdote book launches. It goes against the laws of probability, but I've done it. I put it down to rigorous training and self-discipline. The trouble is, you see, if you go to one, you can't stop yourself from going to another, and another, and so on. And before you know it, you're going to one every week. I suppose the only other solution would be for Ned Sherrin to stop writing them, but that would be cheating somehow, wouldn't it?'

'I know! It was at the National Portrait Gallery. Portraits by children, for some charity.'

'Ah, a dim memory is surfacing.'

'There were all these portraits,' Patricia explained to Michael and Anne. 'You know, of Princess Diana and Margaret Thatcher and so on, done by five-year-olds. And Ted said in a loud voice, "Call those paintings? Why, a modern artist could have done them." And then you made a fuss because you couldn't smoke.'

'Yes, well, not above making an arse of myself, I'd be the first to concede . . .'

'But the *first* time we met was at a dinner party in 1987 in Pembridge Square.'

She was beginning to sound like one of those 'Embarrassed by Lapses of Memory?' people who advertise on the front page, bottom right-hand corner, of the *Telegraph*.

'Pembridge Square? Pembridge Square? I don't believe I know anyone who lives in Pembridge Square . . .'

'The Gossett-Paynes.'

'. . . except, of course, for Mark and Candida Gossett-Payne. Well, well, well. Nice to meet you again, Patricia.'

I could see out of the corner of my eye that this is where things were going to get eggy. Davey had slid into the hallway during the latter part of the conversation and was beginning to darkle and glower dangerously. It looked as though he had decided to take against this spirited and charmingly high-breasted creature. He rightly guessed, I suppose, that I would rate her above him as a companion for a walk or boating trip. This is not how things were to be, however.

'Er . . . and of course you must know David,' I said, bringing him forward.

Her reaction was rather extraordinary, looking back. She moved forward and dropped to her knees . . . hardly necessary since she is only six inches taller than him at most.

'David!' she said, gazing into his eyes. 'I'm Patricia. We met, do you remember . . . ?'

She went into her Mrs Memory routine, while Davey fixed her with a liquid stare.

'My *God*, but look at you now!' she cooed. 'Will you . . . David . . . will you give me a kiss?'

Well, I mean for heaven's sake . . . as if he were a toddler or dribbling grandsire. He played up to it very well, I'll give him that: a flirty look from under the lashes and a modestly presented cheek. But stuff my arse with figs if she didn't try and work the head round to a proper lip-to-lip snog . . .

She's your friend, Jane, and I'd give even unto half my collection of bow-ties to prong her where it counts, but I have to say that I'm not quite sure she's balanced.

We all moved into the morning room for coffee, Davey overcoming a marked inclination to simper, while we discussed thoughts for the weekend. Simon trundled in politely: all *he* got from Patricia was a casual wave of the hand. Twigging to the drift of our conversation he remarked that today was the last day of the East of England Show.

'Really?' said Patricia in a slow drawl that betrayed such contemptuous indifference that Simon went red. She turned to Davey and asked him what he thought of David Mamet.

'East of England Show, eh?' I said to Simon, who was standing there, polishing his toe-cap against his calf. 'Sort of agricultural thing, is it?'

'Well . . . oh well, you know . . . I'm sure it's not very interesting to people who aren't . . . very interested in that sort of thing.'

'No?'

'It's very popular here, though. Round here, I mean. In Norfolk and so on.'

'Oh ah. Sheep-dog trials and the like, I suppose?'

'Um, not exactly . . . this is East Anglia, really. Not many sheep.'

'Well, Norwich terrier trials perhaps. Cromer crab racing. Norfolk turkey knobbly-throat competitions.'

'There's rare breeds and there's displays and stalls and some show-jumping and . . . but it's . . . as I say, it's not very interesting, I expect.'

'You love it, Simon, you know you do,' his mother said. She and Michael had been in private conference in the corner. Bedroom and mealtime arrangements, I assume. She turned to me. 'He's absolutely potty about it, you know. Hasn't missed a Show Thursday in years. I'm surprised you aren't on your way there now, darling.'

'No, well I thought I ought to . . . you know, greet our guest and see if anyone else wanted to . . . but it's probably not . . .'

'Simon, old thing,' I said, 'if you've room, I'd love to come along. That is, if it isn't a bore for you?'

David turned round, startled. Patricia gave me what writers used, inexplicably, to call a 'level' look. Of . . . what? Scorn? Relief, possibly? Heaven knows. Anne looked pleased and Michael, rather distracted that morning, nodded benignly. Simon, either out of courtesy or genuine feeling, expressed delight.

'No! Not at all. Be a pleasure. We can go in the Austin-Healey if you like. Unless anyone else . . .'

What on earth had possessed me I really cannot say. An agricultural fair . . . in blazing July . . . in East Anglia. Rare breeds . . . Show-jumping . . . Fat pigs . . . Clay, in all probability, pigeon shooting.

We left straight away, just Simon, Soda and myself. My horror at the prospect of massed farmers aside, I found myself unable to calculate whether I was pleased or piqued to see Patricia and Davey form such an instant bond of apparently mutual devotion. Naturally, I've known girlies form attachments to the younger male before now – there's that icky media notion of the toyboy after all – but in the tennis score of the bedroom most girls in my experience would rather Love Thirty or Love Forty than Love Fifteen. Men, of course, are a whole other issue: they start at Love All and stay there until they're dragged from the court.

The East of England Show, I was disturbed to learn, takes places outside Peterborough, on the way to being a two-hour drive from Swafford. My face must have betrayed my misgivings.

'You should have come last month instead,' said Simon. 'Last month was the Royal Norfolk Show. That's only in Costessey, half an hour away.' Costessey, it became clear despite its spelling, is pronounced 'Cossy'.

Simon then embarked on a story that will be deeply familiar to you, Jane.

'I took my cousin Jane to the Royal Norfolk,' he said. 'Do you know Jane?'

'My god-daughter,' I yelled above the wind-rush.

'Ah. You probably know then that she's not very well.'

I nodded.

'I had thought that perhaps a day out might be good for her. Unfortunately she collapsed during a baling demonstration. Terrible.'

'Terrible,' I agreed.

'I thought she was a goner, I'm afraid. You've never seen anyone so pale. The St John's Ambulance people wanted to take her to the Norfolk and Norwich. That's a hospital.'

'Sounds a reasonable idea. Probably more appropriate than a restaurant, say, or a football stadium.'

'She came round a bit in the tent, though, and I took her back to Swafford. She didn't want to see a doctor. Just went straight to bed. She was there for a couple of days. Davey read to her every afternoon and Dad hired a proper professional nurse. Dad's her uncle.'

'She seems quite well now,' I ventured. 'I saw her in London.'

'Yup, bit of a recovery. I'm not too surprised. You see that with pigs sometimes.'

Cousinly affection takes strange forms.

As we drove to Peterborough, I mused on the peculiar

pronunciation of Costessey and entertained Simon and Soda by improvising a limerick.

> *There was a young girl from Costessey*
> *Whose pubes were curly and glostessey*
> *Her thighs and her arse*
> *Were smooth as mown grass*
> *And her cunt was dark, dank and mostessey.*

'Brilliant!' Simon almost swerved off the road in joy. 'That's absolutely brilliant.'

When we arrived at the show ground, he repeated and repeated the limerick to his chums, of which there were many present. The poetic spirit, as you can see, is capable of flourishing in even the most barren and unpromising soil. Simon, for whom poetry is a closed book in a locked cupboard in a high attic in a lonely house in a remote hamlet in a distant land, kept saying to his friends, 'This is Uncle Ted. He's a famous poet. He actually made up a poem in my car as we were driving over!' And then he would recite it. The circumstance of being a 'proper poet' seemed to transform the limerick and confirm upon it something approaching the status of Art.

Reminded me of a trick we used to pull when hard up in the Dominion days. The Dominion was and still is a drinking club just round the corner from the Harpo, probably not your scene, dear. I used to wastrel there in the late Fifties and early Sixties with Gordon Fell, later 'Sir' Gordon, the painter and cultural icon (or so he was described the other week in an article by my daughter Leonora). The ruse was to get Gordon absolutely tanked up on the syrupy Old Fashioneds that he favoured and then start him talking. As soon as he mentioned in the course of conversation someone who wasn't actually a bosom-buddy of anybody in the room – let's use the name Tiny Winters, for instance – we would ask:

'Tiny Winters . . . Tiny Winters . . . Remind me, Gordie, who's he?'

And Gordon would splutter out some description of who this chap was. We would look puzzled and then firmly shake our heads.

'Nope. Simply can't place him.'

This would enrage Gordon, as well it might, Tiny Winters

or whoever being in fact perfectly well known to us. 'You know Tiny! *Tiny!* Everyone knows Tiny!' Gordon would hoot indignantly.

We would appear to struggle with our memories.

'What does he look like?' someone would wonder at last.

'Well he's . . . oh, give us a piece of paper for the Lord's sake . . .'

Tra-la! Victory. Out would come the charcoal and within five minutes we would be possessors of a genuine Fell. Even in those days you could get £50 for the crudest of sketches. The cruder the better, in fact.

'Oh *that* Tiny! Gotcha. Yes, of course, how *is* old Tiny then?'

One of us would slip the paper into a pocket and hurl off in a cab round to Cork Street and come back to share the spoils, old Gordon none the wiser.

Of course that shite-arsed little weasel Crompton Day had to go and tell him all about it one afternoon. Next time we tried the scam, Gordon took extra care over his portrait, tongue out, eyes swimming in concentration. We were simply panting with pleasure, this looked like seventy-five quid in the bag at least. When he finished we went into our usual 'Ah, *now* I know who you mean' routine, but before we could slip the portrait off the bar he had picked it up and was starting to tear it into narrow strips before our horrified eyes.

'There you are, dears,' he said, handing out a thin ribbon to every one of us. 'One each.'

Sod. After that you could never get him to draw so much as a map to show you the way to a restaurant.

Anyway, my limerick did the rounds of the show, much aggrandised, as I say, by its status of being the work of a known poet. Not that it could be sold like a Fell sketch, of course. Poetry doesn't work like that, oh no. It just shoots straight into the public domain. Still, mustn't mount that weary old hobby-horse again.

You don't really want to hear about 'The Day I Went to the East of England Show', so I will skip details of the gripping display of synchronised John Deere tractors, spare you the full story of the Suffolk Punch competition and save my descriptions of the titanic struggle between the Dereham and District Beet Growers and the Neane Valley Mangel-Wurzel Breeders (Incorporating the North Cambridgeshire Tap Root Association) for another time.

Simon, paucity of imagination and dullness of wit aside, is at least a civil figure and he never yielded to any temptation to abandon me to the depredations of the numerous hat-wearing ladies who skimmed and dipped from tea-tent to tea-tent like dragon-flies in August. In as much as agricultural fairs were a new experience for me, and every man in his sixties should take especial pleasure in any new experience however apparently grotesque, I cannot claim that it was the grisliest afternoon of my life. Simon allowed Soda and me numerous pit-stops in the beer-tents and sandwicheries and even suggested that we track down a Rothman's bus which he knew would be in attendance. I stocked up on armfuls of free Rothies, filled in a questionnaire and charmed the sashes off a couple of the heavily fucused popsies who were staffing the bus, a converted double-decker gaily trimmed in the Rothman's livery of blue, white and gold. Reminded me of my youth when cigarette girls were as common a sight at theatres, cinema premières and nightclubs as charity-beggars are today. Thing is, the chances were you could shag a ciggie girl in the lavvies for a fiver in those days: I've a strong feeling that the sticker-vendors of the Save the Children Fund and the bucket-shakers of the Cystic Fibrosis Society would scream for the police and sue you for optical rape if you so much as flicked an eye below the level of their necks in today's caring Britain. There has been a relentless and disturbing rise in moral standards over the years. It worries me.

We left the jamboree at six, trailing many shiny floating balloons that bore the glamorous logos and exotic colourings of cattle-feed suppliers and manufacturers of slow-release fungicides – it would appear that Michael likes to sit round after dinner and giggle at helium-enhanced voices.

As we drove back, Simon pestered me for more limericks. 'Do one for Swafford,' he insisted.

> *There was an old woman of Swafford*
> *Whose hair was gigantically coiffured*
> *When asked for the reason*
> *She said 'In this season*
> *I need all the shade that is offered.'*

'Not bad. It wasn't very rude, though, was it?'
'Soda liked it,' I replied, wounded.

'Now do a limerick on me.'

'Hum . . .'

> *There was a young man named Simon*
> *Who hated the art of rhyming*
> *He thought it a shame*
> *That his very own name*
> *Could only be mated with hymen.*

'You're absolutely bloody right, there. Hymen was my nickname at school. Did you know?'

'Let's call it an inspired guess,' I said.

'Okay, what about one for yourself?'

> *There was an old lecher named Ted*
> *Who was known to be useless in bed*
> *When parting a bush*
> *He'd fumble and push*
> *And screw the poor mattress instead.*

Simon was fascinated by this concept. 'Does that really happen?'

'What, missing the opening, you mean? Certainly. All the time.'

Not to have known that, it seemed to me, meant that the boy must either be a virgin or else have been seduced by a woman experienced enough to guide him in without so much as a moment of outslip. Lucky beggar.

The homebound trek from Peterborough, as so often happens, seemed appreciably shorter than the outward haul.

Davey, in a replay of the moment of my arrival on Sunday, was drooping on the front steps.

'Hello, young beast. And where's your girlfriend?'

He turned his head away to disclaim the appellation.

'We bear gifts,' I said. 'Look, for you a fat pig fashioned of rarest homespun and with finest kapok stuffed.'

He took it. 'It's rather funny,' he said. 'Thank you.'

'The lady who sold it to me wondered if I had sat for the artist. This was a little rich as she herself favoured nothing so much as a common cormorant or shag struggling in an oil-slick. None the less, I think you will agree there is a more than passing resemblance between this excellent pig and my wise and wicked self. If you were to stick a pin in it I should leap and yowl.'

'I would have liked to have come, you know.'

Ha! Where is an outreach counsellor with a diploma from the University of Dunstable and a government grant, when you need one? I waited until Simon and Soda were out of earshot, smoothed Davey's ego with descriptions of how turgid and unamusing the afternoon had been and toddled into the house to dress for dinner. For tonight was to see the Logans playing host to the county, a black-tie event.

No one else was about, so it wasn't until we foregathered in the foregathery that I discovered Mother Mills was to be of our party.

Oliver Mills. I don't know if you've met him. He was padre of our regiment back in National Service days. He's seen the dark since and defrocked himself. That at least is his story: it is my belief, founded in idle gossip, that he became frankly too hot for the army or the church to handle. His taste for butch subalterns and zesty young rankers knew no bounds. There was an episode I heard about in '59 that may well have been the straw that broke the camel's back. A general, inspecting a platoon of glowing cadets, soon to be passed out, stopped in front of one especially doll-like ephebe.

'You, sir! Name?'

'Cyprian Manlove, sir.' (Or whatever)

'You a gentleman of sound moral fibre?'

No reply.

'Well, sir?'

Whereat the unfortunate boy burst into tears and scampered from the parade ground. Hanged himself by his Sam Browne, leaving a note that begged his mother's forgiveness. Nothing proved, naturally, but he was known to serve at the altar in chapel and it wasn't long before Oliver folded up his stole and plunged head first into the secular. The boy hadn't been exactly Mother Mills's type, but in those days buggers couldn't be choosers.

Oliver's first lay billet was with the BBC, a haven for the bent and faithless if ever there was one, where he directed most of those dreary kitchen-sinkers that everyone pretends were the golden produce of the golden age of television, though frankly I'd rather watch John Major dry than sit through any of that self-righteous ullage ever again. Most of the playwrights responsible have died from alcohol poisoning and socialist disillusionment by now, thank God, and Oliver, as you know, specialises these days in rich and loving period adaptations of the classics and fuck the workers, though he wouldn't thank you for saying so. You never knew such a one for writing priggish round robins to the press: 'Sir, We the undersigned are horrified at the government's attempts to cut the Arts Council grant/impose VAT on corduroy trousers/privatise Dickie Attenborough', you know the sort of mealy-mouthed sludge I'm talking about: he'll round up all the usual suspects at the Harpo Club and get them to agree to be set down as co-signatories. Once tried to get me to append my name to a screed wailing about the Net Book Agreement, whatever the badgery fuck that might be. Thoroughly amiable and amusing companion (if you like your wit tied in frilly bows) but, when the socialist bit's clamped between his expensively capped pegs, as humourless a lump of dough as ever held a torchlight vigil outside the South African Embassy or stuck an AIDS Awareness ribbon on an unwilling first-nighter.

'Quid pro quo,' I had said. 'First, you sign a letter I'm writing that urges the government to bring back town-square flogging for graffiti and littering . . .' I had notably crabby views on that head just then, the wall opposite me in Butler's Yard having recently been sprayed in lettering that looked like upside-down Arabic.

Naturally, Mother Mills had stalked away baffled. For all that, he and I were on good terms and he greeted me heartily on Thursday night at Swafford when I pottered in, freshly tubbed and scrubbed, for my pre-dinner glass of the nasty.

'Well, if it isn't the Happy Hippo,' he said – Christ, I hate that old nick-name – 'and beaten to the watering trough by a better man.'

'Hello, Oliver,' I wheezed, 'and what plucks you from Kensington?'

'Same as you, angel. R&R. Mother's been as busy as a big brown bee these last few months. She's come to replenish her tissues.'

'But still sucking up the vodka, we note.'

'Not since Barbara Cartland described Fergie as vulgar have we heard such a grubby pot have the Nigella Nerve to call such a Katie Kettle black.'

I ignored him and poured myself a few fat fingers of the Macallan as he twittered on about his new love.

91

'Dennis. A name as romantic as fly-spray, but so sweet and trusting and heavily cocked. I'll take another voddie while you're there.'

'What does he do, this Dennis?'

'Anything I ask.'

'For a living.'

'He's a social-security clerk if you must know. I met him on a Pride march.'

There are times when you envy faggotry, and times when you don't. At least we plain old hetters never have to set up house with clerks and welders and shop assistants. Call me a snob and call me unkind, but how Oliver can bear the idea of ignorant dull-witted oafs from Clapham or Camberwell farting in his bed and scratching their balls in front of his cheval-glass, I cannot imagine.

'And what about you, Ted? We understand you've been squiring love's young dream about the lawns and meadows.'

'Barely spoken to her.'

'No, no. Not the breeder. I'm talking about the caramel-thighed Hylas of the fens. The Rupert Graves of the Iceni, as you very well know.'

I did, but had affected to misunderstand.

'Are you by any chance referring to my godson?'

'Please, Ted. You're a poppet when you're yourself, but not fit for firewood when you're all stiff and grumpy. Throw your mother some line or she'll have a miserable time.'

Well, put like that, a man can hardly in all charity keep up a chilly front.

'You'll find him a pretty little piece, I'll not deny,' I conceded, easing myself into a chair. 'Intense as all get out, mind you.'

'Don't I know it. While you and Simple Simon were dwile-flonking with the rough bumpkinry, he took me out on his little dinghy, *much* to the chagrin of the Patricia element, who was too scared or too high-heeled or too tightly stockinged or too lah-di-Mayfair-dah to climb aboard, but wanted sinful Davey all for herself none the less. And *we* know why, don't we?'

'We do?'

'Well, of course we do!' Oliver looked at me in amazement, saw that I was genuinely adrift and then became puzzled himself. 'Don't we? I mean, darling. I assumed you were here for the same . . .'

At this point the door opened and Max and Mary Clifford strutted in.

'Ah, Ted . . . returned from your adventures.' Max extended a languid hand. Born in Liverpool, yet with an accent and manner that makes the Duke of Devonshire sound like Ben Elton. A self-made man who worships his creator, as someone said about somebody else, or somebody else said about someone. His wife Mary is of Welsh stock – Wrexham, if memory doesn't deal me a dog-turd, and is also possessed of vowels like a line of Lalique icicles.

She proffered a powdery cheek and wagged a waggish finger. 'Now Ted, I hope you're going to be *very* well behaved and *very* sober tonight. The Bishop and his wife are coming over this evening and the Draycotts will be here too, so best party manners.'

Un-yippee and un-hurrah.

'That goes for you too, Oliver. No atheistical talk, we beg.'

Said as if *she* were throwing the party and this was *her* house.

'Is he Heidi or Lorraine?' Oliver wanted to know.

Mary looked blank. 'He's Ronald, Oliver. Ronald and Fabia, I think their names are. They used to be at Ripon.'

'I think what Oliver wants to know,' I said, 'is whether the Bishop is High Church or Low Church.'

'Thank you, precious,' said Oliver.

'Oh, nothing like that,' Max pronounced with authority, taking two sherry glasses deftly in one hand. 'Solid public-school hymnbook. No nonsense.'

'Looks like Molly Moderate,' I said to Oliver.

'Hm . . .' Oliver looked at his nails dreamily. 'Pity. I'm best at twitting the low rent, as it happens. Bishop-baiting,' he explained to Mary, 'is one of Mother's specialities.'

'Now Oliver,' Mary screeched. 'I absolutely *forbid* . . .'

'Forbid what?' Michael had arrived, hair sleekly brushed back, sapphires winking in his shirt front.

'Oliver's threatening to tease the Bishop this evening.'

'Really?' Michael looked towards Oliver, who jiggled the ice in his glass in lazy salute. 'I think he's more likely teasing you, Mary.'

'Oh.'

'But, you're welcome to try your luck, Oliver. I believe Ronald used to box for the army. Isn't that right, Max?'

'So they tell me, Michael. So they tell me.'

93

Max has mastered a particular tone of voice with which he addresses Michael. It tells the world of a special relationship, a close and secret bond that shares its own private joke about the world. It drives me absolutely potty, as you can imagine. I knew Michael long before Max and his kind. There is a simultaneous envy (I know that Max, as a fellow boxwallah, can talk turkey with Michael in a way denied to me) and a protectiveness. I feel like Piggy in *Lord of the Flies*, left behind when Ralph is borne off with the others to explore the island. 'But I was with him before anyone! I was with him when he found the conch,' I want to cry.

In the event the Bishop went largely unbaited. Twenty of us sat down to dinner. I suppose I had better give the guest list and you can tell me in your letter back whether you need further details.

> Michael and Anne
> Ted
> Patricia
> Max and Mary Clifford
> Rose (Michael's ancient Austrian aunt, never said a word)
> Oliver
> Simon
> David
> Ronald and Fabia ✠ Norvic (the Bish and Bishess)
> John and Margot Draycott
> Clara (the Cliffords' daughter – skinny, wears a brace)
> Tom and Margaret Purdom (local squirearchy)
> Malcolm and Antonia Whiting (local literati, to please me. Ha!)
> YOUR MOTHER

Yes, I thought that was worth leaving to the end. You could have felled me with a cocktail-stick. Your mother. Rebecca Burrell, née Logan. In the flesh.

Five minutes before we went in to dine, the full complement, as I thought, having been mustered, a peal was heard from the doorbell and there she stood. With luggage, with presents for the boys, with all the useful clever gifts from Fortnum's that city-dwellers bestow on their deprived country cousins – rustic pies, stone-ground loaves, Norfolk honey, grain mustard and wind-dried lavender – with, in short, all the paraphernalia that betokens a long and cosy stay.

'Bex!' cries Michael, falling on her neck. Then he beams at me. 'So, kiss my sister, Ted.'

She was sporting a beady, I-know-you're-wearing-dirty-underpants sort of face but with the trace of a smile lurking in its margins. I'd seen her four years ago, at Christmas. Michael had been hoping to forge a rapprochement then I suspect, but it hadn't really worked. I was too rebarbative, Rebecca was at her spiky worst and Pamela Pride, as Oliver might say, had woven her wicked web all too easily. With so many people there it had been possible for us to ignore each other. It's going to be harder these next weeks.

So Jane, give it to me straight: did you or did you not know that the She-Beast of Phillimore Gardens would be coming? If so, I hate you and hate you and hate you for not warning me.

We were seated apart at dinner which was some kind of a relief. I had been given the treat of walking Patricia in and sat between her and the squire's wife, Margaret. Simon sat at his mother's end of the table next to Clara Clifford and engaged her in conversation without vomiting at the sight of the particles of food that were getting caught in her brace, which is more than I could have managed. David sat at Michael's end, unostentatiously avoiding meat. He had to parry the ludicrous remarks of Antonia Whiting, some of which drifted over to my end.

'Malcolm and I are trying to set up a South Norfolk Festival of Poetry and Prose. We think Jeyes of Thetford might sponsor it. Malcolm's worried that the "J-Cloth Festival" might not sound right. What do you think?'

Oliver, largely thanks to Mary Clifford's witless proscriptions earlier on, was at his most disgraceful. Talk of festivals reminded him of an anecdote and he discoursed at length about the erotic adventures that had attended his visit to the Venice Film Festival last year.

'You won't *believe* the trade that you can find trolling up and down the Dorsoduro,' he said. 'After a week my back-pussy was like a wind-sock.'

'What's a back-pussy?' Davey wanted to know.

'We were rather disappointed in Venice, weren't we, Tom?' Margaret Purdom put in hastily.

'The prices in Harry's Bar were ridiculous. Absolute scandal. For two Bellinis you had to pay . . .'

'There was one boy,' Oliver continued, 'who worked behind the guichet at the Academia. I got him to come back to the Gritti with me only to have him deliver the sweetest warning. You see, he was possessed of the most enormous . . .'

The door opened and Podmore came in to clear away the soup plates. Oliver was equal to the occasion. He knows better than to talk loosely *devant les domestiques*. Barely pausing for breath, he put up a hand to one side of his mouth, as if to shield Podmore from corruption, and continued, '. . . the most enormous C-O-C-K . . .' spelling the word out in a loud and frantic whisper. Podmore's chin wobbled a fraction and Margaret Purdom let out a small scream, but Oliver looked pleased with his social adroitness.

'It was so sweet,' he went on, once Podmore had departed, 'Gianni, for such was his name, anxiously explained, in one of those divinely dusty Italian voices, that he was afraid he might hurt me. "Carissimo," I said, "I'll grant you it's a monster, but after what I've been through this last week you'll be lucky if it touches the sides. It'll be like a paper boat up the Grand Canal." Still, that's enough of me. You much of a traveller, Bishop?'

Patricia nudged me. 'Oliver makes it all up of course, doesn't he?' she whispered.

'Naturally,' I said. 'Nobody has sex any more, straight or bent.'

'What on earth do you mean?'

'It's the great paradox of the age. Before permissiveness came in, everyone everywhere was at it like randy goats. But the moment the young started to insist on talking about it all the time, you couldn't get laid if you were a table at the Savoy. As soon as something becomes a Right you can't bloody do it any more. Self-consciousness, you see.'

'In *Gerald's Fortnight*, my third novel . . .' Malcolm Whiting said.

'I just think it's all so unnecessary,' the Purdom offered from my right.

'Unnecessary?' Oliver's ears had pricked up at the other end of the table.

'Hear, hear,' said Max.

'The protagonist of *Gerald's Fortnight* . . .'

'The day sex becomes unnecessary,' said Michael, 'will be a dark one indeed.'

I was glad he had decided to join in. There is nothing worse than a Jew sitting and listening to a conversation. They nod their heads with a fraudulent air of rabbinical wisdom that makes you want to set about them with staves.

'Do you mean sex is now unnecessary because of artificial insemination?' asked Simon, having a pitiful stab at sounding sophisticated.

'I'm not saying hex itself is unnecessary . . .' Margaret Purdom is one of those ghastly upper-middle-class people who can't quite bring themselves to pronounce the 's' in sex. 'I just mean the endless *talking* about it and showing it on television and rubbing our noses in it.'

'Does it shock you, Mrs Purdom?' asked Oliver.

'Of course not . . . it's just so uncalled for. There was a thing on the other day . . .'

'What about tea drinking?'

'I beg your pardon?'

'Tea-drinking,' said Oliver. 'Do you object to that on television?'

'Well, of course not. I don't see . . .'

'Nobody *calls* for tea-drinking though, do they? I mean, in television dramas, the camera could easily show the kettle boiling on the hob and then cut discreetly away. But no, they have to show the whole thing. The warming of the tea-pot, the pouring-out, the plopping of the sugar-cube and the slow sipping from the cup. Isn't that "unnecessary" too? Isn't that completely uncalled for?'

'Hardly the same thing, Oliver,' said Max.

'No, of course not! Because no one is shocked by tea-drinking, are they? They are shocked by sex but they daren't admit it. I could respect that Mary Whitehouse creature and her moral minority if they had the Betty Balls to admit that they were in fact frankly and deeply shocked by the spectacle of naked coupling on a public screen. Shocked to their winceyette knicky-knicks. But, instead, they think it's more impressive to give off a tiresome worldly air. "I'm not *shocked*," they say, "oh good heavens no. I just find it all rather boring," as if Tessa Tedium were the Chrissie Crime.'

While Ma Purdom struggled for a reply (to an argument that I suspect Oliver had trotted out many times before . . . probably on one of those 'The People Grill the Producers' shows that the BBC now inflict endlessly on us in a futile attempt to crawl to the audience), bold husband Tom leapt to her defence.

'Yes that's all very clever-clever,' he said, 'but you can't argue that the world isn't in an unhealthy moral state.'

'Wouldn't think of it, dearest. People lie, cheat, rape, swindle, kill, maim, torture and destroy. Bad thing. People also pop into bed together and cosy up. Good thing. If we imagine fucking is a sign of moral decay we're being just a little bit stupid-stupid, aren't we?'

'I still don't see why we have to go *on* about it all the time,' said Margaret.

'*Gerald's Fortnight* was accused by critics of . . .'

'If you really want to crack down on promiscuity among the young,' said the Bishop, 'then you should surely fight for sex scenes on television to be more realistic. Show the whole thing with actors that look like real people instead of like models. Once children know about the squelch and the stench and the whole slippery mess of it they may become less anxious to try it out until they have to.'

Bit hard on the Lady Bishop I felt, but a point well made. Patricia at this point, heated by such saucy talk, started consciously or unconsciously to rub her leg against mine. It was good to have a woman's thigh pressing against me and, victim of the primal curse on man, which is a need to show off to women, I embarked on holding the company spellbound for a while with my sparkling theories on art and life.

Oliver, being the bitch he is, tried consistently to undermine me with bitter little interjections. I held my own, naturally, but refused to allow the conversation to sink into sterile mud-slinging.

'Returning to the subject of sex for a moment,' said Michael, during a pause which followed a more than usually platitudinous observation from Simon. 'When I bought Newsline Papers Ltd, I called a conference of interested parties to see whether we should stop showing naked women in the pages of our tabloids.'

'Interested parties being bricklayers and spotty teenagers, no doubt?' said Oliver.

'Being psychologists, sociologists, feminists, moralists and representatives of religions,' said Michael. 'The bricklayer and the teenager I can cope with. I said to these experts, "Pretend you own this newspaper. If you can't turn it into profit in six months you're out of a job. What do you do?" Well, you never heard such nonsense in your life. "Let's have more *good* news", "Make it a *family* paper", "Show women in a positive light", "affirmation", "family values" . . . I slapped on the table in front of them a copy of the rival paper. "This is the competition," I said. "It sells millions every day. It is the opposite of everything you have mentioned, but it sells. Why? Tell me please, why? Because people are stupid? Because people are cruel? Because people are ignorant? Because people are savage? Why?" And they answered, "Because it's there. It sells because it's there." "The *Independent* is there too," I said, "and the *Christian Science Monitor* and *Spare Rib* and the *Morning Star*. They are there too, but they don't sell. Give me a better answer." But no better answer came.'

'Of course not. Because what they wanted to say,' said Max, 'is that newspapers should be under *their* control. *They* know better.'

'Well, who's to say they don't know better, Max?' Michael said. 'Perhaps they do know better about many things. About selling newspapers they don't know better, that I will say. I tried running for a few weeks without naked ladies and the circulation dropped. We put the naked ladies back in and the sales rose. What else could I have done?'

'You could have gone into another fucking business,' said David with sudden and extraordinary ferocity.

The whole table froze in a fraught and deathly silence. There was something terrible about such savagery from such a source. Few things are more sphincter-winkingly embarrassing than a family row at the best of times. I could hear Patricia beside me holding her breath.

'Well, Davey,' said Michael, 'I did go into another business, if you remember. I sold the newspapers.'

'And someone else bought them and is profitably printing pictures of naked ladies to this very day,' said Max.

'Well, thank God it isn't my father!' David was trembling at his own courage but otherwise he managed to maintain a steadfast front.

'Davey is very concerned with the whiteness of my soul,' said Michael ruefully, much as a husband might joke about his wife's solicitude for his waistline.

There was a sudden outbreak of little local conversations

and no single topic dominated the party again for the rest of the dinner.

Davey left the table with the ladies but Simon stayed for the port, his demeanour failing hopelessly to project an air of being simultaneously grown-up, respectful, blasé, grateful and impassive.

Max slid down to my end of the table and put an arm to my shoulder.

'Well, that was a sticky one, I think,' he said in a low voice. 'Of course, little Davey can do no wrong, can he? The sun shines out of little Davey's rear end, doesn't it? If Simon had said such an unctuous and insolent thing, not that he would, there would have been hell to pay.'

I remembered that Max was Simon's godfather and found myself amused that he should show such loyalty. I felt bound to reciprocate and soon we were at it like a couple of old generals taking sides over a rematch of Waterloo.

'Well, he may have been a tad unctuous, but it was brave, it was spirited and it was felt.'

'Sodding cheek and you know it, Ted.'

'So, it's better to be drained of imagination and ideals at birth than to risk losing them later on, is that it?'

'Simon isn't devoid of imagination *or* ideals. It's just that he has manners and decency enough to respect others.'

'The kind of manners and decency that question nothing, challenge nothing and achieve nothing.'

'Oh pish, Ted. As if you believe a word of that. You're the most cynical man in Britain and you know it.'

'Never, Max,' I said, 'never, ever tell a man he is cynical. Cynical is the name we give those we fear may be laughing at us.'

'Don't get all gnomic with me, you old fraud.'

The trouble with Max, repellent as he may be, is that he is not quite as stupid as one would like him to be. Not that he's brilliant, it's just that he's always just a tiny bit brighter than would be convenient.

'This is a silly conversation, Max.'

'You're right. If the truth be told, I just came over to steal a cigarette off you. Can't cope with Michael's enormous cigars.' I obliged him and he puffed on it like a schoolboy. 'Heard about your dishonourable discharge from the rag. Sorry about that. Quite agree with you over the Lake man. His plays get worse and worse. Pleased that Rebecca's arrived, are you? You and she . . . weren't you . . . once upon a long ago?'

'I believe I'm not the only one,' I said, then wished I hadn't.

Max flashed his eyes at me and then down to the stem of his glass. 'Well, well. Now who on earth can have told you that, I wonder?'

'These things get about.'

'No they don't. Oh no they don't. Only happened once. A Christmas some years back. In this very house. And I thought we'd been so very discreet. Well, well, well. *There's* a mystery. Can't be the lady in the case, can it? Fancy that, just fancy that.'

I wriggled a bit on this hook. It was hardly my intention to land David in the poo; in his relation of the Great Shooting Sabotage (you'll have read that by now, Jane) he had only told me the story of Rebecca and Max in the night-time as an incidental detail. He hadn't even understood it himself at the time.

In casting about for a convincing way to change the subject, I recalled something that Donald Pulsifer the wild-life photographer had once told me. The way to confuse and pacify an angry gorilla, he said, is to start hitting yourself. If you make a blistering assault upon your own person, slapping your cheeks, punching yourself in the stomach, tearing at your hair and clawing at your face, the animal will stop in its tracks, tilt its head and – likely as not – come forward to cuddle and caress you in sympathy, licking your wounds and cradling you like a baby.

'Can't deny it was a shock to see Rebecca coming through the door this evening,' I said, deciding to test Pulsifer's theory. 'We had a furious row at Jane's christening. Well, that's what I tell the world. The fact of the matter is I was drunk and I was dreadful. A couple of years earlier Rebecca had nourished something of a *tendre* for me, you see. To her I was rather more than a casual bedmate. My first wife Fee had run off with that American Open Field poet and I had become a sodden and available mess. Then Patrick Burrell started lapping and sniffing around her loins and she gave me an ultimatum. "If you don't marry me, I'll up and marry Patrick," she said. "Then marry the daft turd," says I. "What the fuck do I care?" That was bad. Very bad. She kept to her word, duly wed the oily rat and out popped Jane, for whom I was chosen as godfather, as much, I believed, to prove to me that she was "Happy! Ha, ha! Blissfully, blissfully happy," as anything else, and I accepted to show that there were no hard feelings on my side either. And then at the . . . what do you call them . . . wakes? That can't be right, at the christening party . . . there must be a proper name for them . . . I did a very stupid thing.'

'Oh yes?' Max was sucked in now and seemed to have lost interest in my knowledge of his own little secret.

'I found Rebecca alone in the conservatory. I said to her that I missed her. I said to her that I wished I hadn't let her marry Patrick.'

'Oh, you idiot.'

'It was true. Damnation, it was true.'

'What use was that to her?'

'Well I know that now, don't I? I had imagined, in my champagne blur, that she would be touched. Instead of which she smashed fifteen panes of conservatory window and roof in her fury. I let it be put about that she had been repelling my unwanted advances.'

'Well, that certainly explains a great deal,' said Max. 'Do you know, I have always wondered why Rebecca freezes at the sound of your name?'

'Well, now you know.'

'Lord, Ted, I'd've thought you knew women better than to have made a blunder like that.'

This egregious man-of-the-world matiness hardly qualified in my book as cradling my head and licking my wounds, but it was an improvement on the icy stare of a minute ago.

'Let's have you down this end, you two,' called Michael. 'We're going to have some fun with the ladies and those balloons.'

So we filled our lungs with helium, crept into the drawing room and made the women scream.

An evening of games followed, the details of which you won't be anxious to hear. I rather shone in charades, fooling everyone with my vivid portrayal of an army of rabbits calling a truce.

'It *must* be *Watership Down*!' everyone cried.

Ha, ha. It was *War and Peace*. Warren Peace, do you see?

Simon made an arse of himself as guesser in a round of 'In the Manner of the Word', on account of never having heard of the word 'archly'. I'm afraid he is rather an oaf, that boy.

I tried to get Oliver alone to quiz him about our earlier, interrupted, conversation, you remember the one I mean?

'*Patricia . . . wanted sinful Davey all for herself . . . And* we *know why, don't we?*'

'*We do?*'

'*Well, of course we do! Don't we? I mean, darling. I assumed you were here for the same . . .*'

But Oliver proved elusive, and after bidding goodnight to the non-resident guests, we all wound our ways to our several beds.

And now it is Saturday morning, an equestrian party has departed for trottings, canterings and gallopings about the park, my neck is stiff, Podmore has promised to provide a late breakfast and this letter is done.

Yours aye

Ted

Five

12a Onslow Terrace
LONDON SW7

27th July 1992

Dear Ted,

What a long letter. How beautifully printed. How absorbing. How alarming. I shall answer your numerous questions one at a time.

Patricia: Yes, I did know that she would be joining you at the weekend. I saw no special reason to tell you. She is not spying on the spy if that has been worrying you. She is there simply because she wants to be. As you discovered, she is recovering from an unhappy love affair. I am *very* interested in her comings and goings, however, and would beg you to watch closely there. Patricia is very vulnerable and I want her to come to no harm.

Mummy: I had no idea that she would be coming down, although I am not surprised to hear it. I am very grateful for the elliptical (is that the word?) way in which you have filled me in about your relationship with her. She often moves from place to place without telling me, there is nothing unusual in that. She knows nothing of the reason for your

104

visit (nor does Patricia) although both of them are aware of my leukaemia, as are the Logans.

Michael: I am sure he will consent to your request. If he doesn't it hardly matters, you will just have to be an unofficially inquisitive guest instead of a licensed writer-in-residence.

There are now a number of specific things that you can do for me.

Firstly: Please stop using Latin tags in your letters. You should by now be beyond the stage of having to demonstrate your superiority over me. The same goes for pointing out spelling mistakes and incorrect usages.

Secondly: Enquire about the twins, Edward and James. You have hardly mentioned them. You say they are 'staying with family'. What family? Where? Why? When are they returning? This may be important.

Thirdly: Find out how Oliver is and what brings him here.

Fourthly: I need more information about Aunt Anne. You told me nothing for instance of her reaction to David's outburst about Michael's newspaper holdings at the dinner-table on Thursday.

Fifthly: On no account mess around with Patricia. She is very special and not to be trifled with.

Sixthly: You have talked only about the guests. The house is full of other men and women. There are indoor and outdoor servants, there is Podmore. I have heard nothing of them.

Seventhly: Constant vigilance; constant awareness; constant observation; constant openness.

I shall write no more because I want you to get this as soon as possible.

Much love

Jane

II

Swafford Hall
Swafford
DISS
Norfolk

25th July 1993

Jane –

As you can see, I'm at Swafford! You'll never *imagine*
who's here too! Your mother for one, looking fantastically
elegant, and . . . wait for it . . . Ted Wallace, your long-lost
godfather. I *wish* you could make it over too. You've always
said you wanted to get to know him. As far as I can tell he's
here for simply ever, so why don't you come on down? He
and your mother seem to be getting on rather well, which is
a bit of a surprise – David tells me they used to hate each
other.

And what *about* David?! Everything you said seems to be
absolutely true, though there is the veritablest *queue* for his
attentions. I'm having to fight off that dreadful Oliver Mills
as well as Ted and even, I think, your mother, just to get five
minutes alone with him.

Who else is here? Oh, Max and Mary Clifford, natch, and
their daughter Clara who's rather squinty and peculiar and
unfortunate. Michael's been a bit quiet but we had an inci-
dent-packed dinner party on Thursday, lots of local worthies
present, including Ronald Leggatt, the Bishop of Norwich,
and his fat wife, Fabia. The Draycotts were there naturally,
those dreary literary people the Whitings, and some other
couple I couldn't place.

As soon as we sat down, Oliver started behaving dreadfully,
telling all kinds of shatteringly inappropriate stories and talking about sex in a loud voice, so I gave Ted who was sitting
beside me a swift kick to get him to try and change the
subject. Big mistake! I think you have been well off not
knowing that man. There are football hooligans in gaol who
could fairly claim to be more sensitive and less piggish.

'I blame this ghastly obsession with therapy,' he said, on

the subject of everybody's obsession with sex. 'It's a short space between "therapist" and "the rapist", after all.'

'What's wrong with therapy, Ted?' I asked – I hope not too snappishly. I didn't want to give the impression that I'd been under one myself.

'Well, it comes down to which damned language you choose, doesn't it?' he said, in an extravagantly patient voice, as if I were a two-year-old. I think he is one of those kind of men who would talk to Marie Curie as if she were a drooling illiterate.

'Are you talking about sexual discourse here?' Malcolm Whiting asked.

'No, he's discoursing about sexual talk,' said Oliver.

'I wrote a book called *The Love Tree* which you may have . . .' the Whiting idiot started to say.

'I'm saying this,' Uncle T. interrupted. 'In the old days, when we thought that our souls were at stake, Latin had all the authority and it was the curate or the curé who did the curing. Now, in the technical age, we say psyche for soul, and therapist for curate, Greek being the language of science. Mind you, with all this New Age wank around, we've turned to Anglo-Saxon too and the world has started to blather on about "healing". Same process – holy, sane or healthy: cure, therapy or healing.'

'You really don't see a difference, Mr Wallace?' asked the Bishop. 'You don't perceive different kinds of ill-health?'

'Different kinds of "unholiness", you mean? Well. If I break my leg I go to see my old friend Doctor Posner. If I break my heart I go to see my old friend Doctor Macallan.'

'Doctor Macallan?'

'He means whisky,' your mother explained, while directing an acid "Why-can't-you-shut-up-and-leave-well-alone?" look at Ted.

'Ah,' said the Bishop, 'and suppose one of your children were sick in some way?'

'Loopy?'

'If you like. I assume you wouldn't fill *them* up with whisky?'

'It's always struck me,' said Max, 'that if someone believed they were Napoleon I'd send them to someone else who believed that they were the Duke of Wellington. That'd sort them out.'

'Few people are spiritually unhealthy in quite such a clear-cut way, however,' the Bishop said.

'Ah well, "spiritually" is your word, you see,' replied Ted. 'One man's "spiritual ill-health" is another man's "lack of self-esteem" is another man's "oversupply of blood-sugar" is another man's "holistic imbalance". You pays your exorbitant fee and you takes your worthless choice. The fact is nothing can ever be truly cured *or* therapied *or* made whole.'

'Whatever do you mean?' Michael asked. This was getting dangerous.

'Everything rots. At the risk of special pleading, only art can halt the process.'

'What a load of pompous balls, darling,' said Oliver. 'Gone are the days when art bestowed immortality. "So long lives this, and this gives life to thee" and all that wank. The invention of the camera gave us all eternal life. The Dark Lady and the Golden Boy of the sonnets are no more immortal now than Oprah Winfrey or the contestants on the "Wheel of Fortune".'

Ted wasn't having any of that. 'You don't believe that for a moment and besides, it isn't what I meant. You must surely confess that artists, certainly dead ones, are more intelligent, sensitive and intuitive than any therapist with a degree in psychogibber from Keele university or any scurfy outreach parson with a diploma from King's or for that matter any mad Druid channelling energy with hot hands and a lump of amethyst.'

'But honey, we all know that art is what drives people mad.'

'Oh, artists are mad, Oliver, I'll give you that. Every man Jack and every woman Jill of them. All practitioners of the spirit are mad. Show me a sane psychotherapist and I'll show you a charlatan, show me a holy priest, saving the Bishop's reverence, and I'll show you an apostate, show me a healthy New Age healer and I'll show you a mountebank. But who's to say that sending a patient to a recital or an art gallery isn't a better balm for hurt minds than forcing them to talk about their relationship with their mothers or stuffing them full of Holy Bread?'

'But you do distinguish between the mind and the body I suppose?' Rebecca said. 'I mean, you wouldn't send a man with a physical disease to an art gallery, surely?'

'Of course he would. That's why the Tate is already so full

of lepers,' said Max, earning rather a cheap and obvious laugh, I thought.

'The anti-hero of *The Love Tree* is brought down by . . .'

'No, no.' Ted was getting het up now. 'A mechanical fault can be corrected and medicine is perfectly competent at that. But it isn't healing, it isn't *making whole*.'

'And healing can only come from art?'

I felt we were drowning in precisely the sort of conversation we shouldn't be having, but I honestly couldn't see any way out of it. All the Logans, David, Simon, Michael and Anne, were staring at Ted, practically open-mouthed.

'Put it this way,' replied Ted, 'we're all grown-ups. Even the religious amongst us are no longer superstitious. Nobody happy and confident believes in ghosts or telepathy or miracles. But art abides. It is the only thing that not only cannot be disproved, but can actually be tangibly and incontrovertibly proved.'

He looked round with an indecently smug expression on his face, as if challenging us to disagree. Most of us just gawped down at our dinner-plates in embarrassment. It couldn't have been more killingly awful if he had taken out his whanger and stuffed it in Lady Draycott's ear. David stared at me in consternation and Rebecca shook her head sorrowfully. Then Simon, stupid clod-hopping Simon, above whose head the whole undercurrent had flowed (if that makes sense), started to speak.

'Well, I think that there are *some* things that can't be explained . . .' he began, but mercifully Michael galloped to the rescue by talking about his newspapers.

Even that wasn't safe ground, mind you. It provoked a very strange scene with David blurting out how he'd always hated Michael owning tabloids. The young can be so puritanical, can't they? I can remember being a bit like that at his age, but not quite as daring. Michael took it like a lamb, but all in all it had turned into a very odd dinner party.

But what was Ted up to? I mean he does *know*, I assume? Perhaps I should take him aside and tell him not to meddle? Unless his slobbery grins mean nothing, he's desperate to sleep with me, so I should be able to get him to behave. He spent all of yesterday banged up in his room 'writing', which probably means drinking his shame away.

It's such a pity you aren't here, Jane. Surely those doctors will have finished their tests by now? I don't know how you can bear to miss all the fun. I reluctantly confess that Oliver ought to be first in the queue as his need is greater than mine, but my Lord I'm looking forward to it all . . .

All my love

Pat

PS: Blast, I've missed the Saturday post, so you won't get this till Tuesday at the earliest.

III

Swafford
28.vii.92

Jane,

Disaster. Absolute fucking disaster. I don't know how it happened and I don't know how I'm going to tell you. I am tempted to run from Swafford squealing the words 'Fly, fly! All is lost!' It may be that flight will be pre-empted in any case, by a swift and savage ejection. The threat hangs over me like the sword of Damocles. That's Greek by the way, so it's allowed . . . which brings me to this point: where the *hell* do you get off telling me to avoid Latin tags? Amongst the dwindling number of perks that come with old age are included:

A) a literal and metaphorical presbyopia which allows distant schoolgirls and distant schoolboy Latin to come sharply into focus

B) a contempt for self-image and the opinion of others

C) the respect and deference of one's juniors (or – if that is too Latinate for you – 'the high thought and fealty of one's youngers').

Or so I had fondly imagined.

We'll make a deal: I will lay off the Latin if you promise never EVER to use words like 'special' again. Thank you.

Now, to explain the disaster.

How much do you know about computers? A great deal more than me, I should imagine. The machine I'm using at the moment is the first I have ever touched. I think of it really as no more than a socially ambitious type-writer. It belongs to Simon and has been transported to my room together with its printer and a simply baroque quantity of cabling. It lives on the writing-desk and hums irritably like the engine-room of a submarine. When I haven't used it for a while the monitor succumbs to a fit and gaudily coloured fish swim quietly to and fro across the screen, which eccentric mannerism I find strangely endearing. The computer has a device attached to it called a MOUSE, on account of the

111

squeaking noise it makes when it is grabbed and rubbed along a hard surface.

All I know about the use of the thing is that I have to SAVE all the time. This soterial requirement has no evangelical basis, but is said to keep me from accidentally erasing the things that I am typing. You give the work you are saving a FILENAME. My letters to you are stored by the computer in a little envelope on the screen. The envelope is called TED'S FOLDER and the letters are called JANE.1 and JANE.2. I may call them letters, but the computer calls them FILES. This is something of a misnomer as they are nothing like a file, but that is neither here, there nor anywhere. Be patient. This is getting somewhere.

When I sat down at the computer this morning to write this I decided first to reread my last letter to you so as to remind myself of its contents. The procedure for this is relatively simple. I point my mouse at the FILE I need to look at, then twice in rapid succession I depress a button on the mouse's head and, as if by technology, the text of the letter appears on the screen.

As I was preparing for this operation, I noticed for the first time that on the screen, inside TED'S FOLDER, next to the FILENAME of every document, there is printed a lot of incidental information of a wearisome technical nature: SIZE, KIND, LABEL, things of this kind, followed by numbers and abstruse acronyms. There are another two columns which say 'CREATED' and 'LAST MODIFIED'. I realised that these descriptions refer to DATES. In other words, just by looking at a file you can see when it was first written and when you last made alterations to it.

Well, blow me down if I didn't discover that JANE.2, my last letter to you, claimed that it was 'Modified on 27/07/92 at 20.04' – or five past eight yesterday evening. Now, I know for a fact that I was sucking down pre-dinner cocktails in the library with Rebecca, Oliver and Max at five past eight yesterday evening. I also know for a fact that I haven't so much as looked at the computer since my marathon session on Friday and Saturday, the 24th and 25th.

I looked through the text to see if it had indeed been 'modified'. I couldn't *find* any alterations, but then you see, anybody could have accidentally pressed the space-bar while reading the letter through and this would have counted as modification enough to change the ascription under the FILENAME heading.

Well, next I thought I was being absurdly paranoid. How could I be sure that the computer knows the date anyway? For all I know it believes that this is a cold December night in Heidelberg at the height of the Holy Roman Empire. To test this (as I could find no way of instructing the computer to divulge to me its idea of the day of the week) I wrote a brand-new letter and then looked to see what date it was stamped with. There is no doubt about it, the computer is accurate to the minute.

This can only mean that SOMEBODY has read my last letter to you. This would never have happened if you'd allowed me to communicate in MANUSCRIPT (that's English for handwriting).

I don't know who the culprit can be. This machine belongs to Simon and he certainly knows how to work it . . . he has some ridiculous program stored here which lists the Swafford estate's game-chick population and records the progress of the shooting season. His familiarity with computers might be said to count in his favour perhaps, since he is unlikely to have been so dumb as to have made an alteration to the text of my letter and then saved it in such a way that I, a complete novice, can tell that it has been tampered with. On the other hand, we do know that Simon is not one of nature's brightest specimens.

David perhaps? Perfectly possible, except that he is so obsessively honest and 'good' and strait-laced that I imagine he would pluck out his eyes rather than catch himself reading another man's letters. The bottom-bitingly horrible thought that occurs to me, if it turns out that it was Davey, however, is that he has therefore read my less than complimentary remarks about his fucking poem. Ooya.

It cannot have been Oliver, Max or Rebecca, that we can say with certainty. They were with me from seven fifty-five until the end of dinner. The rest of the house-party, Simon, David, Clara, Michael, Anne, Mary and Patricia, were all downstairs by twenty past I reckon, so unless I can prove that the Butler Did It we may have to send for Poirot.

But that's not the point really, is it? The worry is not *who*, but *what next*? It was a damnably long letter and besides being stuffed with the indiscreetest of gossip, it would reveal to anyone that I am being paid by you to sniff around: hence my fear that I may be about to be shown the door. For the moment I am brazening the thing out. Damn technology. Damn you. Damn me and damn whoever is responsible.

Next we come to the Seven Proclamations of Onslow Terrace which you nailed up in your last communication.

1. Stop using Latin
We've dealt with that one.

2. Enquire about the twins
Hum. The twins have been staying, in answer to your question, with Anne's sister Diana, who lives, as I'm sure you recall, near Inverness. Edward suffers from asthma and the air in Scotland is believed, at this time of year, to be less harmful than the air in Norfolk. James and Edward are inconsolable if parted: therefore they have gone together. But you'll hear more on that subject under Proclamation Four.

3. Find out how Oliver is and what brings him here
I really didn't know at first what you meant by 'find out how he is'. He is . . . Oliver, I thought. As to what brought him here: his exact explanation last Saturday was 'R&R', which perhaps you didn't understand. It is Eighties-speak and means Rest and Recreation or possibly Rest and Recuperation, at a pinch Rest and Relaxation. *Not* Rock and Roll, nor Rhyme and Reason, nor Rough and Ready, nor Radicals and Revolutionaries, nor Rum 'n' Raisin: not any other damned thing, just plain Rest and Recreation.

There is a pleasing American saying: 'If it looks like a duck and walks like a duck then it probably is a duck.' Oliver looks like a man in need of R&R and walks like a man in need of R&R, I reasoned. Therefore he probably is in need of R&R. I couldn't imagine why you wanted me to find out more.

Ever your obedient, however, I bearded him yesterday morning after breakfast. He sat in the library, filling a shaft of light with cigarette smoke and emptying the newspapers of gossip.

'Morning, heartsworth. Guess which little play at the Nash is sold out to the end of its run?'

He was referring of course to Michael Lake's *Demiparadise*, the cause of my fall, currently wowing them at the National Theatre.

114

'It would hardly have been worth my making a fuss about it,' I said, defending my attack on the piece, 'if I thought it was going to fold in a fortnight. It was because I *knew*, absolutely knew, that the public would eat it whole. That's the point.'

'If there's one thing Teddy can't bear, it's a successful left-winger who's stayed left-wing. Every time you think of Michael Lake and his kind, Gertie Guilt scampers up and swings her handbag right into your solar plexus, doesn't she?'

'Oh, Oliver, not this conversation.' I sank into a chair opposite him, the slant of sunlight falling between us.

Oliver and I had been on an Aldermaston march together, had joined the same Labour club (West Chelsea, naturally . . . nothing too hairy or tattooed) and contributed to the same periodicals, which in those days were so left-leaning they needed the support of Moscow to keep them from falling over. I couldn't have been happier than to seize upon the Prague Spring in 1967 as a perfect excuse to leave, in every sense, the party. Oliver always pretends that I betrayed him, betrayed my principles and betrayed that non-existent heap of prejudice and ignorance, the 'people'. Of course we all know that the real traitor, Oliver's necessary Judas, was none other than his beloved History. He has got to the age now when he considers it worth foisting on the world lamentably evasive and heavily edited editions of his journal, or 'Daisy Diary' as he refers to the work privately. The years 1955 to 1970 have just been published, lots of sanctimonious ordure heaped on *my* head, but very little about his disgusting basement-nightclub activities, naturally. Just a few mealy-mouthed phrases about the 'awakening of the gay identity' and arse-wash of that nature. Most of 'Daisy' consists of media gossip and his usual monocular interpretation of politics. 'Them' are callous and shiftless, 'Us' are heroes of the people.

'Not this conversation?' he said. 'What would you rather speak about? The smelliness of the working man and his ingratitude in refusing to have heard of you?'

'My breakfast is just digesting,' I said. 'I refuse to have it brought to the surface by a man lecturing me on political morals from the comfort of a rich leather chair in a million-aire's country-house library.'

'A political truth is a political truth whether spoken from a working man's pub or a gentleman's club, dearest, and well you know it. But,' he added sweetly, sensing that I was ready to confound him with a reply, 'you're right. Let's talk of cabbages, not kings. Simon tells me that without rain, the winter barley is going to be looking pretty jolly silly soon. What's more, Hetty the Hose-Pipe Ban will shortly be paying a visit unless Clara Cloud can be pinched and made to cry.'

'Talking of Clara,' I said, wondering whether there was some accidental significance in Oliver's choice of that Christian name. 'What's going on with the Clifford product? Is she . . . I mean . . .'

'If you mean, is she two faggots short of a *corps de ballet*, then no, darling. She's fourteen, she's got a little bit of a squint, her teeth stick out, she has no friends and no bust and nothing can make her happy. You could hardly expect her to be the life and soul of the party, now, could you?'

'What about you? Everything up to snuff?'

'Oh lor, we're about to be quizzed on Safety, I can tell. Mother's very safe, thank you, baby, and very sound. Socialism is still her only communicable disease.'

'You've lost a bit of weight, though.'

'In the days when I grew up, when Fitzrovia was the heartland of the civilised world and Quentin was still Crisp, losing weight was held to be rather desirable. Nowadays it would appear to be a flag of shame. Just because we like to take it up the Gary Glitter, darling, it doesn't mean we have to grow fat to satisfy the fears of our friends.'

'Oh, for goodness' sake will you stop expecting me to tread everywhere with precious little tippy-toes of political correctness.'

'Darling, the real political correctness in this country, as you very well know, is to stuff the minorities and howl "Sanctimony, sanctimony" at anyone who dares suggest different.'

We just can't help it, Oliver and I. We wouldn't be able to discuss prospects in the Danish football league without bickering.

'Well, it's wonderful to see you looking so fit, then,' I offered.

'Ha, well, that's where you're wrong, you fat Ted. The real reason I'm losing weight is because my Dennis won't let me eat anything worth eating. I may have a cute figure, but I've also got acute angina.'

'Oh, my dear Oliver, I'm very sorry.'

'It's only chest pains, not the real thing. But my sweet Dennis chooses to interpret it as a Warning.'

'So you've come here to escape his eagle eye and stuff yourself as full of good food as you can?'

'Something like that, Ted, yes.'

So. There you have it, Jane. That answers Proclamation 3, I hope.

4. More information about Aunt Anne

Later that same morning Davey dragged me off round to the stables to say hello to the horses and hounds. Annie came clattering into the yard on her return from the morning gallop.

'This is a first,' she said, dismounting. 'Are we about to see you ride, Ted?'

'Given our respective weights, it would probably be fairer if the horse got on my back and rode me,' I said.

A groom came to take Annie's mount.

'Could I have a word, Lady Anne?' he asked.

'What is it, Mr Tubby?'

'That's Lilac. Simon reckon she's sick.'

We clustered round the stable door of the horse in question. Lilac is a large bay mare belonging to Michael. She stood at an angle, her head pressed against the side wall, a forlorn attitude that may or may not have betokened illness, and certainly seemed to indicate a rather depressed outlook on life. Horses strike me as being so perpetually dull of eye and stupid of demeanour that it is never easy to determine, as it might be with dogs, what state of health they are in.

'Simon was here for the morning rounds and noticed she want taking her feed and she was circling round and round and there was blood in her spittle,' said Tubby.

'But she was all right yesterday, was she?'

'She was ever so well yisty, Lady Anne.' (Forgive the attempts at rendering the dialogue, Jane dear. It's rather a challenge.) 'She come in from pasture full of spirit.'

'Oh dear, have you any idea what it might be?'

'Simon want certain, he's afraid that might be ragwort poisoning or maybe grass fever.'

'Oh, dear, I do hope he's wrong. Surely we would have noticed if it was ragwort? It takes time, doesn't it?'

'That can come sudden, Lady Anne, so Simon say.'

Who was supposed to be the expert, I wondered, Simon

or this paid professional? A case of passing the buck, I supposed. If the horse suddenly went mad and bit everybody, it would be Master Simon's fault not the groom's.

Davey stroked the horse's muzzle and blew gently up its nose. 'I wonder,' he said, starting to open the stable door, 'if . . .'

'*NO*, Davey! No!' Annie screamed. 'Come away from there *at once*!'

David leapt back from the gate as if it had been surging with high-voltage electricity. Tubby looked discreetly away, but I felt free to goggle.

'I'm sorry, darling, I didn't mean to shout.' Anne's breath, like the mare's, was snorting from her nostrils as she wound down from her peculiar outburst. 'Ill horses can be very dangerous. Very temperamental.'

David was scarlet with bafflement or embarrassment or fear or rage or frustration. 'Lilac knows me as well as anyone . . .' he managed to say.

Anne gained full command of herself, anxious to preserve a front before Tubby and myself. 'I know, darling, I know. But until we know what's wrong with her, there's always the danger of infection. There are a number of things horses can get which humans can catch, you see.'

'When did I last catch *anything*?' asked David.

Annie turned to me brightly. 'I'm popping into Norwich to see my dentist in half an hour,' she said. 'Why don't you both come along? David can show you the sights.'

I sat in the front of the Range Rover next to Anne, with a subdued, if not sulky, David in the back.

'The twins will be coming home tomorrow,' she said. 'Angus and Diana are off on their hols.'

'And Edward?'

'He's been taking a new treatment out of his asthma season, all through the winter and spring. So far there's been no trouble, so we do feel we can risk him coming home. If it starts up again we may have to rethink. There's a place in Switzerland Margot was telling me about. I miss them dreadfully.'

She had surprised the world and herself when, at the age of forty-eight, she had waxed pregnant with twins. I remembered them as eighteen-month-old blobs at Christmas '88 when last I had visited Swafford.

'They'll be on their way to being five soon, I suppose?'

'That's another reason to have them back. Their birthday comes in another fortnight.'

David perked up after Anne had dropped us off somewhere near the centre of town and driven off to keep her appointment.

'Do you know an interesting thing about Norwich?' he asked as we stood about on the pavement.

I doubted there was one, unless he was referring to its distance from London, but expressed the required ignorance.

'There are exactly fifty-two churches in Norwich and three hundred and sixty-five pubs.'

'Is that right?'

'So they say. That means you can get drunk in a different bar every night of the year, and repent at a different altar every week of the year.'

The odds, then, were a pleasant six-to-one on that we would stumble across a pub before we encountered a church. Probability took a powder that day however, and I found myself being marched by Davey into the close and asked to admire the flying buttresses and exquisitely proportioned apsidal east end of the great cathedral. The flying buttresses and exquisitely proportioned apse of a great barmaid would have exerted infinitely more powerful a pull, but I allowed myself to be led. I mused that it had in all probability been twenty years since I had last stood inside a cathedral. The smell of the stone and the particular perfection of temperature and atmosphere, neither warm nor cool, neither dry nor humid, is common to all Norman and Gothic ecclesiastical interiors and contributes much to the mystery and grandeur of such creations. He says.

David took me outside to the cloisters where he showed me the armorial bearings of his mother's family.

'And where do you think your father's ancestors might be recorded?' I asked.

'In the Bible, I suppose.'

'Do you like being the seed of Abraham?'

'You don't count as Jewish if it's only your father, you know.'

'So I believe.'

'The trouble with Jews,' said David, settling himself on a small ledge within an open archway that looked on to the central lawn of the cloister, 'is that they don't have any sense of nature. It's all towns and businesses.'

'Are you talking about Jews in general, or one Jew in particular?'

'Well I think Daddy is actually more rurally minded than most, wouldn't you say?'

He can afford to be, I thought.

Interpreting my silence as disagreement, David folded his arms and thought for a while.

'Why don't you sit down?' he asked at length.

'Do you really want to know?'

'Yes,' he said, surprised.

'The reason I don't sit down,' I said, 'is that lately I have been growing the most luscious and luxuriant crop of piles.'

'Piles?'

'You must have heard of piles. Haemorrhoids.'

'Oh, haemorrhoids. Yes. Daddy gets those. He has a cream and an applicator. I've seen them in his bathroom cupboard. He says I'll get them one day because piles are a Jewish man's affliction. Piles and mothers. What causes them?'

'They come with age and sedentary habits. The only cure is to have them lanced with a knife. A cure that is crueller than the disease.'

'I thought you said on Thursday night that nothing could be cured.'

'Touché, you young sod.'

'*You* aren't Jewish are you?' asked David after a pause.

'Sadly not. Despite the piles.'

'You are a pretty urban sort of person though, wouldn't you say?'

'Only nor'-nor'-east,' I said. 'I know a fox from a fax machine.'

'Simon thinks *I'm* the urban one in the family because I don't approve of killing. He says city people have lost all idea of the importance of life, so they concentrate on the importance of death.'

'That sounds to me a little too sophisticated to have come from Simon.'

David laughed. 'Well, he probably read it in the *Shooting Times*.'

I felt in a pocket for a Rothie. David looked scandalised.

'What's the matter?' I said. 'The Victorians used to fit ash-trays in their pews, you know. Sermons were judged by cigar length. A four-inch sermon, a five-inch sermon, a full Corona and so on.'

'Never!'

'Swear to God.'

'Try telling that to a tour-guide.'

I conceded the point and went without.

David gazed up at me. 'Do you know why Mummy wouldn't let me go into the stable to tend to Lilac this morning?'

I shook my head.

David sighed and chewed his lower lip. 'She doesn't like me to use . . . she's *afraid*, you see.'

'Afraid?'

'I can . . . sometimes . . . almost . . . I know you'll laugh . . .'

'I won't laugh,' I promised. Not audibly, at any rate.

'I can sometimes *talk* to animals.'

Well, I thought, I sometimes talk to the wall. But I knew that was not what he meant. He meant, of course, that the animals talked back.

My son Roman, who is not far off Davey's age, once claimed that he could understand a mouse he kept in a cage in his bedroom.

'And what does this mouse talk about?' I had asked.

'He tells me how much he would like a friend.'

A feebly transparent plea for another pet mouse, I had thought, and duly shogged off to Horrids to buy one, on the strict understanding that they guaranteed its masculinity. It occurred to me later that perhaps it had really been a plea from Roman himself. He often grew lonely in London, once the initial excitement had worn off, on those occasions when his mother packed him off to stay with me in school holidays: too young for his sister Leonora – he had been conceived, after all, as a last-ditch attempt to create something that might hold Helen and me together – too young to accompany me to the theatre, too old to be entertained by a nanny.

It struck me now that, idyllic as Davey's childhood might seem from the outside, he too had cause to be lonely. He does not share the agricultural or sporting interests of his brother and (presumably) his local age-mates; his manner, while not precisely forbidding, does give off an air of remoteness, of separation from the herd, of – to use Annie's word – disconnectedness. It is natural for a child of sensitivity and intelligence to withdraw. Better to flaunt your independence than risk rejection. Animals are welcome friends because

121

they never judge. Adolescent girls, as is well known, become so infatuated with their ponies that they have been known to wedge the morning sugar lump in their labia and lie back to have it nibbled from their drooling quims. The unconditional love an animal can offer, love without guilt, rejection, violence or demands, has great appeal for the young. They are of course too stupid to see that even the most intelligent creature does things only for food. Love, for an animal, begins and ends with din-dins.

'So you talk to animals?' I said.

'They trust me. They know I don't want their eggs, or their milk, or their coats, or their strength, or their flesh, or their obedience.'

'A large number of them want each other's flesh though, don't they? Or do you only talk to vegetarian animals?'

I could have kicked myself when I saw how sarcastic that question had sounded in David's ears. I had meant it quite seriously.

He stood up. 'We are meeting Mummy at the Assembly House,' he said. 'It's a bit of a walk. We should be on our way.'

Anne and I sat munching flap-jacks in the tea-rooms of the Assembly House. David had begged to be allowed to trot across the road to the City library.

'I never thought I'd be doing this,' said Annie.

'Doing what?'

'Biting. I had quite made up my mind that I was in for all sorts of terrible injections and fillings.'

'Clean bill of health, then?'

' "If I have teeth like that at your age, Lady Anne, I shall count myself a lucky man." '

'Double-edged compliment.'

'Any compliment will do at our time of life, don't you find?'

'It's been such a while since I received one,' I said, 'that I can't really answer the question.'

'Oh, poor little Tedward. I'll offer you one then. You've been in Norfolk only a week and you already look a thousand times better than you did when you arrived.'

'That's a compliment to yourself and your hospitality, my love, not to me.'

'Oh poo, you're quite right. Well, I'll tell you how wonderful it is to have you around, then.'

'Angel.'

'No really, Ted. It is. I do hope you're enjoying yourself. You must say if there's anything you need.'

I opened my hands to indicate that not princes nor popes could provide me with more.

'What about you?' I said. 'A happy bunny?'

'Blissful.'

'No storms on the horizon?'

'Why should you say that?' She frowned a little and became busy with the tea-pot.

'No reason, no reason. I just sometimes think it's a strange life for you. Living in the house you grew up in, but . . .'

'But with a husband from another world? Oh Ted, really! I get the best of everything. My own lot and all the financiers and politicians and artists and writers and odd-balls that Michael attracts.'

'That's a list that would make many in this world vomit.'

'Well, put like that, it does sound rather dreadful, but I'm so lucky really. Let's face it, I'm not awfully bright and Michael is such a good husband. I mean, it would be obscene if someone in my position complained. Simply obscene.'

I let her pour out another cup for me.

'I'm not saying,' she went on, 'that I don't get upset when the newspapers write awful things about him. Comparing him to that ghastly Bob Maxwell, for instance. Calling him a corporate raider or a financial pirate and an asset-stripper. If they *knew*, Ted! They haven't seen him in tears when he has to sack people.'

Haig used to weep over the casualty lists, I thought to myself. Never stopped him from sending them over the top though, did it?

'He cares, Ted. He's decent. I'm so proud of him. The boys are so proud of him.'

'That much is very clear, my love. *I'm* proud of him too if it comes to that.'

'I mean, Ted, it is enough for me just to be a mother and wife, isn't it? If you can say, at the end of things, that your life's achievement was a family, that doesn't mean you failed. Not everybody has to create things, like Michael and you.'

So Anne was at that stage, I thought. 'I may not have composed the Ring Cycle or founded ICI, but I brought up four children.' Brought up four children with the help of a quantity of maids, nannies, nurses and hirelings that would have been better employed running a medium-sized boarding school.

'My dearest of dear, dear old things,' I said, and I may even have patted her hand. 'Firstly you have to confess that, in fact, you do a great deal. I don't suppose there is a committee, a trust or a charity that doesn't have you on its board. People may laugh at Lady Bountiful, but what you do needs to be done, is done, and couldn't have been done without you.'

'Thank you for saying that, Ted. I must confess one does feel underappreciated sometimes. They have such awful types around on the charity committees and school boards and councils these days. So snide and picky and sneery. They just expect me to smile and nod like the Queen. So often, when I suggest things, I simply get laughed at, as if my job is only to appear on the letter-head and wear a big hat.'

I could picture those meetings all too readily. The ginger-tached, tinted-lensed, cheap-suited, signet-ringed, loafer-shod nobodies suffering from razor-burn and irritable-vowel syndrome who import Korean strimmers or run golf driving-ranges and now populate all the boards and committees and magistrates' benches of the country, what would they see in this Lady Anne Ponsonby-Smythe-Twistleton-Lah-di? Conservative, Labour or Liberal, they would consider her a useless joke.

'Wouldn't it be lovely,' I could imagine Annie saying brightly, 'to ask the Duchess of Kent to open the borstal's new lavatory-complex?'

Sniggering glances are exchanged and dandruff rains down on the agenda-papers as heads shake slowly in disbelief.

'With respect to the lady chairman, that would be highly inappropriate,' says some builder of executive homes, by which he means, 'We'll do the thinking, thank you, pet. You just shut your posh mouth and sign the frigging cheques.'

Poor old darling, committing the crime of doing no more than trying to be nice.

'What you do,' I said, 'is valued. Good God, your family alone! Wouldn't I rather have four fine sons ready to do something in the world, than four flabby poems mouldering in the *Oxford Book of Modern Poetry.*'

'But you've got children as well!'

'Helen's got them. I'm a Bad Influence. I think I know my godchildren better than I know Roman or Leonora.'

'Ted, that's a terrible thing to say. I know you must be a wonderful father, if the way you treat Davey is anything to go by. You treat him as an equal.'

'That's conceited of me. I should be treating him as a superior.'

'Oh dear, I do know what you mean. He isn't being a nuisance, is he?'

'Good Lord, as if! I should imagine that child's school reports would compare favourably with those of St Agnes.'

'Do you understand what I was talking about when I said I was worried about him? Am I just being hysterical? You see, it's so difficult for him. Growing up under the shadow of someone like Simon. I sometimes . . . here he is!'

David hove into view, swinging a carrier-bag full of books.

'And what have you two been talking about?'

'The characteristics that distinguish the ten-year-old Macallan from the eighteen. I was telling your mother that the ten-year-old, cheaper as it may be, is the better glass.'

'I quite agree,' said David. Saucy thing.

As we walked to the car-park I asked him what he had taken out from the library.

'Oh, just books.'

As it happens, I managed to catch a glimpse of one of the titles when he slung the carrier-bag into the back of the Range Rover.

Staunton's Equine Anatomy was the title. Hah-lah.

That completes my report, for the time being, on Lady Anne, although I would like the chance to quiz her on what she had meant by 'the shadow of someone like Simon'.

5. On no account mess around with Patricia. She is very special and not to be trifled with.

This is unworthy of you in every particular. I ought, I suppose, to be flattered that you imagine Patricia would *allow* me to 'mess around' with her. Or do you imagine that I would stoop to rape? Or in her case, stretch up on tip-toe to rape?

I have no doubt she is 'special'. Who the bloody hell isn't? It's a short step from using the word 'special' to ending conversations on the telephone with 'I love you' instead of the more usual and desirable 'Good-bye' or 'Fuck off, then'.

Your warnings were redundant in any case, for it is she who has been messing with me.

She found me on the hammock after lunch, relaxing with the *Telegraph* and a glass of the particular.

'Game of croquet, Ted?'

'Well,' I replied, laying down the paper, 'I can see the hoops, but where are the mallets and balls? Or are we to use flamingos and hedgehogs?'

'They're kept in a trunk in that hut,' she said pointing to the simulacrum of the Villa Rotunda. Hut, for goodness' sake.

I happen to be rather good at croquet. I don't know why this should be, there is no other game at which I am anything less than an embarrassment. I played tennis with Simon yesterday: the boy had only to stand solemnly in the centre of the court and pat the ball gently over the net to have me wheeling, slapping, panting and thrashing like a Newcomen engine. Oliver, who was watching, said the spectacle put him in mind of a windmill tilting at Don Quixote.

The gentle, spiteful art of croquet, however, is more suited to my low centre of gravity and high sense of malice. We played, as is best, with two balls each, I with my fascistic favourites black and red, Patricia taking yellow and blue. My skills took her a little by surprise, I think; she is adept at the game herself, and the first circuit of the lawn was completed in a concentrated silence, broken only by the thlunk-shimm of roqueted balls fizzing out of bounds.

As we approached the final hoops however, Patricia gave up all attempts at winning and became inclined to coze. It seemed she had what I believe is known as an agenda.

'Ted, why did you behave like that on Thursday night?'

'Behave like what?'

'You know perfectly well.'

Thursday was the night of the big dinner party. As you will see from my chronicle of the event, I behaved in exemplary fashion throughout. As far as I can see, it was Oliver, and to some extent Davey, who crapped in the salad on that occasion, not me. I said as much to Patricia.

'Whatever it is that is going on here,' she said, 'can only be ruined by your scepticism and contempt. You may think it's all very funny, but I should have thought you had more respect for a godchild than that.'

126

Respect for you, Jane, or respect for Davey? I really was completely lost by now.

'Thoughts, Patricia,' I said, 'as you may imagine, are beginning to burgeon and bubble in the primal soup of my mind, inchoate and confused, like protozoic life-forms. Some of the more likely-looking specimens might one day evolve into sentient beings, but for the moment my planet seems to be eons behind everyone else's in the race for civilisation. When you say "whatever it is that is going on here", you mean precisely . . . ?'

'If you want to sit and snipe from the sidelines, then fine, Ted. But I'm warning you, if you blow it for the rest of us, I'll . . . I'll kill you.'

'Blow *what*?'

'Oh, for goodness' sake . . .' Patricia threw down her mallet and glared at me. 'You're just a wart-hog, aren't you? A great fat vicious wart-hog!'

Turning on her heel she stamped off to the house, muttering and choking with emotion. As I watched her go, I became aware of a figure looming towards me from the corner of the lawn. Rebecca approached, a trugful of strawberries on her arm, a broad grin on her face.

'Still the same magical touch with women, Ted?'

'Some people,' I said, bending to gather the croquet-balls, 'cannot take defeat.'

'Oh, come now, Ted, it was more than that surely? You tried to goose her while she bent to play the ball.'

'Certainly not,' I replied. 'Nothing can have been further from my mind.'

'Then you are not Ted Wallace but an imposter and I shall go and ring the police.'

'Well, naturally any bending woman in a short skirt causes some kind of reflex on a summer's day, but I assure you it is a reflex buried deep by years of frustration and remains fully under my control.'

'Then what was it all about? Come and sit on the steps and tell me everything.'

We sat with the roundhouse behind us.

'What is going on here, Rebecca? Just what the hell is going on?'

'Darling, you've been here longer than I have. You tell me.'

127

I'm afraid at this point, Jane, I half gave away our little conspiracy.

'Well, it starts for me like this,' I said. 'Bumped into Jane a couple of weeks ago. She knew me, but I felt the completest fool not recognising her.'

'I think we know whose fault that is, darling.'

'Yes, well, whatever. Went back to her place and she told me about the leukaemia and such like.'

'Did you get an earful of God?'

'There was talk of miracles certainly. Something emanating from here, from Swafford. She claims to be . . . well . . . cured.'

'Don't I know it? Ecstatic letters have arrived at Phillimore Gardens praising the Lord and rejoicing in many wonders.'

'Do you believe her?'

'Like you, that's why I'm here, darling. To find out. As it happens, we share the same doctor, Jane and I.'

'And what does he say?'

'Well, you know doctors. He is surprised by the remission but cautious as cautious can be.'

'There definitely has been a remission then?'

'No doubt about that.'

'Hum.' I sat and thought for a space while Rebecca started in on the strawberries.

'But what has any of that,' she asked, 'got to do with Patricia's splendid description of you as a wart-hog, a great fat vicious wart-hog?'

'Does she know about Jane's miraculous recovery?'

'Sure to. Best buddies.'

'Who else knows?'

'Search me, darling. It was last June I understand. Simon brought her back prostrate to this house from the Norfolk Show, white corpuscles practically oozing from her pores. Michael and Anne were here of course, Simon and Davey had an exeat from school to celebrate the finishing of their exams, can't be sure who else. Oh, Max and Mary, they were staying at the time, I'm almost sure.'

'So do any of them believe in this miracle?'

'Don't ask me.'

I grabbed a fistful of strawberries and thought for a while.

'Well, I don't think Simon believes. He told me the other day about Jane's collapse. Compared her overnight recovery to that of pigs he had known.'

'Romantic bugger.'

'Oliver on the other hand . . . He seems to know something. I'm almost certain he does.'

'If there's truffle, Oliver will snuffle it out, you can be sure of that.'

'And Patricia clearly thinks that I am in on it, but scoffing sceptically up my sleeve.'

'Well, that's certainly how you sounded the other night at dinner, isn't it?'

Rebecca was alluding to a conversation I had with the Bishop and others about 'healing' and 'therapy'.

'You do see, don't you, my dear, that this talk of miracles is preposterous?'

'Well, I know one thing, darling, and that is that Jane should have been dead by the end of June.'

'Why did you never let me know? Why did I only find out by chance that my only god-daughter had leukaemia?'

'Fat lot you'd've cared. It would have taken more than a dying god-daughter to get you to raise your red eyes from the whisky glass. I know what you've been like. Oliver tells me of your exploits. Not that he needs to – I read the newspapers. A glitterati drunkard rampaging around Soho and the West End insulting everyone you meet and sweating your fat arse over a bar-stool with your fellow has-beens, puking bile at everyone under fifty and tearing great chunks off hands that dare to feed you.'

'Rebecca . . .'

'But of course you've been sacked now, haven't you? Suddenly you need your rich and powerful friends to help you out of the tank of bitter piss you've been drowning in for the last twenty years. You'll slobber with doe-eyed sympathy and moon with paternal concern – why, darling, you'll even cut down on your drinking and go boaty-woaty with your godson like a white-haired old saint – so long as underneath you can remain the same cynical, evil-minded old turd that the world knows and loves.'

There, in a nutshell, you have your mother. I suspect I am the only man in this world who has dared to spurn her. It may have been all of two decades ago but to a mind like hers this is no time at all. Revenge for Rebecca is a dish best served ice-cold, nestling in a *coulis* of vitriol, garnished with sprigs of belladonna and thrown hard into the poor bastard victim's face.

I arose, brushed the strawberry stalks from my lap and walked away, saying not a word.

On my way to the house I collided with Clara the cross-eyed Clifford.

'Good afternoon, Mr Wallace,' she said, 'I was just coming to fetch you.' At least, that is what I think she said. I won't try and emulate her lisp, poor dear.

'Oh yes? And why is this?'

She looked steadfastly at me (and at some other unidentified object a hundred and twenty degrees to the west). 'Uncle Michael would like to see you in his study.'

The visitor to Lord Logan of Swafford's study is put in mind of Ernst Stavro Blofeld's headquarters. Control consoles, electrically operated curtains and projection screens, telecommunication devices, globes containing whisky decanters and large-screen videophones represent only the visible and identifiable elements of gadgetry.

'Choose a city for destruction, Mr Bond. Which is it to be? New York? Leningrad? Paris? No, wait! London! Of course! Goodbye Piccadilly, farewell Leicester Square, as you British are so fond of saying.'

'Ted!' Michael half-rose from his chair, a cigar in his mouth. 'Forgive me for summoning you like a disorderly corporal. I'm awaiting a call from South Africa.'

'Business or politics?' Michael is well known for dabbling his hands in the affairs of nation states. Around the walls there are hung photographs of him beaming at the camera in varying postures of intimacy with World Leaders: an arm around Walesa, stiffly side by side by Mandela, toasting Yeltsin with a shot-glass of vodka, sharing a preposterous gilded Louis XVI sofa with Arafat, on the golf course with James Baker and George Bush.

'So what's the difference? There's a tobacco company I'm looking at in Johannesburg. South Africa's the coming state, you know.'

'I admire your optimism.'

Michael backhanded away a waft of cigar smoke and with it the reservations of any so small-minded as to doubt him. 'So. Tedward. What do you want to know?'

I didn't understand what he meant at first. Then I saw and a big smile spread across my face. 'You'll do it? You'll co-operate?'

'My lawyers and I receive an absolute right to veto?'

'Certainly.' I nodded vigorously. As if it would ever come to that.

Instantly, Michael pushed across the desk a sheaf of papers, densely type-written in narrow margins, secured with green thread fasteners.

'Read and sign,' he said. 'Initial where I have initialled, full signature where I have signed in full.'

Ah, the ways of the mighty. 'Do I *have* to read it?' I asked.

'Tedward, so plaintive, like a child with homework. Your "Ballad of the Workshy Man", that must have come from the heart. Me, I read documents twenty times this size on the crapper before breakfast.'

'No wonder you've got piles,' I said.

'You knew I have piles?' Michael frowned.

'Fellow-sufferer,' I said hastily. 'One sees it in the way you sit down.'

'You writers! Not workshy at all. All your work is done observing people.'

Sweet of him to choose to believe that. 'So tell me,' I said, mimicking one of his favourite opening phrases, 'what exactly is in all this?'

'Standard contract for an authorised biography. Rights of injunction. Don't worry, there's nothing that stops you from making full royalties. Talking of which, you owe me one penny.' He opened the palm of his hand and stretched it across the desk.

'I do?' I looked up in surprise.

'In law,' said Michael, 'a contract is meaningless without consideration. Someone must pay someone. You will see in the document you are signing that in consideration for the sum of one penny, I agree to co-operate in your biography, known hereafter as The Material. So. One penny please.'

Fazed by the combination of legalese and earnestness, I fumbled in my trouser pocket for a coin.

'Do you have change for a five-pence piece?'

'Certainly.' Michael caught my shilling, opened a drawer, took out a small strong-box, shook inside it with his fingers and drew out two tuppenny bits. 'And four is five,' he said. 'Shake, business-partner. We have a deal.'

I stood to shake his hand and was disconsolate to see him burst out laughing.

'Tedward! Smile! Deals are causes for celebration.'

'I'm sorry,' I said. 'I think I am overawed by your solemnity.'

'It was your first lesson in how we work. Up to the moment of signature and handshake is grim determination. The moment the ink is on the paper and the hands are clasped together, we are locked in an ecstasy greater than love.'

Michael placed two tape-recording machines on the desk and pressed their record buttons.

'One for each of us,' he said. 'Just so we know where we stand.'

Thus, interrupted only by two calls from Johannesburg, fourteen faxes from there and elsewhere and a call to tea, we sat while Michael embarked on the story of his life.

I will save the details of the conversation for a long weekend, Jane. Let it just be said that Much Has Become Clear.

This morning however, an oddity.

I slouched in to brekker, hoping to catch the bacon before it had turned to leather in the tureen, and sat myself down, as usual, alone with the *Telegraph* at the end of the dining-room table.

Patricia came in, flushed and excited.

'Ted!' she cried. 'I'm so glad to have caught you.'

'Have a coffee,' I said, a little frigidly. I find it difficult to treat a girl who has recently called me a wart-hog with any real warmth of manner, however much I may want to jam my cock up her funnel.

She was not much interested in coffee, however. She had something on her chest. Lucky something.

'Ted, I want you to forget everything I said to you yesterday afternoon.'

'Ah.'

'I'm just so terribly sorry. I really don't know what came over me. I was quite unbearably rude.'

'Not at all, not at all.'

'And I talked such a great deal of nonsense.'

At this point, Simon loomed in looking for Logan, a worried look on his customarily vacant face.

'I think he's working in his study,' said Patricia. 'Anything wrong?'

'Oh, not really. Well, it's Lilac, actually. Dad's hunter. She seems no better. Just wanted to let him know, that's all.'

And off he lumbered, leaving Patricia and me alone once more. She continued with her rather strained apology.

'I can't think why I was so horrid to you. I've been under a lot of pressure lately. I think that must be it. You've probably heard that my . . . that Martin, the man I've been living with, he left me. I get very . . .'

'My dear old girl,' I said. 'Please. Think no more about it.'

'I suppose I imagined at that dinner that you were getting at me. All your talk about therapists. I've been seeing one, you see, and I thought you must have known and were mocking me.'

'Patricia, I would never for a moment . . .'

'Well, of course I realise that, now. I lay awake last night thinking what a brute I'd been to you. You were just talking in general. How could you possibly have known?'

'It was entirely my fault for jabbering on in such a thoughtless fashion. I should be apologising to you.'

She smiled. I smiled back. Somewhere deep in the trouser region the neglected old worm twitched and wriggled in his sleep.

She kissed me on the cheek. 'No hard feelings?'

'Of course not, my dear,' I lied.

I watched that magnificently constructed arse swing out of the room and allowed those hard feelings to subside in my lap. A high arse, ledging out from the coccyx; the kind of arse you can stand a tea-pot on.

But Jane, what the deuce had she been talking about? Didn't fool me for a second. The smile was too bright, the kiss on the cheek too theatrical. I recognise pride thwarted when I see it. She was apologising because she had been told to. Hm. Thinks.

I return now to my schedule and address Proclamation the Sixth:

You have talked only about the guests. The house is full of other men and women. There are indoor and outdoor servants, there is Podmore. I have heard nothing of them.

What do you want, blood? I am not one of those easy aristocratic types who can walk with kings nor lose the common touch. I'm a tight-arsed bourgeois masquerading as *déclassé*. Give us a break, baby-doll.

Of the servants I know by name I can tell you this. There is Podmore, first name Dick, who looks and behaves more like a disbarred time-share salesman than a butler, but then that is how all butlers have looked for years now, even in ducal households (as if I really know). Upper servants have lost the knack of seeming to have no provenance, no private life, no family and no sexuality. One look at Podmore and you can surmise all too readily that he was born in Carshalton Beeches, that he flirted with the Teddy Boy movement in the 1950s before moving with his wife Julie to Norfolk (just great to get away from all that traffic and what was then called the rat-race . . .), that he has his eye on a retirement condo hard by a golf course in Florida and that he can't understand why Logan hasn't replaced the french windows in the main drawing room with sliding patio doors.

Not much else to say about him really except that I suspect him of being a closet nance, Mrs Podmore or no Mrs Podmore. He has a way of eyeing Davey up that argues something of the gaysexualist.

Julie Podmore acts as housekeeper, her duties largely comprise bossing the maids shrewishly and lowering her head whenever she passes a house-guest. She is in her fifties, of medium height, weight and fuckability: she dyes her hair. Beyond that I know nothing to her credit or detriment.

The only maid whose name I can remember is called Joanne. I remember her name because she has a combination of ample thighs and noisy tights. As a result she makes a frishing noise whenever she climbs the stairs or walks the corridor. To match the thighs she sports a cantilevered bust: I should imagine she has to make an effort to lean backwards at all times in order not to fall over. The other maid is woundingly plain and will never rise in her profession until she learns that guests are unlikely to be interested in her brother's exploits on the speedway track.

There are kitchen staff into whose eyrie I have not penetrated, but I can tell you that the cook's name is Cheryl and that she bakes a sinful egg custard. Liberality with the nutmeg is the key here, I fancy.

Venturing outside we encounter Alec Tubby, the chief groom. He is stoutly Norfolk and entirely without discernible character. His son Kenny assists him in the muckings-out and rubbings-down around which stable life revolves. He will be a bit depressed at the moment on account of the vet expressing dark forebodings this afternoon as to the chances of Lilac pulling out of her decline.

A splendour called Kate supervises the kennels and, as is

traditional with such specimens, presents to the world a handsome beard and moustache. It must take at least a square yard of stout blue corduroy to trouser her arse alone. She is rather fun as a matter of fact, and a pleasure to talk to. She has persuaded me to puppy-walk some of the young hounds, which is a thing that needs doing at this season and which I find highly enjoyable. There is something tirelessly entertaining about the way puppies widdle.

Further afield we find Tom Jarrold, the gamekeeper. He is aggressively jealous of his cocks, hens and chicks and can spot a no-good townie like me a mile off. We have little to say to each other. Henry, his assistant, aspires to be no more than a carbon-copy of Tom. Simon seems to be the only person alive who can communicate with either of them. Jarrold has a hare-lipped daughter, Katrina. Not just hare-lipped, actually, but hairy-lipped too. Nature can be unbearably cruel.

The only other member of staff to mention is Valerie, Michael's secretary or PA. She keeps herself very much to herself and is only here on certain days. I have not determined if there is a pattern. When she is here she dines alone, in Michael's study, guarding the telephones. This is her choice apparently, since she has been offered a place at table amongst persons of rank and tone.

I really am afraid, my angel, that there is nothing more I can tell you. But, as required by the last of your dictats, Proclamation Seven, the Four Constants will ever be my guide.

Constant vigilance; constant awareness; constant observation; constant openness.

So rest assured that I shall not cease from mental strife, nor shall Simon's computer sleep by my hand, till we have built Jerusalem in Norfolk's green and peasant land.

Assuring you, madam, of my good faith in this and all matters.

Yours (for Logan-Wallace Biogs Plc)

Ted Wallace (CEO)

Onslow Interiors

12a Onslow Terrace • South Kensington • LONDON SW7

URGENT FACSIMILE TRANSMISSION

To: Patricia Hardy, c/o Logan, Swafford Hall, Norfolk
From: Onslow Interiors Ltd
My fax: 071-555 4929
Your fax: 0653-378552

For the private and personal attention of Miss Hardy

Dear Miss Hardy,

You suggest in your letter that you might consider
making an approach to E.L.W. to raise the question of
his recent remarks on the subject we discussed.

We would recommend with <u>extreme</u> force that you do not
make such a move. T. is not an expert in this field and
has no knowledge of the details.

I trust this warning has come in time to save you
making an unfortunate mistake.

Unable for the moment to join you for meeting as
suggested.

Letter follows

Yours

J.S.

136

LOGANGROUP plc

To..Jane Swann
Company...Onslow Interiors
Fax No. 071 555 4929
From ....Patricia
Fax No. 0653 378552
Page..1 of 1

Jane,

Bother! If your fax means what I think it
does, then I've screwed up. Gave Ted an
earful yesterday. Called him a foul and ugly
old wart-hog. Hard to take those kind of
words back but I had a go just now in the
breakfast room.

I told him that I've been behaving
irrationally on account of Martin leaving me
and that I had had a go at him because I
thought _he_ had been having a go at me. <u>Think</u>
he swallowed it. He leered what he imagines
is a debonair smile and started dripping egg-
yolk down his shirt, which I think is a sign
of forgiveness.

You really should have warned me though.
Does he really not know what's going on? And
why are you concerned with what he thinks or
believes anyway? He's not here on a
commission from a <u>newspaper</u> is he? The mind
boggles. Come to think of it, Michael
announced last night that Ted is writing his
biography. They've been closeted together for
hours and hours. What's <u>that</u> all about?

Wildest apologies, do come down soonest

Pat

If you encounter any difficulties with this transmission, please call Valerie Myers on 0653 378551

IV

David closed the book and let his eyes lose focus as he gazed up at the ceiling-rose. By eleven o'clock the light had faded enough to silence the chimes of the stable clock. Two hours had passed by since then. In an hour he would be ready. For the moment it was safest, so excited was he, to relax his whole body and concentrate on nothing.

He thought of a circle and within that circle, another circle, within that another and another and another, allowing his inner eye to zoom at speed through the endless ring of rings, finding a central glowing spot that in its turn changed into another circle which itself contained yet more and more circles. It was like a dive into the centre of things and diverted the mind from any base or worldly thoughts. The technique came from a book on yogic meditation he had bought last holidays and worked extremely well so long as one was capable of concentrating with the utmost force while at the same time remaining entirely relaxed.

The time went surprisingly quickly in this state and David already knew, without looking at his bedside clock, when it was two o'clock precisely.

He stood naked before a tall mirror, breathing deeply. The night was warm but he would need some protection. He chose a T-shirt, baggy track-suit bottoms and a pair of trainers. No socks or pants. Taking from the bedside table a torch, an apple and a small jar wrapped in sheets of Kleenex, he left the room.

A gibbous moon, he had heard it called. Half and half. Enough light to see, enough dark to conceal. Light was not important, really. In his present state he felt he could accomplish the mission blindfold.

His trainers loomed white beneath him in the shadow of the house and against the greasy black of the grass, white flashes pumping back and forth. Looking up, he saw Orion's belt twinkling on its waist and the dog star spinning blue to the east. The sound of his trainers scuffing the grass died in the velvet deep of the night.

'All the air,' he whispered to himself in the rhythm of the running and panting, 'a solemn stillness holds. All the air . . .

a solemn . . . stillness . . . holds. All the air . . . a solemn . . . stillness . . . holds!'

He was there. The long shadow of the clock fell on the stable yard and a warm savour of horse manure rolled towards him.

Soft as a moth he flitted to the door of the corner tack room. Inside, another smell awaited him, the perfume of saddle-soap and dubbin, so rich that it made him cough. Holding his breath, he felt for the wooden stool, picking it up by the carved hole in the centre of its seat. A loose item of tack, a bridle or unfastened martingale, fell to the ground with a brittle ring as he lifted the stool clear, but he knew that the sound penetrated no ears but his own and those of the horses, who knew what he was up to and approved.

He reached Lilac's stall and unlatched the top section of the gate. Lilac, as though she had been waiting, moved her head forward to welcome him.

'Hello,' said David, mind to mind, with no movement of lips and no stirring of breath or vocal cords. 'I've brought you an apple.'

Lilac took the present, like a patient with no appetite who knows they must eat to keep up their strength. While she was slowly masticating the apple, slewing it from cheek to cheek, David pulled off his T-shirt and slipped out of his track-suit bottoms. Feeling that it was ridiculous to be naked but for a pair of trainers, he took those off too and stood bare in the moonlight.

He shivered a little and felt a colony of goose-pimples start up around his legs.

'Are you ready, old girl?' he asked, again without use of his voice. 'I am.' He stooped to take the jar and its tissue wrapping from the pocket of his track-suit. The torch he could do without.

He exerted the gentlest pressure on Lilac's shoulders as he opened the lower gate and stepped in clutching the stool, but she made no move to make for the open yard. Slowly, he closed both gates together and they were alone in the absolute dark.

She was very peaceful, only a light sweat testifying to her terrible illness. She stood in silence, one rear hoof from time to time clopping the flagstones. David moved down her side, his body touching hers as he felt his way to the end of the stall. The heat from her flanks awoke the great heat in him and as he raised himself up on the stool he felt his glans push through the foreskin and his whole cock stand higher and straighter

139

and harder than it had ever stood before. He straightened up on the stool, a hand steadying himself on Lilac's hindquarters, and slowed his lungs to the rhythm of Lilac's own breathing. She was oestrous and would not kick back with her legs as she might when off heat. Even had she been, David knew that she would welcome him.

When he was ready and he knew they were as one, he pushed two fingers into the jar and gathered up a thick lump of Vaseline. With his other hand he brushed Lilac's tail to one side. Obediently she gave a twitch and the tail hung high above, leaving him free to work with both hands. Below the dock and anus the outer lips were easy to find and within them he could feel the clitoral hood and below it the soft tissue of the inner labia. Delicately pushing with his finger he found what he thought must be the urethra and gently he traced his finger down to the easy tender squash below. As if to confirm his discovery, Lilac blew gently from her nose and stamped a foot.

David worked the bolus of jelly into the vaginal opening, finding that his fingers slipped easily in and out. What Vaseline was left over he used to anoint himself, although he was already supplying himself with his own thin stream of juice.

The cock went in with splendid ease, its straight slicked hardness pulled further through by a quick spasm from Lilac. The wall closed all around to suck him deeper in and David gasped with the blinding joy of what he felt. A hand either side of the root of her tail, he experimented tentatively by pulling himself marginally back and pushing himself marginally forward. The sensation blinded his head with stars. A millimetre this way, a millimetre that, hooves thundered in his brain and the hot crystals in his stomach were smashed into billions of burning grains. The absolute rightness and holiness and perfection and beauty of life charged through him. In this position he could stay for ever, he and the whole kingdom of life – animal, plant or human, locked in a whirlwind of love. The other time it had all been too quick for him to feel this ecstasy: that had been with a woman and there had been tension and the need to talk in words.

'You are whole, Lilac,' his voice inside him called to her. 'With this gift of pure spirit I pronounce you whole and healed.'

The lights in his head spilled and toppled and spun in desperate agony as he pushed and pushed, unable to believe the unsurpassable depth and intensity of the tumult of pleasure that was overwhelming him, and then there flashed one great white sheet of light in his head and he felt the surge of his spirit course and course and course and course and course as though it would never stop.

As he finished, forcing the last drop, the Vaseline jar tumbled to the ground with a clatter and Lilac whinnied in alarm, pulling in her great ring of muscle with a bruising clench.

David winced but stayed calm, knowing that Lilac would subside too if he was still. The tension in her flanks eased away and she relaxed the muscle, letting David pull out.

He stood there for a moment, hot hands on her side, exultant and exhausted. At last he stepped down to pick up the wad of tissues that had wrapped the jar and began with care to wipe Lilac down, talking to her all the while.

Out in the stable yard he shivered sharply as he put on his T-shirt. He looked down at the spongy dangle of his cock.

'You must be sparing of this great gift,' he said to himself, 'very, very sparing.'

Six

Albert and Michael Bienenstock grew sugar beet in a part of Hungary that in 1919 was redesignated Czechoslovakia. This act of cartographical tyranny had transformed Michael into an overnight Zionist and, inspired by a childish sense of adventure and the inflammatory writings of Chaim Herzog, he took a boat to Haifa in 1923, under a proud new name, Amos Golan. Golan, Michael had satisfied himself after extensive, and in Albert's view preposterous, researches into family history, was the Bienenstocks' true Israelite patronymic. Golan was a fit name for a man travelling to claim his homeland for his people.

'Sailing into trouble,' said Albert, words with which he was later to mock himself.

Albert's own son was named Michael in honour of his foolish uncle, to the great consternation and scandal of Albert's cousins in Vienna. Tradition held it to be bad luck for members of the same family to share a given name. Albert was not a traditionalist. He had no religion, he had no real sense of Jewishness. He was a farmer and a horseman, closer to the anti-Semitic Magyars of the old Habsburg Empire than to the scholarly gabardine beetles of shtetl and city, who scuttled about the streets with their heads down, cravenly hugging the walls when the gentiles walked by, as if fearful of catching or perhaps transmitting some terrible disease.

As a young man in 1914, Albert had fought for his Emperor. Rigged up like a chocolate soldier in gleaming cuirass and nodding plume, Albert the Blue Hussar was among the first to charge the Serbian guns in the early weeks when the Great War was a small Balkan affair that nobody believed could matter. Later, the proud troops of horse humbled by the titanic ordnance of the twentieth century, Albert was appointed to their reassignment as no more than drays and dispatch ponies, pulling with lowered heads the carriages and ambulances that shuffled behind the lines in the frozen Carpathian mountains or relaying fatuous messages between staff and field. With ironic resignation he told himself that loyalty to a great moustache in Vienna was no more stupid than loyalty to a great beard in Jerusalem. By the end however, he had seen too many white worms crawling in the eye-sockets of too many dead comrades, and too many living comrades frying up the livers and lights of too many slaughtered Cossacks with baby faces. He exaggerated the symptoms of some light shell-shock he sustained during a bombardment and was happy to be transferred to a remount division in that district of Romania known as Transylvania, where he was to sit out the war processing the remnants of the cavalry.

Albert possessed a very special gift with horses. He understood them far better than did the equestrian instructors and veterinary surgeons of the Imperial Army, a fact which generated ill-feeling in some of his brother officers. Others preferred to trumpet Albert's skills as a healer, making extraordinary claims which he was always quick to repudiate.

'There is nothing so mysterious about what I do,' he said. 'I am patient with the animals. I show them that they are loved. I keep them calm. The rest is up to nature.'

Such protestations were so much spitting in the wind. Albert's reputation grew and was even extended to humans, the result of a stupid incident over his batman, Benko. This foolish soldier had allowed his foot to be stamped on by a frightened stallion one afternoon. Instead of reporting the injury immediately to an orderly, Benko had kept quiet and allowed the wound to fester overnight. The next morning, when he hobbled in with the morning coffee, Albert had questioned him.

'Why are you limping so badly, Benko?'

Benko had burst into tears.

'Oh, sir!' he cried. 'Would you take a look at it? I daren't go

143

to the surgeon, for I know he will amputate from the knee. He never does anything else.'

It was certainly true that there existed many standing jokes about soldiers who had made the mistake of visiting the regimental sawbones. There was one private, they said, who rather lost his head and went to see this doctor with nothing more than a migraine – after which he lost his head completely. This joke worked better in Romanian than in Hungarian. Another story concerned Jana, the local whore. One day a soldier called Janos had gone to see the doctor with a genital wart. He was never seen again, but Jana set up her stall only a week later.

Understanding Benko's reluctance to make an official appointment, Albert agreed to examine the foot, but could not help wincing with disgust when Benko gingerly pulled off his boot and sock. He was not a hygienic soldier, indeed had not in all likelihood separated that boot from that foot in many weeks. Benko saw Albert's gagging reaction and immediately began to gibber with fear.

'It's gangrene, isn't it, sir? It's gangrene and I shall lose my leg! I know it, I know it.'

'There, there, you stupid boy. Let me see.'

'No, no! I'm done for, I'm done for!'

Albert took him by the shoulders and spoke into his eyes. 'Listen to me. You must be very calm now. You must breathe slowly and deeply. Breathe very slowly and very deeply for me.'

Trembling, Benko tried to obey. Albert kept on talking to him, firmly but with kindness, until he was satisfied that the boy had wound down from his hysteria. Horses were easier, you could communicate such confidence without words.

'Now I'm going to look at your foot. Be sure there is no real problem with your foot. It is sore and it smarts, but that is not the end of the world.'

Benko turned his head away in squeamish terror as Albert took a deep breath, stooped and pressed his hand to the swelling, which was purple with poison. Immediately, a small splinter flew from the centre of the wound, followed by a jet of pus.

'There,' said Albert, 'that's better.'

Benko turned round to stare at Albert. 'Better?'

'Yes, I'm sure you will find that your foot will mend now.'

'You place your hand on my foot and you say it will mend?'

'No, no, I merely . . .'

But it was too late. Around the barracks the rumour flew. 'Benko's foot was black with gangrene . . .'

144

'Bienenstock himself nearly fainted at the stench . . .'

'Just put a hand . . .'

'A hand that seared with heat, Benko says . . .'

'Nearly burned him . . .'

'Just rested it for a second . . .'

'Would have had to amputate from the knee . . .'

'Look at the boy now . . .'

'Skipping like a terrier . . .'

'Bienenstock is a strange man, I've always said so . . .'

'Not Christian, you know . . .'

'Not even a proper Jew . . .'

'Never seen in synagogue, according to Corporal Heilbronn . . .'

After a while even Albert himself began to wonder what he had done. He was sure that he had seen that splinter fly, he was sure that the smell he recoiled from was nothing more than the Limburger reek of filthy socks, he was sure that his 'skill' lay in no more than the ability to comfort, to comfort in the proper sense, to make strong, to fortify. But the damage had been done, and from that day Albert never knew a moment's ease amongst his men. A horse that he had 'miraculously' nursed to health had later gone mad, throwing a recruit, who broke his back and never walked again. Everywhere that Albert went he saw the sign of the cross or of the evil eye. Then Benko, silly superstitious Benko, made an appointment with his commanding officer and asked to be reassigned to other duties. Serving Captain Bienenstock made him nervous. A week later Benko died after stepping on a landmine.

'He trod with *that* foot,' the men said. 'Bienenstock's curse.'

Albert's loyalty would never be given again: so he swore when he returned in 1919 to his neglected Hungarian fields, soon to become his neglected Czechoslovakian fields. Michael his brother, who had stayed behind with Imperial blessing to tend those fields that the people of the Empire might have something to sweeten their war, had not been a good farmer. The Zionist bug had bitten him early in the Gentile's Quarrel, as he called it, and he had higher things to think of than the husbandry of, as it were, alien corn.

After Michael's departure, Albert spent the next ten years working to become the largest grower of beet in all of Czechoslovakia. In 1929 he set the seal on the triumphant achievement of this ambition by building a small refinery on his land and marrying the daughter of his foreman, a small girl with brown eyes and lustrous hair. Within a year she bore him a son, Michael, and in the spring of 1932 perished in the delivery of a daughter, Rebecca. Albert tried, but he could not save her. Grieve as he might, he could still reflect that it was perhaps as well that he had not succeeded in nursing her back to health after the doctors had pronounced her all but dead. His reputation as an unholy sorcerer had followed him back home and even rabbis, who were supposed to be above the credulous herd, shunned his society.

Albert needed no one. He had proved his point. He was a superb agriculturist. Now, alone with his two tiny children, his wide fields of beet and his sugar refinery, he yearned to leave the country that was no longer his own. Besides Yiddish and Hungarian, his mother tongues, he had had to learn German and Romanian for service in the Hussars and since then the languages of his new government, Czech and Slovak.

'I am leaving before Prague is taken over by the French,' he told his factotum, Tomasz. Albert held, all his life, a peculiar horror of the French tongue, unaccountably believing it to be far more difficult to master than any other in Europe.

But how could Albert leave? Who would buy his beet fields? Who would give him a good price for a private refinery? Where would he go? Many in his village spoke of America, but America meant only New York; Jews were not welcome in the farmlands. Albert's brother Michael, or rather Amos, urged him by letter to come and join him in Palestine, where he and his new wife Nora had given the world a pair of brand new sabra children, Aron and Ephraim, who were growing up to be the new Jews of the new Jerusalem.

'After all, you're something of a sabra, yourself, Albert,' he wrote.

Albert was puzzled by this remark. A Jew could only call himself a sabra, he had understood, if he was born in the land of Israel. A learned friend explained Amos's meaning.

'Your brother is making a friendly joke, Albert. "Sabra" is also a word for a kind of fruit. A prickly pear, spiky on the outside but sweet and soft on the inside.' As good a description of Albert as anyone ever found. He had been forced to be prickly however, for his estate was large and took a great deal of energy and skill to run, with markets so deeply corrupt, inflation so crazily high and the people so grindingly poor. He had been forced to be prickly because his real, calm, loving and rational self was mistaken for the black soul of a hypnotic wizard.

A week after this letter from Amos had arrived, Adolf Hitler was elected by the German people to be their new Chancellor. Albert was disappointed. Hitler did not seem to him to be a suitable leader for the Germans; the anti-Semitism, he supposed, like everybody's anti-Semitism, was an unpleasant noise that meant very little. Albert was rarely bothered by anti-Semitism. He had often felt a little that way himself when he heard Hasidim sounding off on the subject of the law or Amos and his friends sounding off on the subject of Zion. It was not that Albert was ashamed of being Jewish, it was rather that he was damned if he was going to make a big fuss about it. He was a father and a farmer, that was all.

Another week later a very surprising thing happened. An English gentleman arrived at Albert's house, accompanied by an interpreter from Prague. Albert was beside himself with excitement to have a real Englishman within his walls. Of all the peoples of the world the English were quite his favourite. It had been a matter of great relief to him that he had not come into any hostile contact with them during the course of the war, for he was sure that he would have been greatly tempted to cross the lines and join them. He liked their formality, their tweed suits, their respect for horsemanship, their ironic humour and their lack of show.

Albert seated the Englishman and the interpreter in leather chairs in his study. He rang for Tomasz, his servant.

'The gentleman will take tea?' he asked the interpreter. He hoped that the Englishman would not think that his ringing for a servant amounted to ostentation. It really was perfectly usual for Albert to drink tea at this hour and for Tomasz to be summoned by a bell and commanded to prepare it.

'Tea would be delightful, my dear sir,' the translator replied in grand Hungarian. He seemed to Albert to be attempting to out-anglify the Englishman with his pre-war pomposity and pre-war whiskers.

Once tea was poured, Albert sat politely upright and waited for the purpose of this visit to be revealed. Sipping from his cup as though he were attending the smartest party on the smoothest lawn in Berkshire, the English gentleman delivered himself of a short sentence and then cocked his head good-naturedly towards the interpreter. The voice was light and pleasant, with soft 'r's and a gentle falling inflection. The interpreter smiled broadly and declared:

'Mr Bienenstock, I represent His Majesty's Government in London.'

What splendid words! Albert's head became dizzy with excitement, then dizzier still as, over the next hour, the Englishman explained his mission.

The British Empire – another splendid phrase! – was deeply sensible, the Englishman said, of her complete dependence upon the cane sugars that originated in her far dominions of Australia and the West Indies. Were there ever to be another war in Europe – and the Englishman protested that this eventuality was held by his masters to be quite discountably remote – naval tacticians were of one mind in their agreement that the seas that bounded the British shores might be all but cut off from vital supplies of hot-weather commodities, of which sugar was the most vital . . . well, after tea perhaps. The British had never in all their long history – really a most unpardonable oversight – grown sugar beet on any domestic basis. They had no expertise on the subject whatsoever. That it could be grown was not a matter that admitted of the least doubt. Sugar from cane, they were fully aware, was not a realistic possibility, owing to their weather, which Mr Bienenstock doubtless knew was capricious to a nationally celebrated fault. Sugar beet however, the staple of Mr Bienenstock's fertile native plains, seemed perfectly suited to the British climate. It was after all, was it not, akin to the carrot, the turnip and – one must assume – the beetroot? The British farmer was known for the splendour of his carrots, his turnips and his beetroots; surely the cultivation of their close cousins *Beta Rapa* and *Beta Vulgaris* could not be beyond him? The Ministry did feel, however, that someone was needed to guide them, a man who knew all aspects of the vegetable, as it were from field to sugar-bowl. Mr Bienenstock's name had been put forward to Ministry representatives in Prague as being one of the most authoritative in the sugar world. Would Mr Bienenstock consider making the journey to England, in two years' time, to counsel and instruct the ignorant farmers there, to manage test beds, to supervise refinery construction and to oversee Britain's first tentative production of the crop? To use a meteorological metaphor, the British Isles were in drought and needed a man like Mr Bienenstock to shower them with his knowledge and expertise. Her Majesty's Government would pay a generous salary for this work and take pleasure in defraying any such expenses in the matters of travel and resettlement as might arise. The English gentleman himself was in no doubt that should Mr Bienenstock be desirous of such status, he could during this time apply to become a full subject of King George and be assured of a favourable outcome.

The government of this same majesty would also be pleased, subject to Mr Bienenstock's agreement, over the next two years to buy, at a fair market price, all his fields and his refinery in Czechoslovakia and to send out a number of British agriculturists to experience with him two full cycles of the beet, in growth, harvest and refinement. The government of Czechoslovakia was most anxious to help in this matter, Britain's friendship with the vigorous young democracy being an established fact in a fickle world, a relationship to be relied upon in these trying times for Europe.

The Englishman and Czech translator would leave Mr Bienenstock now to digest this proposal. His decision could be given over the next few weeks. Really most excellent tea. The best the Englishman had tasted on the Continent. Good afternoon to you, Mr Bienenstock. Such charming children.

If Albert had got down on his knees and covered his head to beseech God to grant him all that he desired he could not have framed a prayer that so exactly delineated his requirements. Albert managed to maintain his dignity enough not to reply there and then, sending word to Prague three days later that he would be pleased to assent to the English gentleman's scheme and that he was looking forward to offering his hospitality to the agricultural experts London chose to send out to him.

The English farmers, Mr Northwood, Mr Aves and Mr Williams, arrived later that year. They impressed Albert as being both intelligent and respectful, proving themselves attentive and exceptionally apt pupils in the art of sugar. Harry, Paul and Vic, as they insisted they be called, were kind to Michael and Rebecca, who responded by taking to English as though the language had been planted inside them at birth and had been only waiting for this one chance to flourish. Albert picked up the spirit and substance of the language very quickly too, but suffered great teasing from young Michael, who could not understand his father's inability to master its textures.

'No, Father. It's not "Wick Villiams" or a "vunderful willage". It's "Vic Williams" and a "wonderful village".'

'I can't say those letters.'

'That's mad!' Michael would hoot, outraged by such absurdity. 'If you can say "Villiams" and "willage", of course you can say Williams and village.'

'Old weterans stick to old vays,' Albert would say with deliberate cussedness.

During those two exciting years for the Bienenstock household, all the talk was in English and of England. The visitors spoke of pubs and clubs, of cricket and soccer, of Oxford and Cambridge, of Leslie Howard and Noël Coward, of crossword puzzles and fox-hunting, of Huntley and Palmer biscuits and Mazawattee tea, of the BBC and the GPO, of Guy Fawkes Night and Derby Day, of the Prime Minister of Mirth and the Prince of Wales. Albert unearthed in a bookshop a copy of *Der Forsyte Saga von John Galsworthy* and found himself growing ever impatient to become part of this kindly, ordered world with its town-squares and sea-side hotels, its cosy fogs and rattling taxis, its politicians in top-hats and duchesses in white gloves.

On the boat over from Bremerhaven (one last look at poor Germany and poor, poor Europe), while Rebecca was being sick over the rails, little Michael raised the subject of their names.

'Harry says . . .' every statement of Michael's for the last year had begun with those words, 'Harry says that English people might laugh at the name Bienenstock. Harry says it sounds like a kind of bean soup.'

'Oh dear,' said Albert. 'We don't want people to laugh at our names. We must think of something else.'

It was a year later, when they were already well settled in just outside the town of Huntingdon, that Michael himself came up with the splendid idea. His best friend at kindergarten was called Tommy Logan and Michael, writing Tommy's name many times all over his exercise book, as best friends do, noticed that 'Logan' was really 'Golan' rearranged.

Albert was delighted. 'Logan,' he kept repeating to himself, 'Logan . . . Logan . . . Logan.'

'You see, Father!' said Michael. 'We have made an *Anglo* version of *Golan*!'

Six months later the two children walked with their father from the Naturalisation Department of the Home Office towards the Lyon's Corner House in Trafalgar Square.

'Uncle Amos will be so pleased,' said Albert Logan, subject of the King.

Tommy Logan's reaction however, back at the Huntingdon kindergarten, had been one far removed from pleasure.

'You've stolen my name!' he howled. 'You horrid *Jew*, you've stolen my name. How dare you! I'll never talk to you again, you stinking *Jew*.'

'However did they know that you are Jewish?' Albert had wondered when Michael related this falling-out to his father.

'Miss Hartley told them on my first day,' Michael said. 'She said that everyone was to be nice to me, because decent people have forgiven us for killing Christ.'

'Is that so?' said Albert and a small furrow appeared on his brow.

But furrows were not for Albert's forehead, they were for his fields. The government test beds in Huntingdonshire were the sensation of the day and for a short season the talk of England.

'BRITAIN TO BEET THE WORLD!' a page-five headline in the *Daily Express* had declared above a photograph of Albert and a government agriculturist standing proudly in front of their 'experimental' acres.

'This unprepossessing vegetable, no more in reality than a turnip with a sweet tooth, could be the key to Britain's future prosperity,' a leader writer declared.

The members of the British public were less sure.

'Will sugar from beet be purple?'

'Can it be turned into proper English cubes?'

'Is it more fattening?'

'Will it taste of soil?'

'Can beet be baked in a pie?'

'Can I grow it in the garden and make my own sugar?'

'Is it fair on the colonies?'

'You can bet they won't be serving it in the Tate Gallery tea-rooms.'

Over the next four or five years, the smiling Hungarian in tweed plus-fours toured the south coast and East Anglia in his holly-green Austin, bestowing government grants and agricultural advice on puzzled but welcoming farmers. Michael and Rebecca continued with their studies at Miss Hartley's kindergarten in Huntingdon, a town to which Albert was by now greatly attached, despite initial misgivings.

'Oliver Cromwell?' he had cried, when first he had heard. 'Oliver Cromwell came from here? The king-killer?'

151

He simply could not believe that the otherwise loyal and respectable townspeople of Huntingdon could be so sincerely proud of their wicked son, that disgrace to English history, the British Lenin. In time however, he learned to forgive the Lord Protector who was, after all, a gentleman farmer like himself and had been pushed by dread circumstance, not by Bolshevism or bloodlust, into the events that led to that awful January morning in Whitehall. The people of Huntingdon, in their turn, learned to love the strange Czechoslovakian with the charming manners, perfect English children and inexplicably Scottish surname. They were less sure about the refinery whose construction he had supervised and which he now ran. It gave off a sickly smell of burnt peanut-butter which would hang over the whole town on windless days. The creation of a second refinery in Bury St Edmunds gave young Michael his first lesson in management technique, however, and can be thanked for that.

One rainy afternoon, when Rebecca and Michael were playing on the floor of their father's study, an engineer came to call on Albert. He left a 600-page report, full of technical drawings and scientific data, which he was anxious for Mr Logan to approve.

Michael watched that evening as Albert sat with the report on his lap.

'Have you got to read all that?'

'Read it? What do I know from pressure-gauges and amps? This is what I do.'

Albert riffled his thumb through the pages of the report and opened a page at random. With a red-inked pen he underlined a few words and flipped through to another page where he circled some numbers, writing a large question mark in the margin. He did this four or five times before scrawling at the bottom of the last page the words, 'Can the sub-station take the extra load?'

Michael happened to be outside the study a week later when the engineer called again.

'I've checked and checked and checked the figures you queried, Mr Logan, and so have my colleagues, but we're blowed if we can find any error.'

'Ah. I'm so sorry, my dear fellow. I must have made a mistake. I should not have been doubting you.'

'Well, we do like to be thorough, sir. We were pretty sure about the sub-station too. Then, you'll never guess, but the contractors telephoned to say they had made a miscalculation with their tolerances. They should have been greater by ten per cent.'

After Albert had shown the grateful and admiring engineer from the house, he addressed Michael, whom he had seen lurking in the corridor.

'You see? Now they have checked so many times that everything is sure to be fine.'

'But the sub-station? How did you know?'

'Sometimes you make a lucky guess. Believe me, you can always rely that sub-stations cannot take the load and you can always rely that another man's pride will do much of your work for you.'

II

One day, it was during the holidays, the very week before Michael was due to start his first term at boarding school in Sussex, Albert summoned the children to his study. He was looking very serious and spoke in Hungarian, a sure sign of distress.

'I have just had a letter from your Uncle Amos,' he said. 'It means that I shall have to go away for a little while. This is a good time for me to take a holiday. You, Michael, will have to go early to your new school. I have telephoned the headmaster and he will be happy to look after you. You will stay at home, Rebecca, and be looked after by Mrs Price.'

'What is it, Father?' asked Michael. 'What has happened?'

'Our cousins living in Vienna, your Uncle Rudi, your Uncle Louis and your Aunts Hannah and Roselle and all the children, they would like to leave Austria and come to England. I can help because I have my British passport. But I must go there myself. A tiresome necessity, but a necessity all the same.'

The next day Albert had gone to London to see his old friend in the Foreign Office, the English gentleman who had visited him in 1933. Albert forbore from making any reference to Britain's 'firm friendship with your vigorous young democracy', the 'established fact in a fickle world' of which the gentleman had spoken on that afternoon in Czechoslovakia. It was not for Albert to question Mr Chamberlain's tea-party with Hitler.

The gentleman from the Foreign Office listened to Albert's story and confessed the matter to be a little out of his sphere. He recommended a man he knew in another department and was kind enough to write Albert a letter of introduction.

The man from the other department, perhaps because his name was Murray, had not taken to this Logan with a middle-European epiglottis.

'Really, sir, I am not sure what you mean by "taking a stance". We have a large number of British Jews like yourself coming here every week, all making representations of this nature. I say to all of them what I am going to say to you. There are wheels within wheels. You must understand the precarious state of diplomacy currently obtaining on the continent of Europe. After recent hard-won successes in Munich, His Majesty's Government is hardly in a position to make demands on Germany as that long-suffering country struggles to express a coherent sense of her national identity and establish a proper place at the world's table. It is precisely the sort of hysterical rumour-mongering that you and your fellow . . . that you and your fellows are engaged in that can upset the delicate balance of negotiations and threaten peaceful relations.'

'But my peaceful relations are already being threatened,' said Albert with the unselfconscious wordplay that only a non-native speaker of English can achieve.

'Really! If you insist on founding your understanding of a power such as the new Germany on the hearsay of a brother in Jerusalem . . .'

Albert knew enough to hold his tongue in the presence of a triumphalist Munichois.

'You are of course free to travel where you will, Mr "Logan", but I must warn you that if you transgress any law of the German Reich you cannot expect protection or immunity from us. I would recommend that you wait a little while. If your family is sincere about coming to England they must satisfy firstly the requirements for emigration laid down by their home government.'

'But they have no home government, sir!' Albert cried, sounding, he was painfully aware, exactly like the kind of whining Jew that he and much of the world most despised.

He never told Michael or Rebecca how completely his faith had been shattered by the indifference and disapproval that he met at the hands of His Majesty's Government that day and on the four days following, as he wore out the waiting-room chairs of Whitehall and the patience of the few functionaries who consented to see him. Had he lived to see the Battle of Britain and the Blitz, Michael persisted in believing, Albert's belief in the British might have been at the very least partially restored. Michael was to find out later from Uncle Louis the full extent of his father's disillusion and despair during that painful week, as he was to find out the details of all that followed.

Arriving in Vienna, Mr Albert Logan, famed grower and refiner of beet, summoned his cousins by messenger to the hotel he had chosen to favour with his custom. Here he met his first reversal, here the sharp point of the Truth began to press against his new-grown English hide.

The messenger returned half an hour later with a letter. Albert took some notes from his pocket with which to pay the youth and was astonished to see the money being snatched roughly from him without a word of thanks.

'Steady there, young fellow,' said Albert in his most patrician officer's Viennese.

The messenger spat on the carpet, a fleck of yellow spittle landing on Albert's shining brown brogues. 'Jew-lover,' he said with contempt and stalked from the room.

Albert shook his head with disbelief and opened the letter. Now the sharp point of the Truth pierced the skin and started to push through. His cousins could not attend such a meeting, they explained with profuse apology. In order to comply with the laws of Austria under the recent Anschluss, they were obliged to wear yellow stars on their coats. Persons with yellow stars on their coats, they assured Albert, were not allowed inside hotels like the Franz Josef.

Mohammed took a cab to the mountain. Cousins Louis and Rudi and their families were all crowded together in one small room in a part of the town that Albert, who knew Vienna well from his old days in the Hussars, had never thought to visit. He was shocked to see them, shocked beyond bearing, more shocked than he had ever been before. The white worms in the eye-sockets of his comrades and the frying livers of the young Cossacks had not shocked him more: in this small room the sharp point of the Truth finally forced itself deep inside him until it tore at the walls of his heart. Albert leant on his Swaine, Adeney and Brigg's umbrella and cried like a baby for a full quarter of an hour while his cousins clustered about him in concern.

Albert had known and then forsworn loyalty to the Emperor Franz Josef, whose cavalry he had loved; he had known and now forswore loyalty to two King Georges and a King Edward, whose country and people and history he had revered. In that awful little room with its imponderably hateful smell, a smell that took all the dignity and colour and strength away from his family and all the dignity and colour and strength away from him, his tweeds, his expensive luggage and his small blue passport, in that dreadful stinking room he swore a new loyalty, to his people – his stupid, moaning, helpless and cosmically irritating people, whose religion he scorned, whose culture he despised, whose mannerisms and prejudices he abominated.

★

With lies, with cunning, with the use of old army contacts and above all, of course, with the use of money, Albert procured the papers necessary to allow his cousins to leave Vienna. Besides Louis, Rudi, Hannah and Roselle, there were four children, Danny, Ruth, Dita and Miriam. He took them by train to Holland and thence by boat to Harwich in England. He stayed in Huntingdon long enough to introduce them to Rebecca and her nanny Mrs Price, and then he drove down to Sussex to call on Michael's headmaster, Dr Valentine.

'Here is money enough to pay for his schooling for the rest of time,' he said. 'You shall see it please that he acquires an excellent scholarship to his public school.'

'Well, I think that rather depends, Mr Logan, on how intelligent the boy is and with what diligence he applies himself to his work. Scholarships are hardly something you can . . .'

'Michael is most intelligent and most hard-working. I will see him now please.'

A boy was dispatched to fetch young Logan.

While they awaited him, Albert addressed the headmaster once more. 'Another thing to say, Dr Walentine. It is possible that you may imagine my son and myself are Jewish people.'

'Really, Mr Logan, I had given it no . . .'

'It is to understand that we are *not* Jewish people. Michael is not a Jewish boy. He is a Church of England boy. I am going away into Europe now, but I have friends here in England. If it arrives in my ears that any one single person of the school suggests or makes it said that Michael is a Jewish boy it is possible that I shall come back to take him away and that I strike you with my fists, Dr Walentine, with strength enough to kill you.'

'Mr Logan!'

'Here he comes now. We shall go to a walk, he and me . . . him and I.'

The flabbergasted Dr Valentine was left to ponder this alarming threat while Michael showed his father the lake, the pony paddocks, the cricket field and the woods where he and his friends played cowboys and Indians.

Albert spoke in a mixture of Yiddish and Hungarian. Michael replied in English.

'You are seven years old now, Michael. Plenty old enough to know the facts of the world.'

'It's all right, Father. I've already been told.'

'You've been told?'

'The man wees inside the woman and she has a baby. Wallace told me. He's the senior boy in my dorm.'

'What a child. I'm not talking about *those* facts, which you can tell your friend Vollis, have nothing to do with urination. I am talking about the real facts.'

'The real facts?'

'Tell me, Michael Logan. What is your country of birth?'

'Hungary,' said Michael, puffing up his chest.

'NO!' Albert turned and gave his son a violent shake. 'Not correct. Tell me again. What is your country of birth?'

Michael stared at his father in amazement.

'Czechoslovakia?' he suggested, frightened.

'NO!'

'No?'

'No! You come from England. You are English.'

'Yes, of course, but I was born . . .'

'You were born in Huntingdon. You grew up in Huntingdon. What is your religion?'

Michael had never seen his father like this before. So strong and so angry. 'Church of England?'

'YES!' Albert kissed him. 'Good boy. You have the idea. You must never, ever, upon pain of your life and my eternal curses, tell a living soul that you are Jewish. Do you understand?'

'But why not?'

'Why not? Because the Germans are coming, that is why not. They will tell they are not coming, but believe me they are coming all the same. The Nazi Germans are coming and they will take anyone away who is Jewish. So you are not Jewish and your sister is not Jewish. You know no Jews, you see no Jews, you have conversation with no Jews. You are Michael Logan of Wyton Chase, Huntingdon. Your uncles and aunts from abroad live with you. They are Lutheran Christians.'

'And you live with me too, of course.'

'Of course,' said Albert. 'I live with you too. Of course.'

Six months later Michael had received a letter with an exotic postmark.

'Jerusalem!' one of his friends shouted. 'Logan's got a letter from Jew-rusalem.'

'My uncle's with the army in Palestine,' Michael said nonchalantly. 'The Mandate, it's called.'

'Logan's a Jew!'

'Bloody am not!'

'Miserly jewy Jew!'

'What's going on here?'

Michael turned in fear as Edward Wallace shouldered his way to the front of the press. Wallace was a senior boy and known to be capable of merciless mental bullying.

'Loganstein's got a letter from Jew-land.'

'He's a Jew. You can tell. Look at his nose.'

'He's a Roundhead, that's for sure.'

Roundheads, in school slang, meant those who were circumcised, as distinct from Cavaliers, who were not.

Wallace looked down on Michael, his eyes darting wickedly back and forth across the boy's face as if coming to a decision. Michael braced himself. His mouth was dry and he felt faint with apprehension.

Wallace spoke at last. 'Don't be stupid,' he said. 'Logan's not a miserly Jew, he's a miserly Scot like me. And I happen to know, Hutchinson, that you are a Roundhead too and what's more your nose is bigger than anyone in the civilised world's. It's so big in fact, that there's talk in the papers of East End children being evacuated into your left nostril until the end of the war.'

A tidal wave of mocking laughter swept over Hutchinson at this and Michael had to clamp his muscles tight to avoid wetting himself with relief. Wallace turned to him with a sly smile.

'Bags I have those stamps, McLogie, I collect 'em.'

Michael tore the corner from the envelope and handed them over with a beam of gratitude. Wallace clipped him round the ear and told him not to grin at him like a monkey or he'd kick him in the slats.

'Sorry, Wallace.'

Michael had then run to the school rears to read the letter in private. It was from his Uncle Amos. To this day he regrets never having read it more closely. The quickest glance was all he would allow himself before tearing it into tiny shreds and flushing it down the lavatory.

All he would ever be able to recall of the letter were a few phrases. Uncle Amos wrote that Michael's father had been shot by the Nazis two days after Chamberlain had declared war on Germany. Something about Berlin. Something about living in the ghettos and spreading warmth. Albert Golan was a hero of the Jews and a great man. Moisha Golan, his son, should be very proud and should always remember.

The next day Uncles Richard and Herbert, as Louis and Rudi now called themselves, came to pick Michael up from school.

159

III

All the money had gone, naturally. All the money from the sale of the farm in Czechoslovakia, all the money earned from his work over the last few years for the Ministry, all the money raised against his interests in the two refineries. Michael's next three years at Dr Valentine's prep school were assured. After that . . .

'I shall certainly get a scholarship,' said Michael. 'And I shall get a job in the holidays and pay for Rebecca's schooling too.'

'You aren't yet ten years old, Michael,' said Aunt Roselle, now Aunt Rose. 'We will pay for your school. We all have work, we will look after you both. We will be proud to have you as a son and daughter.'

Michael had found jobs however. Every day of his school holidays was engaged in earning money. Firstly he had worked for a bakery in Huntingdon as delivery boy and then, after his scholarship took him to public school, he called the family together and made a suggestion.

'Mrs Anderson is getting very old,' he said. 'She wants to sell her shop. Why don't we buy it?'

'How could we afford to do such a thing?'

'We can sell this house and be able to live over the shop. I've made enquiries. There is room enough for all of us. It's a tight squeeze – Rebecca, Ruth, Dita and Miriam will have to share a room, Danny and I will sleep behind the counter – but we can manage.'

Logan's Sweets and Smokes was known in the family as Michael's Shop. Michael did the books, having the most mathematical turn of mind in the family. He understood coupons and the rationing system, he understood how to barter and he understood how to keep customers loyal.

One evening Aunt Rose knocked on his bedroom door.

'Michael, it's Happidrome on the wireless. What are you doing there? Come downstairs.'

She opened the door and saw Michael holding a large book.

'This is my customer book,' he explained. 'Every time a customer comes into the shop I talk to them and find out what they like. I list their favourite tobacco, or cigarette, or brand of sweets, and each night I make sure I have learnt it. Take the book. Ask me.'

A bewildered Rose had opened a page and offered the name 'Mr G. Blake'.

'Godfrey Blake,' said Michael, 'lives in the Godmanchester Road and smokes forty Player's Weights a day. He buys one packet of Craven A a week for his wife, who only smokes at weekends. He has a son in the army in North Africa and a daughter in the WAAF. He's an assistant ARP warden, injured his hip at Passchendaele and is secretly in love with Janet Gaynor. He has a weakness for humbugs and I always give him one or two if he's out of coupons. He gives me half a crown for cleaning his car on Sundays.'

'Woosh!' said Aunt Rose. 'Mr Tony Adams?'

'*Wing-Commander* Anthony Adams,' said Michael, 'flies a desk at RAF Wyton. He has a sweetheart named Wendy, a land-army girl working near Wisbech, and he rides there to see her twice a week on his motor-cycle. He smokes Parson's Pleasure ready-rubbed, which they don't sell in the Officers' Mess, and he likes aniseed balls for himself and Fry's Five Boys chocolate for Wendy.'

'Michael. Why have you learnt all this?'

'Because these people smoke and eat sweets. The first time Mr Blake came into the shop he was just passing. Now he walks the extra half-mile to us twice a week. When the business grows after the war, people like that will be important.'

'When the business . . . ? Listen to him. Michael, it's just a shop.'

'It's a seed, Aunt Rose. Now, I have to go back to school next week. You and Aunt Hannah will be looking after things weekdays. I will leave this book for you. See if you can try to learn everything in it too. Everyone should know it off by heart – Danny, Dita, Miriam, everyone – so when they help out at weekends and after school they can make the customers feel important.'

In the family's eyes, Michael's destiny was as inevitable as if he had been born Prince of Wales. He was a force and that was that.

During subsequent school holidays, as the war came to a close, so the proper expansion of the business, the full germi-nation and growth of the seed, began. A paper round was added, early-morning work for Danny and his sister and cous-ins; bread, potatoes, flowers and an increasing range of tinned foods began to crowd the shelves of the small retail area until Michael and Richard decided that it would be worth their while to buy the house next door, knock through the party-wall and create a small version of a Home and Colonial Store.

In 1947 Michael won a scholarship to Cambridge which he turned down.

'We can really concentrate on things now,' he said.

A call-up the following year to National Service could not be turned down however. His old protector from prep school, Edward Wallace, who had deferred service until after Oxford where he was now finishing, persuaded him to join him in applying to the Royal Norfolk regiment.

'Not a very smart outfit, which is perfect as we'll be cocks of the roost. Plenty of time for race-meetings and women.'

One afternoon, during his officer training in Wiltshire, Michael read a short story by Somerset Maugham which gave him the idea he had been looking for. It concerned a young man who found himself in need of a packet of cigarettes in a Midlands town one afternoon. He walked along the streets searching for a tobacconist: the better part of a mile he walked before he found one. Instead of going on his way and thinking no more about it, as an ordinary person might, this young man retraced his steps to the place where he had first stood. 'I shall open a tobacconist's here,' he said to himself, 'there is clearly a need.' His shop was a magnificent success. 'How childishly simple,' thought the young man. For the next twenty years he travelled Britain walking the streets looking for cigarettes. Whenever he had to walk far, there he would open another shop. He was a millionaire by the age of thirty-five.

'Well, Tedward,' said Michael to his friend Wallace, 'God bless Mr Maugham.'

'Don't you think,' said Wallace, 'that others might have tried it first?'

'What you have to understand, Tedward, is that "others" don't try anything. They leave it to people like us.'

'You can count me out, darling one,' said Wallace. 'Sounds like work.'

A year and a half later Michael met Lady Anne Bressingham, which gave him something to work towards. She was eleven when they met and Michael not quite twenty, but he knew as surely as any man ever knew a thing that she would grow into the woman for him.

Wallace accused him of being a pervert.

'No, no, Tedward, you don't understand. It is in the smile. She has the right smile. At the moment she is a bony girl, but I know what she will become. It is never the eyes alone, or the beauty, or the figure, it is always the smile. When she smiled I knew at once. It is that clear.'

By 1955, Wallace had cause to remark that Logan news-agent-tobacconists were as familiar a sight in every English high street as dog-turds and Belisha beacons.

'Clothes rationing will end soon,' said Michael. 'People will want good, well-made clothes, brightly coloured and cheap. These new teenagers will want jeans from America. It is time we looked into the matter.'

At a party in 1959 to celebrate the publication of Edward Lennox Wallace's *Odes of Fury*, Logan took the rising poet aside.

'I'm going into publishing, Tedward. We've bought APC Magazines Ltd. What do you think of that?'

'Women's magazines and children's comics.'

'Chiefly. But we have other titles too. *New Insights*, for instance.'

'*New Insights* is older than God and just as dead.'

'So tell me, who should I employ to nurse it back to life? They say Mark Onions is a coming talent.'

'Stanley Matthews knows more about poetry and literature than Mark Onions. Mark Onions couldn't nurse a sick vole.'

'Perhaps I should ask my best man.'

'Your *what*?'

'Anne and I are to be married. I was hoping your waistcoat would be the one to hold the ring.'

Over the next sixteen years Logan's collection of companies was transformed into a kingdom and then into what the world could only call an empire. The genius, everyone agreed, lay in the grasp of detail, in the flexibility of strategy and in the remorseless gathering of comprehensive and grindingly techni-cal intelligence. In the Fifties Michael had picked up a tele-phone to sell his highly profitable valve-manufacturing plant the moment he had heard from a friend in America about the development in the labs of an object called the transistor.

'But it will be a long time before they come on to the market,' the friend had warned. 'Vacuum tubes have years in them yet.'

'So I'll get a good price for the factory now. Do you think I will get such a good price next year when everybody knows about this transistor of yours?'

Logan bought into vinyls and man-made fibres in the early Sixties and sold out five years later, just before wool and cotton and leather came triumphantly back into fashion. The teenage daughter of a management employee had told him that nylon was definitely out, square and dud.

The high-street outlets were redesigned, at massive cost, to include aisles and trolleys so that the customers could help themselves to their goods and pay at a cash desk. An unpleasant proceeding, but one which Logan was convinced showed the way forward. The name of these new supermarkets was changed from Logan's to Lomark Stores. All companies, in fact, that Michael acquired traded either under their original names or under new titles which had nothing to do with their owner. The word 'Logan' was used only by the parent corporation in the stock-market listings. 'Nobody likes a smart-arse,' Michael said. 'If my customers thought that the man who sold them marshmallows and cigarettes was the same man who published their magazines and manufactured their televisions, they would start to desert me. They have their pride after all.'

The financial world knew, naturally, and smiled on what was then a rare treat for the markets, a diverse group of businesses controlled by one holding company; a company that was not afraid to borrow and to expand; to divest here and reinvest there. Every skin Logan shrugged off left pickings on the Stock Exchange floor, every corporate marriage or rape was blessed with profitable issue.

Michael's family of second and third cousins proved a sore trial to him, however. Only the ageing Richard showed any aptitude for business: he died in 1962, followed soon by his brother Herbert. Their children were uninterested in the empire. Michael wanted very much to help them, as his father had helped them, but they preferred to help themselves, moving to London, marrying into established Jewish families and making a quieter way in the world.

'You're not our father,' Danny had said to Michael, refusing an offer of money. 'You mean well, but you will keep trying to swallow everything and everyone up.'

Michael was hurt by this. He had a great gift, to make work for thousands, to make money for thousands. It was his duty, surely, to use this gift. Certainly to use it with kindness and consideration. No one treated their workers better. No magnate of comparable power and standing could claim to know the first names and family histories of so many of his employees. No magnate of comparable power welcomed so enthusiastically the arrival of a Labour government. He paid his supertaxes like a man, never grumbling in public, however horrified he might have been in private. After the disasters of devaluation and the rising inflation of the 1970s he could never feel again any great respect for party politicians or interest in their short-term squabbles. He reserved his political energy for global matters, preferring crafty Third World statesmen with their fly-whisks and djellabas to the dull-witted borough councillors of Westminster. His style of beneficent paternalism was regarded with contempt by the domestic political parties but his even-handedly distributed money was welcomed by all.

Michael's sister, Rebecca, he never expected to be involved in business. He had high hopes that she might be a perfect second wife for his friend Wallace, whose poetry Michael could not begin to understand or enjoy, but whose successful editor-ship of *New Insights* had given him real pleasure. She married instead a man called Patrick Burrell, a perfectly ghastly fellow in Michael's estimation who incessantly and gracelessly both-ered him for money but at least provided the closest thing Michael ever had to a daughter, his niece Jane.

'Since you always claim that you need money for her sake,' Michael said to Burrell at last, 'I will settle money on her once and for all. A million pounds is hers and hers alone. I will start an account tomorrow. She can have the cheque-book herself when she is twenty-one. If any school fees need to be paid or clothes to be bought for her meanwhile, you will let me know, Patrick, won't you?'

Burrell had taken this badly and some years later sent a telegram to Rebecca from New York informing her that he had found someone else. Michael had been unhappy for his sister, but relieved to be rid of the connection.

A connection he was sorry to sever had come a little more than a year after Rebecca's marriage. It had been drawn to Michael's attention that Edward Wallace had been stealing money from the magazine; not a great deal, it was true, but it was not the scale of the embezzlement that had been at issue so far as Michael was concerned. It took him some time to forgive his old friend. He watched in great despair as the poet declined in creativity and charm while increasing in girth and drunken misanthropy.

In 1966, Michael knelt before the Queen and arose a knight.

In 1975, he stood to make his maiden speech in the House of Lords as Baron Logan of Swafford. A year later, at the age of forty-six, he came to the decision that he had earned the right to divert his magisterial powers of concentration into the matter of starting a family. He began with a son, Simon. Two years later Anne obliged him with another boy, David. It was after this birth that she persuaded Michael to pardon and absolve Wallace his peculations.

'I can see that you miss him, darling. Let's ask him to be David's godfather.'

Nine years following this, when a woman might reasonably forgive or even thank her uterus for slipping quietly into desuetude, Anne found herself pregnant again, this time with two boys at once.

IV

In 1991, with the twins approaching their fifth birthday, Edward, the younger by fifteen minutes, showed signs of developing serious problems with his asthma. This inspired Lady Anne to order a regular nightly patrol to monitor his breathing.

One hot night, with the air thick with pollen and spore, the twins' nanny, Sheila, was heard to shriek in horror. She ran down the nursery passage howling for Lady Anne.

Edward, she wailed, was blue and lifeless in his bed. Dead, not breathing at all. Quite dead. Most awfully dead. Anne and Michael ran for the stairs, their hearts jumping with panic and terror.

Meanwhile the two older boys had been awoken by the same screams and commotion. They hurried straight to the twins' bedroom in equal alarm. Simon took one look at Edward's immobile form and started to pump the lifeless child's arms and legs back and forth, perhaps in some dimly remembered re-enactment of first-aid instructors at school or more probably in imitation of the procedure of vets when dealing with suffocating piglets.

'No!' David had shouted. 'Let me!'

He pushed aside his older brother, who was now pummelling the ribs with some violence. Anne and Michael arrived in time to see Simon being elbowed roughly away.

Then they saw, they all saw, David kneel at the bedside and lay a hand gently on Edward's chest. Immediately, absolutely at once, they are all agreed on this, the child twitched and started to choke and whoop. Michael and Anne were too excited at first, too concerned with calling the doctor and seeing Edward to hospital, to ponder much on what they had witnessed. Michael remembered, though, that when he had taken his older sons aside and told them that they must go to bed, David's hand in his felt scorchingly hot, where Simon's was cold.

Some weeks later Michael took David aside.

'Davey, we must talk about your talent.'

'My talent, Daddy?'

'You know what I mean when I use that word. Your healing. I should have spoken before.'

Michael related to David those episodes from the life of Albert Bienenstock that he had previously kept from him: the healing and then the death of Benko, the persecution that followed and the suspicion and ostracism of the community and its rabbis.

'Your gift, you see, is not something that the world will welcome.'

'But why does Mummy look at me sometimes as if I'm ill or as if I've done something wrong?'

'She's confused, Davey. You must try to understand.'

David nodded. Michael went next to speak to his wife.

'Tell me truly, what are your feelings about Davey's gift?' he asked.

'Gift?' Anne looked at him in surprise.

'The gift he used to bring Edward back to life.'

Anne turned away, but Michael took her by the shoulders and brought her round to face him.

'You know what we saw, Anne.'

'I know . . .' she said.

'It confuses you and worries you.'

Anne nodded.

'We must make sure,' Michael said, 'that Davey's life will not be disrupted. We cannot allow the thing to be known.'

Anne considered this in silence.

'You're thinking of your father, aren't you?' she said.

'I'm thinking of Davey. Just of Davey. He is not to be treated as a freak.'

'But darling, you can't really . . .'

'We'll say no more.'

'I agree,' said Anne. 'We should say no more.'

More had to be said, however, the following year. Michael's niece Jane arrived in the midsummer of 1991 for her last stay at Swafford. She had spent many months fighting the exhausting cruelty of her disease and was not expected to survive for many weeks longer. All she wanted now, she said, was the peace of the countryside and the love of her uncle and cousins; these she would take away as a memory to comfort her last few sterile days in hospital.

Her collapse at the Royal Norfolk Show was held to be the onset of a terminal and irreversible decline. Simon had been forced to drive her back to Swafford himself despite being too young for a licence and surer of tractors than of Jane's twitchy BMW. He had carried her white and feeble form easily up the stairs, 'light as a plucked partridge, really,' and laid her on the bed of the Landseer Room. The room, the doctors agreed, in which she would shortly die.

During the first week of her confinement David and Simon were able to visit her. Simon would look in each morning with fruit, flowers and stories of life on the estate, and in the afternoons David would come with a book and sit by the bed, reading and chatting until dinnertime, never minding if Jane drifted in and out of sleep while he talked.

On the boys' last morning at Swafford they went in together to the sick room, solemn and elegant in their school uniforms, to bid her farewell.

'You look like dreadful pale undertakers,' she said. 'You shouldn't. I feel so much better today.'

The boys departed feeling greatly hopeful. A week later Jane was out of bed, professing herself not just better but truly cured. Cured not only in body, but cured all through. She felt more well now than she ever did before the leukaemia had come. She claimed that her previous life had been that of a caterpillar and that now she was reborn as a free and perfect butterfly.

Anne asked her, very seriously and in private, if she believed that there was any tangible cause or agency involved in this cure. Jane prevaricated, hiding behind a wide and tangled linguistic bush. Her words were of angels and grace and purity and becoming. Anne went away puzzled and alarmed.

Michael's visit was more straightforward.

'My love, we are so happy. So happy that you are better. However this may have happened, it is best, do you not think, to celebrate it in peace as a quiet and wonderful thing that took place in the privacy of what I hope you will always think of as your family home?'

'Whatever you say, Uncle Michael.'

Logan's friend Max Clifford was staying at this time and Michael wanted to speak to him on the subject too.

'It's just this, Max. You know what devils journalists can be.'

'We've sacked plenty in our time between us, eh?'

'Jane is going to London for tests. It may be that she is right and, as does sometimes happen with leukaemia, she has truly managed to overcome the illness. We don't want, we *really* don't want any publicity attached to this. Newspapers are so

169

hysterical when it comes to anything connected to cancer and there are always religious or mystical freaks who have something to sell. Jane herself is not quite in her right mind about things yet . . .'

'There have been rumours, Michael. Mary tells me she heard her praying in the woods yesterday.'

'Max,' said Michael, 'this is precisely what I mean. While she is so disturbed it is essential that everything is played down.'

'Mm,' said Max. 'She was kneeling there on the ground. A lot of Druidical guff apparently and a great deal about David.'

'If you are my friend, Max,' Michael was very sharp now, 'you will say no more on this subject. Not to me, not to anyone.'

The following year however, it was made clear that, despite Logan's injunctions, word *had* spread. Firstly, Ted Wallace arrived with a quaint story about wanting to write Michael's official biography, a claim that Michael frankly found absurd and a typical, Tedwardly piece of transparent deviousness. Anne had the idea in her head that Wallace might prove a 'steadying influence' on David, but it was clear to Michael that he was there, as usual, to upset apple carts and set pumas among pigeons. The Logans found it difficult to talk to each other about David. Michael wondered if his wife might be in some submerged way envious of the genes David had inherited from Albert Bienenstock. Perhaps she found Ted's worldly cynicism a welcome relief. Perhaps she even welcomed the idea of Ted corrupting David with alcohol or initiating him into Norwich's few sad specimens of harlotry, anything to upset the delicate balance of the qualities in her son that she found so disquieting. Michael considered all these possibilities carefully. To appease her and because it was better to have a man like Ted inside his tent pissing out, than outside pissing in, Michael concealed his misgivings and made a show of being pleased to see the old drunkard at Swafford. He never went so far as to *trust* him; that would be insanity. Instead, he required Podmore to maintain a discreet watch and found out from this that Ted appeared to be in constant postal communication with Jane. Podmore had been quite happy to take it upon himself to do some dusting around the computer currently installed in the Landseer Room and as a result of this zealous housework Michael had discovered, much to his surprise, that the contents of Ted's letters revealed an apparent ignorance of what had been going on as far as Davey was concerned.

Meanwhile, Oliver Mills had invited himself for a few weeks, then Max and Mary Clifford had asked if they might come with their daughter Clara, a girl they never usually took anywhere if they could help it, embarrassed as they were by her unfortunate appearance. Jane's close friend Patricia Hardy was the next to arrive. When Rebecca rang her brother to see if she might too 'pop down for a week or so', Michael began to grow seriously worried. He felt the thing was growing too fast. He knew, in business terms, how hard it was to keep things secret. You cannot cap a volcano. True, the house-party now convened at Swafford constituted none but close, if not trusted, friends, but for how long could such a state of affairs be maintained?

Encouraged by his discovery of Ted's ignorance and innocence in the matter therefore and suddenly acutely aware that a best friend is a best friend, however many times he might lie to you and steal from you, Michael decided to accede to the original request and tell his life story to that old fraud Edward Lennox Wallace. It was, perhaps, the best and clearest way to get Ted up to speed and on-side.

On the second day of their talk, which Michael found he was enjoying immensely, Ted revealing himself to be a surprisingly appreciative listener, the news about Lilac broke and the urgency and importance of their collaboration impressed itself all the more clearly on Michael's mind. There was no *evidence* that David was behind the recovery in Lilac that had the vet scratching his head in astonishment, but there could be absolutely no doubt whatsoever, so far as Michael was concerned, as to the provenance of this miracle, nor, it would seem, was anyone else in the house uncertain. The business of Lilac, coming when it did, destroyed whatever illusion Michael may have had that he was controlling the situation. He broke with all restraint and told Ted everything, not even omitting his differences with Lady Anne in the matter or the details of his sordid involvement in the reading of Ted's letter to Jane. Since the day he had read Uncle Amos's letter from Jerusalem telling him of his father's death, Michael had never placed himself at another's mercy. He did so now.

'There you have it, Tedward. The unvarnished truth. So what do I do? Is Davey's gift meant for the world? Do I roar it from the battlements? Or is it a curse that should be hidden away in shame? Do we call for a priest? A doctor? A shrink? You are the boy's godfather. Advise.'

'Hum,' said Wallace. 'Hah.'

171

'Well?'

'I shall need some time. I have ideas. For the moment I'd recommend you sit tight and do nothing.'

'Do nothing.'

'Often the wisest course. In my case, I must think.'

'Think? Think? What's to think?'

'Well, to be truthful, Michael, a man doesn't like to learn at the age of sixty-six that everything he's always believed in makes no sense.'

'And what have you ever believed in, Edward Wallace?'

'Oh, you know, little things. Little things, like how hard it is to write a poem.'

Seven

12a Onslow Terr.
28th July 1992

Dear Ted,

I think you must be there now. Patricia tells me that you and Uncle Michael have been 'closeted together' for some time.

It's time for me to come down. You can give me the fruits of your conversations with Uncle Michael when I arrive tomorrow, after my final tests. Can you understand now why I have been so excited? I'm so pleased that you have been sharing in this with me.

You can talk to Patricia and Mummy now and let them know what you've been up to. But not a word to anyone outside Swafford, of course.

Look after Davey though. Make sure he keeps up his strength and isn't made to feel isolated or used.

When Davey first told me how he had healed Edward I knew that my decision to come to Swafford had been meant. Was 'miracle' really too strong a word? I don't think so. Surely you can't now either. Tell me this isn't going to change your life, Ted, and I'll call you a liar.

Much, much love

Jane

PS: My most urgent and final 'proclamation' as you like to call them is this: Smile! We are loved. We are loved. Everything is going to be wonderful. Everything shines. Everything is as it could only be and must be.

II

From the diary of Oliver Mills:
29th July 1992, Swafford Hall

Everything has come to a head, dearest Daisy Diary. I write this in tumbling confusion. It's eleven at night and in three hours' time I shall . . . well I don't know what I shall, but it will be the terror of the earth and that's a fact.

I mentioned yesterday that the Hearty Hetties of the household were getting all dismal about some horse, a hunter owned and ridden, as they say on race cards, by Michael himself. The name of the beast, Lilac, besides being camper than a jamboree of Danish scouts in Spandex briefs, betrays the Jenny Gender. Lilac is a big brown mare and the Cox's Orange Pippin of Logan's eye. Yesterday, as I made most meticulous mention, she began to display symptoms of something madly amiss. Vera Vet pronounced that it had all the hallmarks of Ragwort Poisoning. The common ragwort, dread thing, possesses some alkaloid which degenerates the liver: no Auntie Dote is known to man. Horses don't usually eat Rachel Ragwort as she's bitterer than a forgotten poet, but Lilac was grazing in the park at the front of the house last week and might have nibbled away without noticing. Yesterday she was seen to be bleeding from the mouth like Chopin, circling round and round and leaning her head against the wall looking dismal: this means a Dysfunction of the Liver, sure as eggs are oval. Terminal. Incurable. Why horses possess livers I can't for a moment imagine. I've yet to see one with a voddie and tonic. However, I mustn't rattle on, there's lots to write and do before beddies: oh my, is there ever lots to write and do. Dysfunctions of the liver, according to Vera Vet – real name Nigel Ogden, and rather a choice arrangement, as it happens, amber corduroys sheathing the second most provoking bottie in Norfolk – are a guaranteed one-way ticket to Horsy Heaven. Nige would leave Simon and Michael with a day to think what they wanted to do with Lilac and return on the morrow (i.e. today) with a humane killer, should disposal – which Vera Vet frankly recommended, so excitingly harsh, so maddeningly cruel, so thrillingly unsentimental these country people – be the preferred Oprah Option.

Dinner last night, Daisy, was thuswise rather a forlorn affair. Simon, naturally, was all for a bash on the head and a quick sale to the glue factory. Probably would have bought a jar of reconstituted Lilac and used it to mend his wellies too, heartless beast.

I was thinking 'Go on, Davey boy! Lay on with your hands. Don't just sit there . . .' and so I bet were Patricia and Rebecca. Annie was looking daggers at all of us and at Davey especially, so he stayed quiet. If there is such a thing as telepathy then my silent screaming entreaties should have deafened his cute little inner ear. There was a sparkle in that velvet eye and a flush to those nectarine cheeks that bespoke something, I'm sure of that. There could not be a more clearly heaven-sent and angel-scented opportunity to test his powers than the War of Lilac's Liver and he must know it.

Michael was very quiet, as he has been most of the week. He looks worn out, poor lug. He spent the afternoon and early evening closeted with Ted Wallace which, let's face it, would shag out a Jack Russell. I give up with Ted. When I think back to the merry piglet I knew in the Sixties and early Seventies and then look at the mud-encrusted lump that confronts us today I want to weep. He won't let anyone in. The cheap pose of the cantankerous old griffin is bad enough in the talentless journalists and layabouts he associates with, but in Ted, who once had a real helping of that thing called talent, it's heartbreaking. You try and talk to him, try just to bring him out of his private hell and he can't bear it, as if emotional frankness were a distasteful social boo-boo, like saying 'pardon' or fitting a candlewick cover to your loo-lid. All I want to do is see him break down. Whoops, sounds cruel. I mean by it that I just want to hear him say, *once*, 'I know, Oliver. It's awful. I've lost it and I hate it and you must forgive me if I get all choleric and sour. Inside, I'm still the Happy Hippo with a heart. Help me.' Would that be too much? It would transform him, I'm sure it would. But you can't get in. The bolts are drawn.

Aside from anything else his attitude is far from simpatico on the Davey front. I cannot understand why Annie encourages his attentions in that quarter. If anything is guaranteed to break the spell it will be Ted's crapulent can't-impress-*me* scepticism.

All in all, with Ted wearing his worst 'what boring children you are' face, Michael glowering at one end of the table, Annie nervous as a grass-hopper at the other, and the rest of us in varying states of electric tension in between, a pretty glum dinz all round. I shot off to bed early. Cheryl Chest was beating her terrible tattoo and I needed my pills and the soft snog of Sandra Sleep.

A strange waking this morning. I thought at first that Vesta Vision was playing the giddy goat with me. 'This is it,' I moan to myself. 'Next, the tingle down the arms, then the tightness in the throat, finally the big cardiac club that fells me once and for all.'

I stared at the vision helplessly. It was that of a fiendish child, or rather two fiendish children, for it was doubled, like the split-field effects they used to employ to indicate drunkenness in zany Tony Randall comedies. You were supposed, in that tradition, either to clutch your head and groan 'Uh-oh, too many Martinis,' or to gurgle, hiccup and ask the barman for another and another, all on account of how Doris Day doesn't understand you.

I was not drunk, however, and was certain, as I always have been, that Doris Day understands me perfectly. Nothing symptomatic of coronary unpleasantness, just the double demons.

I closed my eyes tight and opened them again. Still the same identical child-beasts. The one on the left spoke.

'He's awake.'

The image on the right giggled and I realised that Mother had been reacting like a hysterical old ninny. It was all simply explained.

'You're the twins,' I manage to croak.

'Yes we certainly are,' says the one on the left.

'Which is which?'

'He's Edward and he's James,' they chirrup simultaneously, which is no help.

'Can't you wear badges with letters on them so we know?' I suggest.

'Ha, ha! We like people not knowing.'

I look at them for a while.

'You're James,' I decide, pointing at the one on the left.

'How do you know?' he says, disappointed.

'Ha, ha! I just knew.'

'No, go on, tell.'

'Well,' I say, 'your breathing isn't as dramatic as Edward's and I happen to know that Edward has asthma.'

They glare at each other with recrimination. James starts to try and imitate Edward's gulping breaths. I know I will always be able to tell them apart though, because now that I look, Edward's chest is notably larger than James's and his shoulders set more upright.

'You had quite a bad turn last year, didn't you?' I ask.

Edward responds with great pride. 'Simon thought I was a sodding goner. Looked very bad he said. Blue as a still-born runt.'

'But somehow you pulled through?'

James and Edward exchange glances. 'Mummy says we're not supposed to talk about it.'

'Never mind,' I say. 'I'm Oliver, by the way.'

'We know that. How do you do?'

'How do you do?' I reply, with matching ceremony.

'Do you want to hear a good joke?' asks James.

'Always want to hear a good joke.'

He clears his throat grandly, as if about to recite 'Gunga Din'.

'Knock knock.'

'Who's there?'

'I done up.'

I pray this isn't going to be one of those tiresome non-jokes that children inflict upon us without understanding them themselves.

'I done up who?'

'Eurgh!!' They scream with delight. 'You done a poo! You done a poo!'

So pleasing to have someone on my level at Swafford at last.

'Well, you must leave me now while I dress. Any idea of the time?'

With the practised ease of synchronised swimmers they each inspect a watch.

'Twenty-five past nine,' they chorus.

'Anyone still at breakfast?'

'Everyone else is round the stables. We're not allowed because the horses make Edward wheeze.'

'The stables?'

'Mr Tubby came round to say that Lilac's ever so better.'

Yippy-dido! I fling on my clothes and streak round to the

178

stable yard. Vera Vet is stepping into his Volvo. Lovat green cords this time, not quite such a good colour for him, it seems to me. Simon, Davey, Michael, Anne, Patricia, Rebecca, Ted and the Cliffords are all there.

'Let me know if there's any change. It's really most . . .' He shakes his brown curls. 'I've seen recovery before, but never so fast.'

We watch his car disappear. Michael turns towards Lilac's kennel or whatever they're called, where Simon stands stroking Lilac herself: she certainly looks in my ignorant estimation as bright of eye and glossy of coat as one could wish. David lurks modestly in the background, tracing patterns in the dust with the point of his shoe. The Cliffords, Rebecca and Patricia are staring at him.

'So what are we all hanging around here for, then?' Michael wants to know. He claps his hands. 'She's a mare, not the Mona bloody Lisa. Let's go inside. Ted, we'll get on, shall we?'

Michael and Ted return to the house. Simon pats Lilac and goes off to talk to Tubby the groom. I take my courage in both hands and snaffle David, much to the boiling rage of the others.

'Well,' I say brightly, 'there's a mercy. I don't have a thing in black. If there'd been a funeral I should have looked horribly festive.'

Annie trolls over. 'Any plans today, Oliver?'

'Well . . .' say I.

'Like to come on the lake again?' Davey suggests, eyes round and lovely.

Annie checks this move.

'Looks like rain,' she says, scanning the cloudless sky. 'There's talk of it anyway. Today or tomorrow. Why not go into town? See a film or something?'

I get the sitch. She wants her boy-child safe in a city, not standing on the lawn laying hands on her guests like Bernadette at a fête.

'Good idea,' I say.

Whatever happens I plan to ask Davey about the horse. Did he press a hand to her flank, pop a crystal in her ear . . . what?

'All right then.' Davey doesn't look too excited, but he's game. It may be my turn. Nothing wrong with Rebecca so far as I can tell, Patricia's in a bate because that Rebak piece

179

jilted her and Clara just needs a squint corrected and her teeth pushed in. I could do that myself with enough follow-through. No question in my mind or, I hope, Davey's: Mother's angina comes first.

Bitch it . . . I'm out of voddie now. I shall steal down for a bottle . . .

. . . Betterness. Much of betterness. No one saw me, full flask of Stolly by my side, now I can concentrate. Where had I got to? Davey and Mother's Day Out. *Much* to tell.

We walked round the corner to where my Saab was quartered.

'What's on?' I asked.

'On?'

'At the cinema, bum-brain.'

'Oh . . .' He kicked a stone. 'Who cares?'

I started in on the questioning as soon as the car had cleared the driveway. 'Now, Davey. Darling. I want to know everything.'

He looked across at me with a smile. An overwhelming urge to run my tongue around and into his lips threatened to unseat my reason. Dreadful. Simply dreadful. I'm an Esau girl, these days. Give me an hairy man, not an smooth, that's my glad cry. Davey has a power though, oh Jessie, does he ever have a power. Mother knew that she was going to have to be very, very careful.

'Look,' I said. 'Time for Trudie Truth and her cheer-leader chums Connie Candour and Fanny Frankness. I know and you know about Jane. I know and you know about Edward and his asthma. And now we have Lilac and her magic liver.'

David breathed out deeply and drummed his heels in the footwell.

'I have to find out, Davey. I'm sick myself, as you know. I must find out what's been going on.'

There was a pause while he wrestled with his . . . I don't know, conscience or pride I suppose. 'I have very hot hands,' he said at last. 'Feel.'

He offered me his hand. It was a warm day so I wouldn't have expected a cold feel from a fish, but Davey's hand . . . cub's honour, Daisy . . . it scorched. Not a wet heat, nothing sweaty, but Lord, hotter by far than 98.4°F, I would swear to that.

'Bloody hell, darling! That's, that's . . .'

'I've always had very hot hands, you see. When I saw Edward lying there I knew that my hand on his chest would help.'

'So that's it, is it? That's all you have to do?'

Davey shook his head. 'No. You see I tried that with Jane when she was here last month and nothing happened.'

'Nothing?'

'Not a thing. The leukaemia is deep in the bones you see, the platelets of the blood are manufactured in the marrow. I knew I would have to . . . have to get right inside her.'

Oh my God, thinks Mother. He fisted her. The little darling fisted her.

'When you say . . . get right inside her?'

Davey hovered on the brink. He's never told anyone, I think to myself. He's on the verge of pouring it all out. All the secrets of his sorcery.

'You see . . . there's . . .'

He dries up.

I take the next turning in the road, down a little lane and towards a wood. Fuck the cinema, we can find out what was on and pretend we saw it.

The sound of the ratchets of the handbrake bring him out of his trance.

'Where are we?' he whispers.

'Let's go for a ramble and you can tell me everything.'

A sign on the fence surrounding the wood says 'Private', but I figure we're unlikely to run into anyone. David springs over like an antelope as I straddle the wire clumsily, snagging a perfectly good pair of Ralph Lauren chinos.

The copse is no more than three or four acres. Beech, ash, oak, brutes like that. Very quiet in that muffled way that woods have.

'You were saying, Davey,' I say as we penetrate the gloom, 'that Jane's leukaemia wasn't sensitive to touch alone?'

'I've always known you see . . . and you swear you'll keep all this to yourself?'

'Swear, swear and double-swear. Cross my heart and hope to go bald.'

'I've always known,' he says, 'that the gift – I call it *the* gift not *my* gift – I've always known that the gift comes from here.'

He stopped, knelt and pressed a palm against the earth.

181

I nodded. David looked like staying on the ground so I got down and sat beside him.

'It's the power of Everything. The word is "channelled". The power of Everything can be channelled through me. But I have to be strong, you see. I have to be . . . pure.'

'You see' was becoming his trademark phrase. He wants me to see. He desperately wants me to see.

'Pure, Davey? What do you mean by pure?'

'I'm very healthy myself, you see. I'm never ill and I never get spots or infections or anything like that. This is because I only eat pure food. Not the meat of animals or plant matter that has been artificially forced. My family used to think I was a crank when I was younger. Most children go through a phase of vegetarianism, but they aren't as committed as I have always been. Now I think they understand. They never talk about it though.'

'So you believe that this diet in some way makes your body purer for this channelling?'

'That's only part of it. You see, there are other kinds of purity. My spirit must be pure. It cannot afford to be contaminated by anything impure.'

'So you think there are spiritual equivalents to meat and non-organic vegetables?'

'You could put it that way, I suppose.' Davey lay back and looked at the roof of the wood.

'A pure mind in a pure body, then?'

'Yes. But you see I am human, aren't I? I mean, I am a human being.'

I was glad he was sure of that. I couldn't have coped if he'd claimed to be an angel.

'And as a human being,' he went on, 'I feel hunger and cold and pain like everyone else. All kinds of hunger.'

Ah. I dimly saw what he was trying to say. He needed assistance, here, I felt. Mother came to the rescue with polished ease.

'You mean that you worry about your other hungers? Fleshly hungers, shall we call them?'

'Mm hm.' He nodded. 'When I first had a wet dream . . . it was only a year ago, which is late, but so what?'

He threw out this embarrassing fact like a challenge, giving me the impression that he had been teased at school for lagging behind in development.

'So what indeed? I didn't mature in that way till I was sixteen,' I lied helpfully.

Davey was not interested in Mother's genital development. 'I caught up anyway,' he mumbled. Mother was aware of this. Mother knows how to inspect a trouser bulge, I hope.

'Anyway,' said Davey, 'I had one of those dreams. When I woke up I didn't know what to do. I knew that I couldn't allow such a terrible waste.'

'Er . . .'

'It's not just my hands, you see. I knew that every part of me could heal. My blood and my . . . my . . .' He broke off, unable to find a word.

'Seed?' I suggested.

'Mm. My seed. So I couldn't afford to waste any of it with cheap . . . you know.'

Wow!

'So, are we perhaps saying, Davey,' I said carefully, as if I were Socrates exploring a premise with Alcibiades, 'that the "way in" to someone's body you talked about earlier might in fact be through your seed?'

'Of course,' said David. 'But just so long as I am pure and only use its grace to heal. I must never use it to give pleasure to myself.'

'So . . .' again the utmost delicacy seemed to be required, '. . . so in Jane's case the only way to help her was . . .'

David sat up and looked straight into my eyes. Hypnotic little baggage.

'We talked about it very fully,' he said. 'Jane understood what I was suggesting. She decided that even if the gift were not to work, at least it would be something . . .'

'At least it would be a kind and helpful experience for you and a comfort and pleasure for her?'

'Exactly!' Davey smiled. 'I wasn't very . . . anyway it doesn't matter, the whole point was to heal Jane, not to "make love" in that sense.'

'And so your seed entered her body.'

'That was on my last night before I had to go back to school. We'd arranged I should visit her bedroom late.'

So intrigued had I been, Daisy, by the prospect of these two cousins at it like knives in the stilly watches that the other, obvious, thought hadn't entered my head.

Lilac . . .

I'd have to tread carefully here.

183

'And we know,' I said, 'how wonderfully that particular . . . er, treatment . . . worked in Jane's case. So when it came to helping Lilac, you no doubt . . . ?'

'The same thing, that's right.'

All inhibition gone now. Said as matter-of-factly as you could wish. Amanda Amazement and Diana Disgust were denied any access to my features as I reacted to this. It was necessary to react as though he were telling me about nothing more remarkable than a trip to the sea-side.

'So that would have been last night,' I said.

'Yes. Last night.'

A wistful grin now, true love recalled.

'I know some people would find it disgusting,' he went on. 'A human and a horse, I mean. But they don't understand the connection between life and nature and grace. It was truly the most natural thing in the world.'

I hastened to agree with him and he lay back again, content to have his secret shared.

Where did all this leave Mother, you'll be wondering, Daisy mine. Well, Mother was heating up like a milk pan in a kiln. If this fifteen-year-old faun with the curling lashes and take-me-now lips was the future of medicine in Great Britain, then a lot of people were going to be queuing up for a cure if ever word got out.

'And Michael and Anne. Your parents. They don't know about this . . .' I searched for a neutral phrase, 'this aspect of your healing?'

He shook his head.

'It would worry them. Daddy's quite proud of me, I think. He values the gift. But Mummy's frightened, I can tell.'

She'd be frightened a whole size bigger if she knew, thought I.

There he lay and there I sat. All that power swimming in his fuzzy little ball-sack: all that fatty deposit lining my aorta and waiting to be cleansed away.

I've always tried to be honest with you, dear Daisy. I told you about the felching episode in the Finsbury Park nightclub. I was manly and frank on the subject of the bondage queen who tried to bite off my nipples in his flat in Hyde Park Gate. I confessed openly that I allowed that gorilla of a policeman in New York to slap my legs with a towel and call me his bitch-pig slave. I can be honest here too, and admit that even if I had not been diagnosed as suffering genuinely from angina pectoris I should have laid claim to it there and then without a moment's thought.

God, it has to be faced, can be astonishingly sweet. When I was a priest, and I'd be the first to admit that I only joined up because I liked the bells-and-smells aspect, the cotters, the thuribles and the sung versicles, I thought God was a capricious prig. Here was I, burning and yearning to serve, and there was the horrid, horrid Bible, never a book that I thought much of, telling me how damned and abominable I was. Couldn't have been pleaseder to hand in my notice and flounce from the chancel never to return.

But – and you know this, Daisy, better than anyone, you who know my inmost heart – there was what we can only call a Void in Mother's life. I've tried my bloody best, I've fought with my tiny fists for the oppressed and the hurt in the world, I've put my talent into things that matter and I've made an effort – unlike Wallace – to live a decent life. I know lots of nasties wouldn't think being pissed on in New York or rimmed behind a bush on Hampstead Heath is decent, but you and I know, Daisy, what decent means.

Now, here was Glenda God giving me the chance to be physically whole in a way that exactly suited the very passion that Big Brenda Bible had always claimed to be unclean. God makes things fit, you have to hand it to Her.

I said to David.

'I'm unwell. Do you think . . . do you think you could help *me?*'

I prayed a little prayer that angina wasn't the kind of affliction that a laying-on of hands could cure.

Davey smiled. 'Of course I can help you, Oliver. It's what I'm here to do.'

A great smarting wave of blood rushed up the nape of my neck. When I spoke, my voice was husky.

'Here? Now?'

David shook his head. 'I don't think so. I'll visit you tonight. That would be better.'

'I'm in the Fuseli Room, slap next to Ted Wallace. I can hear his snoring clearly enough so . . .'

'All right then, you come to my room. You know where it is?'

I nodded, not liking the way such practicalities lent the tryst a squalid air.

We got back in the car, tea-ed at the Scole Inn and

returned to Swafford singing the praises of *Unforgiven,* which I'd seen and in whose details I gave David a good briefing.

Well, Daisy. Here we are. It's a quarter to two. Thank God I never travel without my breath-spray or a spare tube of Man Glide. I'm off to Davey's Den. Wish me luck, my darling.

III

Astonishingly, Mother Mills came down to breakfast after me on Thursday morning. A man takes pride in always being the last one down and I didn't enjoy being beaten.

'Morning, Ted,' Oliver trilled as he came into the dining room.

'You're revoltingly cheerful,' I said, propping the *Telegraph* against the marmalade jar.

'Am I? Am I? Yes, I suppose I am,' he replied with a giggle, practically skipping to the sideboard. 'I could eat a horse. Which, let's face it darling, we all may well have been forced to do had little Lilac not made such an am-az-ing recovery yesterday.'

Hell and turds, I thought. Here we go. 'With the best will in the world, Oliver,' I said with a firm rasp, 'can we please find something to talk about this morning other than bloody miracles?'

'You still can't bear it, can you, baby? The proof that there truly are more things in heaven and earth than your puny, fusty, narrow philosophy ever dreamed of.'

'I wonder if a man in your condition should be stuffing himself with quite so much fried food,' I said, eyeing with revulsion the heaped kidney and sausage that he plonked down on the table next to me.

'Ho-ho!' he said, returning to the sideboard. 'A man in my condition?' He began to fill another plate, flourishing the serving-spoon like a cocktail waitress. 'I'm sure I don't know what you mean by "a man in my condition". What condition?'

I stared up at him, quite unable to hide my dismay. 'Oh, no . . .'

He beamed with what he no doubt considered an inner radiance and I considered a vile smirk.

'Oh yes. Oh yessy-yes-yes.'

'Don't tell me *you've* had the bloody laying-on-of-hands treatment as well?'

'I'm whole, Ted. As cured as this bacon and twice as hot and sizzling.'

'Well,' I gave him a sour look as he sat down beside me with a wince, 'the little Miracle Worker doesn't seem to have had the kindness to heal *all* your infirmities, does he?'

'Meaning?'

'You've got the piles that afflict us all, I note.'

'Oh *those*,' he said, with a smile, 'they'll pass in time no doubt.'

'Humph. I'd be more inclined to trust good old Preparation H myself.'

He waded in on his gargantuan breakfast. Despite my irritation I found myself impressed by the confidence of his demeanour and the unquestionably genuine sparkle in his eye.

'Be serious, Oliver,' I said. 'Do you honestly believe that you have been cured? Completely cured?'

'I've thrown away my pills, Ted. I feel . . . oh, it's impossible to put into words how I feel. Davey is a gift from God. A gift from Glenda herself.'

'And his touch . . . did you feel this warmth that everyone talks about?'

'Darling,' said Oliver, a forkful of kidney hovering in front of his mouth, 'it is simply the hottest thing I have ever felt in my life. It burns like a soldering iron. My word, how it burns. Right inside the deepest deeps it burns.'

I knew now that I had to do that thing that I hate most to do. I had to think. I had to sit, close my eyes, press my hands to my ears and analyse, like a chess-player or a code-breaker. The most dreaded activity a man can undertake. I hadn't done it since last I wrote a decent poem.

I decided that the Villa Rotunda would make the ideal cogitarium, but that it would be madness to go there without fortification. I left Oliver to swim in the riotous grease of his breakfast and his self-satisfaction and made my way to the library.

Morning drinking times are matters of great debate. The threshold moves inexorably the more alcohol becomes a habit. I can remember a time when I thought it was impossible to take a glug of anything stronger than tomato juice before twelve o'clock. Twelve o'clock became half past eleven, became eleven, became half ten, became ten and so on. This was before the great puritan backlash of course which has made drinking a private vice never to be shown the light at lunch-times. Alcohol is the great secret of our age. If the public knew, if they had the remotest idea of the amount of drinking done by our politicians and leaders, they would be shocked to their boxers. Fortunately, journalists, as is better known, are inebriates too, so they have an interest in keeping a lid on things. The number of Members of Parliament who aren't what doctors would call a functional alcoholic is astoundingly small. Alan Beith is a teetotaller, I seem to remember, and Tony Benn gets by on tea and pipe-tobacco; they are the only dry parliamentarians I can think of for the moment. Any others are doubtless abstemious because they have been told by their doctors that one more smell of brandy would kill them. I've seen Chancellors and Prime Ministers pissed as rats, judges too and news-readers and chairmen of transnational giants. A well-known television political commentator told me at the Harpo once that the war in Bosnia, from which he had just returned, was run exclusively on alcohol. Skirmishes and strategies are entirely ordered according to supplies of slivovitz and vodka.

Alcohol is the prime determining factor of human history: the dethronement of British Prime Ministers, civil strife in Russia and the ruin of whole financial structures can be traced back to the glass. We are led to believe that it is only football hooligans who can't handle it; the fact is that it's too big an issue even to think of confronting. Thank God. For, having said all that, we get by on it far better than we manage without. Total abstainers make rotten leaders of men and incompetent husbands, lovers and fathers. Drunkards hiccup, belch, fart, vomit and stain the front of their trousers with piss. Puritans never reveal any of their functions, and it's a short step from denying the world access to your own base physicality to denying others the right to any base physicality of their own.

Special pleading on my part, no doubt. Perhaps we hear once more the light footfall of Pudoria, Goddess of Guilt. I think, as much as anything, that I had become annoyed with myself for taking such a noticeable drop in drinking since I had arrived at Swafford. Not annoyed with myself, more infuriated by the kindly approval of everyone else.

'Ted, you look so well!'

'This seems to have been something of a rest cure for you, Ted.'

'Wendy Whisky is becoming offended by your inattentions, dear.'

That kind of junk. It took a considerable effort to remember to have an ostentatious drink from time to time, merely in order to stop them from strewing rose-petals in my path and chalking up another cure to Davey.

I headed for the library therefore to see if I couldn't push a couple down my throat before giving myself over to thought.

I believed I had the place to myself, but a snivel from a deep wing-chair in the corner told me that I had female company.

'You all right, Patricia?' I said, coming up behind her. Should have coughed my approach, I suppose, for I gave her one hell of a turn.

'Please, Ted! You shouldn't sneak up like that.'

She had been crying steadily for some time.

'Very sorry,' I said. 'Everything all right?'

'Well, what does it look like, you fat idiot?'

'Contrary to popular belief,' I said, 'it only makes it worse to take it out on someone else. I don't think you'll find insulting me very helpful.'

'Is that your attempt at sympathy?'

'It's practicality, which is kinder than sympathy.'

She wiped her nose. 'Well I certainly don't need a cross between G. K. Chesterton and a fucking calendar motto.'

'You still thinking of that Martin Rebak?' He was the underling of Michael's who had ditched Patricia.

She nodded. 'Got a letter from him this morning. I thought perhaps he might have tired of his new infatuation. He's just married her.'

'Then clearly he has tired of her,' I said.

'Oh, give it a rest, Ted.'

'Well, what do you want me to say? That he is not worth your tears? That you'll get over it? That it's always darkest just before the dawn and that time heals all wounds?'

'I need David, that's what I need.'

'And what do you think he can give you?'

'Hope,' she said. 'A sense of worth.'

There you have the modern Briton. It drives me to a frothing frenzy when politicians return from inner cities saying, 'What the people of this town need is Hope,' as if we could all respond with a glad cry of 'No sooner said than done, old sport,' as we gather up a handful of Hope from the sideboard, stuff it into a Jiffy-bag and send it off to Liverpool 8 by the First Class post. What these bleeding hearts mean is Money, but they're too greasy to say so. Hope may spring eternal in the human breast, but you can't suck it off another's tits, it has to lactate in your own. Not the kind of message to give a girl in Patricia's state, I supposed. As for a sense of worth . . .

'The best way to mend your spirits,' I offered instead, 'is to do something for someone else.'

'Meaning?' she asked coldly.

'Meaning, why not do me a favour?'

'Such as?'

'Such as, when this strange little holiday is over and we're back in London, why not oblige me by allowing yourself to be taken out to dinner? Le Caprice is an olive-stone's throw from my flat. We could eat a good dinner and then you could let me lie you on a litter and lick you like a lolly.'

She stared at me. 'I'm young enough to be your daughter.'

'I'm not fussy.'

'This is your idea of grief therapy is it, Ted? Coming on like a randy goat?'

'I'll leave you to think it over. My evenings get pretty booked up, so you'll have to be quick.'

'You're serious, aren't you?' she said, stopping me with a hand, which I took in mine.

'I'm a fat old man, Patricia. It's hard enough to find women of my own age who aren't prostitutes, but a young thing like you . . . well it would be a rare treat. Possibly my last ever. Thighs unpitted by cellulite, breasts that stand up like begging dogs. How often do you think I am granted such pleasures these days?'

'And what makes you think I would consent to being slobbered over by you?' she asked, withdrawing her hand.

'Your innate kindness,' I said, going over to pour myself a large glass of sherry. 'The knowledge that you would be making me quite cretinously happy.'

'It's a hell of a thing to ask.'

'Ha ha!' I said triumphantly. 'And just why is it such a hell of a thing to ask?'

'What do you mean?'

'You said that it was a hell of a thing to ask. Why should you think that?'

'Well, for your information, my body is not something I offer around like a tray of canapés.'

'And why not?'

'Why not? Why not? Because I happen to set some store by it.'

'So,' I trumpeted, 'why do you need Davey to give you a sense of worth if you already have one?'

'Oh, for heaven's sake. Of all the cheap . . .'

191

'You've made it extremely plain that my offer of love and companionship is a far lower offer than you consider you have the right to expect. You value your body and your favours far above mine.'

'There's a big difference between valuing my body and valuing myself. You didn't offer me love and companionship, you asked me to lie out and be licked.'

'Which is a man's clumsy way of asking for love, as well you must know. If I had said that you were the most beautiful woman I had laid eyes on for years and that I most desperately wanted you near me, you'd think I was taking pity on you. Thursdays are pretty good for me,' I said and buggered off, leaving her to stew.

I headed for the Villa Rotunda, notebook and pencil in one hand, sherry-glass in the other. Clouds were gathering on the sky-line and the long-promised bad weather looked to be approaching at last. Clouds boiled in me too and rumbles of thunder sounded in my head.

It was dark and cool inside the summerhouse. I sat on the wooden box of croquet mallets and fired up a Rothie. The last two days, I make no bones about it, had left me feeling bewildered and isolated. On the first page of the notebook I began to write down a list of the contradictions that were driving such hard nails into my mind.

They say writing lists is anal, the mark of an 'anal retentive'. I am almost certain no one who uses that moronic phrase has the least idea what it means. The critic Edward Wilson once described Charles Dickens as an 'anal dandy'. I don't suppose he knew what the fuck he was talking about either. Listing things, as I do with words when preparing a poem for instance, seems to me to be a far cry from a compulsion to store objects in my bottom. Only the other day Oliver and I had been admiring the new Swafford Hall writing-paper that Michael had ordered from Smythson's in Bond Street and which Podmore had distributed on bureaux and tables in the bedrooms, book rooms and drawing rooms of the house.

'Ooh, I just think stationery is so delightfully anal!' he had squeaked. Oliver that is, not Podmore.

'Why *anal?*' I had asked testily. 'Why not renal or cranial or pulmonary or nasal or testicular? I mean, what on earth has it got to do with arses? It makes no sense.'

'Don't be difficult, dear. Everyone knows that stationery is anal. It's an established fact.'

We go through phases in infancy of wanting to lodge things either in our mouths or in our bottoms, we are told. We develop into orally or anally retentive types. As a smoker, drinker, guzzler and biter of biro ends, I might be considered oral. I can understand that: the above-stated itemries are all taken by mouth. Apparently, however, as a drawer-up of lists and a lover of good-quality paper, I am also anal. Does that make sense? Of course not. What possible use do such categorisations have, beyond providing people like Oliver with an opportunity to make flip dinner-party remarks?

Anal, my arse. I like my lists. This particular list was very important. Compiling a list for me is like laying out a formal garden in the rubbishy wilderness of my mind. Anal. Pah.

I chewed the end of the pencil, orally retaining several cedar-wood splinters, and then I began to write.

1. Edward, Jane, Lilac and now, possibly, Oliver have apparently been cured by David's placing his hands upon them.

2. A hot hand placed on a human body is, surely, no different to a hot compress, a hot flannel or, come to that, a hot buttered tea-cake placed on a human body. If heat alone could treat cancer and asthma and heart disease, then the medical world would have told us about it.

3. Therefore David's hands are transmitting some power other than heat.

4. My understanding is that electricity, magnetism and gravity are the only physical fields of force in the universe. A molecule or an atom, or whatever they are called, cannot be moved by any other power. Well, there are a couple of others, but they only exist on paper.

5. The only other force worth considering, I have always held, is the creative force in man, such as might write a poem or right a wrong.

6. There is such a thing as the power of suggestion, however. One human mind is capable of being hypnotised

or persuaded by another. We have faith, we have Hitler, we have advertising. But faith *healing*? Come off it. Pain may be mental illusion, but tumours and clotted arteries are not. Besides, there's the vet and, it would seem, Jane's doctors.

7. If all this is true: if David is capable of changing molecular structure – for this is what we are discussing – then the world should know about it.

8. I am David's godfather. What do I think of the morality of allowing him to be (a) splashed all over the newspapers, (b) pushed back and forth between scientists and fanatics determined either to prove him a fraud or to overblow his gifts?

9. What do I mean 'gifts'? Gifts are things that are given. That necessitates a giver. Why should God waste his time giving the power to heal? What happened to free will and the duty of man to get on with life without the impertinent interference of his creator? And what about the millions who will die every year never having been given a chance to be healed by David? Children in Africa with eaten-away faces? Paraplegics in Peru? Lepers in Libya? The blind in Bali and the deaf in Delhi? It's senseless, senseless, absolutely senseless. Even the flawed and spiteful God we have wouldn't be cruel enough to give his children just a handful of healers to go around four billion.

10. And if God did give us a healer he'd be damned sure that the one chosen would do more than heal. They'd preach abstinence and salvation and hellfire or some such damned thing to go along with it. Whereas all David does is witter on about half-arsed namby-pamby Green crap and dribble a load of maundering pantheistic bollocks about Nature and Purity.

11. There again. Music is a gift. Painting is a gift. Even poetry is a gift. Palpable talents and charisms enough exist which improve man's fate on earth, why not one of healing? It may be that the giver is not God, but genetics and evolution. After all, there is evidence that

David's power is congenital, inherited indeed, as are the gifts of many musicians.

12. But. But, but, but. To be a great musician the gift alone is not enough. You must live amongst men and suffer and understand. Above all you must WORK. Nothing of any value that I've ever seen man achieve on this earth has ever been accomplished without work.

13. Oh yeah? Why are you fighting it so hard, Ted? What's your problem? Face the evidence of your own eyes.

14. Evidence of my eyes? What have I actually seen?

15. Oh, come on. Evidence of your own ears, then.

16. Hearsay.

17. It's 'hearsay' to you that Mexico exists. Do you really doubt it?

18. All right. All right. But that still leaves the problem of David. I swore an oath at the font. His father, my friend, looks to me for guidance. For once in his life he doesn't know what to do. I can help.

19. That's right, you can help. You can . . .

I broke off. The sound of voices was approaching. Two people, deep in conversation. They stopped under the open window of the Villa, the rear window that gave out on to the lake.

'This, I think, is a quiet spot.' The voice of Max Clifford.

'Very quiet.' The voice of Davey.

I locked myself into a kind of gaping immobility, like an uncoordinated child playing musical statues. They were only yards from where I sat and the smallest sound from inside the summerhouse would be as audible to them as their speech was to me.

'Now then. I'll get right down to it, David. I've seen Oliver this morning.'

No reply.

'He wouldn't say what had happened, but it's clear that something has. Something of a similar nature to the

195

extraordinary recovery that Mary and I witnessed in your cousin Jane earlier this year.'

'It's quite true. Oliver's heart is mended now.'

Clifford gave an admiring laugh.

'Amazing. Quite amazing.'

'It's not really amazing, you know. Not to me.'

'I suppose these activities take something out of you?'

'Yes. As a matter of fact they do take something out of me.'

'It's merely . . . I feel rather absurd making this request. I appreciate it's not like asking someone to lend you a book or to baby-sit for the evening.'

'You can ask me anything you like, Max.'

'My daughter Clara has . . . certain things wrong with her.'

'I'm sure I can help her, Max.'

'She's not *ill* exactly, but she is, well, odd. She's so awkward and clumsy and . . .'

'And unhappy.'

'Very difficult to take her out anywhere. People stare, you know. The strabismus and the buck-teeth are bad enough. But she makes absolutely no effort to be graceful or . . .'

'Yes, I know. I would be very happy to see her and do what I can.'

'I don't know exactly what your technique is. If Mary and I could help in any way?'

'Well, the thing is, Max. You have to trust me, you see. I would rather that you weren't present when I am with her.'

'Of course, of course. Whatever you say. But you are fully up to strength? I mean, you're not an especially strong boy by the looks of you. We don't want to exhaust you.'

'I am quite strong really. My spirit is very quickly replenished. So long as I don't waste it.'

'Splendid.'

They fell into a silence. I stretched a cramped leg out as noiselessly as I could. Perhaps they had walked away. I contemplated rising and going over to the window to peep down. Then I heard the sound of a pebble splashing into the lake and decided that they were still there. Another couple of pebbles were thrown before David spoke.

'What have you said to Clara about me?'

'Well, we did mention that it was a possibility that you would like to help her.'

'And how does she feel about that?'

'Clara is fourteen years old and will do as she is told,' Max said sharply. He must have realised how callous this sounded, for he quickly added, 'Not that she *needs* to be told, I should say. No, she's very keen. Her squint and her teeth and her bloody uncoordinated gawking. They are a great trial to her. To all of us.'

'Where is she now?'

'With Simon somewhere, according to her mother. Mucking around in the stables. Mucking *out* in the stables, more likely. Would you like me to send her to you?'

'This afternoon if that would be all right. After lunch.'

'Yes. Yes, you should eat first, I expect. Er, where exactly will you do it?'

'I'm not sure, Max. Perhaps we might go for a walk. But it really has to be private. We must be absolutely alone.'

'As you say, as you say . . . I'm very grateful. Mary and I are both very . . .'

Max's voice faded and I was left, once more, to myself.

I turned back to my notebook and completed, for the time being, my list.

20. I may have the evidence of my own eyes soon. Best, I think, to suspend judgement until then.

I looked in on Michael before lunch. He was dictating a letter. Smoother and more assured he looked than when last we had talked. His business face, I supposed. He appeared to be pleased to see me. There again, he had appeared to be pleased to see me the week before when, as I now knew, he had in fact been excessively vexed by my presence. For all I know, no one in the world has ever been pleased to see me, but some have been better at hiding it than others.

'Ahoy, Tedward! And how goes the morning?'

'Just wanted a word, Michael.'

'Thank you, Valerie. I'll talk to Mr Wallace now.'

'Yes, Lord Logan.'

Valerie slipped out, closing the door behind her.

'So, what do you hear, what do you say?'

I sat down in the chair opposite the desk. 'You've heard about Oliver?'

Michael sighed and drummed his fingers against the side of his head.

'Annie was in here. Very upset. She said she had told Davey yesterday not to see anyone without telling her first. She is furious that he disobeyed. "Of course he disobeyed!" I said to her. "If my Uncles had told me, when I was his age, 'Don't do any more work on the shop, Michael. Sit and listen to the wireless or read a book, but no more thinking about business and customers and money,' do you think I would have taken any notice? Never on your life." But Annie was not satisfied.'

Michael sighed again and unzipped a fresh cigar. 'So tell me, Tedward, what do you think now?'

'What do I think? I don't know. However . . .' I smiled a conspiratorial smile, 'I may know later today.'

He frowned. 'Later today? So what happens later today?'

'Michael, do you mind if I don't tell you? I won't let anything occur which shouldn't occur, you have my word.'

'And do I have your word that your word is worth anything?'

'I like to think it's worth at least the air it's spoken with.'

Logan grunted his assent.

'You're going to talk to Davey, then?' he asked.

'Perhaps,' I said. 'I'll let you know this evening.'

'Jane will be here by then. She comes down this afternoon.'

'Yes, I know,' I said. 'We shall have a full house: queens and knaves.'

Logan rose and we repaired for a pre-lunch sip in the library, where Oliver's friskiness and excessive show of good health quite put me off my schooner of fino.

IV

Meals at Swafford gather in formality during the day. This is common in the grander houses of the kingdom. I expect Lévi-Strauss or Margaret Mead, were they living, could explain this phenomenon by stripping away the lacquer of smart country-house tradition to reveal a solid anthropological teak of tribal taboo beneath – as it is we shall no doubt have to look to arse-witted Sunday-paper style-writers for explanation. Breakfast, to the delight of my traditionalist self, is, as it should be, a more or less servantless affair, Podmore only coming in with fresh coffee and toast when summoned by screams or bells. The sideboard is topped with a row of gleaming tureenery containing, in addition to the bacon, eggs, sausages, mush-rooms and wrinkly fried tomatoes we might expect, the three great K's of English breakfast lore – Kedgeree, Kippers and Kidneys (keenly devilled); the length of the dining-table is rhythmically dotted with dishes of marmalade, with pots of coffee and tea, with silver toast-racks and jugs slopping to their crystal brims with the juice of orange, tomato and grapefruit. A Hepplewhite satinwood side table is matutinally spread by Podmore into a fan of national and local newspapers. Periodic-als are provided too, *The Spectator*, *Private Eye*, *The Oldie*, *Country Life*, *The Field*, *Norfolk Fair*, *The Illustrated London News*, *The Economist*, *Investors Chronicle* and *Beano* for the twins. It is my custom, as I have said, to contrive to come down last and have the room to myself. I stay there for an hour or so, until the first easings of mid-morning flatulence push me to the lavatory. If St Peter were to ask in what time or place I should like eternally to be suspended for the infinite length of my heavenly career, I could certainly choose half past ten on a summer's morning in the dining room of Swafford Hall.

Dinner, when guests are invited from outside, is a formal full-fig feast. The ladies slip into off-the-shoulder frocks and the staff into over-the-shoulder modes of food dispensal – white gloves, fork-and-spoon service, effulgent napkins wrapped about the bottle necks. Wine and conversation flow, cheeks and candles glow. Even when the house interns alone are present, a certain elegance of protocol is maintained. The women are taken in draped on the arms of their men at eight and shag off *en masse* for coffee in the drawing room at elevenish, leaving the hairy element to crack nuts and jokes over the port. This much-maligned procedure, Simon told me the other day, originated in Victorian days when women were anxious to keep from their husbands, brothers and sons the alarming news that they possessed bladders and urinary tracts. Whatever its basis, I find the custom highly satisfactory. Anne has the delightful habit of calling us into the drawing room, when she believes the sexes have been segregated for long enough, by performing gentle Schumann sonatas on the piano. One loves to play at being civilised, but one does need rich friends to meet the rising costs of such an exercise. Civilisation, after all, is not an attitude of mind, it is an attribute of wealth. Dinners at Swafford, to my mind, are very nearly as fine as breakfasts.

Luncheon lies between these two in ceremony as in chronology. The library serves as the muster station and pre-prandial lapping-pool of choice; thence we are gonged to the dining room for solids. Podmore brings in the dishes and dumps them at Anne's end for her to dole out down the table. It is the quickest meal, puddings are often sent back untouched, the imbibal of anything stronger than iced water is uncommon and conversation tends to the stilted. The British are uneasy about domestic weekday lunches; the work ethic is in us ingrained so deep that even the leisured classes like to behave as though midday eating is a tiresome intrusion on a life of toil and honest diligence.

As we made our way into the dining room on this day, my appetite already ruined by Oliver's rude health and Anne's distraught demeanour, the atmosphere within doors crackled with the same kind of tension as prevailed without. It is a mark, I have often noticed, of God's cheap sense of literary cliché that he so often chooses to provide climatic conditions that reflect our inmost moods. The day of Jane's christening, for instance, which I think of as the Day of Rebecca's Curse, was a streaming, soaking day, to match the sodden weeping that attended it. The weather that accompanied the scene of Helen's departure from my house and life with a screaming Roman and a coldly sniffing Leonora was bone-chillingly frosty, imparting an iced numbness that exactly suited my mood. And the day, if we cast our minds back all those pages ago, that saw my expulsion from the *Sunday Shite* was clear and warm and free and bright. Today's bristling electric menace, while overdone like all God's effects, could not be said to be inappropriate.

Michael was silent, Anne brittly garrulous. I watched Clara, who in turn cast quick covert glances towards a flushed and expectant David. Simon was, rarely for him, moody and unresponsive. Max contented himself with suave responses to Anne's chatter. Patricia, Rebecca and Oliver wittered about London things. The twins, who might have brought some zest to the table, ate in the nursery. Mary Clifford said nothing, until towards the end of dinner when she tried to press pudding on a reluctant Clara.

'You really should, dear.'

'I'm not very hungry, Mummy.'

'No, but I think a slice of treacle-pie would be a good idea. Don't you, Davey?'

This megalithically foolish remark caused Max to bite his lower lip and Oliver to raise his eyebrows. Davey was about to reply when Simon butted in.

'It's pretty good pie actually, Clara. If you don't finish yours I'll have it, don't you worry.'

'Simon is one of those who can gorge himself like a pig and not have an ounce of flesh to show for it,' said Anne, cutting Clara a slice. 'He's already had three helpings.'

'It's two actually, Mum,' said Simon sending his plate along for the third. 'Got to keep my strength up, we're moving the pigs out to the fields to glean this afternoon. Do you want to come along, Clara?'

Clara looked helplessly at Simon, her eyes big and watery under their thick lenses.

'Clara and I thought we might go for a walk, Simon,' Max said. 'When you say "glean",' he went on effortlessly, 'do you mean they actually get by foraging for themselves, or do you supplement their diets? I've always wanted to know.'

While Simon explained I watched Clara turn with lowered head back to her bowl and poke at her pie in misery. I fancied, this forlorn moment aside, that in fact she looked a little better than she had on arrival at Swafford the previous week. Nature, it seemed to me, was sure to right Clara's defects in time without Davey's mystical interference. Look at American girls. At the age of fourteen they look as if they're recovering from a traffic accident: their mouths are caged with wire, their legs and backs strain in corrective stockings and splints, their skin is lumpy from acne, their upper lips fuzz with down, their sad little bras are stuffed with Kleenex and their eyes slither independently in all directions but forwards. Yet by the time they reach eighteen they have become almost too beautiful to bear, with teeth like indigestion tablets, eyes to dive into, skin you want to lick all over, fresh boobs and postures new. No armpit hair, however, which I believe to be a calamitous error. Have you ever let honey-suckle live up to its name? Ever drained its honey? When you take the flower and pull the stamen through, a delicate shining drop of nectar swells up at its head. A bead of sweat bulging at the tip of a woman's axillary hair is as beautiful. Your true connoisseur of women delights in the great meaty reek of the female essence, not the sterile lemon top-notes of deodorants and creams. The French understand this, about the only thing they do understand – apart from French of course. Think of those giddy Baudelairean *amants* burying their heads in comedy actresses' sweat-soaked how-dare-yous. Haaa . . .

Please excuse me. We return to the luncheon.

Michael stood. 'You'll forgive my leaving,' he said. 'I have work to do this afternoon. But I trust we'll all be here at four to welcome Janie when she arrives?'

Nods all round.

I left as soon as possible to commence my stake-out in secrecy. It was a difficult undertaking to reach the Villa Rotunda without being seen from the house. A number of the guests, I knew, would be in the drawing room that overlooked the South Lawn at the back of which the villa stood. I had, therefore, to skirt the entire lawn in a wide loop and achieve the summerhouse from the rear. This necessitated the nego- tiation of much thick vegetation. The bushes and shrubs had set themselves the happy afternoon task, it soon came to my notice, of attempting to knock from my hand, by the use of cunningly upthrust roots and protruding twigs, the cup of coffee I had foolishly decided to take with me on the journey. By the time I had grunted myself through the rear window of the Villa there was no more than an inch of coffee remaining, much supplemented by garden detritus. An inch of after-lunch- eon coffee, I reflected, is better than a centimetre and I drank it gratefully down, leaf-fragments, thunder-flies, twig-bark and all. None the less, the spillage of so much was shortly to cause me a moment of panic, as I was to discover.

Settling cosily on the croquet trunk once more, I watched a spider swing from the ceiling and pondered, like Robert the

Bruce before me, on the problem of effort. To stand up takes effort, to move about takes effort: simply to be still, to do no more than endure, even that takes effort. Effort is expended strength. Strength comes from food. We carry on because we eat. But *creative* effort? How is that expense replenished? Where does creative energy *come from*? From food also? Then how can it be that a poet, say, who once could write, can suddenly write no more? Not, surely, because he has stopped eating spinach? David thinks he has a creative energy that comes from . . . from God knows what. From nature, from some intricate connecting web, a sustaining field of force such as they talk about in that absurd science-fiction story with Alec Guinness, the one that Roman amazed me by calling an 'old' film . . . may the force be with you . . . if that was an old film to Roman – *Star Trek*, was it called? Something like that – then what was *Duck Soup*? . . .

'It's burning! It's burning!'

An excited voice outside the window. I leapt to my feet. The coffee cup fell from my lap and smashed on the floor.

Not David's voice. Nor Clara's.

I went to the window and looked out.

There below me were the twins, squatting on the pathway that ran between the rear of the Villa Rotunda and the edge of the lake. One of them had a magnifying-glass in his hand, the other was holding a snail. A sizzle of steam rose from a small hole in the snail's shell.

'Hoi!' I shouted.

They turned in guilty alarm and then smiled when they saw who it was.

'Hello, Uncle Ted.'

'We're experimenting.'

'Well, you shouldn't experiment here,' I said.

The twin holding the magnifying-glass frowned.

'Why not?'

'Because . . .' I sought for a reason. 'Suppose your brother David were to see you. You know what he thinks of cruelty to animals.'

'That's all right.'

'Davey's in the woods somewhere.'

'He went with Clara.'

'Ages ago.'

Ages ago? *Ages* ago? I looked at my watch. Ten past three.

Damn you, Ted, you fat buffalo. Damn you, you great

wallowing tit. You've slept for forty minutes. If you'd had a whole, full cup of strong coffee, perhaps . . .

I hurled myself down the front steps of the Villa and round to the twins.

'Where?'

'Where what?'

'Davey and Clara. Where in the woods did they go?'

They shrugged.

'*We* don't know.'

They pointed across the lake.

'Somewhere.'

'Shall we go and hide and seek them, do you think?'

'No, no. You stay here. I just wanted to . . . catch up with them. Have a word.'

'Right ho.'

'We'll stay here.'

'You bet. We'll be here.'

'Right here.'

'Just exactly here.'

I marched off around the lake, cursing my lazy old body. It was entirely my point. Energy. Effort. Where does it go?

I stamped through the damp pong of the lake's edge, my feet tearing up the tangle of glasswort, marshwort, mallows and kingcups beneath. Ahead lay the small woodland copse where Davey and I had walked on our first day. It was more humid now, the air bursting with vapour and, above, the clouds thickening to the colour of cuttlefish ink.

I stood in this spinney and listened. Larks, chaffinches, thrushes and flies squeaked, chirruped, throstled and buzzed. Small pockets of midge eddied and bounced in the gloomier thickets. I walked towards the darkest, densest part of the copse as quietly as a heavy man can when the ground beneath him is carpeted with dried twig and crackling bark.

Somewhere ahead of me I heard David's voice, very low and husky. Bending double, I edged towards the sound, lifting each foot high off the ground and placing it down with all the strained delicacy I could manage. The effort caused me to pant and blow like a steam-roller. Sweat gathered in my eyebrows.

'So you see, the spirit must find a way in,' I heard David's voice explain.

'Spirit like air?' Clara asked.

I came to a stop behind a briar bush and peeped through. In a small clearing, less than the length of a long cocktail bar away from my cover, I could see Clara and David, seated on the ground. Clara was sideways on to me but I could see David's face clearly. He was wearing charcoal-coloured jeans and a white T-shirt. His knees were drawn up a little and he had laid a hand on Clara's shoulder. I breathed as quietly as I could.

'No, not like air, exactly. You must know about men's spirit. The spirit that makes life.'

Clara giggled. 'What, you mean like . . . *sperm*?'

A bead of sweat rolled down and stung my eyes. The light was fading and the air was charged enough to make the skin prickle.

'It isn't a joke, Clara. If this spirit is very pure and very holy, it can make the person receiving it very holy and very pure too.'

Clara stared at him. 'You aren't going to . . .'

I swallowed. This was not what I had been expecting. Not what I had been expecting at all.

'I've been thinking. You see, the problems you would like me to help you with are all up here.'

David traced his fingers around her face.

'Usually, you see, I would implant the spirit deep within you . . .'

I suddenly thought about Oliver's piles at breakfast and wanted to choke. A warm fat drop fell on my head with a slap. Blast, I thought. Some fucking wood-pigeon. Another drop landed on my arm. Rain.

'. . . but I think what would be best in your case,' David continued, 'would be for the spirit to be introduced here.'

He ran a thumb between Clara's lips.

'You mean I'd have to *drink* it?'

David sighed. It was apparent to me that he was not finding the naïveté of Clara's response at all sympathetic.

'Your father explained, didn't he? He told you that I have the power to help people. He told you to trust me and to do what I said, didn't he?'

Clara nodded. She did not appear to be happy.

'The way to take in the spirit is for me to suckle you, as a loving mother might suckle her young.'

Clara did not reply.

'You must think of how the pure living spirit will enter you and make you whole. It will heal your eyes and your teeth. It will fill you with power and beauty.'

205

'What will it taste like?'

Splendid child. I found myself taking to her very much. Poetry lies in practical detail.

'It will taste of everything you love. Of honey and sweet warm milk.'

'Aniseed?'

'If you like aniseed it will taste of aniseed.'

'I *hate* aniseed.'

'Well then, it won't taste of aniseed. What is your favourite flavour?'

'Worcester sauce.'

'Mm . . .' David paused. I could imagine him wondering how much conviction it would carry if he claimed that his pure holy river of spirit would indeed taste of Worcester sauce. 'Your mind will create whatever flavour it desires,' was the best he could come up with.

'Will it *look* like Worcester sauce, then?'

'Never mind how it will look!' David was becoming exasperated.

'It's starting to rain, now.'

'The rain is good. It's clean and pure and quite warm.'

I edged further forward for shelter in the bush; the bramble around me combing my hair with violent scratches.

David had mastered his irritation and spoke now in a calm hypnotic coo.

'Clara. You have been told to trust me and you trust me. You have been told I will help and I will help. I will lie back like this, all right? Now, I'm going to take your hand and put it here, just on my jeans like this.'

'What's that?'

'You know what that is. You must know, surely? Just feel it for a moment. Feel how warm and firm it is. It is where the spirit comes from. That's right.'

Clara's body obscured my view of the details of this woodland scene. I could see David's face looking up to the trees and his toes curling in their shoes. I could see Clara's shoulders and the back of her arm. A rumble of thunder sounded far away and the rain began to spank the leaves.

'Now,' he said. 'Just undo me here and . . . that's it. Gently though.'

'Is this what they all look like?'

'Surely you've seen one before?'

206

'A girl at school showed me a magazine. It didn't have this loose skin though.'

'OW! CAREFUL!'

'What have I done? What have I done?'

'No, no. It's all right. But you must be more gentle. It's extremely sensitive, you see. So, nice and easy.'

'It's very hot.'

'Yes, that's right. It is. Very hot. The heat comes from the spirit that is going to make you well and whole. Now, I want you to bring your head down.'

'I don't like to . . .'

'Clara . . . it's very simple.'

'But that's where you do . . .'

'What?'

'That's where you do pee-pees.'

'Clara, please! It is completely clean. So clean that it can purify your whole body. You have to trust me. What would your father say if I told him you had failed to trust me?'

'All right, then . . .'

Through the riot of brambles I saw her head dip down and David's right hand press against the nape of her neck.

'Easily,' said David. I imagine he was grateful that the girl's teeth protruded outwards, not in.

'Wimbledon,' she replied, or so it sounded to my ears. It may be that she said something else. I supposed that any word spoken under those circumstances would come out as Wimbledon.

'Birmingham!' she said, proving me wrong.

'Drain the spirit,' said David, the downward-facing palm of his free hand clutching and releasing the litter of the spinney floor. The rain was falling fast now, bouncing from a tree-stump beside his head. 'Yes. Don't stop. Keep going. Yes. At any moment . . . at any moment you will feel the spirit . . .'

Any moment? Christ the young are extraordinary. I would have had to lie there for half an hour just to warm myself up.

'Yes . . . yes . . . yes . . . *yes!*' David's voice rose into song. But suddenly, with a violence more powerful than that of the thunder rolling in the distance, a deep voice bellowed from out of the darkness behind them.

'NO!! NO!! LET HER GO!!'

Four things happened at once.

Ted Wallace fell forward into the bramble bush in surprise and tore his wrist on the brambles.

David howled in agony.

Clare tore her face from David's lap, a stream of crimson and cream bubbling in her mouth.

Simon crashed through the bushes and hurled himself into the clearing, his face white with rage.

I pulled myself free of the thorns and watched as Clara staggered forwards into Simon's arms, gagging and sobbing. David sat up and stared down at the torn and bleeding mess in his lap. His magic pecker seemed, luckily for him, to be in one piece, but Clara's lower teeth had scraped a gash along the underside and peeled back a curl of flesh.

Simon, one hand holding Clara's head against his shoulder, looked across at his brother. His shoulders heaved and his tongue flicked across his lips as he searched for words. The rain streamed down between them and the wild electric smell of freshly soaked forest rose from the floor.

At last Simon found utterance.

'Physicist . . .' he shouted, '. . . heal thyself.'

Poor old Simon, illiterate as ever.

He turned and spoke in Clara's ear, as the approaching thunder shook the copse.

'We can't have you going into the house looking like this. Come on, I'll take you to Jarrold's cottage. You can clean up there.'

Clara clung to him as they left the clearing. The front of her dress was soaked and stained with rainwater, blood, semen and lumps of freshly vomited treacle-pie.

'You can't leave me like this!' Davey shouted after them. 'Simon! Come back!'

They disappeared into the wood. David rocked himself backwards and forwards, the rain flattening the hair against his scalp.

There sat a child, I supposed, much in need of a godfather. Sighing, I took a handkerchief from my pocket and stood up. He watched my approach silently, quivering like a snared rabbit. His breath caught the upper register of his vocal cords as he inhaled with huge gasps.

'You saw?' he managed to say.

'Don't talk,' I said. 'Not a bloody word. Can you stand?'

He took my arm and struggled upwards, wincing like the very dickens. Poor fucker.

Eight

When Gordon Fell was knighted in 1987 he threw a celebration binge afterwards at the Savoy. Not the Dominion Club of course, as it should have been, but the Savoy. Well, no matter. During the party he described to us the ceremony at Buckingham Palace. Gordie hadn't been the only man there that morning to be knighted, naturally. The Queen contrives to process dozens of candidates in one hit. They are disposed, it would seem, in rows of chairs, as at a lecture, while a band of the Guards plays anus-contractingly inappropriate tunes like 'A Spoonful of Sugar' and 'Chitty Chitty Bang Bang' in the background. Gordon was due to kneel and be dubbed next in line after the self-important fool sitting beside him. This pompous little pip-squeak had wriggled his way into the chairmanship of some large charity or another and was now coming to collect what he regarded as his due reward.

The figure had introduced himself with pride and whispered, after Gordon had told him his name, 'And what do you do, then? The diplomatic, is it?'

'I'm a painter,' Gordie said.

'Really?' said the fellow. 'Not one of those awful moderns, I hope.'

'Oh no,' said Gordon. 'Of course I'm not a modern painter.

I was born in the sixteenth fucking century, wasn't I? I'm an Old Master, me.'

Not quite Buck House language perhaps, but justifiable under the circumstances. The chap turned his shoulder on Gordie, disgusted that he could be sharing an honour with such an animal. Gordon pointedly scratched his groin and yawned.

Anyway, the turn came for the charity weasel to kneel and be serviced. It so fell out that his investiture into the Knights Commander of the Crawling Toads, or whatever order it was that he was in line for, took place unaccompanied by melody, the band being engaged in taking the sheet music of 'Consider Yourself' off their stands and replacing it with 'Born Free'. Her Maj's sword tapped the man's shoulders in hushed silence and he rose to an upright position with becoming dignity, bowing his head with a crisp snap that would have shamed an equerry. As he did so his nervous, uptight and excitable system delivered itself of an astoundingly sustained and quite start-lingly loud fart. The monarch stepped backwards, which was all part of the programme as it happened, but which seemed to everyone present to be an involuntary reaction to the man's violent rip. The expression on his face as he trailed miserably down the aisle was one of deepest woe. Every person in the room stared at him or, worse, waited until he was level with them and then averted their eyes. Gordon, passing him in the aisle as he made his own way to the steps of the throne, murmured in a growl audible to all, 'Don't worry, old boy. She'll be used to it. Keeps plenty of dogs and horses, don't forget.'

The lips of the Queen, according to Gordie, were seen to curve into a smile at this and she detained him in conversation for longer than anyone else. When he returned to his seat next to the still-scarlet farter, Sir Gordon rasped out, in time with the band which was now operative again, 'Bo-orn free, a-free as the WIND BLOWS.'

Being the vindictive sod he is, Gordie didn't stop there, naturally. In the mêlée of press that gathered outside the palace and especially around him, he was asked how the occasion had gone.

'That man over there,' Gordon said, pointing at the chap, who was standing with his wife and only a photographer from a local Hampshire newspaper to bolster his self-esteem, 'let out the most extraordinary fart, virtually in the sovereign's face. Quite astonishing. Some kind of anarchist, I suppose.'

The pack flew to the spot like flies to a cow-pat and the pathetic creature was last seen streaking down the Mall, his silk topper bouncing on the pavement behind him. He lost his hat, his reputation and in all probability his wife in one Gordon Fell swoop. Never insult a painter. Not worth it.

I had always reckoned that this man's experiences counted as the most embarrassing a human being could undergo. I had not known, however, what God had in store for me that stormy Norfolk afternoon.

I walked a wincing David to the edge of the west drive as the rain streamed down upon us. Slow progress: he was bent forward, the handkerchief pressed to his groin, and capable only of shuffling geriatric steps. We got there in the end and I told him to shelter under a tree until I returned. Back at the house the first person I bumped into was Rebecca.

'Ted, for heaven's sake!' she hooted. 'You look as if you've just emerged from a swamp.'

'Don't have time to talk, Rebecca,' I said. 'Can you save a life and lend me your car?'

'Why?'

'I'll explain later. Bloody urgent. Please.'

She shrugged. 'Help yourself, darling. It's round the back.'

'Bless you. And, Rebecca? Another boon. Simon will be returning to the house in the next half-hour or so. I wonder if you could give him this note?'

I grabbed a sheet of house writing-paper, scribbled a message for Simon and sealed it in an envelope.

'Dark, dark mysteries,' said Rebecca.

'Terribly important, old carrot. You won't forget? Promise?'

She promised.

'And the car-keys?'

'Under the visor.'

I hadn't driven since the army, and even then sparingly. In those days you passed your test by going to the adjutant and signing a piece of paper which entitled you to command any vehicle from a motor-bicycle to a three-ton lorry. I didn't doubt I would manage, however. When I considered the number of dickwits who seemed capable of perfectly competent driving, Simon for example, I couldn't believe that it would be beyond me.

Rebecca's Mercedes was under cover in the garage behind

211

the stable yard, a convertible with the blasted roof down. Electric roof at that. After fiddling hopelessly with the ignition key for five minutes – fucking thing wouldn't even *turn* – I hared off to find Tubby. He got the car started and roof up, quick as pigshit.

I contrived, with great discomfort, to fit my belly under the steering-wheel only to encounter my first problem.

'The fucking thing's only got two pedals!' I yelled.

'That's automatic,' said Tubby.

He wasted ten valuable minutes in painstakingly explaining the workings and I edged out of the garage and headed for the west drive as fast as I could. I reached it without actual collision on the way, but it was a near thing, the edge of the park being liberally furnished with stone Portland vases and quaint rustic benches. I could barely see: the rain was still coursing down and I hadn't the faintest idea where the windscreen-wiper switch could possibly be hidden.

I slewed to a halt at the end of the drive, churning up mud as the car skidded on to the grass of the park itself.

Davey was lying under a cedar, motionless.

Fuck, I thought. He's been struck by lightning. Should never have told him to shelter under a tree.

It was not as bad as that. He had fainted, but not, I decided, from loss of blood. The handkerchief was stained, but not swamped. I bent down and tried to lift him. Not a heavy boy, but too much for me. Matters would not be helped by discs slipping and joints locking up.

'Davey!' I called in his ear. 'Wake up. Wake up, Davey, wake up.'

His eyes flickered open and he stared at me.

'Come on, boy. You've got to try and stand. I've got us a car and we're going to a hospital. Get you put right.'

He tried to get to his feet too quickly, as though there had been nothing wrong with him. The pain caught up with him sharply and he fell against me with a whimper. From that half-standing position I was able at least to drag him to the car and push, lever and pack him into the passenger seat.

'Oh, Uncle Ted,' he kept saying. 'Uncle Ted, Uncle Ted.'

'Sh! I've got to concentrate on this fucking car.'

'On the string common,' he woozed like a drunkard.

'What?'

'On the . . . steering . . . column. The windscreen-wipers. There.'

The wipers helped, but it was still a nightmare drive. The road threw up the most tremendous mist of water and some deep memory inside me kept prompting my left foot to attempt a clutch manoeuvre when I wanted to slow down. The only pedal for it to meet was the brake, on which it would stamp with great force, causing us to aquaplane on the spray to the hooting terror of the traffic.

David seemed to be amused by my oaths and grunts and remained alert enough to direct me to the Norfolk and Norwich Hospital.

It was only as we slid to a stop outside the doors of the casualty entrance that a true realisation of the fraught nature of this call impressed itself upon me. Michael would expect me to manage this without involving him or his family in any publicity. I turned to David.

'Whatever I say by way of explanation, Davey, you must remember and repeat. Do you understand?'

He looked at me dumbly.

'What?'

'I will explain who you are and how you came by this accident. You will not diverge from my explanation by one syllable. Do you understand? We don't want Clara dragged into this. Nor your parents if we can help it.'

'What are you going to say?'

'I don't fucking know yet, love, do I? Oh, now what?'

A knuckle was being rapped against the glass on my side of the car by a man in a bright-yellow plastic waistcoat. Unable to find a way to wind down the window, I opened the door, pushing the man off balance and into a puddle. I heaved myself out of the car and went to his aid.

'I'm terribly sorry . . . terribly sorry. Oh dear, oh God. You're all wet.'

'You can't park here,' he said, ignoring this frippery incidental. 'Ambulances only.'

'This is an emergency,' I said. 'Besides, I don't know how to park. If I left the car here, you wouldn't be kind enough to put it somewhere for me, would you?'

'I *beg* your pardon?'

I went around the bonnet and helped Davey out of the car.

' 'Ere!' the fellow shouted. 'I'm not going to . . .' He caught sight of the crimson hankie pressed to the fork of David's jeans and the words of recrimination died on his lips. 'You'd best

213

hurry in,' he said. 'The car'll be round the back. You can pick the keys up from my booth.'

One is always hearing a great deal of liberal waffle about the terrible state of the National Health Service. Waiting lists, cuts, low morale: you can't help but soak up the thrust of the moronic yapping we have to put up with every day from the professionally disenchanted and humourlessly self-righteous wankers of the left. Even a sceptical old reactionary like me is, willy-nilly, influenced by this kind of talk into imagining that all NHS institutions are crowded with desperately sick patients lying about in the corridors on straw palliasses waiting for the health authority's one overworked, under-rested teenage doctor to come and tell them to pull themselves together.

Not a bit of it. Not a bloody bit of it. It may be that the Norfolk and Norwich Hospital is an exception – East Anglia, it must be admitted, cannot be described as an area of massive inner-city tension; one supposes the average medical emergency involves bumpkins bitten by coypus or tourists overdosed on flapjacks and churches. I expected, none the less, to find at least a measure of squalor and overworked hysteria. But when Davey and I walked in through the automatic electrically operated doors and reported to the reception desk I felt less like a soldier dragging his wounded comrade into the filthy Crimean field-hospital of popular left-wing imagination and more like Richard Burton checking in to a five-star hotel in Gstaad with a tipsy Elizabeth Taylor on his arm.

'Oh dear oh dear,' clucked the little granny behind the desk. 'Someone's been in the wars, haven't they?'

'This young fellow has met with an accident,' I said with a hearty wink. 'Usual thing, you know. Caught the old man in his zipper, poor sod.'

'Whoops!' she said. 'I'd better have your names then.'

'Ah, Edward Lennox.'

Davey's eyebrows rose.

'And your son's name?'

'David,' I said. 'His name is David.'

'Do you have David's National Insurance card with you, by any chance?'

'Oh lor, came straight out without thinking of it, I'm afraid.'

'That's all right, dear. You can fill in a form later. Meanwhile, if you wouldn't mind taking a seat, a doctor will be out to see you as soon as possible.'

'Got that?' I hissed to David as we sat down. 'David Lennox. Accident while peeing.'

He nodded. He was very pale, his hair was still damp and his lower lip oozed blood from where he had been gnawing at it in pain.

He sat there not speaking, just staring blankly at the clock on the wall.

'You'll be fine,' I said, interpreting his silence as fear. 'They'll know what to do. Probably happens every day.'

'The thing is . . .' said David.

'Yes?'

'These jeans. They are 501's.'

'501's? I don't understand.'

A nurse was walking towards us, radiating welcome, confidence and disinfectant.

'David Lennox?'

'The thing about 501's,' whispered David urgently into my ear as he stood, 'is that they have a button-fly, not a zip.'

He was led away and I sat there punching my thigh with an angry fist.

Bloody American fashion. Fuck it. Fuck them all. *Button-fly?* Who ever heard of such a thing? Button-flies were for demob suits and old wedding trousers. *Button-fly?* Buggering fuckety-cunt, this was going to be just wonderful. Button-fly. Absurd.

After twenty minutes of this lonely fury, a tall white-coated woman with steel-grey hair gathered in a vicious bun strode towards me, a dangerous light in her cold blue eyes.

'Mr Lennox?'

'Yup, that's me.'

'Dr Fraser. I wonder if I might have a word with you?'

'Yes, yes. Absolutely. Absolutely. How's Davey doing?'

'This way, please. I have a small office.'

I followed obediently, beguiling the time on our short walk by making amusing observations on the weather and the state of the traffic, just like a real grown-up daddy.

Dr Fraser – Margaret Fraser if the identity tag attached to her coat was to be believed – closed the door of the office behind her and pointed to a seat.

'Mr Lennox,' she said as I sat down, 'I wonder if you would be good enough to tell me the nature of your relationship with David?'

'Well,' I said breezily, 'some days good, some days bad. You know what adolescents are like.'

'That's not quite what I mean, Mr Lennox,' she said, going round to sit behind the desk. 'You are the boy's father, is that correct?'

'For my sins.'

'Perhaps you can explain, then,' she unclipped a biro from her breast pocket, 'why David should say to me: "The pain got worse in the car, partly because Uncle Ted is such a terrible driver." Those were his words, Mr Lennox. "Uncle Ted".'

'Really?'

'Really. Now why should a son call his father "Uncle", I wonder?'

'Well, I *say* "father", but I mean *god*father, obviously.'

'Godfather?'

'Godfather,' my voice sounded dry and reedily inadequate, 'you know, which is *like* a father, isn't it?'

'You are not related to David?'

'Not really.'

'Not really. I see.'

As if making out a prescription, she took a small white notepad from a drawer in the desk and started to write on it.

'Why,' she asked as she wrote, 'obviously?'

'I'm sorry?'

'You just told me that when you said father you meant godfather, "obviously". Why obviously?'

'Well . . .' I began to feel a great need for a Rothie, 'I suppose it isn't that obvious, now you come to mention it. You being outside the family, nothing would seem obvious to you, would it? I mean, other people's lives . . . mystery. Blank mystery. Wouldn't you say?'

'But *you're* outside the family too, it would seem.'

'Ah well . . . yes. In that sense. Mm.'

'David's injury, according to the papers from the front desk, was sustained when he caught his penis in a zipper.'

Penis, what a ghastly word. Not right from a tall woman with chilly eyes and solid breasts.

'Yes, zipper, that's right.'

'Although the jeans he is wearing . . .'

'Have a button-fly. Yes, well, obviously he changed out of the original trousers.'

'Obviously again?'

'Well, there he is, you know. Having a pee, catches the

pecker. *I* didn't know what to do. So I rushed and got another pair of trousers for him and then . . .'

'You were present when he was urinating?'

'No, well, obvi . . . *naturally*, he called out, didn't he? I rushed up . . .'

'*Up?*'

'To the bathroom . . .'

'All this took place in a bathroom?'

'Yes! In a bathroom. What did you expect, a bakery? A hair-dressing salon?'

She wrote down a few words.

Her silence and patience were excessively irritating. I moved a hand to the pocket of my jacket.

'I hope you aren't thinking of smoking, Mr Lennox?' she said without looking up. 'This is a hospital.'

I sighed. She spoke again, still writing.

'Why are David's clothes so soaked, I wonder?'

'It's been raining, Dr Fraser. It's been raining for most of the afternoon. Or hadn't you noticed?'

'Yes, Mr Lennox. I had noticed. Such weather causes us to be very busy with serious accidents, Mr Lennox.' I was beginning to hate the way she kept repeating the name. 'But to return to your story. As I understand it, David's little misadventure took place in a bathroom? I can understand, at a stretch, why he might change trousers after his accident, but why he should then stand outside in the rain . . .'

'I had to get the car out, didn't I? Look, why all these questions? Surely this kind of thing must happen often enough . . .'

'I am happy to be able to tell you, Mr Lennox, that it is in fact pleasantly rare for a child to be admitted to this hospital with human bite-marks to the penis.'

'Ah.'

'Yes. It is even more rare for a busy casualty surgeon to be obliged to listen to stories of bathrooms, urination, zippers and changed trousers when it is plain to the meanest intelligence that the mud-, semen- and blood-stained jeans and hysterical state of the boy in question tell quite another story.'

'Ah,' I said, 'well . . .'

'What makes this case rarer still is the fact that the child has been brought into casualty by a man I immediately recognised as the poet E. L. Wallace, but who gives his name as plain Edward Lennox.'

217

'Well, for goodness' sake, if you knew who I was in the first place . . .'

'This E. L. Wallace claims to be the boy's father,' she went on, 'and when this is exposed as a complete fabrication, he asks me to believe that it was "obvious" that he meant he was really only the godfather.'

'Which I am.'

'I think, Mr Wallace,' she said, resting her chin on her hands, 'that you should tell me the name of the child's real parents now, don't you?'

I ignored this question. 'I'd like to speak to Davey, please.'

'I am sure that the police, when I ring them, would disapprove of my allowing you to do any such thing.'

'The police? Have you run mad? What on earth have the police got to do with anything?'

'Please don't shout, Mr Wallace.'

'I'm sorry, but look . . .' I leaned forward and lowered my voice. 'All right. Let's talk as grown-ups and mature people of the world now, shall we? I confess that the story about the zip was a little bit of a white lie. But surely, just because a pair of lovers suffer an unfortunate mishap . . .'

'David is fifteen years old, Mr Wallace. I have no doubt that in the Bohemian world that you inhabit . . .'

'Yes, yes, yes. Never mind about your rancid second-hand ideas of Bohemia. The young must be allowed to experiment surely? I mean . . .'

'I have a boy of David's age myself, Mr Wallace!'

'Well, if it comes to that, Dr Fraser, so do I.'

She looked at me aghast. 'You do?'

'Certainly. And if the same thing happened to him, do you think I would kick up a great stink about it? Of course not. Make a fuss and the whole thing gets blown up out of proportion. You know what the young are like. Guilt, resentment, anger, aggression. No, no. The last thing in the world you should do is make some big deal out of it. That's not Bohemianism, that's plain common sense. I absolutely forbid the involvement of the police. And leave the parents out of it too, that's my advice. I'll see him now, if I may.'

She stared at me with round eyes, the notepad forgotten.

'Well!' she said finally. 'I must say for sheer bloody nerve you take first prize, Mr Wallace. This is what is meant by "poetic licence", is it?'

'Oh, for hell's sake!' I had frankly had it with this stiff-

218

bosomed prude. 'You're a doctor, not a damned social worker. Don't you have some oath that forbids you from gossiping about the private lives of your patients? I mean, Jesus, woman, what is it with this country? Why do bossy creatures like you insist on sticking your inquisitive noses into other people's affairs all the time? Just stitch the boy's prick up, give him some pills and send him on his way. What the hell business is it of yours how he got his injuries and with whom? Just leave us alone, will you?'

'It may interest you to know, Mr Wallace, that I am a magistrate. A Justice of the Peace.'

'And a member of Calvinists Against Cocksucking and Housewives Against Fellatio, no doubt. What you do in your private life is a matter of complete indifference to me. And what a young boy does in his should be of equal unimportance to you. You're a doctor, your job is to heal, not to preach.'

She gave me another hostile glare and reached out her hand for the telephone. 'If I don't have the name and address of David's parents this minute, Mr Wallace, I shall call the police.'

I sighed. 'Oh, very well. Very well. And I suppose you want the name of the parents of the girl too, so you can fuck up two families at once, is that it?'

'Girl? What girl?' She stared at me in astonishment.

'What girl, what girl? What do you mean "what girl"? Did you think he was being sucked off by a giraffe, for God's sake?'

'No, Mr Wallace. I assumed that *you* were the other party.'

It was my turn to give the look of pop-eyed amazement.

'WHAT? You thought *what*?'

'Please, Mr Wallace, lower your voice.'

'You thought *I* . . .'

I've spent a lifetime having people of Dr Fraser's stamp throw words like 'Bohemian' at me, but I truly believe that if I have a fault it's that I'm not as dirty-minded as most. They call me a cynic and sceptic too, but that's because when I see a thing I call it what it is, not what I want it to be. If you spend your life on a moral hill-top, you see nothing but the mud below. If, like me, you live in the mud itself, you get a damned good view of clear blue sky and clean green hills above. There's none so evil-minded as those with a moral mission, and none so pure in heart as the depraved. All the same, it was probably stupid of me not to have seen what she had been driving at.

'If there has been a mistake, Mr Wallace,' she was saying, 'I

assure you I am very sorry, but you must see that it is my duty
to establish the facts in cases like these. The parents are . . . ?'

'When I tell you,' I said, 'you will understand why I am
worried about any police involvement and subsequent publicity. The boy's parents . . .' I paused dramatically, '. . . are
Michael and Anne Logan.'

Her mouth dropped open.

I nodded heavily. 'Precisely.'

'Do you know, Mr Wallace,' she said, 'I thought David
looked familiar from the first. I've met him. Lady Anne and I
serve on the same bench.'

'Is that right?' Big bloody surprise. I could picture her sent-
encing poachers and flashers to death with relish. 'Well, it so
happens that there is a young girl staying at Swafford at the
moment, Clara Clifford. She is the daughter of Max Clifford,
whom perhaps you also know?'

'I know *of* him of course . . . I didn't know he had a daughter.'

'She's fourteen. Now, to cut a long story short, I was walking
in the woods at Swafford this afternoon and I heard a scream.
When I got there I discovered that youthful eagerness and
inexperience had brought Davey to the pass you have witnessed. Unfortunate and embarrassing, but hardly a matter for
the police.'

She gave me another long look.

'And you really are David's godfather?'

I raised my right hand. 'Poet's honour.'

She smiled and for the first time I saw the ghost of something
attractive and even erotic lying behind her skeweringly blue
eyes.

'If you like,' I offered, 'you can take an impression of my
bite-mark. Isn't that usual forensic practice?'

'I think what I'll do,' she said, rising to her feet, 'is go and
have another word with David. Would you mind staying here
for a moment?'

'No, no. I can read your letters.'

'Nothing very interesting there,' she said with a laugh. 'You
will find an ashtray in the middle drawer however.'

I composed a little present for her in the notepad.

There's a beautiful doctor called Fraser
With a glance like a surgical laser;
If you're guilty of sin

She'll stare at your chin
And save you the price of a razor

Underneath I wrote, 'Limericks are the best I can come up with these days. I'm only sorry there are no good rhymes for "Margaret" . . . with love Ted Wallace.'

Under that thick ice, I thought, lay the perfectly preserved remains of a passionate heart. I believed I knew exactly the kind of sounds she would make at the moment of orgasm. Something between a creaking gate and a pouncing jaguar. Humby-ho. I would never get a chance to prove myself right.

Davey stood a little sheepishly by the reception desk while she took charge of his paperwork. A thoughtful nurse, or perhaps Dr Margaret herself, had given him a handful of glossy magazines to hold in front of his groin. Behind them protruded a thick white bandage.

'I've used sutures,' she told me. 'They will dissolve in one or two days.'

'No permanent damage?'

'He'll find it a little painful to pass water for a while and even more painful to . . .'

'Quite.'

'Otherwise he'll be fine. I'm sure he's a good healer.'

'You speak truer than you know,' I said, to a thunderous look from David.

'I've also given him a tetanus booster and some antibiotics.'

'And he can redress the bandage himself after each piddle, can he?'

'Oh, he'll have no trouble, will you, Davey?' she said, laying a hand on his shoulder.

'I'll be okay,' he mumbled, writhing like a pint of live bait at the embarrassment of being talked about over his head as though he were a five-year-old.

The journey out of Norwich passed in silence. I was too preoccupied with avoiding bollards and lorries to talk and David had his own thoughts to contend with. Once we had cleared the city boundary and settled ourselves behind a pleasantly slow-moving van, I felt relaxed enough to speak.

'Fortunately,' I said, 'that doctor is a friend of your mother's.'

'She said. Will she tell Mummy anything?'

'No,' I said. 'I don't think so.'

'I might,' said Davey, greatly to my surprise.

'Well, if you think that would be a good idea.'

He shifted uncomfortably in his seat. 'She has to know what Simon did. It was wicked. It was evil.'

'Now, hang on.' I took my eyes off the road for a second to look at him. 'What would you expect Simon to do? I mean he comes upon a scene like that . . .'

'He knew. He knew perfectly well what was happening. He knew and he was jealous. He wanted to humiliate me and destroy me. He's always been jealous, you see. He's like the brother in the parable of the Prodigal Son. He can't bear being ordinary and he can't bear Mummy and Daddy thinking I'm different and special.'

'And that's what you are, is it? Different and special?' It still stuck in my craw to repeat that ghastly word.

'You know I am, Ted.'

'At the risk of sounding obvious, isn't everyone?'

'Well, that's true as well. I don't actually believe that what I do is anything so extraordinary. I think anyone could have my power if they really wanted it.'

'Even me?'

'Especially you! You've already had that power, when you were a poet. You wrote "Where the River Ends", didn't you?'

'I've always thought my power as a poet came from studying form and metre and, of course, the poems of others, not from tapping some mystical source. And,' I thought it was about time to give it to him straight, 'I hate to disappoint you, but "Where the River Ends" is not about the purity of nature and its contamination by man.'

'Yes, it is. It's about pollution.'

'It's about the fact that the poetry of Lawrence Ferlinghetti and Gregory Corso was included on the school syllabus.'

'What?' He stared at me as if I had gone mad.

'Poems are inspired by real things, real shitty, concrete things. I was making a bitter joke about how the pure well-springs of poesy were being fouled by people I thought of as inadequate and talentless nobodies. I deliberately used the tired old metaphor of rivers running to the sea just to satisfy my desire to describe those poor harmless American poets as floating turds.'

'Well,' said Davey, shifting again, 'I don't see what difference that makes. Your poem still has my meaning, doesn't it? The river starts as pure and then, as it goes through each town and through the city and to the sea, it becomes darker and dirtier and more disgusting. Your poem still says that. I don't suppose anyone who reads it knows about those poets. It *is* about purity.'

'Yes, but the point is you can't start a poem by wanting to write about some capital-letter idea like Purity or Love or Beauty. A poem is made of real words and real things. You start with the base physical world and your own base physical self. If some meaning or beauty comes out of it, then that is, I suppose, the wonder and relief of art. You want gold, you have to go down a mine to hack it out of the ground, you have to sweat your guts out in a filthy forge to smelt it: it doesn't fall in gleaming sheets from the bar of heaven. You want poetry, first you have to muck in with humanity, you have to fight with paper and pencil for weeks and weeks until your head bleeds: verses aren't channelled into your head by angels or muses or sprites of nature. No, I don't see that my "gift", such as it ever was, has anything in common with yours at all, Davey.'

David chewed on this for a while. 'So what exactly are you saying?'

'I don't know, my old darling. That's the bugger of it. I don't know.'

A car behind me honked its horn and I noticed that I had slowed down to under thirty miles an hour. It occurred to me that with clever gadgetry you could easily chart the emotional state of a driver from his variations in speed and aggression at the wheel. I considered the idea of cars having sensors installed which would pick up driving inconsistencies and calculate their cause by reference to some electronic table compiled by a competent psychologist. The data selected from this table would then send signals to a display on the roof. 'Attention! The driver of this car has just had a terrible row with his wife.' 'This driver is besotted with his new mistress.' 'This driver is in a foul bate after being unable to find his spectacles this morning.' 'This driver is in an even, equable temper.' I was convinced, as that retired police commissioner used to say, that it would constitute a major contribution to road safety. The only flaw, I supposed, lay in the possibility that experienced drivers were more adept than me at driving consistently whatever their mood.

We caught up with the van ahead and I shook myself from this pointless reverie. This is the worst of driving, your thoughts get sucked into long tunnels, as into a sleep. You don't, as it were, breast the waves of thought, you are borne along by them and you end up drifting.

I glanced across at Davey. He was slumped in his seat in that slack-jawed, eye-glazed lolling stupor at which adolescents excel.

'Perhaps it would help,' I said, 'if you told me more about the exact nature of your powers. I think I have a goodish idea, but you can fill in the gaps.'

'All right.'

By the time the hedgerows had leapt up by the roadside and the gables of the hall were flashing behind the parkland trees, I believed myself to be more or less, as Max Clifford would say, 'up to speed', Lilac and all.

I dropped Davey off at the back of the house before re-stabling the car. He was to slip upstairs, unseen if he could help it, while I explained to the household that the poor angelic mite was all fagged out after a hard day's mending bumblebee wings, healing bruised buttercups, smiling sweetly at the rain-drops and generally being David. Once he was safely between the sheets he could be visited without anyone being the wiser as to the local details of his injuries.

Simon was waiting for me in the garage yard. I stopped the car and pulled myself out, leaving the engine running.

'It's nearly seven,' he remarked, a hint of complaint in his voice. I had arranged in my note to him that we should RV here at half past five.

'Never mind about that,' I said. 'You manoeuvre this bastard thing into its hangar. My driving days are over.'

His enthusiasm for cars got the better of his grumpiness. He climbed in, nosed the Mercedes into the garage and switched off the motor. I stood in the yard waiting for him to come out. The rain had stopped and everything shone and dripped, fresh as a washed salad.

Simon remained in the gloom of the garage for an inexcus-ably long time.

'What are you doing in there?' I shouted into the darkness. 'Singing the bloody thing to sleep?'

He emerged two or three minutes later, edged round the car and closed the double doors of the garage.

'There was blood on the front passenger seat,' he said. 'I wiped it off.'

'Ah. Good man. Now, if it's seven, I had better go to my room and change.'

We walked back towards the house.

'I got your note, Uncle Ted. I haven't told a soul. I wouldn't of anyway.'

'Wouldn't *have*,' I muttered.

'Oh, sorry. I never get that right.'

'Well don't *apologise* for it, for God's sakc.'

Simon had a quality that seemed to bring out the mental bully in me. All bullies become more and more irritated by their victim's acquiescence in being bullied, which inclines one to bully all the more.

'Are you cross with me?' Simon asked.

'I am excessively annoyed with myself, as it happens,' I said. 'Annoyed with myself for being irritable with you, annoyed with you for allowing me to be irritable with you, annoyed with myself for allowing myself to be annoyed, and most of all annoyed with myself for being stupid.'

There were too many 'annoyeds' and 'irritables' in that sentence for Simon to be able to decipher its meaning, so he changed the subject.

'Is Davey all right?'

'He'll live. I banished him to his bedroom. And what of Clara?'

'She'll be okay. I sent her to bed too.' He bent down to pull up a weed from under the cotoneaster that grew along the wall around the side of the house. 'I suppose Davey is furious with me?'

'He thinks you're jealous of his powers. He thinks you deliberately chose your moment to crash through the woods and humiliate him. He thinks you are evil.'

Simon gaped. 'That's pathetic.'

'Well, perhaps. And what's your point of view? What do you think of Davey?'

He thought about this.

'He's my brother.'

'Yes, yes. But what do you think of him? What's it *like* to have him for a brother?'

'I can't really remember *not* having him as a brother. He can be a pain. I mean, let's face it, he is a bit weird. And he really pisses me off with all that bloody anti-blood-sports stuff. I mean, he claims to love nature so much, but surely he can see that we wouldn't have all these copses and spinneys if it weren't for the pheasants. Everything would be flat fields for thousands of square miles. The woodland doesn't just support

225

game-birds, you know. There's wild flowers and wild mammals and insects that completely depend on shooting.'

'Of course, of course, of course.' I wasn't in the mood for a lecture on killing. 'I'm talking about the other side of Davey.'

'Look, here's Max,' said Simon and I received the impression that he was relieved to be spared the necessity of answering.

Max was standing outside the front door in a dark suit, looking up at the sky with benevolent approval, as if it were a junior management executive who had successfully cut back on their workforce without provoking a strike.

'Ted. Simon. Splendid,' he said as we approached. 'Rain's stopped. Glorious evening.'

'More on the way, actually,' said Simon.

'You seem very cheerful, Max,' I remarked.

'And you look like shit, old boy.' Which, I suppose, I did. My skin and scalp were scratched by brambles and my clothes were devastated by rain, sweat and mud.

'I'll go in now,' Simon said. 'See you at dinner.'

Max took my arm and walked me to the lawn. 'As a matter of fact, Tedward, I *am* cheerful.'

'Really?' I said, frigidly. I hated it when Max used Michael's name for me.

'I might as well tell you, if you hadn't already guessed, that I asked Davey to see what he could do about Clara.'

'Has she been ill?'

'Oh, come off it, Tedward, you know perfectly well what I'm talking about. Anyway, David did see her. Always found the boy an intolerable little prick, if you must know. Hated having to ask him a favour. So goody-goody. Nothing in this world less bearable than an anti-business snob. He'll spend his father's nasty money when the time comes, right enough, don't you worry. But, well . . . I can't deny his ability. I don't know what he did. It must have been very intense. Clara's absolutely knocked out by it.'

'And it's worked?' I stared at him. It had never crossed my mind that, after Simon's intervention, David's cure might actually have been effective. Aside from anything else, in crude physical terms, she had not appeared from my angle so much to have swallowed her medicine as to have spewed it down her front.

'I've just spent half an hour with her in her room.'

'You mean her teeth are straight and her eyes look in the same direction?'

'Well, no. Obviously he can't alter her appearance just like that. But *inside*, Tedward! I've never seen her so cheerful and so . . . confident. It's absolutely miraculous. We've sent that girl to psychiatrists and nuns and summer camps and God knows what. It's unbelievable.'

I agreed and nodded enthusiastically while he gibbered on.

'She wouldn't tell me how he did it, but I wouldn't care if he fed her eye of newt and ear of bat. The squint will correct itself soon, apparently, and the teeth too. And she's just so much . . . oh, you'll see. You'll see.'

'Fabulous,' I said. 'Bloody marvellous. But look, I must bath and change if I'm not going to be late for dinner. See you at the bin.'

Oliver was gliding up the stairs as I made the hallway.

'Well!' he said, turning at the sound of the front door. 'Another happy meeting of the Somme Re-enactment Society, I see.'

'Yes, most amusing. I got caught in the storm, if you must know.'

'I think the storm got caught in you, dear.'

I headed up the stairs towards him. 'By the way,' I said, 'has Jane been asking after me?'

'No, heart. There was a message to say she can't come till tomorrow.'

'Why not?'

'More tests. Doris Doctor just refuses to believe. They probably want to exhibit her at the Royal College of Surgeons. Shall we bustle? We mustn't be late for din-dins.'

I wallowed in my bath, gazing at the sky and clouds painted on the ceiling, a tumbler of the ten-year-old clutched in my fist. I wished I could wash myself clean of everything. I wished Jane were here. I wished I was back in London. I wished I wasn't so old, so confused and so cross. At least there was whisky. A bottle, that's all I asked for, a full bottle of . . .

As I peered through the mist of steam at the angels looking down on me from their *trompe-l'œil* heaven, a small thought arose somewhere in my mind like a bubble of marsh gas. I dropped my whisky glass in surprise. Other thoughts began to pop to the surface, each lighting the other in a lightning path like will o' the wisp. Could it be possible, I wondered? Did these sudden zig-zags of light lead anywhere, or was the parallel of ignis fatuus appropriate and the whole burst of thoughts nothing more than a false trail into the swamp? Hum . . .

I reached out an arm for the telephone handily placed in an alcove by the bath.

Nine

Podmore's felt hammer gonged the conversation to an end. I replaced the receiver and hauled myself from the tub. Years ago I discovered, and you may find this useful, a trick which enables one to dress quickly after a bath. The problem with clothing oneself when not fully dry is that one's shirt and especially one's socks will frot and rub frictively against the skin. They won't slide easily on: a man can pull a shoulder muscle or crick a neck trying to wrestle with clothes in a damp post-balneal state. My discovery is that the use of a good old-fashioned bath-oil will solve this problem. It leaves the skin smooth and sleek as a seal's and sir's shirtings and half-hosements will practically leap from the floor and wrap themselves around him in a gladsome twinkling.

I was therefore able to glide serenely into my underlinen and stand before the mirror, patting my well-rounded tummy while I considered the little errands that had to be completed before dinner. Just two essential visits would . . .

I was distracted by the sound of moans and gasps floating through the wall from the Fuseli Room next door, where Oliver was billeted. I finished dressing, brushed my hair and came out into the corridor. Oliver emerged at the same time. He looked guiltily towards the door of his room.

'Ted, you double beast. Were you listening just now?'

'Listening? To what?'

'I'm afraid Mother was enjoying a quick one off the wrist. I'm a noisy lover when it comes to myself.'

'My dear old Oliver,' I said. 'When my life is so impoverished that I find I have nothing better to do than listen to an old man wanking, I will put a bullet in my head.'

I had been listening, however. A man does. I parted from Oliver at the top of the stairs.

'Just have to pop back and check something,' I said. 'Think I left a packet of Rothies in my room.'

I hurried back along the corridor and towards the passageway where the children slept. Having paid my respects to Clara, a fruitful conversation, I slipped down the stairs and out of the front door. I skimmed across the drive, panting like a dog on a hot day, crossed the front lawn, skirted the west drive and achieved the park from the side. After all, I didn't want to scramble up and down that bloody ha-ha again. The sky was thickening to charcoal as new storm clouds gathered, but the light, although mucky for a July evening, was perfectly good enough to see by. I picked my way carefully through isolated heaps of horse dung, confident that Tubby would have stabled the horses against the bad weather and that I would escape rape or trampling from a loose stallion. I found what I was looking for and bent down to get a closer look. Satisfied, I straightened myself with a grunt and returned to the house.

Only Max, Mary, Michael and Oliver were in the small drawing room when I arrived. Michael and Mary were sitting on a sofa in the corner, talking quietly while Oliver presided over the drinks tray.

Max was peering out of the window. It gave out in the direction of the Villa Rotunda and the lake beyond, so I knew he couldn't have seen me crossing the front lawn.

'Simon was right,' he told the room. 'More storms on the way.'

'Ar, these country folk, they ben know,' Oliver croaked.

'That is the worst Norfolk accent I have ever heard,' I said.

'Then you haven't heard real Norfolk people talking, dear. Their accents are *much* less convincing than mine, I can assure you. Pour you a whisky?'

'Larger the better,' I said.

I approached the sofa where Michael and Mary sat.

'But Michael, *everyone* should know,' she was saying.

'Mary, believe me, I'm delighted. Delighted. Let's leave it at that.'

'But Michael, don't you feel that you have a duty? I mean this gift is something remarkable, something that must be *used*.'

I hovered behind the sofa, not wanting to interrupt.

'I don't know, Mary. I just don't know. You see Annie doesn't like . . .'

'What doesn't Annie like?' said the woman herself from the doorway. Acutest bloody hearing you could think of.

There was a fractional pause – too short for a court of law to read anything into, but long enough to embarrass Michael – before Oliver came to the rescue.

'Voddie dear, that's what you don't like. You're a gin girl. Voddie makes you grumpy. So I'm pouring you a full Jilly Gill of lovely Jenny Gin.'

'Thank you, Oliver.'

I caught Anne's eye, which was filled with a pleading expression that I found hard to interpret. She gestured to the far corner of the room, away from the others. I joined her there and we pretended to inspect an Oakshett acrylic portrait of the Logan family.

'I've just seen Davey,' she said in a low voice. 'What's wrong with him?'

'Ah,' I said. 'Bit knocked up, that's all. You might as well know that he . . . he had a session with Clara this afternoon.'

'Oh, no . . .'

'They got caught in the rain. Both fine. Just a bit tired. As a matter of fact, Max believes Clara is wonderfully improved.'

'She is?' Annie shook her head sorrowfully. 'Davey said something about a row with Simon, but he wouldn't tell me any more. What happened?'

'You might as well face it, Anne. No point fighting. That boy is a miracle worker. There can be no question about it. Don't you agree?'

She started to speak.

'Don't you agree?' I repeated slowly.

She looked at me and caught her breath.

'Oh, Ted!' she whispered. 'Oh, Ted, you wonderful man!' She tugged at my sleeve like a child. 'I *knew* I could rely on you. I *knew* it!'

'Rely on Ted?' Oliver's voice burst in on us. 'I find that hard to believe,' he said and presented Annie with her gin.

'Ted has been an angel and promised to take the twins

ballooning at Brockdish tomorrow,' said Annie brightly. 'So sweet of him.'

'Balloonists at Brockdish? They sew up the end of a pair of Ted's drawers and then fill them with hot air, do they?'

'No, Oliver,' I said. 'They take a life-sized nylon replica of your ego and ask you to talk into it on any subject. That's how it's done.'

'Wit isn't quite your thing, my love,' said Oliver. 'Just a little too cumbersome, you see.'

Rebecca, Patricia and Simon were the last to arrive, Patricia giving me a secret little grin as she came in. She's been considering my offer, I thought. How delightful.

II

'There should have been twelve of us to dinner tonight,' Annie announced as we filed into the dining room. 'But Jane hasn't come yet and Davey and Clara are having early nights. So we'll have to have Max, Oliver, Mary and Simon on that side and Rebecca, Ted and Patricia on this.'

'It's dark enough to be winter,' said Michael, closing the shutters.

'Cosy,' said Oliver.

'Gloomy,' said I.

The first course was a smoked goose-breast, and things were going well conversationally until Patricia asked whether Lilac was still healthy.

'She's fine,' said Simon. 'Perfectly all right.'

'The most wonderful thing,' Patricia said. 'I mean, that vet was so absolutely sure, wasn't he? Ragwort poisoning. I looked it up in the library. It's a chronic condition that causes irreversible liver damage. How *can* Lilac be all right?'

Simon mumbled something about vets being as capable of making mistakes as anyone else.

'We must face facts, Anne,' said Mary. 'I know you don't like talking about it, but something has got to be said, hasn't it? Apart from anything else, Max and I are just so *grateful* to Davey.'

Simon cut into a slice of goose-breast with a violent scrape of his plate.

'I'm very glad that you are happy,' Anne said. 'And I'm very glad Clara is happy.'

'And Oliver,' said Max. 'Oliver's happy, too.'

'Oh, yes,' said Oliver. 'I'm happy. I can eat disgusting food again and voddie up without fear.'

'And I'm happy,' said Rebecca. 'Happy about my daughter.'

'And you must be happy too, Anne, Michael? You must be happy about Edward,' said Patricia.

'And Simon must be happy about Lilac,' said Mary.

Simon nodded uncomfortably.

'It's so *silly* not to talk about it!' Mary went on, her eyes shining. 'As if it's a guilty secret, instead of a wonderful, wonderful miracle that has made everyone happy.'

I laid down my knife and fork with a clatter. Now. It might as well be now.

'Well, I'm sorry to piss on this parade,' I said. 'But I'm not fucking happy. I'm not fucking happy at all. In fact I'm as miserable as bloody sin.'

'Of course you are, you miserable old shit,' snapped Oliver. 'And you deserve to be, too. Christ almighty, what a piece of work you are.'

'Hold it, hold it!' Michael thumped his hand down on the table. 'What is going on here? This is a dinner table. Please!'

'I'm sorry, Michael. You're the host and whatever you say goes, but I think Edward Pissing Wallace has it coming to him.'

'Hear, hear,' said Rebecca on my left.

Oliver pointed a spoon at me. 'You still don't believe in Davey's power, do you, Ted?'

I looked across at Anne and shrugged my shoulders. 'If you must have it, then I'll tell you. No, I don't believe in Davey's powers.'

'You see! He just can't take it.' Oliver's voice was rising in pitch. 'He is granted this one chance, as we all have been here, a chance which most people would never be permitted in a thousand lifetimes, he's granted this *one* chance to pull himself up by his boot-straps, this one chance to lever himself out of the swamp he's been stuck in for all these years, this one chance to raise his eyes upwards and see the beauty of things, and what's his reaction? "I'm not fucking happy. I'm miserable as bloody sin." Of course he's not happy. What we've experienced this last week is nothing less than a divine revelation. A divine fucking revelation and we can all see it, all of us can see it and celebrate it. We've got at least that little inch of humility that allows us to shout and weep with unreserved joy. All of us but bloody-minded, pig-headed, stone-blind, stone-deaf, Doubting Ted.'

There were tears in his eyes. I looked down at my plate in embarrassment.

'I'm sorry,' Oliver said. 'I'm sorry, Ted. But the fact is, I love you, you stupid turd. You're a friend that I love. We all love you. But you're such a . . . such a . . .'

'It's all right, Oliver,' said Rebecca, 'we all know what he is. It's just this, darling,' she said, turning to me, 'why won't you accept what you can see? Why would it hurt you so much just to face the truth?'

'What truth?' I asked.

'The truth,' said Oliver, 'that there is such a thing as the Operation of Grace.'

'The truth,' said Rebecca, 'that there really is something out there.'

'I'm not interested in what's out there,' I said. 'I'm interested in what's in here.' I thumped my chest.

'*Christ!*' Oliver banged down his fork. 'Why do you have to say things like that? Why do you have to say things like that? This isn't a fucking sixth-form debate. There are no prizes for smart-arsed remarks here.'

'I must say,' said Max, 'it's a bit odd that a poet of all people should be the only one unconvinced by all this. What's happened to your sense of mystery, your imagination?'

'No,' I said, 'it's not odd at all. If I was interested in mysteries and the imagination, I would have become a physicist. I'm a poet because I'm very mundane. I'm only good with what I can taste and see and hear and smell and touch.'

'Oh here we fucking go again, Pamela Fucking Paradox . . .'

'It's not a paradox at all, Oliver.'

'So is that why you came here, then? Just to pour cold water all over us? Just to sneer up your snotty sleeve? If you can't take it seriously, why try and ruin our happiness?'

'Of course I take it seriously. I take it very seriously indeed. Jane is my god-daughter and Davey is my godson. Whether you believe it or not I am very serious about that. Very serious indeed.'

'Well then, why . . .' Rebecca began, but was interrupted by Anne.

'I'm pressing the bell for Podmore,' she said. 'I would rather we didn't say anything while he is in the room.'

We sat in stiff and strained silence while Podmore cleared away the plates and served up the main course. I drank down two big glasses of wine. I was hot and uncomfortable. Oliver, opposite me, alternately glared and shook his head in sympathy. I had been touched when he had said he loved me.

Michael was revolving the stem of his wineglass and frowning. He threw little puzzled glances at me from time to time. Simon was scarlet and deeply uncomfortable. Max, Mary, Rebecca and Patricia had formed a strong bond and twittered loudly about the weather and politics. Every silly assertion seemed deliberately aimed in my direction, as if daring me to challenge their united front. It was like being sent to Coventry at school.

At last Podmore departed.

'Seconds away,' said Oliver. 'Round Two.'

'Tedward,' Michael said, sawing at a roast potato. 'I don't understand. You are denying everything? Everything that I told you?'

'It's not a question of denying, Michael. I don't deny anything you said about your father, I don't deny anything you . . .'

'Woah, woah!' said Oliver. 'Just a Molly Moment. Michael's *father?*'

I looked towards Michael, who shrugged and nodded his assent. I told the story of Albert Bienenstock and his horses and Benko, his batman. Not news to Rebecca or Anne, obviously, but everyone else, even Simon, was amazed.

'Well, you see!' said Patricia, nudging me. 'It's inherited. Skipping a generation. The whole thing's inherited.'

'Oh, I don't doubt that,' I said. 'I'm sure of it, in fact.'

'Well what *do* you doubt, for God's sake?' demanded Oliver, thoroughly exasperated.

'Look,' I said, 'you might as well all know the reason I came here. I was asked.'

'Asked?'

'By Jane. I bumped into her in London a couple of weeks ago. She told me . . . well, she didn't tell me very much in fact. She told me that her leukaemia had gone and that there had been some kind of miracle at Swafford last month while she had been staying here. That's all she told me. She wanted me to find out the rest for myself.'

'Which you have.'

'Which I have.'

'So what's the problem?' asked Michael.

'There's no problem,' I said. 'No problem at all.'

'But Davey?' said Oliver. 'What do you think about Davey?'

'Do you really want to know?'

'*Yes!*' Oliver screeched.

'Steady on, Oliver,' said Michael.

I could well appreciate the note of hysteria in Oliver's voice. I tried to sound as neutral and dispassionate as possible. I really had no idea how anyone would react to what I had to say.

'I think that Davey . . .'

The door opened.

'What is it, Podmore?' Annie asked in a tone of voice that, for her, was distinctly sharp.

'I beg your pardon, Lady Anne. There is a telephone call for Lord Logan in his study.'

The annoyance around the table was colossal. I was relieved. The diversion gave me a few minutes to collect my thoughts and arrange what I had to say in some kind of coherent order. If I'd had a piece of paper and a pencil I would probably have jotted down headings. Anal old Ted.

Michael stood up. 'Damn,' he said. 'I'm sorry. If it has come through on my study line it must be America and it must be urgent. I shall be as quick as I can. Please hang on for me, Ted. I want to hear everything that you've got to say.'

We passed a fraught three minutes in silence. I drank another glass of wine, to looks of recrimination from everyone.

Michael returned and closed the door behind him.

'I'm sorry about that,' he said, resuming his seat. 'Ted, go on, please.'

'What was I saying?'

'Oh, Lord save us, he's drunk now,' said Oliver. 'You were going, Teddy bear, to give us the benefit of your expert opinion of Davey.'

'That's right,' I said. 'Well, I think the key is this. David is a sensitive boy and a proud boy.'

Max laughed and the others joined in. Oliver snorted his contempt.

'That's it, is it? "David is a sensitive boy and a proud boy." End of analysis. I think you've said enough, dear. If anybody is proud and sensitive, it's Edward Wallace. Too proud and sensitive to believe what conflicts with his lumpish theories or to admit it when even he can see that he's wrong.'

'Leave it, Oliver!' said Michael in a tone fierce enough to make everyone jump. 'I want to hear what Ted has to say. Now more than ever I have to hear it. You'll find out why. For the time being, just be quiet.'

I stared at him in some puzzlement. He looked back at me with an expression of great intensity and – I believe I recognised it even then – of great fear. With the benefit of hindsight, it must certainly have been fear. At the time I couldn't understand the look at all.

'Well,' I said, slowly, 'as I say, David is proud and sensitive. He loves poetry and he loves what he thinks of as Nature with a capital "N". He is not quite as intelligent as he would like to be, but then which of us is? He is not unintelligent, you understand, he is intelligent enough to glimpse valuable and serious

237

ideas and to be maddened that they are beyond his reach. Because so much that he prizes is out of his intellectual grasp he imagines he can leap at the truth of things by intuition or with the help of some deeper agency, some spirit of nature. He cannot believe that God could have granted him the sensitivity to respond to beauty and ideas without also giving him the mental equipment or artistic talent to participate actively in them. I don't think any of this is uncommon with a fifteen-year-old. It would be bizarre and horribly inappropriate if David was in fact as intelligent and precocious as he wanted to be. The intellect grows, like any other part of the mind or body. Davey is different from most children, however, because he is so extraordinarily sensitive. Some sensitive children just suffer in silence. But David is extraordinarily proud as well as extraordinarily sensitive. He hates his inadequacy. He cannot bear it. It has driven him to a miserable and dangerous hysteria. Some proud and sensitive children in similar situations fantasise that their parents are millionaires. Davey's father already is, so that would hardly be feasible. Some fantasise that they are foundlings, or aliens, or special agents, or capable of unsupported flight, or invisible, or possessed of supernatural powers. And that is what David has chosen. Supernatural powers. It wouldn't usually matter, because under normal circumstances everyone around such a child would tease or straight-talk its delusions away. But you have all fed them, which is absurd and irresponsible and, I believe, immensely dangerous. Davey's hysteria has grown and grown and overtaken the entire household.'

I took a giant swig from my glass of claret.

It was Oliver, naturally, who broke the silence. He stared at me with disbelief. 'How can you sit there and say all that? We know what we have seen.'

'No you don't,' I said. 'You haven't the faintest idea what you've seen. Believe me when I say this. David is possessed of no extraordinary powers whatsoever. There is nothing miraculous he has done or can do. He is a very, very, very ordinary child with a more than ordinary helping of, as I said, pride and sensitivity . . .'

There was a noise outside the door and we all straightened into silence again.

The door did not move.

'Come in!' shouted Michael.

Still no response. With a click of irritation, Michael strode to the door and opened it. The corridor was empty. Michael looked down it to right and left.

'Oh dear,' said Anne, 'do you think Podmore has been listening?'

'Probably just the wind,' said Michael, closing the door and returning to the table. 'There's another storm on the way.'

It was true that wind had begun to howl around the windows and down the flues.

'Carry on, Ted,' said Oliver, with a savage growl. 'I think you were saying that we are all very irresponsible and absurd and that Davey is a very, very, very ordinary child.'

'A very ordinary child who needs a great deal of kindness and understanding if he is not to slide into hysterical chaos,' I said.

'But you're a mass of contradictions,' said Max. 'You've just admitted that Michael's father's powers could have been inherited and now you say that there aren't any powers.'

'I have said no such thing.'

'He is drunk,' said Patricia. 'If anyone needs kindness and understanding, it's *you*, Ted.'

'I need my share, certainly,' I said.

'We can all play armchair psychiatrists, can't we, Ted?' said Rebecca. 'We could, for instance, examine the mind of the ageing poet.'

'Quite,' said Oliver, 'the man who believes that spirituality is his province and his alone. The man who thinks that a glimpse of art and the infinite is only granted to hairy-arsed curmudgeons who drink hard liquor and understand Ezra Pound. The man who struggles so hard for his own poetry that he has developed a theory that denies the possibility of inspiration in others. "If I have to flounder in the mud sweating and straining, then it must be true that everyone else on earth has to as well." That's your grand "philosophy", isn't it? The sight of an innocent child given grace as a divine free gift just chokes you to death, doesn't it?'

'You may think I appear very graceless,' I said. 'But you must . . .'

'Graceless, darling? Why ever should we think that? Your own inspiration dried up years ago and you've lived on rotten credit ever since. As an ugly old fraud yourself, anything of any beauty or authenticity has to be mocked and rejected. Graceless? Lordy Lord, no.'

'Let's leave character out of it for the moment,' said Max,

with boardroom crispness, 'and concentrate on facts. Do you deny, Ted, that Edward's life was saved?'

'No,' I said. 'I have to confess that I cannot deny that.'

'And Lilac?' said Oliver. 'And Jane? And me? And Clara? Can you deny us? Look at what's in front of your great fat nose, man!'

'All right, Oliver, calm down,' said Michael. 'Let's get this straight, Ted. Are you saying that my son has absolutely no powers whatsoever?'

'*No!*' I cried. 'No, I am *not* saying that! I think he is a remarkable and wonderful boy. I think he is, in his own way, a miracle. Not magical, but uncommon enough to be a miracle in this world. I think he has powers that are as rare as they are beautiful.'

'I'm going mad!' said Patricia clutching her hair. 'You said a moment ago, "David is possessed of no extraordinary powers whatsoever. He is a very, very, very ordinary child." Your exact words. And half a minute later . . .'

'I stand by every word I have spoken,' I said.

There was an almost unanimous shout of rage at this perversity. It was brought to a shocked silence by Anne.

'Oh be quiet, all of you!' she stormed. 'You just don't see, do you? You just don't see! You told Ted that he couldn't see the truth when it was right under his nose, but it's not Ted, it's you. It's all of you. Ted is absolutely right. Everything he has said is absolutely right and consistent and you just can't see it.'

'Annie! My love, I don't understand!' Michael stared across at his wife in bewilderment.

'I'm sorry, Michael,' I said. 'I've been playing games with you.'

'Games? You've been playing games?'

'Well, not games precisely. Just getting a bit of my own back perhaps. *Allowing* you to misunderstand. You asked me whether or not I thought your son had any powers whatsoever and I said that he did. I said that he was a remarkable and wonderful boy. What you don't understand, what only Annie understands, is that *I wasn't talking about Davey.*'

Still he couldn't see. None of them could see.

'Not talking about Davey?'

'No,' I said. 'I was talking about *Simon*.'

'What?' Oliver whipped round on Simon, who sat there, fork

hovering in front of his face, and mouth open in consternation and alarm.

'Oh look . . .' he said. 'Come on, Uncle Ted . . . I mean . . .'

'I'm sorry, Simon,' I said, 'but the truth must be told.'

Anne leant forward and placed a hand on Simon's arm.

'Ted! Annie! Explain . . . please, tell me what's going on,' said Michael.

'You saw yourself how it all began two years ago, Michael,' I said. 'For the time being we'll call it the first miracle. You came into the room when Edward was lying suffocated and almost unconscious from asthma. Simon did what any sane human being would do. He pumped the boy's arms back and forth and tried to get the breathing started. He pummelled the ribs. A few seconds later, sentimental hysterical David elbows him out of the way, frightened by such violence and completely ignorant of the need for it. He has just laid a hand on his chest when you and Annie walk in, at the very moment that the results of Simon's commendable first-aid became apparent and Edward is starting to cough and splutter. You see the hand laid on the chest and you instantly think of your father, who despite his own obvious good sense was very nearly bamboozled himself into thinking that he had done something extraordinary with his batman's sore foot. Some time later you tell Davey this story and the stupid boy, who had probably only laid his hand on the chest to feel for the boy's heart-beat or something equally useless, believes he has inherited a mystical power from his grandfather.'

'But . . . you can rationalise *anything* like that,' said Patricia. There was a hint of doubt in her voice, however.

'Rationalising a sunset doesn't make it any less beautiful,' I said. 'Nor is it designed to. Simon is thoughtful, practical, unsentimental and kind. He is also entirely without ego. It never occurred to him to take credit or demand thanks for what he did. Davey on the other hand . . . well, just think about it. Just consider the sequel. Michael and Annie decided that Davey's miraculous healing of Edward should remain a secret. Michael because he didn't want his son to be hounded or feared in the way Albert had been, Annie because she could see what Michael believed and how much it delighted his sense of separate family pride. She was also afraid that Michael might think she was in some way jealous of Davey's apparent gifts. Which, of course, is precisely what you *did* think, isn't it, Michael?'

Michael nodded.

'And the point is this. In spite of the pact of secrecy and silence, word of Davey's powers did get out. How? I'll tell you. Davey made damn sure word got out, that's how. I had it in a letter from Jane recently. "When Davey first told me how he had healed Edward," she wrote. It wasn't part of Davey's plan that his magical gifts should go unrecognised. Jane told Patricia and Rebecca, they told Max and Mary and Oliver. Davey announced his status as healer and miracle worker to the whole bloody world.'

'I think I'll go now, if I may, please,' Simon said, half-rising from the table. He had been listening to all this with acute dismay and unease.

'No, Simon . . . I beg of you,' Michael said. 'I beg you, stay.'

Simon dropped reluctantly back into his seat. Everyone was looking at him and he hated it.

'So you are saying that it is really *Simon* who has done all this healing?' said Patricia. 'He is the one who inherited his grandfather's gifts?'

'Certainly Simon has inherited Albert Bienenstock's powers,' I said.

'Simon. A healer . . .' said Michael shaking his head.

Simon himself sat there, simply squirming with embarrassment, poor lad.

'Michael, can't you see what I've been saying?' I said. 'Your grandfather wasn't a healer. His powers were the powers of calm good nature, amiability, decency, selflessness, courage, modesty and sense. Prosaic you may think, but what is poetry if not the compression of the prosaic? Such qualities as Albert Bienenstock possessed may have seemed as dull as coal, but taken all together, concentrated in one man, they refined themselves into a diamond. That is what Simon has inherited. Isn't that enough for you?'

It was *not* enough for them.

'I'm sorry to go on about this,' said Patricia, 'but you're avoiding the obvious point, Ted. What about Jane and Lilac and Oliver and Clara?'

'Exactly,' said Oliver. 'If modesty and calm good nature can cure leukaemia and liver failure then I think the world should know about it, don't you?'

I poured myself another glass of wine. The stuff was going down me by the gallon and swishing in my belly. The wine, together with the unaccountable nervousness I was feeling and the adrenaline that was pumping around me, was starting to cause my guts to bubble and squelch with wind.

'Davey really believed that he could cure sickness,' I said, suppressing a wet fart. 'I think we can be sure of that. He concocted some weird fantasy about having to be pure in order to channel his mysterious power.'

'Pure?' asked Michael.

This was going to be extremely difficult.

'I suspect he had discovered somehow, perhaps with wounded animals, that he could not always effect a cure with a laying-on of hands. He developed a bizarre theory. Pure and natural were the keywords. What he meant by them, God knows. Nothing more coherent or convincing than what an advertising copy-writer means by them, I suppose. Davey decided that he had to be as pure and natural as an animal. Pure and natural as a ladybird, of course, not pure and natural as the ladybird's cousin, the dung-beetle. Pure and natural as a gazelle, not pure and natural as the hyenas that bite into the gazelle's eyeballs and feast on its intestines. His ideas of purity and naturalness seem to have more in common with a Victorian hymnbook for children than any real understanding of the physical world. All things bright and beautiful and no things dark and foul. But at the same time Davey was undergoing puberty, don't forget, an event not covered by Victorian hymnbooks, an event as dark and foul as you could imagine. Davey happens to be a voraciously sensual child. Those of us around the table who are male can remember what our gonads and gametes were up to when we were fifteen, I'm sure. In my case they're still up to it, but without the up-springing violence of old. Davey was mortified to discover one morning that he had succumbed to a wet-dream. This presented him with a problem. Why had God and Nature packed his body with this nasty fluid? How could he remain a pure, pretty little buttercup while such a squirting horror dwelt within him? He reconciled it this way. Semen was a life-giving spirit, he knew that much. So long as he avoided the lustful outflow of this spirit, it would remain pure, would in fact be the purest, most potent essence imaginable. He decided that his semen . . . I hope you're ready for this, Annie . . . was the ideal channel for his healing. When his cousin Jane arrived for her stay at Swafford he was presented with the ideal test-case for this belief. He persuaded Jane that the laying-on of hands would not be enough and that he needed to impregnate her with his spirit. It's a technique many a leader

243

of religious cults has found invaluable. In Davey's case, desire and appetite were submerged and I am sure he sincerely believed that his only motivation was to heal and to help.'

'Oh, Davey . . .' Annie whispered. She had been completely unaware of this feature of her son's mission and emission and I felt a bit of a pig letting her know so publicly.

'I'm sorry to have to tell you that it is highly probable he tried the same trick with Lilac,' I added.

Jaws hit plates and Oliver started to throw mental daggers at me.

'Only Oliver can tell you,' I said, feeling he deserved it, 'what technique was employed in his case.'

Heads swung towards him. Poor Oliver, not a good dissembler.

'Look,' he said, licking his lips. 'We all believed, didn't we? Some of us still do. Everything Ted has said has been bigoted and circumstantial. He hasn't disproved a thing.'

'You seduced my son?' said Michael.

'No, bugger it, he seduced me! He told me . . . Jesus, it sounds absurd if put like that . . . Look, if you have to have it described in language that Wallace would understand, then yes, Davey fucked me up the arse. And I'm better, aren't I? It was Davey, though. *Simon* hasn't done a thing for me. I've barely spoken to the oaf all week. It's Davey! Of course it's Davey. Why the hell are you listening to this fat sod? What about Jane and Lilac?'

Mary and Max exchanged horrified glances. They were thinking about Clara, poor dears.

'I can explain about Lilac,' I said. 'I'm afraid the whole episode was entirely my fault.'

'*Your* fault?' Michael frowned.

'Yes, it's the stupidest thing on earth. I telephoned the vet, Nigel Ogden, this evening. I asked him to confirm that Lilac really had been suffering from ragwort poisoning. He said it was the only condition that could explain the depression, the bleeding from the mouth, the aimless circling, the leaning against the wall, the abdominal pain, the loss of appetite, the diarrhoea, the raging thirst, everything. But I had had an inspiration in my bath this evening, you see. Like Archimedes. I may not be a vet, but no one could deny that I am a drunkard. What if, I asked the vet, what if Lilac had been *drunk*? Really, really soused. Off her saddle and pissed out of her mane. Nigel thought about it for a bit and had to confess that he had never seen a horse drunk, but that he supposed the symptoms might be similar to those he witnessed. It would affect a horse badly, he imagined, since it is very difficult for them to vomit. It wouldn't explain the bleeding from the mouth, however. But I had an answer to that, too. I won't go into the reasons, but early in the morning on the second day of my stay here I dropped a full bottle of ten-year-old malt whisky into a bucket in the west park, where Lilac and her fellow four-footers have since been grazing.'

'You did *what*?' gasped Patricia.

'Yes, I know it sounds mad, but it seemed the right thing to do at the time. We can go into it later. The point is, this evening in the bath, the moment I remembered that incident, things clicked into place. I crept out before dinner to inspect this bucket. The bottle had cracked open and whisky had oozed out. There were blood marks on the cracked glass. Lilac, with irreproachable taste, must have discovered this unexpected treasure while out in the park the day before yesterday and licked and sucked and lapped at it happily for most of the afternoon. Barley can never have been presented to her in so pleasurable a form. She didn't get all of it, you'll be pleased to know, just enough to give her a good time and a really vicious hangover. It truly is as simple as that.'

They all stared at me in silence. Then Simon began to laugh.

'Drunk!' he said. 'So Lilac was drunk. Do you know I *thought* it couldn't be ragwort! Alec and I spent a whole day checking the field, because it does grow round here. You have to check, you know. It's no good using a weed-killer, because funnily enough they just make the plant more palatable to horses. Drunk!'

Oliver banged the table. 'All right!' he said, face whitened in anger. 'That might be true. *Might* be. But . . .'

'Clara,' interrupted Max heavily. 'What about Clara? Are you saying that boy dared to . . .'

I thought I would have to tread carefully here.

'You will be pleased to know that Davey did not attempt to do to Clara what he had done to Jane and Oliver and Lilac. He tried this afternoon to feed her some stuff to do with his spirit . . .' I thought that was near enough the truth to be acceptable, they could take the phrase as literally or metaphorically as they chose. 'But Simon prevented him. What you thought you were doing sending that poor girl to Davey I have no idea.'

'We wanted to do what was best,' said Mary helplessly. 'It seemed the right thing.'

'Look, far be it from me to lecture you both,' I said, 'but Clara is the most downtrodden young thing I have ever seen in my life. You make it abundantly plain to everyone that you are ashamed of her, you tick her off in public for her awkwardness, which naturally makes it ten times as bad, and you give her, it seems to me, absolutely no indication whatsoever that you love her or enjoy her company.'

'How dare you?' Max shouted across the table. 'How bloody dare you?'

'Oh be quiet, Max, he's right and you know it,' said Mary. 'Of course he's right. Clara doesn't match up to your idea of the perfect accessory and it maddens you.'

Max thought about answering back, but the idea of a public row clearly didn't square with his self-image, so he shrugged his shoulders and relapsed into silence.

'Simon has worked a miracle on Clara this last week,' I said. 'He's had her helping in the stables, feeding the chicks, walking the puppies, swimming in the lake. He's given her confidence and he's shown her that he likes her for herself.'

'No, really, I haven't done anything . . .' Simon started to say.

'She was very shaken by her experience with David this afternoon,' I went on. 'She told me about it when I visited her in her bedroom just before dinner.'

'My, we have been busy this evening, haven't we?' said Oliver. 'Quite the . . .'

'What do you mean "her experience" exactly?' Mary interrupted.

'Well, as I say, Davey can be very intense in his manner. She was a little frightened by it all. As well as demeaned, I should imagine. You've sent her to doctors and shrinks and specialist summer-camps and religious retreats as though she were sicker and madder than a rabid dog. Now you instruct her to go into the woods with Davey to be healed like a leper. Simon happened to see them together and took Clara away. He told her that there was absolutely nothing wrong with her. He told her that he adored her exactly the way she was and that if she dared change a thing about herself he would never forgive her. She worships Simon of course and for the first time in her life she felt loved, simply and properly loved. I think, as far as she is concerned, that is a miracle.'

Mary looked across at Simon.

'Look . . .' he said. Big tears had started to roll down his face. 'Don't be . . . don't be angry with Davey. He never meant any harm. He was just trying to help. He's not bad or anything. He's just a bit confused, really.'

Annie stroked his arm.

Oliver was trembling now. 'What is the *matter* with everyone?' he cried. 'You haven't explained the most important fact of all. Jane. You can't, can you?'

I raised my shoulders apologetically. 'Remissions occur, Oliver,' I said.

'Remissions occur! Loaves of bread will sometimes turn into fishes. Dead men will sometimes walk. Pigs have been known to fly. Balls to "remissions occur".'

'I can tell you all about Jane,' said Michael in a voice so heavy that we all turned to him. 'Bex, I'm very sorry. That telephone call just now. Jane has died. At the hospital. In her sleep. I had to wait until I had heard what Ted was going to say.'

I stared into my wineglass. I suppose somewhere in the back of my mind I had guessed that there was something wrong. When I thought of the over-bright phrases that ended her last letter to me. 'Smile! We are loved. We are loved. Everything is going to be wonderful. Everything shines. Everything is as it could only be and must be.' Silly child.

'Let's go through,' said Anne. 'I don't think we want anything more to eat.'

We rose from the table in silence and processed to the drawing room. Michael comforted Rebecca who sobbed into his shoulder and I put an arm around Patricia.

I felt curiously to blame, as though my breaking of Davey's spell had been the cause of Jane's death and the sudden misery in the household. We sat in a ring of sofas surrounding the large central ottoman, which we all gazed at glumly to spare us the hardship of meeting one another's eyes. With the wind whipping around the house and the rain batting the window panes, our huddled group resembled frightened cavemen staring into a fire.

'She had a relapse this morning,' Michael said at last. 'She thought it must be a mistake. Kept telling the doctors that she was fine and that she had to travel to Norfolk. She died at ten minutes to eight this evening.'

Ten to eight. Exactly the moment the memory of the whisky

247

bottle in the bucket popped into my head. Oh, be quiet, Ted, I said to myself. Get a grip, man.

'And all the time,' said Michael. 'All the time, she thought she was well. Never said goodbye because she thought she was cured.'

'But *me!*' said Oliver, unable to suppress it for any longer. 'What about me? I'm cured, aren't I?'

'Oh, Oliver,' I said. 'Did you really throw those pills away?'

'I don't need them. I don't *need* any fucking pills. Can't you understand that?'

'Then why were you shouting in agony in your bedroom this evening?'

'I wasn't shouting in agony, I was . . .'

Poor old bugger.

'I was *groaning* in agony,' he said at last, with an attempt at dignity. 'There's a big difference.'

'I'll send someone out to Norwich to get some more pills,' said Michael.

'It's only angina,' Oliver said. 'If I stick enough vodka down me to deaden the pain, it can wait till morning.'

Annie slipped out of the room and Oliver looked up at me with reddened eyes.

'Why, Ted? Why did you have to spoil it all? It *could* have been true. Why couldn't you let it be true?'

'Oh, Oliver, I don't know. You're the priest, not me. Isn't it something to do with letting man get on with things on his own?'

'But it was such a beautiful idea. It gave us hope.'

'Don't imagine,' I said, 'that just because you can't be cured by the laying-on of hands or the injection of holy semen that life and the world are therefore hopeless. If you want to talk about the Operation of Grace, why not talk about Simon?'

'Oh, please . . .' Simon stood up. 'Uncle Ted, I'd much rather you stopped talking about me like that. Please.'

I waved a hand at him.

'I'm sorry, old darling. It's been very fraught for you. The more one ages, you will find, the less afraid of sentimental language one becomes. Didn't mean to embarrass you.'

'I have to walk Soda now,' he said backing out of the room.

'Good idea.'

He stopped in the doorway.

'Um, Aunt Rebecca. I'm very sorry about Jane. You have my . . . you know. Deepest . . .'

He turned to go but his path was blocked by Annie. 'Simon!' she said with alarm. 'Davey isn't in his room.'

III

Mary Clifford's first thought was for her daughter.

'What about Clara?' she wailed.

Fatuous woman. As though Davey might have kidnapped her or eloped to Gretna Green with the helpless creature lashed to his saddlebow and struggling to be free. I doubted he wanted to see her or her big buck teeth ever again in his life.

'Clara is in bed, fast asleep,' said Annie.

'Tedward,' said Michael. 'That noise we heard outside the dining-room door . . .'

The same unwelcome thought had crossed my mind. If David had been listening to my pompous and pitiless analysis of his disordered psyche, then the Lord alone knew how he would react. Such a clumsy arse I am, such a hopelessly clumsy arse.

'Oh hell,' I said. 'He can't have gone out on a night like this. He can't have done. Not in his condition.'

'Condition?' Annie grabbed my arm. 'What do you mean condition?'

'Look, there's no time to explain,' I said. 'Davey injured himself this afternoon. He's perfectly all right, but he should be in bed.'

'Dad, why don't you and Mum and Mary and Rebecca and Patricia search the house?' said Simon. 'I'll get Soda and the rest of us can take a look outside.'

Simon took Max and me through to the boot room where he issued us with wellington boots, waxed jackets and torches.

Armed with these, we trooped down into the kitchens and out of the back door, past the astonished kitchen staff. I, as back marker, was the member of the party detained by Podmore.

'Is anything wrong, Mr Wallace?'

'Everything's fine, my old. We're going on a treasure hunt. Such fun.'

Out in the kitchen yard Simon shouted to us above the roar of the wind and the hissing of the rain.

'We'll go first to the kennels. Get Soda.'

Max and I nodded and followed him round the back of the house. Rainwater streamed down the back of my neck.

'Do you really think he might have run away?' Max asked me.

'No idea,' I answered. 'Christ, I hope not. But if he was listening at the door while I was talking about him, he might well feel unable to face us all.'

'And how exactly is he injured?'

'Well,' I said. 'Your daughter bit him.'

Max nodded. 'I see,' he said. 'Yes, I see. The stupid thing is, I never liked the little shit anyway. Always relieved that Simon was my godson, not him. Should have gone on instinct.'

'Not a little shit,' I said, fumbling for the hood of my Barbour. 'Hardly his fault everyone encouraged him to believe he was Jesus Christ, is it?'

We had arrived at the kennels. Soda lived apart from the beagles, who were baying and whimpering in the sheltered part of their accommodation. Max and I talked to them and told them that thunderstorms were a harmless lark, while Simon let Soda out and attached a long lead to her collar.

'She's got a super nose,' he said. 'Davey and I used to play hide and seek with her. Manhunts and that kind of thing. You know.'

He bent down and spoke to Soda in the rushed, excited tones humans reserve for dogs. 'Seek Davey, Soda! Go on, girl. Seek Davey! Seek Davey! Where's he gone, Soda? Where's he gone?'

Soda jumped and barked with pleasure. Never occurred to her to wonder what the fuck we were doing playing games like this late at night in the middle of a thunderstorm. Still, I suppose if you're a dog and are used to watching humans zooming around at high speed in metal boxes, staring at large sheets of paper at breakfast-time and breathing in smoke from short white tubes, then nothing the species does has the power to surprise you.

We followed Simon and Soda out of the kennel yard and round the side of the house. Soda's nose bounced along the ground, snorting and sniffing. Every now and again she would dance off in a wide loop, following some false scent, before returning to the main path.

'Nothing yet,' said Simon.

I looked up at the windows of the house and watched the lights being switched on in rooms on every floor. The indoor search party seemed to be having no luck either. I wondered whether they would have the courage to ask the servants for help.

We arrived at the front door and immediately Soda began to snuffle around the steps, barking excitedly and spinning about in frenzied circles.

'I think she's got something,' said Simon. 'Go on, girl! Find Davey! Find Davey!'

Soda yapped twice and tore off towards the front lawn, Simon holding on to the lead. Max sprinted after them, anxious to show he could keep pace with a spaniel and a seventeen-year-old. I rolled along at a more leisurely jog and caught up with the trio at the end of the lawn. Max and Simon's torches were flashing back and forth, but it was light enough to see that of David there was absolutely no sign. Perhaps he had climbed over the ha-ha and into the park. That is where I had been earlier in the evening, peering at the bucket of whisky. The association gave me an idea.

'False alarm,' said Simon.

Soda was barking and circling furiously in the ditch of the ha-ha.

'Wait a moment,' I panted. 'I was here the other week. It was morning.'

'So?' said Max.

'Well, I followed a trail of foot-prints in the dew across the lawn and this is exactly where they ended. I couldn't under-stand it. That's the morning I went on into the park and dropped that whisky bottle. Thought I'd been going mad. Just a trail of foot-prints up to here and then nothing.'

Simon looked at the lawn and then down into the ditch where Soda still leapt frantically back and forth barking fit to bust. He slid down the ha-ha and shouted at Soda.

'Seek Davey! Go on, girl! Find him, find Davey!'

Soda kept up a stream of excitable yapping and began to scrabble with her paws against the bank. Simon watched for a moment and then took hold of Soda's collar and pulled her back.

'Look!' he shouted, pointing. 'Here!'

We were still on the lawn level, so Max lay on his stomach and looked down, tracing with the light of his torch a line in the turf that Simon was indicating, a line which formed three sides of a large square.

Simon grasped a handful of the grass and heaved. A heavy turf rectangle, about three feet by three, started to come away from the bank. It was uncut at the top edge, which formed a kind of hinge, but Simon wrenched until the whole piece worked free. Max and I, reaching down, helped take the weight of it and drop it into the ditch beside Simon.

As soon as the entrance was revealed, Soda tried to jump in, but Simon kept hold of her.

'Leave, Soda. Leave. Good girl, you're a good girl. Stay there.'

He shone his torch into the hole.

Max and I, lying on the grass above and peering down, could make out the doorway of a tunnel cut into the bank beneath us and see in the light of Simon's torch two bare feet in the mud.

'Is he all right?' I shouted down. 'How is he?'

Simon put his hands around the ankles and began to pull. 'I can't tell,' he said. 'I'll need a hand.'

Max and I dropped into the ditch to help. Max pointed with the torch as Simon and I heaved and more and more of Davy emerged. He had been lying lengthways and unclothed in a tunnel scarcely big enough to contain him. Air-holes, if he had bothered to construct any, would have been penetrated by the rainwater and blocked by wet earth. He cannot have lain there for more than an hour, I thought. None the less, the air would have become appallingly fetid and the soil would have dampened into mud.

I heard footsteps and shouts from the direction of the house. Michael and Annie were running up the lawn, with Rebecca, Patricia and Mary not far beyond.

'You've found him,' cried Annie. 'Where was he?'

They looked down into the ha-ha, where Simon and I were laying David's body in the ditch. Soda licked the mud from his arm and moaned like a rusty gate.

'What's that bandage,' asked Michael. 'There's blood on it! What in God's name has he tried to do to himself?'

'Don't worry about that,' I said.

'He's not breathing!' wailed Annie. 'Michael, his eyes are closed and he's not breathing.'

Simon took one of David's arms, which were lying by his side, and I took the other. We raised them, pulling them back behind Davey's head. We did this several times, slowly at first and then with a quicker and quicker rhythm. Then Simon laid the palms of his hands on David's chest and bore down with all his weight, pushing and pushing. Annie began to cry.

Finally Simon, shaking his head, pinched his brother's nose with one hand and with the other opened his mouth. He leant down and blew into the lungs.

IV

'Look, for fuck's sake, keep up, the pair of you,' I growled. 'I'm ten minutes late as it is.'

'We'll run then,' said Roman. 'Yes sir, we'll bloody run.'

'Abso-sodding-lutely. We'll only bloody run.'

They barged past me and ran up the pavement, turning left and out of sight into Great Marlborough Street.

By the time I caught up three minutes later they were swinging around a lamp-post outside the back of Marks and Spencer's and tutting at imaginary wrist-watches as I approached.

'I'll be over there,' I said. 'In that building. I shan't be more than half an hour.'

'There's a McDonald's in Oxford Street,' said Davey.

'Yeah, can we go over and get a Big Mac?'

'Ten Big Macs.'

'Come on, Dad! It's the last week before school.'

'Yes, yes, yes. Don't badger me. Here . . .' I handed them each a fiver. 'And don't throw up in the street.'

'We'll see you in there. It's just in Oxford Street.'

'See you . . .'

I crossed the street and pressed the buzzer.

'Ted Wallace to see Lionel Greene.'

'Second floor.'

Greene didn't have a great deal to say. Nothing that Michael, as executor, hadn't already told me.

'The estate consists in its entirety of the South Kensington property, four hundred thousand pounds in shares and one hundred and thirty thousand pounds on deposit with the Chelsea branch of Coutts Bank.'

'Seems rather a lot.'

'Would you prefer the shares to be sold?'

'Not sure.' If I donated it all to some leukaemia society I would end up regretting it. Gestures are all very well but they don't fill bellies. Besides, it would look so smug and greasy.

'It's entirely up to you as the sole beneficiary.'

'Yes. I know.'

'And the house, Mr Wallace? Will you be selling that?'

'I'm certainly not going to live there,' I said. 'You should see the wallpaper.'

'I am also instructed to give you this letter,' Greene added, handing me an envelope. The handwriting was appalling and it took me some time to make out a single one of the words. Greene turned discreetly away to allow me to read it unobserved.

Dear Ted,

I'm so sorry. I can't understand what has gone wrong. I need you to send Davey to me at the hospital. I'm suddenly very weak. It doesn't make sense. It doesn't make any sense at all.

The doctors say it is the leukaemia, but we know that can't be the case, don't we? We know that they must have made a mistake.

Thank you for all your letters and for throwing yourself into the work so whole-heartedly. I wasn't wrong in sending you and I haven't forgotten that we have a bargain. I have made a new will which the nurses have witnessed. Spend the money on bringing Davey's gifts to the notice of the world.

As soon as you get this, come with Davey. He will make it all right again.

Love

Jane

'I understand,' Greene said, 'that she died no more than half an hour after writing it. Very sad. I had a brother who died of leukaemia. Terrible thing.'

'Very terrible,' I said, standing.

'Just two things before you go, Mr Wallace. I have the keys to Onslow Terrace here. Would you like them?'

'I suppose so. There are some papers there that I ought to go through.'

I pondered the strange custom by which people's letters, bills and scraps of useless rubbish instantly become dignified with the word 'papers' the moment they are dead. Objects like house-keys, of course, become 'effects'.

Greene handed them over with a ceremonial dip of the head.

'And the second thing?' I asked.

'The second thing is this,' he said, picking up a book from his desk with a shy smile. 'I wonder if you would do me the inestimable favour of signing my copy of your *Collected Works*?'

The boys were sitting in an upstairs section of the 'restaurant', as it liked to call itself.

'Everything hunky-dory, Dad?'

'Yes, thank you,' I said. 'My God, do you really enjoy those things?'

'No, Dad,' said Roman, 'we eat them because we hate them. Of course we bloody enjoy them. Have one yourself.'

'I think not.'

'Go on, Ted,' Davey urged. 'You've got to at least try them, you know. Otherwise you've no right to criticise them.'

'Oh, now hang on . . .'

'I'll nip down and buy you one,' he said.

'Why couldn't he have asked a waitress?' I asked, watching him shoot downstairs.

'Come off it, Dad,' said Roman. 'Don't pretend to be more ignorant than you are.'

'Hum.'

'Do you know, Davey had never had a Big Mac in his entire life until two weeks ago?'

'Yes, I did know,' I said.

'Bloody addicted to them now.'

'Roman,' I said.

'Yup?'

'I know we never really get much of a chance to talk about anything, but I just wanted to say . . .'

'Say what?' he burped.

'Well, I just wanted to say that it's bloody good having you around. I hadn't realised what a . . . what a splendid chap you are.'

He smiled. 'Dad, you've been watching too many bloody American TV movies,' he said.

'I have watched as many American TV movies as I've eaten Large Macs,' I replied. 'At least let me *try* and be fatherly, however badly I may do it. The thing is this, though. I know Helen only carts you off to London when she and Brian go on their August holiday, but if ever you want to hang around the flat at any other time, well . . .'

'Yeah, I don't mind,' he said.

'Good man.'

'So, what's the plan for the rest of the afternoon?'

'Well, it's a rather busy day for me, as it happens. I've got to cut over to the Harpo Club in half an hour. Your sister Leonora wants to see me. I think her boyfriend's run out on her.'

257

'Again?'

'Again. She hasn't got anywhere to live. I might be able to put a house her way. After that, I've got a meeting with a publisher.'

'You writing poems again?'

'This is for a novel, based on . . . based on an idea that came to me last month when I was staying at Swafford.'

'And how long will that take?'

'I've no idea. I've never written one before.'

'No, the meeting. With the publisher person. How long will that take?'

'Oh, no more than half an hour I don't suppose. But then I really ought to zip over to visit Oliver in hospital.'

'Blimey, and what are we supposed to do all this time?'

'Ah, well. I'm coming to that. Let me see . . . hold out your hand.' I took out my wallet. 'I reckon thirty pounds each ought to do it.'

'Yes please!' said Roman. 'Ought to do what?'

'This afternoon's task,' I said, counting out six ten-pound notes into his hand, 'is for the two of you to go along Brewer Street and see if you can get admitted into a dirty movie or bed show. You have to bring me the ticket stubs as proof.'

'And what's the prize if we manage it?'

'The prize, Roman, you ungrateful bastard, is the pleasure of having seen a dirty movie or a bed show. Isn't that enough?'

'All right. You're on.'

'Fine.'

'What exactly is the point, though?' Roman asked, pocketing the cash. 'Is it just to annoy Mum if she ever finds out?'

'It has absolutely nothing to do with your mother. Nothing whatsoever. It's for the good of your immortal souls, if you must know.'

'Fair enough. Just wondered.'

'And the pair of you had better find something to do this evening as well. I'm taking Patricia out to Le Caprice and she may want to come back afterwards.'

'We're going to need more than thirty quid, then.'

'You are one of the few people,' I said, handing him another four tenners, 'who can accurately be called a son of a bitch.'

'Your Big Mac, sir,' said Davey, depositing a plastic tray on the table in front of me. 'With Regular Fries and a Diet Coke.'

'There's no cutlery,' I protested.

'Fingers and thumbs are nature's cutlery,' he replied with a self-conscious smile.

I opened the brown polystyrene box and stared gloomily at the contents.

'Do I really have to do this thing?'

'Yes, sir, you do!' they said.

'A good trick,' Davey offered, 'is to empty the fries into the open lid of the box. There, like that. Neat, isn't it?'

I raised the bun to my face and sniffed. 'What's that pink sauce?'

'Ah, nobody knows. It's the best-kept secret in the world.'

I bit into the warm squashy mess.

They watched me anxiously, like laboratory technicians monitoring a guinea-pig.

'Well, Dad? What do you reckon?'

'Absolutely dis*gusting*.'

'So, another one?' Davey suggested.

'Why not?' I said.